DRAGONBLOOD RING

RING

AMPARO ORTIZ

PAGE STREET
PUBLISHING CO.

PAGE STREET
PUBLISHING CO.

Copyright © 2021 Amparo Ortiz

First published in 2021 by
Page Street Publishing Co.
27 Congress Street, Suite 105
Salem, MA 01970
www.pagestreetpublishing.com

Distributed by Macmillan, sales in Canada by The Canadian Manda Group.

25   24   23   22   21   1   2   3   4   5

ISBN-13: 978-1-64567-316-3
ISBN-10: 1-64567-316-2

Library of Congress Control Number: 2021932092

Cover and book design by Melia Parsloe for Page Street Publishing Co.
Cover illustration by Setor Fiadzigbey

Printed and bound in the United States

TO RENIS

Little brothers don't have rights,
but you can have this book in your name

A world without Blazewrath is nothing to fear. We knew how to entertain ourselves long before the sport was created! Besides, dragons aren't disappearing. They never will, mate. A world without dragons . . . That would be our true nightmare.

—*Excerpt from interview with Russell Turner, former president of the International Blazewrath Federation, in* The Weekly Scorcher

CHAPTER ONE

Lana

SAVING THE WORLD FROM A DRAGON SUPREMACIST SHOULD totally have better benefits.

I can handle the bodyguards. My former Blazewrath teammates and I have a humble total of fifteen—two per dragon steed and a lone ranger for me. I can even handle how serious they are. Hours before our Transport from Dubai, Daga—the youngest Sol de Noche dragon—tried to play hide-and-seek with the two disapproving suits assigned to her. They also declined her belly rub request. The International Bureau of Magical Matters is officially immune to cuteness.

Our safe house is fine, too. There are worse things in life than living in a four-story manor hidden in Cayey—my hometown here in Puerto Rico. We're secluded in the evergreen Sierra de Cayey, almost two thousand feet above sea level. If I stand on the house's rooftop, I can see a decent chunk of La Cordillera Central, a mountain range that cuts right through the middle of the island from east to west. It's a wondrous collection of treetops and winding rivers. More than a dozen municipalities are part of La Cordillera Central. Even though I haven't visited them, I have a feeling the mountains look best in Cayey, but I might be biased.

The weather's not so great, though. Today is August 17—summery turning point in the rollercoaster ride that's been my 2017 so far—and it's pouring rain. We've had occasional lightning, too. I blame hurricane season. Local weather reports have about fourteen to nineteen tropical storms lined up for us, with at least five potentially turning into hurricanes. Bless the invisible shield surrounding our house. We're spoiled with dry clothes, cool air, and no frizz.

But we can't freaking *go* anywhere.

I get it, okay? Dragon Knights are still searching for us. Those terrorists are desperate to free the Sire, that silver-scaled scumbag we trapped inside the Dark Island, which can only be accessed via the Sol de Noches' magic. These restrictions are meant to protect us.

How am I supposed to stay put when I'm finally in Puerto Rico again after *twelve years*?

How can I reconnect with my roots if they're still out of reach?

The house I grew up in—the house where I found the reason I was born—is a few miles south of this mountain. My requests for escorted visits have fallen on deaf ears. I can't race down the pothole-ridden roads that lead to dragon caves I daydreamed about as a child. There's no chance to see the island's many wonders. I can't eat my weight in lechón, bacalaítos, or pinchos at a restaurant. And I can't visit the beach. I'm in Puerto Rico and I can't. Visit. *The beach.*

"The families are arriving in thirty minutes," says Agent Vogel. "Prepare accordingly."

My personal bodyguard saunters onto the wooden porch, where I've been sulking alone on a rocking chair for the past three hours. Agent Vogel—a sixty-year-old German lady with a fauxhawk—looks out of place in her white linen Chanel suit. It's the only thing she ever wears. She's clutching her Silver wand in both hands, which are covered with black leather gloves.

At least she's brought me great news. Tonight, my friends and former Blazewrath teammates will be reunited with their families. I'm going to meet the people who supported their Blazewrath dreams.

The people who can also help me get out of this house.

If more of us corner our bodyguards, they'll be pressured into contacting Director Sandhar, or even his right-hand woman, Agent Sienna Horowitz. I scan my phone for any new texts from her. My screen flashes my own words with a bunch of "Read" subtitles. It's been like that ever since I left Dubai. Sure, they must be busy, especially if they're catching Dragon Knights posing as bureau agents. But radio silence pushes my mind into drawing maps with dead ends and question marks. Are they okay? If so, why hasn't Agent Horowitz replied?

Director Sandhar hasn't even told the press we're in Puerto Rico. We could be cloaked in Invisibility Charms like this house. We wouldn't leave at the same time. Maybe it's best for the dragons to stay, but we can totally go without causing a scene. I just need to feel like I'm *back*.

Above all, visiting my childhood home is the closure I need. Going back to where Papi taught me about my favorite sport—my purpose— is the last goodbye. Without it, I might successfully start a new life post-Blazewrath, but a piece of the puzzle will still be missing.

"Did you hear me?" Agent Vogel asks.

The sheer willpower it takes not to scream empties me of energy. "How do I prepare? Is there a blood sacrifice I haven't heard about?" I say through gritted teeth.

Agent Vogel is as excited as a dead squirrel. "Not tonight."

"Wait. Did you just make a joke?" I check her pulse. "Vitals are suspiciously good."

She lazily takes her arm away. "Do not touch me."

"What about your head? Have you hit it with anything lately?"

"No."

"You could have a concussion."

Silence.

Normally, I'd crack a smile at my trolling. But this well-dressed lady is acting more like my jailer than an ally. I don't know *anything* about Agent Vogel. What qualifies her to lead this special babysitting mission? Is she some badass bureau agent who's racked up tons of arrests like Horowitz? I doubt she's ever been forced to hide on a mountain because Dragon Knights were trying to hurt her country's dragons. She can't possibly understand how I feel. From the way she's motioning to the living room, I don't think she cares.

"Do you miss Germany?" I tempt fate with a personal question. It might soften her up a bit. Maybe she also wishes she could go home.

Agent Vogel furrows her brow. "That's irrelevant to my request."

Hmm, her guard is up. Must be a yes.

"What do you miss the most?" I press on.

"None of that concerns our current pressing matters."

"Do you have family there? Friends? Maybe even a whole life you had to leave behind?"

Her unblinking stare hardens into ice. "You mustn't keep your friends waiting."

I don't care if she's pissed. I've been pissed for the past four days. And it's only going to get worse if she doesn't cooperate. "Because if you ask me, I'd say I miss *all* of it. I'd pounce at the chance to go back to the place that made me who I am." I shrug. "Wouldn't you?"

For the first time since I've met her, Agent Vogel frowns. I blink three times in case I'm imagining things. Nope—she's still frowning. And she's gazing out to the sloping hills below.

Is it working? Did I make her crack?

Agent Vogel looks back at me. Her frown disappears. "I appreciate your sudden interest in my nostalgia, but I'm confident your friends will be more eager to indulge you."

She waves to the glass door that separates the balcony and the living room.

The sky flashes a bright ivory. A thunderous clap soon follows.

And yet my crashing spirits ring even.

I almost cracked her tough exterior, though. If the others stick to the plan, Agent Vogel could be contacting Director Sandhar before the night ends.

There's just one more person who still needs convincing.

"Good talk…" I push off the wooden rocking chair. I salute Agent Vogel, which always makes her sigh heavily, then make my way into a house I can never call mine.

"MOCK MY ART ALL YOU WANT, BUT MAMI'S GONNA LOVE IT. Beethoven is shaking in his grave!"

Luis García, former Charger and grape aficionado, is treating us to a horrendous piano session. He hits the same three keys over and over like a drunk cat in need of a time out.

"Yeah, he's shaking because he's *mortified*. Please put our misery to an end." God bless Héctor Sánchez. He's trying to push Luis off the bench, but not even the team captain can sway him.

"Mortified of undeniable talent and poise? Please," Luis says.

He has everyone in stitches. Even Mom is covering her mouth as she giggles. It's still a bit weird seeing her have a blast with people she didn't want me associating with a few weeks ago. Mom initially asked to stay at a hotel, but our bodyguards think Dragon Knights could find her faster, even if she used a fake name or a disguise. They want to keep us together—we're easier to protect that way. Not once has she embarrassed me in front of my friends, which I'm immensely grateful for. She's also on my side regarding my requests to visit our old house.

Tonight will be Mom's first time addressing Agent Vogel about visiting our house, though, so I'm hoping she can do a much better job than me.

"Luis, if you don't stop, I'm going to sing," Héctor says.

"NO!" Luis flees from the piano.

Héctor slams the piano keyboard's cover down, then raises a fist in victory. "At last."

I have no idea who thought putting an instrument in this house would be a good thing. Not one of us has a musical bone in our bodies.

What we do have is *food.* Joaquín Delgado, our chef for the night, is currently placing the arroz mamposteao con gandules inside an aluminum tray as big as a guitar. There are also trays with white rice, boneless ribs, oven-roasted chicken, every vegetable known to humankind, and four types of salads, including ensalada de coditos. Mom calls it macaroni salad, which has elicited a grand total of six disappointed sighs from Joaquín's father, Manny. He's sitting on the spacious kitchen island, taking slow sips from his Medalla beer can, and watching *Rambo III* on his tablet at full volume.

This is the most Manny he's ever been.

I do a quick scan of the rest of the area. Génesis Castro puts the finishing touches on the sangria, looking cute in her red apron with a pit bull grilling a steak. Gabriela Ramos is still checking that the charcoal-grey tablecloth is devoid of creases. Edwin Santiago has claimed the couch to himself. He's FaceTiming with Kirill Volkov, the former Russian Blocker who also happens to be his boyfriend.

Victoria Peralta must still be wrangling the dragons for their surprise entrance.

I'm pretty sure none of the bodyguards are lending a hand. They're quick to tell us what to do, but keep their distance when we do it.

Sure enough, Agent Vogel stands by the sliding doors, eyes glued to my every move.

I fight back the urge to stick my tongue out.

The mahogany front doors open.

"Hey…" A sweaty Victoria walks into the dining room. Even though she's in her usual black sportswear, the way she's scowling suggests she wasn't expecting *that* much exertion. "Operation Dragon Surprise is good to go. They made me work for it, but it'll be a success."

"Thanks for setting that up!" Gabriela blows her a kiss. Of course she's the only one who's dressed for the occasion. She's wearing a blush velvet maxi dress and a pair of bone-white booties. Her pink-and-purple hair is styled in a topknot. She calls tonight's makeup the Sweet Summer Look—her face is skillfully decorated in a blend of apricot and peach tones.

I'm in black jeans and a Monsta X T-shirt. No regrets.

But as Victoria walks over to me, I sure as hell start to feel like I might have some soon.

"Hey. Do you have a minute?" I say.

She meets my gaze, an eyebrow raised. "I need to shower," she says firmly.

"This will be quick."

Victoria sighs. "It better be. I smell like decaying flesh."

Not even her pathetic attempt at humor makes me smile. Less than a week ago, I held Victoria Peralta's hand while President Turner canceled the Blazewrath World Cup. My goal had been to provide even the tiniest bit of solace. She'd lost her favorite sport, her purpose, just like me. We were in this *together*. But ever since we got back to Puerto Rico, she's been… different. Not quite as cold as in Dubai, thankfully. She's not a ball of warmth, either. Asking her what's up is useless—I might as well try speaking with the coquíes who serenade us at night.

This *has* to have something to do with the Cup. She hasn't brought it up, but I don't want to bring it up, either. The last thing I want is to make her heart shatter all over again.

"Does your speech consist of staring at me in disturbing silence?" she asks.

"Come on." I lead her to an empty corner in the kitchen. Victoria quietly joins me by the huge cabinet where the glassware is stored. "Are you on board with tonight's plan?" I whisper.

Victoria opens the cabinet. She grabs four glasses, then sets them on the marble counter. "You don't need me. I think you're all better at sob stories."

Did she just insult me? Or am I being too sensitive?

I take a step closer, my arms folded. "The more people we have stacked against Vogel, the faster we can get out of here. And it doesn't have to be a *sob story.* Just tell your mom how much we miss our homes. Génesis needs to help out her dog rescue group, too. This isn't a vacation."

"That's for sure." Victoria wipes each glass with a napkin.

Okay, she's officially being weird. I've never seen her clean anything in this house.

"Is something wrong, Victoria?"

"No, *Lana.*" Her voice rises in pitch when she says my name. It's like she's singing in a Disney movie, but with a thousand percent more condescension. She offers me a glass. When I grab it, she says, "How are you feeling about Takeshi's upcoming trial?"

The glass slips from my hand.

Thankfully, I catch it before it shatters.

"Nice reflexes." Victoria's smiling wider, harder. "Is something wrong?"

God, why is she being *so* annoying? I wipe the glass clean with my shirt, even though it's already pristine. It's better than meeting her gaze. "I'm... fine." I barely get the words out.

My cheeks sizzle white-hot. How am I not supposed to freak out for the boy who's locked in a Ravensworth Penitentiary cell? The boy whose fate relies on me convincing the bureau he's a hero? My favorite Blazewrath player had betrayed Director Sandhar in order to avenge his dragon steed's murder. He also helped me stop the Sire along with Samira Jones, my best friend. She hasn't heard anything about Takeshi at the New York bureau headquarters. Being busy with her Gold Wand certification hasn't stopped her from snooping around, but she's come up short. Whatever Takeshi is going through, I won't know until I see him next week.

"I think that's the cleanest it'll ever be." Victoria motions to the glass I'm wiping.

I almost slam it on the counter. Instead I set it down as carefully as if it were a newborn. "So you won't pitch in tonight?" I give her one last chance to act like she cares about people other than herself. But when she remains silent, I nod. "Awesome. Thanks for nothing, Victoria."

"You're welcome."

I walk away before she tests my patience further.

Luis is turning the TV onto a local channel, which is featuring a Die Hard movie. It's currently competing with *Rambo III* for the title of Loudest Film Ever Made.

SWISH!

Agent Vogel looks out the front porch. "Our guests are arriving soon."

My friends and I all give each other knowing looks. Héctor winks.

It's showtime.

Manny is taking his sweet time turning off his tablet. With the dulcet tones of *Rambo III* gone, the TV sounds even louder. A man is yelling his guts out onscreen.

"Don't be fooled! Those dragons aren't loyal to mankind! They're *killers!*"

A bearded, middle-aged white guy is standing in front of La Fortaleza in Old San Juan. He's holding up a sign that reads KILL THEM BEFORE THEY KILL US. The crowd might be small—about twenty people or so—but it's big enough to warrant a wall of local police. They keep a close watch from the other side of the wood barricades. Most of the protesters are also holding handwritten signs in both Spanish and English. Some of them shout the bearded guy's words into megaphones. It's only now that I notice his T-shirt.

It has my cousin Todd's face on the front.

"You've got to be kidding me…" That jerk would *love* to see himself on a T-shirt. He'd also love to see these losers spewing the same hate-filled speech he'd tossed at me on national television. My silence on his offer to debate him on dragons must've gotten on his last nerve. Now he's sending his brainless hounds to get a rise out of me.

"Don't bring those beasts into this country, Lana! If you let them loose, you're no better than the Sire!" says Bearded Guy. "Is *that* why you let Andrew Galloway die?"

I flinch. He might as well have punched me with a steel glove.

"You watched Andrew Galloway get murdered and did nothing! You're a murderer, too!"

"Murderer! Murderer! Murderer!" The protesters join in a raging chorus.

Someone in the house calls my name. Someone else grabs me.

No matter how loud they are, how tight their grip is, everyone blurs into the background. I can only see and hear the furious people on TV. Focusing on one voice is a waste—there are too many. But I try anyway. I'm speeding through a dark tunnel with no clue how to steer or stop.

"Murderer! Murderer! Murderer!"

The air is thinning around me. Has someone cast a spell to suck it all out? Or did they close the windows? The faster I breathe, the less oxygen flows into my body.

It's been four days since Andrew's funeral. Four days since the world lost a hero… since I lost a friend… I led him to that dragon sanctuary in Brazil. I *begged* him to fight with me.

This isn't on you, Lana, Andrew had told me seconds before Randall Wiggins cast the blood curse that ended his life. *This will never be on you.*

But if I hadn't told him to come with me, Andrew would still be alive. He'd be back home with his mother in Scotland, playing his favorite Garbage song on his black-and-blue guitar.

"Murderer! Murderer! Murderer!"

I hadn't lost a friend.

I killed him.

"I can't breathe… I can't… What's happening…"

"She needs medical attention!" Mom's voice pierces through the exploding landmines.

As Agent Vogel rushes toward me, I sink to my knees, and unleash a sea of tears I had no idea I'd been drowning in.

An athlete doesn't have to practice or play every day to be considered one. A notable example is Rúben Neves, the first Portuguese Runner in Blazewrath history. During the 1971 Cup, Neves led his team to the finals. They lost to Denmark by three seconds. A devastated Neves refused to step foot on the field again. Some called him a sore loser, but he claims he left his spot free for someone better—the purest form of sportsmanship. Rúben Neves will forever remain the first Portuguese Runner. Whether he misses the field or not, nobody can take that away from him.

—*Excerpt from Olga Peñaloza's* Blazewrath All-Stars, Third Edition

CHAPTER TWO

Victoria

THIS IS BULLSHIT.

As vexing as she can be, Lana didn't murder Andrew Galloway. The only things she's ever massacred are my eardrums when she rambles.

Her panic attack had been *awful*. Grief must be eating her up inside.

Vogel and two other agents stand guard outside her room. Her mother is consoling her. We're downstairs waiting for the Calming Charm to take effect. I loathe the Todd Trolls more than I loathe trolls in general. Thank God Génesis turned the television off. Now the living room is as silent as a graveyard. Mami and the other family members are being kept in the front lawn until Lana can join us. They must be wondering what the holdup is.

"*Nothing* happened to Lana," Vogel had told us before whisking her upstairs. "There is no need to alarm your loved ones. All seven of you will go outside together and act normal."

I could teach PhD courses on acting normal.

However, I don't understand why Vogel wants to hide Lana's panic attack. Could she be trying to keep this secret not just from our loved ones, but also from other bureau agents? Perhaps she's mostly determined not to let Sandhar know. If she *is* afraid of him finding out, what role does Lana play in their plan to protect our steeds? Dragon Knights would favor freeing the Sire over harming a teenager. I cannot decipher what the fuck Vogel's angle is.

The six bodyguards nearby haven't told us to keep quiet, yet nobody speaks. I presume we're all still processing what happened to Lana. Manny is the only one checking his phone. A male guard is watching him closely. He seems stressed Manny will make our evening worse.

This is not how I thought our family reunions would unfold.

I never even expected to be back in Puerto Rico so soon.

Lana keeps talking about *home*. When she suggested leaving this mountain, she didn't ask about *my* home. The closest she's gotten is inquiring about the dragon-friendly manor in San Juan we lived in temporarily. But she's never wanted to know where I was raised—the hellhole with a fresh coating of pain on every brick and tile.

Coming home, as Lana puts it, means returning to a life I tried to run from. Lana expects me to stroll past the chipped paint in the kitchen where my stepfather first smashed a vodka bottle… the dented steel in the backyard where he took a bat to the awning… the coffee tables that displayed my childhood photos before he burned my face off them with cigarettes…

My stepfather is in prison, but his memory haunts those walls.

I've offered to buy Mami a new place.

She insists on staying. "That man doesn't get to destroy what's ours anymore," she'd said the day I left for Dubai.

Lana should go back to her old house if she wants. I don't have to do the same.

WHOOM!

Sand dunes stretch for miles in my thoughts. A sun is perched high in the desert sky; white houses are arranged in a familiar horseshoe formation.

The stadium appears. Riotous chants of "Puerto Rico!" erupt from within. The Keeper's goalpost is at the end of the field. The Runners' mountains are on either side.

Fire crackles beneath me as the Sol de Noches fly toward the goal. They're shooting at the seven different Sires approaching. Together, the black steeds scorch their enemies until there's nothing left. I make it to the goalpost unharmed, then throw the Rock Flame through the hoop.

The crowd screams even louder. This time, they chant my name.

"Victoria! Victoria! Victoria!"

I cover my smiling mouth. Those first few images are memories, but the last ones show me events that never happened. They're what my dragon steed conjures to cheer me up.

Gracias, Esperanza, I tell her in my thoughts. *Pero estoy bien.*

Esperanza whines, hitting me with an image of us soaring toward the Dubai stars. She's mumbling again, too, but the words never fully form. She's still too young to speak.

En serio, chica. Ya basta.

She mumbles louder. "D… De…"

That's as far as she's gotten. I presume she's trying to say "Déjame ayudarte" or a similar expression, but showing me a victory I never experienced isn't the most effective way to help.

Then she slips out of my thoughts with another *WHOOM!*

My mood is immediately sour again. If the Blazewrath World Cup hadn't been canceled, this would've been the night President Turner handed us our first-place trophy. That golden cup was *ours.* Whoever thinks otherwise is a loser. I suppose *I'm* a loser for still referring to him as President Turner. There won't be an International Blazewrath Federation. The sport is history.

I can't be a Striker if I'm not playing Blazewrath. I wish I knew what to call myself now.

But even more than that, more than *anything*, I really wish I could still play.

"If you were an adult, I'd offer you some whiskey." Manny is holding his glass to his chest like it's his greatest treasure. "Looks like you need some."

"Jesus Christ, Pa." Joaquín shakes his head. "That wasn't funny. She's *fifteen*."

"Our baby V." Luis pinches my cheeks while making kissing noises. He's lucky he's one of my best friends. Otherwise, I'd send a roundhouse kick to his jaw. "What's on your mind?"

"She's still recovering from your nightmare of a piano performance," says Héctor.

"Ay, mira, canto de charro. That was *talent*, okay?"

They dive into an argument about what constitutes a talented piano player.

Our bodyguards aren't paying attention. One speaks into his Whisperer—they have the same Rolex that works as a magical communication device. When the agent is done talking, he motions to another. They nod. I'm expecting them to head upstairs, but they hold their positions.

They'll lie if I ask them what's going on. How can I trust people who demand that *I* lie, too? I don't mind twisting the truth if it'll get me what I want. Right now, I want to see my mom. I don't want to think about the golden trophy I didn't win, or the house in Loíza I was supposed to never set foot in again. I want to know why Lana has been kept upstairs this long. She's the key to seeing Mami again *and* discovering what Vogel is up to.

"Can I use the restroom?" I ask the bodyguards. They always let us roam the estate without requiring permission, but their hyper-vigilance tonight comes with a brand new set of rules.

Which makes sneaking upstairs a more pressing matter.

I'm escorted to the one on the first floor.

After locking the door, I slide the glass window open and exit as quietly as possible.

CLIMBING THE BALCONIES ON THE FOUR-STORY MANSION'S exterior will never be as daunting as mounting a dragon.

The hard part is not making any noise. I'm tiptoeing as if I'm treading on thin ice. I'm also ducking low enough to avoid detection through the windows. Lana's room is the last one on the fourth floor, right next to mine. My path winds around the eastern wing's balconies.

The house is spacious enough to feel comfortable, with its wide corridors and towering pillars, but it's *nothing* like our home in Dubai. We don't have training rooms. There isn't a gym. The dragons' habitat is outside, and it's much smaller. Our dragons don't have a pool for their water-spitting games.

The Compound had been built on our wildest dreams. It was the haven that nourished our souls in the middle of Pink Rock Desert. With each step up these creaking wooden beams, I hold back tears—I'll never live anywhere that perfect again.

Don't you dare cry right now, Victoria.

Once I reach the highest balcony, I slow down. The wood stops groaning under my feet as I press under a window.

"Are you positive about the locations?" I hear Vogel whisper. She sounds much closer to the window than Lana's room, which is why I go even lower.

"Yes. Six in Cuba. Four in the Dominican Republic," a male agent says.

"But neither of those countries has dragons."

"Exactly," another man says. "They're trying to lead us on a wild goose chase."

"And force us to soften up security here," the first man adds.

"Just what we needed." Vogel sighs. "We have enough stress with Dragon Knights, and now *this*. Do you know where their hideouts are located?"

"Not yet, but it should be confirmed in the next few hours."

"I hope so," says Vogel. "Have there been any confirmed captures?"

"No. Director Sandhar suspects the dragon trappers have one objective."

Vogel says something else, but it's so low I can't hear it. Her colleagues are no better.

I strain to hear more, but it's all gibberish. My whole body goes cold. *This* is what they're hiding—something other than the Sire's followers is close by. It poses yet another threat to us. These agents are making them sound much worse. A Dragon Knight's style is to break Un-Bonded dragons out of their sanctuaries. They serve their gods of wing and flame with the utmost devotion. If they ever hurt a dragon, it's because the Sire has asked them to.

Who the hell are these dragon trappers? What's their objective?

A bedroom door swings open.

"Okay, I'm ready!" Lana's voice brings me back to my surroundings. She sounds much more cheerful—the Calming Charm has done its job. "Let's have dinner."

I tiptoe downstairs as fast as I can.

My appetite is dead. If these dragon trappers pose a threat, and they're running wild in the Caribbean, we need to be prepared. How can we protect our steeds if we don't know anything about this new enemy? We can't solely depend on the bureau. I have to dig deeper after dinner.

I lost my dream of winning the Cup. I lost my future.

But I *refuse* to lose my dragon.

"¡Ahí está mi hija!" Mami says as she sprints toward me.

Mami's the most beautiful woman on Earth. Despite her flailing arms and that lopsided ponytail, her smile is a stroke of pastel in this pitch-black night. She crushes me to her chest as if she hasn't seen me in a hundred years. It must've felt that long to her.

"Hola, Mami…" I hug her back.

She kisses my forehead. Then she gently presses hers against mine. We're the same height—five-foot-two Puerto Rican hobbits. We could also pass as twins. I got her straight brown hair, button nose, and light skin. We look more like Lana's gringa mom than she does.

Back in Loíza, my neighbors would call me La Blanquita, which is similar to saying "the little white girl." Most people in my community have darker skin. Thanks to a crushing history of colonialism and shitty racial stereotypes, I was usually chosen as group leader in school. They didn't care that Héctor was much better at everything, or that Génesis was the smartest person in any room. Being a mediocre light-skinned girl was more admirable than actual talent.

Being a Striker is the only talent I've ever had.

"¿Qué te pasa?" Mami asks me.

As she lets me go, I think of all the times I daydreamed about bringing her the Cup. It was supposed to mark me as a winner. It would erase the nightmares we endured at the hands of the cruelest man I've ever met. The man who fought hard to show me how little I was worth. I never considered the possibility of coming back to my mother empty-handed.

Now I have nothing to show her.

There's a glow in her gaze, warmth in her soft strokes against my cheeks, as if hell will freeze over before she's ever disappointed in me.

It still doesn't soothe me.

"Nada," I lie with a smile that pains me more than any Charger steed crashing into me. "Ven, Mami. Acompáñame a decirle hola a los demás."

I do the rounds saying hello to my friends' relatives. Everyone is warmer than today's weather, especially Héctor and Génesis' parents. All four have the rare honor of knowing me since I was in diapers. Génesis's older sister, Gloria, slaps my butt before she hugs me. Edwin's grandparents laugh at her antics. I introduce myself to them, a soft-spoken couple with Edwin's elf-like beauty. Then I greet Luis's parents and Gabriela's mom. Joaquín and his wife laugh as I high-five Roberto, their five-year-old son. Mami is at my side through it all.

"¡Mucho gusto!" I hear Lana behind me. She's doing the rounds, too, but she's bubblier than I'll ever be. You'd think she hadn't suffered a panic attack minutes ago.

I need to tell her what I heard upstairs. She's the only person on the team who's known for researching things she's not supposed to. She also has the biggest cojones aside from me. If anyone can help me figure this hushed-up business out, it's Lana Torres.

Wait. I just called us a team. We're not a *team* anymore.

I tip my head back, sighing. This will get easier. But does it have to be so hard?

"Un placer, querida," Mami tells Lana as they embrace. "Thank you for everything you've done for our country." She turns to me. "I'm so proud of you for defeating that silver cabrón."

Lana and her mom burst out laughing.

"That's the perfect word for him," says an approaching Manny. "Cheers, Claudia."

Mami pretends to raise an invisible glass of whiskey. "¡Salud!"

"¡Salud!" everyone else repeats.

SWOOSH!

Six black dragons appear in the night sky.

The Sol de Noches have Faded out of their habitat—a grassy cave farther down the mountain. They're inches away from the magical shield. Thank God they haven't ruined their flor de maga crowns. It had been a challenge fixing our country's national flower on their heads. Esperanza is the cutest tropical queen covered in the flor de maga's scarlet petals. Titán, Fantasma, Puya, Rayo, and Daga are also adorable with their new accessories.

They light themselves on fire.

Each dragon breaks formation to fly around in different patterns, drawing on the sky with their flames. Esperanza soars higher than the rest. She's in charge of the biggest piece in this fiery puzzle—a task she gladly accepted. When they're finished, the dragons fly away from their artwork. It's a recreation of every single member of our families here tonight. They're wrapped in the heart Esperanza made out of her fire. The words LOS AMAMOS spark beneath their feet.

"¡Pero qué belleza!" Héctor's mom, Annie, starts clapping.

Soon everyone joins in, whistling and hollering.

Mami is clapping the hardest, and she's even tearing up. "Ellos son perfectos," she says.

The Sol de Noches take a bow. Daga bows so low that her crown slides off. She snatches it with her teeth, then flings it on top of her head, causing an uproar of laughter from her audience.

Operation Dragon Surprise is a success.

I clap along as I inch closer to Lana. "We need to talk. It's urgent."

She falters, but keeps her gaze on the dragons. "Does it involve the plan?"

"Possibly. I think going outside is a bad idea, but I have to explain why, so can we—"

"Here we go again." Lana stares at me like I've incinerated all of her Monsta X albums. She's even stopped clapping. "Victoria, how can you not want to leave this house? What's so wonderful about being cooped up on a freaking mountain? Why are you this selfish?"

It's like she presses PAUSE on the world, and the only thing still moving is the girl who's perpetually oblivious to my needs. Whether she's forgotten about my past, or she keeps choosing to overlook it, I won't tolerate such classless disrespect. But putting Lana in her place would mean discussing why I'm livid. I'd have to prick my wounds and show her I'm bleeding. Her idea of home will never be mine, and she won't get it until I make her.

Fuck that. I don't have to explain myself.

"Victoria. I'm talking to you."

"Then you can keep talking to yourself."

I'm back at Mami's side. She happily feeds Esperanza a boneless rib. As my dragon steed swallows it, her black-and-yellow eyes settle on me. They're narrowed with worry, but she doesn't try to break into my thoughts again. She knows I'll kick her out.

"I missed you both so much," Mami says breathlessly. She tosses another rib to Esperanza. My dragon steed catches it while Mami wraps an arm around me. "Ahora me siento completa."

What I'd give to also feel complete. I don't know what I am if I'm not a Striker.

Tonight I'll settle for being the daughter my mother deserves.

"So do I, Mami," I whisper. "So do I."

The International Bureau of Magical Matters was founded in 1684. It thrived in secret from the Regular community. The bureau's first director wished to go public in 1692 as an act of defiance to the Salem Witch Trials. However, they didn't come out of the shadows until 1743, when a Scottish Golden Horn Bonded with a Regular. The bureau has adhered to the same principle since its inception: protect all living beings from magical threats. There will always be threats it can't foresee. Then there are those it's quite aware of, but is incapable of stopping.

—Excerpt from Julissa Mercado's article "Behind Bureau Walls: The Complicated History of the International Bureau of Magical Matters" in The Weekly Scorcher

CHAPTER THREE

Lana

So THE PLAN ISN'T WORKING.

Or maybe it *is* working, but our bodyguards are too stubborn to admit it. It's been twenty-four hours since the family dinner ended. We feasted on more lechón asado than should be legally acceptable, made fun of everyone's baby pictures, then closed the night off with Luis's cringe-worthy piano skills. We sang out of tune and danced like it was the last night on Earth.

Well, most of us did. Victoria had flat-out refused to partake in any fun.

"My dignity is very important to me," she'd told us. "But knock yourselves out."

She also wouldn't look at me when I dove into my woe-is-me spiel at the dinner table. My proudest achievement is how often I emphasized the twelve years I've been in the States. Héctor's parents, Annie and Jaime, had been quick to agree it's been way too long. Almost everyone chimed in to back me up. A melodramatic Joaquín expressed his fear that exposing us, even if we *were* hidden under Invisibility Charms, would still be dangerous.

Victoria had been deathly silent. The rest of my friends complained to their relatives some more in private. Jacinto, Edwin's grandpa, led the charge toward the agents. Manny relayed his message in English (he sprinkled in some bonus swear words). Agent Vogel nodded, but said nothing. It had been like that the whole time someone went up to her. Not even when the families left did she address anything she'd heard. She just sent us to bed like she's done every night.

Not even the promise of a brand new day can make me feel better.

"Would you like an extra pancake?" Joaquín asks. He and Mom are the only ones at the table with me. The others are either still snoring, or hanging out with their steeds.

From across the dining room, Agent Vogel and a male colleague stand guard. What are they supposed to be protecting us from right now? A spike in our cholesterol levels?

"I'm good, thanks," I say.

Joaquín dumps the pancake on his plate, then steers his wheelchair to the front porch. He loves eating breakfast with the Sol de Noches. They surround him like hungry puppies, waiting for their chance to steal his bacon. Joaquín's not even parked when Daga's euphoric squeal tears through the mountain. I can see her hips swaying at full speed along with her tail, which keeps hitting both Fantasma and Puya. They roll their eyes as they move away from her.

Not even adorable dragons can make me laugh.

I lazily pick at my scrambled eggs. They've gone cold, but I don't have the appetite for them anyway. Am I *really* going to be trapped in this house? There haven't been confirmed Dragon Knight sightings here yet. So far, the only danger the outside world poses are those jerks advocating for the murder of dragons.

I haven't checked the news. The way that guy with the Todd T-shirt had screamed... as if he has any idea what I went through... cutting me down like I'm nothing...

You're a murderer, too!

My fork slips out of my hand. It lands with a loud clang on the plate.

"Honey? What's wrong?" Mom squeezes my hand.

"I'm fine. Just lost my grip."

She won't let go. "How are you feeling today?" Her voice is softer than silk.

Yesterday we sat next to each other in my room after that embarrassing display in front of everyone, and she'd also spoken with the same tenderness.

I'd barely said a word. Don't get me wrong—I *love* having Mom back in my life. This is just so mortifying. All the tears that spilled out, how I plummeted like the whole world sat on top of me. That's not who I am. I can't be the girl who sobs because strangers are guilt-tripping her.

I'm the girl who took the Sire's fire. I saved the world.

But you couldn't save Andrew...

A slight tremor creeps up from my fingertips to my wrist.

I pull away from Mom before she feels it, too. "Tired, but I'm much better."

The tremor persists. I can't focus on last night's hater brigade. Freaking out again is out of the question, especially in public. I fish out my phone. Kitten videos will surely distract me.

"Stay away from social media, okay?" Mom says.

"Why? Has Todd posted something?"

Damn it. I thought I'd stopped caring about his antics. Now I'm wondering how low he's stooping. What if he's calling me a murderer without hiding behind his groupies? Is he trashing Andrew's memory, too? This is a deeper cut than asking Gold Wands to kill dragons. His initial threat hurts other members of society, but bringing Andrew into this… that's a shot at me.

I killed him.

I put the phone between my knees. Pressing them together doesn't stop the shivers. It doesn't rip out the part of my brain that remembers how Andrew had closed his tearful eyes and refused to beg for his life. How he let the Sire shatter all hope of ever seeing his mother, his teammates, his fans, ever again.

"Lana?" Mom's voice is the thin thread tethering me to right here, right now.

I hadn't noticed she's hunching over the dinner table. Her expression is more hopeless than yesterday. She'd given up on getting me to talk. As the Calming Charm worked its way through me, Mom held me as if it's the only thing she *could* do. Not once did she mention calling Papi. He's still in Brazil leading a frantic search for Violet #43, the Brazilian Pesadelo who'd fled after the Sire's ambush at the dragon sanctuary where Papi works. Hopefully, she didn't call him with news of my meltdown afterward. I'd hate to be yet another burden in his life.

The way Mom's looking at me suggests she could definitely use a vacation. It's like she's had to put down a pet she's grown up with. She's facing a loss she's unprepared for.

Then it hits me.

"Do you *miss* him?" I chide. Only a loser like me would forget how much Leslie Ann Wells cherished her favorite nephew.

"No," she says curtly. "What I told you in Dubai about him becoming someone else… that's bullshit, Lana. To me, he changed, but to you… this is who he was all along, wasn't it?"

"Yes." My reply flies out with ease. "He was always the worst."

"And I should've seen it from the beginning."

I want to nod, but that would mean I'm ready for this conversation.

"It's okay, Mom," I say. "You're making good decisions now. That's what matters."

"Stop making excuses for me. I've made enough for the past seventeen years." Mom's blank stare lands on the orange juice she's left untouched. "You were always your father's daughter, and I didn't know how to handle that. You both loved dragons and Blazewrath. You share your Puerto Rican culture. I was on the outside looking in, and I felt this *need* to center myself in everything you did. I wanted you to live more like *me* instead. If I got you to see things my way, it meant you loved me, too. That I had a place in your life and heart."

"Listen. It's fine, okay? I—"

"Todd felt more like family because he didn't love dragons or Blazewrath. He made me feel like I wasn't wrong in my distrust. But he was never distrustful. He was hateful."

"Yeah, but we don't have to talk—"

"I'm disgusted with myself, Lana. I understand if you felt the same way about me."

Mom takes the biggest deep breath I've ever seen her take. She's unraveling, and I get a front row ticket to the years of conversations we've neglected all in the span of a few minutes.

The tremors grow more intense. Now it's both hands. And my tongue feels ten times heavier, wider. I couldn't speak even if I wanted to.

Mom keeps going on about Todd this and Todd that, and I'm here wiping my hands on my jeans under the table but nothing is working and she. Keeps. *Talking*. He must've really posted something today. I can't stomach him dwelling on Andrew's murder. But if Todd is hurting others, or trying to incite violence again, the least I can do is acknowledge it.

"Did he ever say anything to hurt you besides the dragon hate? Because if he did, he's—"

I push my seat back. "Sorry. Bathroom break."

Mom says nothing as I grab my phone. Granted, I'm moving way too fast to even catch anything she might be saying. As I approach the first floor bathroom, I check Twitter first. That's my cousin's favorite platform to bash me. The day after he challenged me to debate him, he'd shared a meme with my face photoshopped on a rattlesnake's body. What a gentleman.

But when I open the app, my timeline is filled with pictures of a building that's been set ablaze. It's located in the middle of San Ignacio, one of the oldest neighborhoods in La Habana, Cuba. The building had been a restaurant. It offered free drinks to anyone who presented bartenders with a used ticket to the Blazewrath World Cup. There were no survivors.

Two hours later, another burning had occurred in the Dominican Republic.

A dragon studies museum in Santo Domingo is in ashes. No survivors reported, either.

This doesn't reek of Dragon Knights. They tend to go after sanctuaries. Maybe they're switching their style up to throw the bureau off. Or is this something else?

Victoria…

She's been so adamant about staying cooped up here. What if she knows more about these burnings? How the hell would she even know about them in the first place?

There's one other person who could be in the loop. Calling Papi usually results in me talking to his voicemail, so I save myself the frustration and write instead: *Bendición, Papi. Any intel on these new burnings in the Caribbean? Please be careful!*

After I press SEND, I march upstairs to Victoria's bedroom.

Who would've thought I'd ever go to her for answers?

"JUST A SECOND!" VICTORIA ROARS FROM BEHIND HER LOCKED DOOR.

She never locks herself in. She could just be changing out of her pajamas.

Or she could be hiding something.

"It's Lana. Open up."

Silence.

Then she says, "One minute!"

Oh, now it's a whole minute.

Sure enough, she takes her sweet time unlocking the door. When I finally walk into her room, Victoria yawns as if she's missed out on seven hundred years of sleep. Her hair is messier than a bird's nest after a hurricane, and she's still in her black sportswear.

"What do you want?" Even when she's exhausted, her venomous tone doesn't relent.

"Why do you look like you haven't slept?"

Victoria locks the door again. "I was up watching *Golden Girls*," she deadpans.

I'd bet a million dollars she's never seen a single episode.

She scurries over to her desk, where her red laptop's open on the YouTube homepage. There's nothing written on the search bar. It's like she scrambled to find the page to hide whatever she was really looking at. And there's a closed notebook next to the computer.

"Are you ever going to explain why you're here?" she says with a stone-cold glare. "Shouldn't you be discussing your escape plans with your non-selfish friends?"

For a hot second, I'm totally blanking on why she'd bring up selfishness.

Then I remember what I said last night. I'm pretty sure she called me worse things behind my back when we were still in Dubai. Also, it's not like I'm wrong. Victoria Peralta is sitting on her high horse yet again, and she's acting like I'm cutting off its legs for funsies.

I won't get any answers if I antagonize her further. And I'm *so* not in the mood to fight.

"My bad, okay? People say ridiculous things when they're pissed. I was out of line."

Victoria's cocked eyebrow keeps rising. It's like she's waiting for something else.

Does she want me to apologize in iambic pentameter? Put on a whole musical production? What more could she possibly need to sweep our crappy conversation under the rug?

"Anyway." I flash her my phone. "Someone burned down buildings in Cuba and the Dominican Republic. Is this why you don't want us to ask the bureau for escorted breaks?"

Victoria digs her fingers into her hair. Whatever disappointment she must've felt in my apology has been replaced with dread. "Fuck..." she whispers.

"That would be a yes. Now tell me what's going on."

"What did they burn?" She takes my phone before I can answer. She's scrolling at warp speed, falling down the same rabbit hole as me. "So this was their plan all along."

"Who are you talking about, Victoria? Also, those burnings happened *after* dinner. How did you know they were happening?"

"I didn't know about them per se." Victoria gives me back my phone. She pulls out her desk chair for me, and once I'm seated, she plops down on her bed. "Vogel and two other agents were talking outside of your room last night. I snuck upstairs to find out if they're hiding your..." She clears her throat, picking at nonexistent hair on her pants. "If they're hiding *us* for reasons other than the ones they're saying. I overheard them talking about dragon trappers in the Caribbean. Specifically"— she meets my gaze—"Cuba and the Dominican Republic."

I lean forward, making sure I heard her right. "Dragon *trappers*?"

"Yes. I couldn't find much, but there are rumors of people who kidnap Un-Bonded dragons in the wild. These kidnappings are rare, since many die in the attempt, but there have been *three* successful kidnappings reported in the past week. Two in Denmark. One in Japan." Victoria yawns again. "The Akarui dragon had been spotted flying over a village in Fukushima about an hour before the burning in Santo Domingo. Once the bureau rushed over to the crime scene, the Akarui disappeared. Nearby residents told local news they heard it cry out in pain."

I don't know what's more shocking—the existence of dragon trappers, or the fact that Victoria has become interested in something other than Blazewrath. She's not lighting up like a park full of Christmas trees, though, so this newfound interest isn't making her too happy.

I wonder if she'll ever be that happy again. If we'll ever get back to how we were on that stage in New York, bonding over our shared heartbreak.

That doesn't matter right now. Stay focused.

"You think the kidnappings and the burnings are connected?" I ask.

"Thanks to you. I'd been so focused on finding more information about these trappers that I hadn't seen anything else online. The bodyguards said the trapper sightings had been in the Caribbean, not Europe or Eastern Asia, which makes me think the bureau was there instead. The burnings could've been a distraction so they could snatch those Un-Bondeds."

That does make sense. "But why are they taking dragons?"

"I haven't figured that out yet. Besides, that's not my only concern." Victoria hugs her pillow tight, scowling at the sheets she hasn't slept in. "One of the bodyguards told Vogel this could be their way of getting the bureau to soften up security *here*."

I freeze. The only dragons here are the Sol de Noches, and Dragon Knights are already after them. How can there be *another* threat we have to protect them from? And what's worse, we don't have a clue what these people want! At least Dragon Knights are forthright. Our bodyguards would die before they confess. If we want answers, we can't rely on them.

"We have to take this up directly with Director Sandhar," I say. "If these jerks are trying to kidnap the Sol de Noches, we deserve to know why. And most of all, how we can stop them."

Victoria nods. "*Nobody's* touching my steed."

I shouldn't be smiling. More terrible people are coming to hurt our dragons.

But watching Victoria Peralta, sourpuss extraordinaire, turn into my tag-team partner in this new mission… having something to concentrate on besides Todd and his vitriol… the guilt and grief over what happened in Brazil…. Who knows if Victoria and I will end up becoming friends? At least we'll be fighting the bad guys together again, and that's good enough for me.

"Lana? You were going to contact Sandhar?"

"Right!"

I don't have Director Sandhar's number, but I do have Agent Horowitz's. I fetch her card from my Wonder Woman backpack and fire off a simple message: *Tell your boss to meet me ASAP. I know about the dragon trappers trying to steal the Sol de Noches.*

FIVE MINUTES LATER, SOMEONE KNOCKS ON VICTORIA'S DOOR.

"Agent Vogel here. Director Sandhar is downstairs. He wishes to speak with you."

This is your fault. First, you run away from the quarterfinals 'cause you knew Scotland would beat Puerto Rico. Don't act like Takeshi Endo and the Sire really kidnapped your dad. I know that was staged. Second, the Cup gets canceled with the stupid excuse that dragons don't want to play anymore? The IBF should be making them play! What am I supposed to do now that Blazewrath's over? Those protesters in San Juan are right—you are a murderer. You killed the most important thing in my life, and someone better make you pay.

—*Anonymous comment left on Lana Torres's BlazeReel profile page*

CHAPTER FOUR

Lana

"**F**OR THE BILLIONTH TIME, MISS TORRES, EVERYTHING IS UNDER control."

Nirek Sandhar, director of the Department of Magical Investigations, sips his latte with the nonchalance of a retiree who's enjoying his first day out of the workforce. He simply can't be bothered with how much I'm tapping my foot on the porch's wooden floor. I don't think he's realized Victoria hasn't stopped glaring at him the whole time he's been sitting with us, or how the house has been quaking for the past fifteen minutes thanks to the Sol de Noches.

They're entertaining themselves by rolling down the mountain.

Daga screeches in utter delight as she tumbles like a scaly eight ball. Puya and Rayo are pretty loud, too, but nothing beats the pack's baby. A reluctant Fantasma only joins in after Titán shoves him with his massive head. Poor Fantasma wails during his descent. Esperanza lets out a belly laugh at his anguish. Génesis and Gabriela are filming them with their phones. The boys are at the bottom of the mountain, proclaiming the first dragon to get closest to the shield the winner. Daga has won every single time.

"This is the cutest thing I've ever seen," says Agent Horowitz. She's claimed the seat to my left, elegant in a pastel coral dress and matching trench coat. Her blonde hair is styled in waves today. "It's good to see them having fun."

It's so weird to see her this close to me when I've spent *days* waiting for her text messages. She hasn't acknowledged them, which is ten thousand times weirder. "You know what's even better? The truth," I say. "Why haven't you contacted me until now?"

Agent Horowitz doesn't look away from the dragons. "It's been hectic at the bureau. My workload has risen like you wouldn't believe."

"Why?"

"Boring stuff, I promise."

"Such as?"

She laughs as she glances at me. "New hires, mostly, and I'm thinking we should consider *you* for a position. You're a natural interrogator, Lana."

My mouth is a thin line. "Hilarious. Now tell me the truth."

"That's precisely what we've given you," says Director Sandhar.

Victoria scoffs. "Is that why you Transported here in a rush? This seems more like damage control than reassurance. You could've texted Lana she had nothing to worry about."

"Exactly. Also"—I point to Agent Vogel's sour expression—"Victoria *heard her* talking about dragon trappers nearby. Why would one of your agents freak out about something you claim to have under control? And *what* are they trying to steal our dragons for? I'm having a hard time picturing some random kidnappers wanting to free the Sire, too."

"Where are they taking the other dragons they've caught?" Victoria adds.

Director Sandhar lowers his empty coffee mug. The man who'd blown up at Takeshi Endo for trying to kill the Sire against his orders is gone. Now he's the master of slow, measured movements, including the way he breathes.

"I'm not at liberty to discuss that, but I didn't come here to do damage control. I wanted to look you dead in the eye"—he looks at Victoria, then at me—"and tell you there's no reason to worry. Messaging you felt impersonal. After all we've been through, the least I can do is make sure you hear it straight from me. I figured it would provide you with a greater sense of calm."

"So you *are* worried about Lana's health." Victoria looks from him to Agent Vogel to him again. "Are you trying to keep her from doing something reckless again? Like saving a dragon at a wand shop or forfeiting a Blazewrath match to save her dad? What would make her act impulsively this time?" She pauses. "Does someone besides our dragons need saving?"

"No, Miss Peralta, but I admire your perseverance," Director Sandhar says.

I can't believe I hadn't thought of that. But I'm also not a fan of how Victoria's suggesting I'm a mess. Does everyone else think that, too? As if *they* wouldn't risk their lives for their own parents! Besides, last night's meltdown won't happen again. I'd simply been caught off guard. That doesn't mean something's wrong with me or that I'm a liability.

I just have to do a better job at convincing others.

I clear my throat, hoping my voice doesn't crack. I sit on my hands, too, in case they get sweaty or start shaking again. "You can tell me if something's wrong, Director. I can handle it."

"We know, but there's nothing to tell," Agent Horowitz reassures me. She's speaking politely, as she often does, but a grim shadow sets up shop on her expression, as if she's picturing me jumping toward the Sire's queued-up fireball again.

I wonder if she looked at Takeshi like that when she started training him as a bureau agent, too. If she had any inkling about what he'd end up doing, if she ever thought about stopping him. Then I remember they also failed at preventing Randall's vengeful spiral. Is this why they're so worried about me? How could they think I'll become even a fraction of what Randall was?

I'm not one of their past misfires. I'm not going rogue.

I. Am. *Fine.*

"Lana?" I hear Victoria calling me.

"My bad. I was just thinking." I shrug at Director Sandhar. "Nothing is wrong?"

He nods, looking down at his coffee mug. "Nothing."

"So Takeshi's trial is still happening next week?"

"Bright and early on Monday."

"And Randall Wiggins is dead already?"

"The Dragonshade poison has killed him, yes."

"And there are no dragon trappers coming to Puerto Rico."

"Everyone here is safe." Director Sandhar is motioning to Agent Vogel, who approaches him. "Brunhilde, please treat these girls to takeout brunch from wherever they wish. Sienna and I will be greeting the other riders and their steeds now. Thank you."

"Yes, sir." Agent Vogel helps me stand, even though I'm perfectly okay.

My mind races with what Victoria said about my health, though. I know I can be… spontaneous. Sometimes it's best to charge into battle. And if Victoria's right about someone other than the Sol de Noches needing to be saved, this conversation is very much not over.

It just can't continue with Director Sandhar or Agent Horowitz.

I have to contact the only person at the bureau who can help me.

"Are you in the mood for bacalaítos?" says Agent Vogel. I've never heard the word 'bacalaítos' pronounced with a German accent, but it's officially my favorite thing ever.

"That'd be great. I have to pee, though. Be right back."

I bolt to the bathroom. After I lock the door, I speak into my red Whisperer.

"Samira? Can you hear me?"

Three seconds later, she yells, "LANAAAA!"

I can't help but crack up. "Stop yelling, you weirdo! How are you?"

"Better now! These tests are taking forever, girl. I finished one five minutes ago, and there were three before that. If I weren't this excited about officially being recognized as a Gold Wand, I'd hate my life. But it's like... these people don't *want* me to get certified?"

"Oh, my God. What happened?"

"I did some research before taking my first test."

"Of course you did."

"*And* there's usually not this many hoops to jump over. When you ace a test, you move on, but I've been asked to retake two tests already. Also, whenever I ask about my scores, one of the instructors keeps insinuating they're better than expected, but I can't tell if it's because I'm really powerful, or if it's because I'm the only Black person getting certified. Am I being too nitpicky? I mean, this *is* the International Bureau of Magical Matters, and none of my instructors are white." She pauses. "Then again, I wouldn't be surprised if everything I fear is true."

"Either way, give me that instructor's name so I can report them to Director Sandhar. Or would you like to report them after your certification is over?"

"Ugh, if it ever actually ends... I don't know how I'll proceed yet, but thanks for the tip."

"Anytime. I wish this person a thousand flesh-eating worms in their T-shirts." Samira laughs, even though I'm one hundred percent serious. "I'm so sorry they're putting you through such a grueling process, but hey, you're *killing it* and you always will. Let them stay mad."

"Yup!" She laughs again. "Give me some good news. What's the gossip?"

"Well, I was wondering if you've heard about dragon trappers and kidnapped Un-Bondeds. There's another group trying to hurt the Sol de Noches, but Victoria and I haven't found much."

"Whoa, whoa, whoa. Did you just say *Victoria*?" Samira whistles loud enough to summon all living birds. "Plot twist for the ages! As for this dragon trapper business, I've heard nothing." She falls silent. I picture her grinning like the Cheshire cat. "Want me to snoop around?"

God, I love those magic words. "That would be awesome. Thanks, Samira. And—"

SWISH!

That's a Transport Charm noise. Someone has either arrived or left.

SWISH! SWISH!

"Lana? What's going on?"

"Gotta go, but please snoop carefully!"

I run back to the porch. Mom, Joaquín, and Manny have joined Victoria and Agent Vogel.

Farther ahead, Director Sandhar and Agent Horowitz are talking to three newly arrived female agents. Since their backs are turned to the house, I can't read their lips.

"Who are they?" I ask Agent Vogel.

"I've sent for your brunch. It'll be here soon."

Manny laughs. "Nice swerve."

"I'm simply stating facts." Agent Vogel waves to the living room. "Let's wait inside."

She walks in first.

Mom is furrowing her brow at me. She knows something's up, too. "Come on, honey," she says as Manny marches into the house. "Let me fetch you a plate."

Director Sandhar whips out his wand. He's talking a mile a minute, staring at his agents with the same intensity he'd shown in the Blazewrath stadium's green room, when the Sire revealed Randall as a Dragon Knight. What could anger Director Sandhar as much as the Gold Wand who murdered his son? He addresses Agent Horowitz, who takes out her wand, too.

"They're leaving," says Victoria.

What if they're off to fight? Whether it's against Dragon Knights or these mysterious trappers, I won't know until much later. I might *never* know—this secrecy is on another level. I could wait for Samira's intel… or I can follow Director Sandhar.

He's raising his wand high.

I snatch Victoria's wrist, then dash out of the porch.

"What are you doing?!" she yells as the female agents Transport.

SWISH! SWISH! SWISH!

Director Sandhar and Agent Horowitz cast their spells at the same time.

I lunge at them alongside a screaming Victoria, swallowed into the blinding white light.

SLAMMING YOUR BUTT ONTO CONCRETE ISN'T THE BEST WAY TO make an entrance.

I'm launched out of the light, groaning upon impact. Victoria lands next to me.

Director Sandhar and Agent Horowitz are a good twenty feet away. They're charging forward to a set of black curtains, which are located at the end of the corridor we've landed in. If you sneak into someone else's Transport Charm, the spell sends you flying from the magic user who cast it. Victoria and I remain undetected yet throbbing in places that'll be sore for weeks.

"Are you fucking kidding me right now? You've just brought us over to God knows where, and we don't have any weapons or backup!" If Victoria were a dragon, I'd definitely have my head bitten off. She's bright red and fuming, as if she's on the hunt for blood.

I hold up a hand. "Don't contact Esperanza yet. We don't know what we're up against."

"As if I'd willingly put my steed in danger."

"Well, you did let her Fade to Brazil and save me."

"A decision I will regret *forever*." Her flaring nostrils are really selling her hatred for me.

"Dragonblood! Dragonblood! Dragonblood!"

The chanting is coming from behind the black curtains.

"Is this… a stadium?" Victoria whispers.

The corridor does remind me of where we played Blazewrath, but the tiled walls are as black as a Sol de Noche's scales. Dimly lit red lamps swing from the ceiling. Each one is shaped like a flame. Unlike Dubai, there's no security, no staff.

"Dragonblood! Dragonblood! Dragonblood!"

A dragon roar drowns out the chants.

Victoria and I gasp.

Then we scramble to the black curtains. We pull them aside just a little, covering ourselves as much as possible, and peek at what lies ahead.

We *are* in a stadium. It only has three floors, but the black stands are full. Everyone wears a mask. Ghosts, devils, jesters, those gorgeous ones at the Carnival of Venice… the list goes on. The audience faces a sandpit shaped like a hexagon. Machines tower over the corner seats. A different dragon species is showcased as its mechanical rendering. They have hollowed-out backs big enough to fit twenty people. The most common dragon is the French Chasseur—a black-scaled beast with golden spots. It's poised to strike with its gold fangs. Only one place features machinery like this. We're in Le Parc Du Chasseurs, a theme park in Nantes, France.

There are two *real* dragons in the pit—a Chasseur and an Akarui. The red-feathered crown atop the Akarui's head shines brighter in the sunlight. Its white scales are a stark contrast from the Chasseur's dark-and-gold blend. Thick metal chains are strapped to their necks and ankles.

"Dragonblood! Dragonblood! Dragonblood!"

"Oh, my God…" I whisper. "Are they really gonna—"

The dragons hurtle toward each other with matching battle cries.

Before the first Rock Flame was thrown, there were many attempts at creating no-contact sports with dragons. One that almost took off was the short-lived Flamebounce. Riders had to jump through consecutive fire hoops in the skies. Their steeds cushioned their falls and launched them back up. First rider to reach the last hoop won. Audiences demanded dragons engage in battle instead. Perry Jo Smith's solution was Blazewrath, but a vociferous few believed it was still too tame. They craved more rage, more fire. They begged for blood.

—Excerpt from Harleen Khurana's A History of Blazewrath Around the World

CHAPTER FIVE

Lana

THIS ISN'T AN ORDINARY FIGHT.

Their chains are long enough to let them slam into one another. The Chasseur's fangs latch onto a spot on the Akarui's neck that isn't covered in metal. It's tugging with all its might. The Akarui whips the French dragon with its tail, swatting it like a bothersome fly. Blood seeps out of the Akarui's neck as the Chasseur unleashes a fireball in midair. The Akarui blows it aside with its own. Then both dragons rush at each other again, their fangs searching for flesh.

"Dragonblood! Dragonblood! Dragonblood!"

This is a death match.

Victoria touches her temples. "Esperanza's freaking out. The others realized we're gone."

"Tell them not to Fade here! It'll only make things worse."

"I *know*." Victoria is silent as she psychically relays the message. Then she looks down at the pit again. "We need to stop this fight, Lana. I won't let these dragons kill each other. And I think that's the Akarui that was kidnapped earlier this week. Dragon trappers are using their captures to throw a fighting tournament, and the bureau knew about it?" She scours the seats, as if she's searching for Director Sandhar and Agent Horowitz, but they must be hiding behind masks, too. "Sandhar would never be in league with them, but why isn't he arresting everyone?"

"The same reason we're not doing anything. This place is *packed*."

"Then let's create a diversion. We could blow something up and make everyone disperse."

Whoa. It's one thing to research dragon trappers behind my back, but now she'll rip this place apart? When did Victoria become more gung ho than me? Or is she suggesting the most chaotic solution because she thinks it's what I'd choose? Me, the so-called emotional wreck the bureau is tiptoeing around, incapable of patience and rational thought. This is where I prove I'm *not* a mess. Stopping this death match will require caution, and that's exactly what I'll use.

Maybe the bureau is waiting for something. Director Sandhar would've charged into battle if he knew he could take these jerks down. Either he really is scared of how many people are surrounding him—which I don't blame him for—or there's another reason he's here.

"Let's observe first, Victoria. Why don't we split up?"

"And search for *what*?"

"Any sign of a leader. Whoever's in charge must be high on the bureau's priority list." I wave at the stands. "If we find the boss of Dragon Fight Club, we can end it."

Victoria points to her face. "We don't have masks."

I tug on my shirt. Looks like I'll be wearing a crop top today. "Help me rip this up."

Victoria and I quickly tear the cloth into two pieces—one mask for her, one for me.

She blinks like a cat that's fed up with human interaction. "What if a dragon dies before we find this leader? I don't want to watch that, Lana. I'm certain you don't, either."

"Of course I don't want that! But the more time we waste arguing, the quicker this death match could actually turn deadly, so let's find this person and force them to call it quits."

I don't care if she thinks I'm a brat. This is our best shot at saving these dragons.

Victoria lowers her head. "Don't get caught," she hisses.

"*You* don't get caught."

"As if."

Victoria takes the right side. I go left.

My gaze is cast down as I weave through rows of screaming attendees. I find an empty seat on the last one. The Venetian mask next to me is yelling her lungs out in Italian. I frame my face with my loose hair. The chances of getting recognized are still high, but it's better than nothing.

This stadium doesn't have box seats like Dubai. There are no marked VIP sections, either. If there are any important people here, they're acting like normal spectators.

A burst of white light sweeps over the pit.

The Akarui's scales are flashing a blinding wall of ivory at its opponent. With a wail, the Chasseur rocks back and forth, then wobbles to the sides. It keeps stumbling and complaining in a high-pitched cry. This is the Akarui's magical advantage—their light messes up their rival's senses, granting them a narrow window for offensive tactics.

The Chasseur fires off more flames than before, but the poor thing is aiming at one of the mechanical dragons. The Akarui flies as high as its chains will allow, then hurls a fireball at the Chasseur's face. As the

Chasseur cries, the Japanese dragon dives back into the pit, zooming past the stands at warp speed. People cling to their seats to avoid being blown away. The Akarui bares its pale fangs during its descent. When the Chasseur finally regains its balance, it spreads glorious black wings, leaping to meet its opponent halfway.

It blasts the Akarui again, but the Japanese dragon swerves.

And sinks its fangs into the Chasseur's neck.

With a swift jerk, it yanks the flesh right off. Crimson splatters the sand below, the nearest mechanical dragons, and some of the people in the first row. The Akarui lands in the middle of the pit, its mouth stained red like its crown of feathers. It watches in poised silence as the dragon at the other end of the stadium collapses, its eyes pressed shut.

The Chasseur is dead.

"Oh, my God…" I'm peeking through my fingers, unable to breathe. This is my first time seeing a dragon's death. No, scratch that—a dragon's *murder*. What kind of horrible people call this entertainment? How has the bureau not stopped this? If Victoria's right, and they've known about it prior to this match, what are they afraid of? My blood runs cold as I remember the dragon trappers near Puerto Rico. This is what they're really after. Capturing the Sol de Noches isn't about setting the Sire free like the Dragon Knights. They want our dragons to *compete*.

"Dragonblood! Dragonblood! Dragonblood!"

The crowd is chanting again. Everyone is clapping, whistling, as they repeat that heinous word like a sacred prayer. I'd thought it was an order they were spewing. Now I think it's what this tournament is called—I'm a witness to a Dragonblood ring.

On the other side of the stadium, right on the first row, a teenage girl is perfectly still.

She's in a red dress, her slim arms crossed. I can't believe I didn't see her before—she doesn't have a mask on. She's not wearing a hood, either. This girl is brave enough to expose her fair skin, her rose-blush cheeks, and a half-grin that could scare off even the creepiest demons.

She raises a hand in the air.

The stadium falls silent.

"Congratulations to our champion, the Akarui!" the girl says in a thick accent. It reminds me of Team Spain during their Cup interviews. "Let's give him another round of applause!"

The crowd obeys. She *has* to be the leader. She's too young to be running such a massive event, but why else would these people do as she commands?

I search for Victoria. Maybe she's much closer to this girl.

I find her crouched figure on the opposite side of the stadium, but she's too high up. I take my phone out to text her. Victoria can sneak her way down while I walk over to help her.

The girl pulls out a Gold wand.

Of course she's a witch. But does she *have* to be the most powerful kind? And that craftsmanship… her wand is only golden on both ends. The middle is gleaming white marble. That's a Julia Serrano design! How did this Spanish witch get her hands on a model made by Puerto Rico's first wand-maker? The only Gold Wand the island has ever known?

"Cecilia! Cecilia! Cecilia!"

SWISH!

The girl named Cecilia Transports in front of the Akarui. It whines as it retreats. It won't even glance at her. Cecilia nods, as if she's pleased with the dragon's fear. Most Un-Bondeds don't care whether you're a magic user or a Regular like me—you're still getting fried. The Akarui's capture must've been traumatizing. I couldn't save the Chasseur, but now I'm even more desperate to get this majestic creature back to where it belongs.

"I have a very special reward for our champion. Are you ready?" says Cecilia.

The crowd's reply is swift. "Yes!"

"Blood Masks, bring me our new guest!"

A dozen people Transport beside her. They're also wearing masks, but theirs are the exact same design—a ruby face with a black dragon claw mark slashed across it. These new arrivals are all decked out in fine suits and dresses.

Silver bureau badges are pinned to their outfits.

These Blood Masks are *bureau agents*? Or did they steal those badges to pose as them? This could be why Director Sandhar hasn't done anything yet. He could've been waiting to confirm their identities. I can't believe he tried to sell me on his "everything is under control" crap. How is *any* of this under control?

The Blood Masks are dragging a handcuffed teenage boy into the ring. The black jumpsuit he's wearing has the Ravensworth Penitentiary logo on the left side of his chest.

I sit bolt upright, a scream lodged in my throat. He's not the polished gentleman I last saw at Andrew's funeral. Now he's a hostage with a black eye and cuts on his swollen cheeks.

"Takeshi…" I whisper breathlessly. Is this why Director Sandhar didn't want me to search for answers? Did he know the Blood Masks had taken him? Why would they even *want* him?

Cecilia aims a spell at Takeshi.

He's forced to his knees, but his expression remains calm.

"Everyone," she says, "please welcome Takeshi Endo to the Dragonblood ring!"

The whole place explodes into applause.

I'm rooted to the spot. Not only do I have to save the Akarui, I also have to get Takeshi out of here alive! I start typing a message for Victoria.

A gloved hand covers my mouth.

I'm yanked out of my seat.

Being the best Striker is about so much more than having perfect aim. Tossing a Rock Flame is one thing. Steering a dragon while your rivals thrash every inch of you is another. Japan has a master Striker in Takeshi Endo. He embodies what every Striker should aspire to: razor-sharp focus, adaptability, and an unbeatable spirit. A good Striker will seize their chance when they spot an opening. The best Striker will create it when their opponent least expects it.

—*Excerpt from Olga Peñaloza's* Blazewrath All-Stars, Third Edition

CHAPTER SIX

Victoria

I NEVER THOUGHT I'D HAVE TO SAVE TAKESHI ENDO.

This guy is a Blazewrath legend, a double agent who plotted the Sire's murder to near-completion, and he's kneeling in front of some witch. Why is she so interested in him?

I can't look at the Chasseur's body. The last time I saw blood spilling out that fast, I'd smashed a bottle into my stepfather's head. As happy as I was to end his cruelty, I wish I never had to in the first place. Just like I wish the French dragon hadn't been slaughtered for sport. I *told* Lana this would happen, didn't I? We should've chosen the diversion like I suggested. Serves me right for trusting the human equivalent of a teen soap opera.

BAM! BAM! BAM!

Esperanza keeps ramming into the dark-tiled wall I've put up around my thoughts. She can neither see where I am nor hear what I'm thinking—my strongest psychic block yet. Even if I implore her to stay in Cayey, she might disobey. I can't afford to lose my steed.

Lana's nowhere to be found. I send her a text message: *What's the plan?*

"Isn't he beautiful?" Cecilia is motioning to the Akarui. "A gift from your country!"

Takeshi is quiet.

"Does he remind you of your precious Hikaru?"

Not a peep.

"I think he's more beautiful than your steed. And even better"—Cecilia flips her flowing brown hair—"he knows how to *survive.*"

As soon as I get him out of this stadium, I'm asking Takeshi for classes on keeping my composure. I would've knocked her teeth out.

Lana hasn't replied. I call her, but there's no response. She could be too emotional over Takeshi to notice. I search for her clothes and her poor attempt at a mask.

What if something happened to her?

There could be Blood Masks hiding in the stands. If they recognized her, they might use her as bait for the Sol de Noches. Perhaps they'd torture her to learn our secret whereabouts.

Wherever she is, I need to get us all out of here *now*.

A distraction is my best chance. I can slip outside and find something to blow up.

Cecilia's nagging voice brings me back to the ring. "Here are the rules! Takeshi will be asked a question. If he doesn't answer, the Akarui will burn him alive. How does that sound?"

These assholes are euphoric.

"Perfect. Let's begin." Cecilia beckons the Akarui forward, and it obeys. "Takeshi, where are you hiding the Fire Drake from Waxbyrne?"

I furrow my brow. This is about a British dragon that used to live in a Florida wand shop? Is she trying to get it to fight in Dragonblood, too?

Takeshi says, "Kill me."

The audience gasps.

"Wow…" Takeshi Endo isn't a quitter. He's devoted to protecting that dragon, though, and it makes him more of a hero to me. Still, I don't want him to die, let alone be burned alive by the same species his steed belonged to. That's unfathomably cruel.

"Are you sure?" Cecilia twirls her Gold wand through her fingers. "This could all be over if you tell me where the Fire Drake is. Nobody has to die."

"Kill me," Takeshi repeats. His scowl game is much better than mine, which is saying a lot.

I have to get outside. The longer I stall, the quicker he and Lana could get hurt.

"You're being a fool, Takeshi. You won't be able to hide her for long. And you're—"

A Blood Mask scurries over to Cecilia in mid-sentence. He says something in her ear. She's smiling wider than Manny whenever he's offered alcohol.

When the Blood Mask retreats, she says, "You won't tell me where she is?"

"No."

"Okay." Cecilia winks at the Akarui, then raises her wand. "How about now?"

Two new Blood Masks march into the ring. They're carrying a short, brown-skinned girl.

Lana.

I shoot up. Then I force myself back down. "Motherfucker…" They *did* catch her, but they're not using her to find our country's dragons— she's Takeshi's bait.

Hurry! They need you.

"Everyone, welcome our surprise guest, Lana Torres!"

Takeshi and I are the only ones not celebrating. He's turned pale;

he breathes heavily as Lana's brought to her knees in front of him. His cool demeanor has melted.

Sandhar and his agents *have* to be watching this. Why aren't they doing something? I check the exits. No one's blocking them. There could still be time to distract these monsters.

But I can't bring myself to stand. Not when Cecilia drifts toward Lana, her upper lip curling like she's Maleficent disguised as a brunette Princess Aurora.

"Hola, Lana. Un placer conocer a vos al fin."

Her accent is from Spain—her 'c' vibrates with the same intensity as the 'z.'

"Vete al infierno," Lana snaps. Even when she's a hostage, she's still a feisty little shit.

Don't be reckless. This witch can kill you.

Cecilia's laugh is cold. "Takeshi, tell me where the Fire Drake is, or Lana burns instead."

Takeshi looks at Cecilia as if she's cut out his heart and fed it to wolves. Then he breathes in deep, fixing his expression into that of a bored student in his least favorite class.

"Don't tell her anything!" says Lana.

But Takeshi doesn't glance her way. "Kill me, Cecilia."

"Stop saying that!" Lana sniffles as she turns to Cecilia. "You have to let him go, okay? He doesn't know where the Fire Drake is. He's only pretending to piss you off."

"She's lying," says Takeshi. "Let Lana go. She has nothing to do with this."

"Don't believe him!"

"Will you please be quiet?"

"*You* be quiet!"

Cecilia claps. "Look at these two little doves trying to save each other. Cute, isn't it?" she asks her Blood Masks. They nod. "But it's getting boring. One more chance, Takeshi."

Someone grabs my arm.

I send an elbow to their face, but my attacker blocks it.

"It's me," Sandhar whispers. He's in a Guy Fawkes mask. Horowitz is in a Jason Vorhees mask behind him. "We'll discuss how you got here later. I need you to come with us."

BAM! BAM! BAM! BAM!

Esperanza won't stop trying to break the wall. I rub my scalp—she's giving me a torturous headache. The crowd suddenly cheers, and Sandhar is pulling me out of my seat. Despite the ruckus, I keep my shit together as much as possible, and remove myself from his grasp.

"Quit telling me what to do. How are we getting them out?" I whisper.

"Leave that up to me. Now come."

"But they're about to *burn Lana*."

"They won't," says Horowitz. "I promise you. They're never getting the chance."

Sandhar lets me go, but he's motioning to the exit. "Hurry."

"Kill me," Takeshi pleads yet again.

Cecilia snaps her fingers at the Akarui. "Burn her."

"*No!*" Takeshi lunges forward, but Cecilia blasts him with a Paralysis Charm. His stiffened body drops inches away from Lana.

The Akarui faces her. She's raising her arms as the dragon opens its mouth.

I fly down the stands.

"HEY!" I'm screaming at the top of my lungs. "BURN THIS!"

Psychic magic is rumored to have been possible in the Age Before Dragons, a historical period not much has been written about. Only a few texts allude to an unidentified Norseman who could perform magic with his thoughts. He built a home out of thorny vines in the woods, cured sick children at a nearby village, and hunted without touching a weapon. Magical history experts still wonder whether this person existed, or if he's merely a story.

—*Excerpt from Corwin Sykes's* Dark & Dastardly: Obscure Magical Folklore & Enchantments for Beginners

CHAPTER SEVEN

Lana

I'VE NEVER LOVED VICTORIA PERALTA MORE.

She's zooming past the Blood Masks on the fourth and third rows. They toss spells at her, but she ducks and rolls like a pro. One of them snatches the back of her shirt. Victoria sends a high kick to his nose, then bolts as blood sprays the floor. The small yet mighty girl is getting closer to the ring's entrance, but the jerks that dragged Takeshi here race to meet her halfway.

"Now!" Director Sandhar is taking off his Guy Fawkes mask and whipping out his Silver wand. Agent Horowitz and dozens of other agents are also revealing themselves in the higher rows. "This is the Department of Magical Investigations! Nobody move!"

The crowd leaps out of their seats.

Calling it pandemonium doesn't do this mess justice. Bureau agents—

the good ones—are flinging themselves at the Blood Masks chasing Victoria. Others are getting banged up every which way as they stop people from Transporting. Some are locked in magical duels with both Copper and Silver Wands. My eardrums vibrate from the constant *SWISH!* of these cowards fleeing. Wherever they go, I hope they get caught.

The Akarui is whining again. It rips out flame after flame to the sky. Then it scorches the mechanical dragons around the pit, as if it's too distraught to focus on one target.

It's totally forgotten about me.

So has Cecilia, who's watching Victoria like a snake about to capture its next meal.

Do something, do something, do something.

"Run to Nirek!" Takeshi yells at me. "He can get you home!" Two Blood Masks are still behind him. One of them is walking toward me, wand at the ready.

"I'm not leaving you…" I hate how my voice cracks at the end, and how I keep avoiding his gaze. But there's a Blood Mask coming my way. I need him directly in front of me so I can knock his lights out and use him as a shield from the other Blood Mask's spells. Takeshi's still handcuffed, but he's *Takeshi*. I'm pretty sure he can fight in a coma.

"Get away from my friends!" Victoria roars as she finally enters the arena.

Cecilia turns to the Blood Mask approaching me. "Stop her."

Crap.

When the Blood Mask walks away, I angle my body toward Cecilia. She's standing above me now, but she doesn't notice. Her wand is still aimed at Victoria, who's sending an uppercut to a Blood Mask's Adam's apple, then jabbing another in the ribs. They both topple down, but it's like cutting off the heads on a Hydra—more keep popping out. Soon they have Victoria surrounded.

They won't hurt her if I take their leader.

"Lana, just go!" Takeshi says.

I ball my fist as I push myself up. My knuckles connect with Cecilia's cheek.

"Ugh!" She falls on her back, losing her grip on her Gold wand.

I throw the wand as high into the stands as I can. Magic users can't perform spells without wands, so she'll have to attack me like a Regular. She tries to get up.

I coil an arm around her neck, squeezing tight.

"Don't move," I whisper in her ear. "You won't like what happens if you do."

Cecilia sucks in a breath, as if I've either shocked or impressed her. "Qué chula…"

Now free from the Paralysis Charm, a wide-eyed Takeshi jumps to his feet. He slams his body into the Blood Mask near him, and the man crashes onto the sand. His mask slips off. Takeshi swiftly kicks him in the head, making him lose consciousness.

Perfect!

"You want your leader in one piece? Let us go!" I say.

The Blood Masks wheel around. Four of them hold Victoria. The others shoot spells at Director Sandhar and Agent Horowitz, who run toward the arena's entrance.

With a roar, the Akarui focuses on me again. A fireball sits at the tip of its propeller. It spreads its wings as the machines burn around us—the arena is an inferno. Thick tendrils of smoke billow across the stadium. Some of the flames lick their way up the vacant front rows.

I'm a sweating, panting disaster, but I won't quit. "I swear to God I'll hurt her!" I squeeze Cecilia's neck more. "Call your cronies off, Cecilia, including the dragon. *Now.*"

"Lana, we have to run." Takeshi motions to the Akarui. "He's going to strike."

"He wouldn't burn her. She commands him, remember?"

Cecilia laughs hysterically. It's as chilling as nails scraping the walls in the dead of night.

This girl is a piece of work, but she's still my hostage. "I won't say it again, Cecilia."

"Ay, está bien. Ganaste," she tells me I've won. Cecilia nods to her Blood Masks.

They release Victoria.

The ones squaring off against Director Sandhar and Agent Horowitz stand down. So do the others battling the rest of the bureau agents.

Victoria rushes over to me. She's glaring at Cecilia like she's wanted to pummel her in a hundred past lives. "You're *disgusting*," she says.

There goes that creepy laugh again.

Cecilia looks to the Akarui. "Burn them."

Are you kidding me?!

Takeshi grabs me at the same time the dragon unleashes its fire. I lose my grip on Cecilia. Takeshi, Victoria, and I dive behind the Blood Masks. None step forward to protect their boss.

She's still on her knees, her arm is raised, taking the brunt of the flames.

Not an inch of her body is burning.

The fire fans out on either side of Cecilia, as if she's repelling the dragon's attack with nothing more than flesh and sheer will.

How the hell is she doing this?!

"Come on!" Director Sandhar screams something else, but I can't hear over the onslaught of spells ricocheting in every direction. He's pulling me up as Agent Horowitz and his other agents are blocking us from the Blood Masks. When Victoria, Takeshi, and I are standing close enough, he points his Silver wand at us.

A glimmer of white light encases me.

Cecilia holds out a hand to Director Sandhar, her palm glowing bright gold.

Then I see her no more.

Hide them wherever you want. Make them run as far as they can.
I'm the shadow that never relents, Professor.
And I'm not alone.

—Anonymous note left in Madame Waxbyrne's private
residence; property of the International Bureau of Magical Matters

CHAPTER EIGHT

Victoria

GRASS BREAKS MY FALL, WHICH ISN'T MUCH OF A COMFORT.

At least I'm not on top of anyone, and no one is on top of me.
I'm smack-dab between Lana and Takeshi, who groan louder than me.

Esperanza wails at the top of the mountain.

She swoops down first, followed by the other Sol de Noches.
Esperanza brushes her snout against my nose. The motion is gentle
enough for me to know she's happy, but she keeps huffing like she's a
Puerto Rican mother about to chase me with her chancla. I hold back
a sigh while she smells me. Heat rolls off her skin as usual, but her
warmth comforts me more than ever—it's confirmation that I made it
out of the ring.

"Sí, sí. Perdón. Tenía que hacerlo sin ti."

She rolls her eyes, as if doing anything without her doesn't have
justification. Then she brushes her snout against me even faster.

"¡Aquí están! ¡Corran!"

Héctor runs as fast as he would during our Blazewrath training
sprints. The dragons retreat to let him pass. He helps me up, wiping sand

off my cheeks. "Where in God's name were you?" Héctor's jaw drops as he looks at Takeshi. "And why is Takeshi Endo in Cayey?"

"Stay where you are!"

Vogel rushes to Takeshi, her Silver wand inches from his chest.

Our steeds' bodyguards surround us. They also have their wands out.

Takeshi raises his cuffed hands. "Brunhilde, I—"

"Director Sandhar's in danger!" Lana stands in front of Takeshi, but there are still wands aimed at him from all sides. "That Cecilia witch was about to kill him! And her Blood Masks are attacking other agents! You have to save them!"

"What the hell is a Blood Mask?" Manny's panting like he hasn't done any physical activity in years. The rest of the team… the *group*… is right behind him. He pulls Edwin and Luis back when they try to approach me. "Start talking, ladies. I might pass out at any minute."

"Everyone, back inside!" Vogel turns to the bodyguard next to her. "Seize him."

"*Wait!* You need to get to Le Parc Du Chasseurs in Nantes!" Lana's back is pressed against Takeshi now. This isn't the time for me to smile at the way Takeshi gulps down hard, or at how he's trying to put some distance between him and Lana. But it's not every day I see a Blazewrath legend act like an awkward teenage boy.

"Our orders are to remain here, Miss Torres." Vogel's harsh tone pulls me back into this disaster of a situation. "Now move. This young man is a Ravensworth Penitentiary escapee—"

"He was *kidnapped*." Why is she so determined to waste precious time? Sandhar is about to be murdered, and here she is acting like Takeshi's her biggest problem! "Your colleagues are dying, Vogel. Now you either get a team together, or call in other agents to ambush those dragon trappers your boss told us not to worry about."

All eyes are on the woman who holds our fate in her hands.

She says, "Everyone get inside right now. Agent Endo stays with us."

Two bodyguards grab Takeshi from behind.

Lana raises her fists. "But you can't—"

"Stop." I launch myself at her before she does something stupid. Then I face Vogel. "Those people in that ring? Their blood is on *your* hands. I hope you can live with that."

Then I drag Lana up the mountain, our friends following closely behind.

"How are you just gonna walk away?" Lana asks. The little shit keeps checking behind her. It's like hauling a golden retriever who's caught a glimpse of a squirrel. "What if they hurt him?"

"They'll most likely interrogate him, so calm down. You're making things worse."

"I'm not the one letting my friends die!"

She yells so close to my eardrum that it starts pulsating. Her intolerable yelling grows louder, but I ignore her. I shove Lana through the open double doors. Her mom and Joaquín barrel toward us with matching looks of concern. A tearful Lana rounds everyone up at the dinner table. She fills them in on what's going on in Nantes while I stand by the entrance. On occasion, I hear loud gasps and a combination of swear words in both Spanish and English.

The dragons are lying in wait near our so-called protectors. Vogel is addressing Takeshi. She seems too relaxed for someone whose boss has probably been eviscerated. Perhaps it's part of her training. It could also be Sandhar's strategy—sacrifice a few for the good of all?

My heart constricts.

Or they could be Blood Masks, too. Maybe even Dragon Knights.

Their insistence in keeping us here... denying Lana a quick trip down the road to her old house... What if this isn't a bureau-approved hideout? What if it's a trap?

Vogel did seem surprised to learn about dragon trappers in the Caribbean. She doesn't emote well enough to be considered a good actress. Perhaps I'm overreacting. The bureau *has* been compromised. What if she's avoiding further involvement for fear of having our location leaked to real Dragon Knights or Blood Masks? She could simply be taking precautions.

Our families were brought here together, for example, and they were escorted to their homes in the same Transport Charm. I haven't spoken to Mami today.

I haven't confirmed she made it back safely.

When I call her, she doesn't answer. I'm used to her not picking up once her nursing duties take over. I can't recall my friends speaking with their relatives today, though. I haven't seen Edwin FaceTiming with Kirill, either. I check my phone's signal—all the bars are on-screen.

I march to the dining room. Lana is explaining how Cecilia can use magic without her Gold wand to a horrified audience. Her mom keeps rubbing the small of her back, but from the way Lana speaks at a mile a minute while welling up with tears, I can see it's not comforting her at all.

"The last time I saw magic like that, it was with Randall Wiggins," she says.

Joaquín nods. "That boy was an anomaly. Cecilia sounds like she could be similar."

"Or worse. But we don't have time to discuss this." I squeeze in between Manny and Luis. "Has anyone spoken with their families today?"

"Nada," says Edwin. "No me contestan."

"Same here. It's like everyone at home is asleep," says Génesis, flashing me a photo of her two pit bulls, Bam-Bam and Boo. "I really hoped to see them on video chat today."

"I haven't gotten any replies yet," says Gabriela. "But my mom could be sleeping in."

"My parents never sleep in," Héctor says in a grave tone. He angles his body toward me, breathing slowly. "You think the signal's been messed with? Or maybe the shield's blocking it?"

Everyone looks at me like I'm holding the keys to the kingdom. Theories rush at me faster than the Pangolin steeds during our quarterfinals match. The signal could be blocked. My phone shows me otherwise so as to not raise suspicions. Or these bodyguards really are the enemy, and they've taken our loved ones—hostages don't answer calls or texts.

I can't be certain of anything. But I don't trust our bodyguards. Even if I did, we could be ambushed when we least expect it.

We have to get out of here.

"Victoria?" says Héctor.

I stand up straight, even though my knees shake at the thought of Mami being kidnapped. Wherever she is, I'll find her, but I need to search for a better place to strategize first.

"We need another hideout," I say. "There could be undercover Blood Masks or Dragon Knights down that mountain right now. This might've been their plan—keep us locked up until Sandhar was out of the picture so they can snatch our steeds."

Lana's mom gasps. "No… They can't… You really think…"

"The thought crossed my mind." Héctor nods. "Where would we hide?"

I force myself not to smile. Our team captain, my lifelong friend, is choosing my side without hesitation. After a few disagreements in Dubai, it's nice to have his support again.

"Our best option is the Dark Island. Nobody will find us there," I say.

"I don't want to be near *him*…" Lana hugs herself, leaning closer to her mom. Gabriela puts her hand on Lana's. She accepts it, but she's glancing at the floor.

She must mean the Sire. I don't want to be near him, either, but I'm not the one who's still processing Galloway's death. Being stuck in the presence of that silver cabrón could lead Lana down a more self-destructive path. I'm willing to do most things to protect us, but as much as Lana gets on my last nerve, I'm not letting her painful memories bubble up to the surface again.

"Okay. We can go somewhere else. Any ideas?"

"I mean, I'm *fine*, but he's just… you know… the worst." Lana can't even bullshit properly.

"Noted," I say. "So. Ideas, please?"

Edwin shrugs, as if the answer is obvious. "El único que conoce los mejores escondites en este mundo está allá afuera. Tenemos que llevarnos a Takeshi. Sin él, no llegaremos lejos."

He makes a fair point. Takeshi *does* know the best hideouts in the world. Besides, leaving him here means torture or death—two options I'd never stand for.

However, taking him with us means fighting off those bodyguards. We'd risk our steeds, too. What if one or more are hurt trying to save a boy who could save himself?

"I'm not *abandoning* him." If Lana were a witch, I would've been hexed a thousand times.

"I haven't said anything."

"But you look like you're considering it."

"Smart people consider all angles. You should try it."

"Ay, dejen la mierda ya." Manny puts his arms between us like he's a referee. "Listen closely 'cause I'm not repeating myself. We're getting out of here, and we need the kid." He jabs a thumb to the door.

"Yeah," says Lana.

I heave a sigh. This will not be easy. Not even with our dragons.

But if I were Takeshi, I'd want someone to help me. I've been a hostage, too, even if it was in my own home. I should never have to feel like that again. Neither should he.

I push my shoulders back. "So what's the plan?"

"I TOLD YOU TO *STAY INSIDE.*"

Vogel's still standing too close to Takeshi. The bodyguards have him surrounded, too.

"Have you heard anything about Director Sandhar? What about Agent Horowitz?" Lana wedges herself between Vogel and Takeshi, creating the human barrier we agreed on.

I'm right behind Takeshi. He peeks over his shoulder as if he can hear my sneakers brush against grass. Either I'm not as sneaky as I thought, or his senses are developed far beyond mine.

The dragons are in a circle at the top of the mountain. Joaquín and Lana's mom are next to Esperanza. Manny and the riders are with me. Each is close enough to knock a bodyguard out.

"I can't disclose further information at the moment, Miss Torres."

"But they're *under attack.* How can you be so chill?"

"We could be next!" Luis adds a touch of drama by yelling. "Aren't you freaked out?"

"You should be!" says Gabriela.

"We're all going to die!" Génesis adds for even more drama.

I love them so much.

"Hey," I whisper to Takeshi. "Tell me the safest location you know. I'll share it with Esperanza, and she'll communicate with the other dragons. We're going to Fade to your new hideout. On my mark, run to Titán. Do you understand?"

Takeshi's nod is so quick I almost miss it. "Sanjay Van," he says.

I have no idea what that means, but I still push my thoughts into Esperanza's, knocking down the black wall I've built brick by brick.

WHOOM!

Vamos a Sanjay Van, I tell her.

She purrs her approval.

Héctor's the first to cross his arms—that's the signal his steed knows the location. Then Génesis, Gabriela, and Edwin mimic him. Luis is the last one to confirm.

When it's my turn, the Sol de Noches spring into the sky.

Esperanza leads them to the base of the mountain. Joaquín and Ms. Wells are on her back.

The dragons shoot fire at the bodyguards.

"Go!" I yell at Takeshi.

We sprint toward the dragons together, with the rest of the group trailing behind us.

"STOP THEM!" Vogel shrieks.

Silver lights whip past me—spells. They're firing every which way. I duck as Takeshi jumps onto Titán's back. Once he's settled, he pulls Héctor up, helping him sit in front. Lana is already on top of Puya along with Gabriela. Manny is climbing onto Fantasma.

I'm a breath away from Esperanza.

Vogel pummels me with the strength of three fullbacks.

"Ugh!"

She pins my throbbing limbs to the grass, magically shielding herself from Esperanza's flames. "Running won't save you, Peralta! You can't protect yourselves from what's next!"

I gasp. "So you *are* a traitor!"

"You impossible girl! I'm a—"

Manny pounces on her.

They both roll away from me as Esperanza stops firing.

I'm heading toward Manny when he yells, "VICTORIA, GO!"

SWOOSH!

Titán, Puya, Fantasma, and Daga have Faded. Esperanza is waiting for me.

I frown at Manny. My worst fear has come true—they're keeping one of us hostage.

"Manny, I can't—"

"VETE AHORA MISMO."

Two bodyguards crush Manny on the ground. He's still screaming as Vogel gets up again.

She sprints toward me.

She deflects Esperanza's fireballs, approaching even faster. Even if I defeat her, I'm still putting Esperanza in danger, and I won't be any closer to freeing Manny without her.

"RESPECT MY AUTHORITY FOR ONCE IN YOUR LIFE, ¡PUÑETA!" Manny roars.

I bolt. My head is low as Vogel's spells shoot past me. While Esperanza keeps her at bay with more flames, I leap on top of my steed, holding on for dear life.

"Vámonos…" I say.

Manny's proud smile is the last thing I see before the world sinks into darkness.

CHAPTER NINE

Lana

THE SIRE'S ROARS RATTLE THE DARK ISLAND. IT'S A TEMPEST bent on our total destruction.

I peer down from the midnight-black sky. The ivory claw-shaped towers are still twisted around him. There are jagged edges where his wings used to be; they haven't grown back since Esperanza wrenched them off. His fire propeller is still caged in ice, too. Dried blood coats the corners in splashes of crimson. No matter how hard he writhes, he can't break free. He's as trapped as I was after signing my Blazewrath contract under his ruthless command.

Good.

This is the least Andrew's memory deserves. The Dragon Knights will never get their hands on his killer. I have new enemies chasing me, but seeing the first one I made in this state fills me with hope. Maybe we *can* beat them.

The Sire bites at the air as he stares at me. He goes faster and faster, roaring even louder.

I flinch. Then I hug Gabriela tighter.

She pats my hand reassuringly. "We're almost there, Lana! Hang on!"

The wind inside the Fade's white tunnel is whipping me hard. My friends and I fly across the beach with its dark palm trees and even darker sand. The bone throne remains at the center of the island. It still has those extended claws at the sides, as if they're prepping to lock someone in.

Not even the Sol de Noches know why it's there. Maybe they'll be able to communicate its purpose better in time—they might be too young to understand what it means.

WHOOSH!

We're tossed out into another night sky. Instead of a beach with coal-colored water, the dragons have taken us to a forest. There are trees and rocky, sloping pathways everywhere. I don't know where we are, but it's totally big enough to hide six dragons. The weather is hotter and stickier than in Cayey. I'll melt into a whole ocean if I go on a walk.

"Keep going east," says Takeshi.

Under his guidance, the Sol de Noches soar toward a sprawling lake. They land a few inches away, right between the trees. There's not a single human or animal in sight. Still, birds are singing in the distance. Theirs is a high-pitched song that clashes with the forest's serenity.

Gabriela helps me dismount Puya. As my friends huddle close, I do a quick headcount.

"Where's Manny?" I ask Victoria.

She takes a deep breath. "He charged Vogel to save me. They pinned him down as I fled."

"No…" I rush to Joaquín. "We have to go back. They'll *kill* him."

"I knew this would happen," Victoria says. She's looking me up and down as if I've kicked her plate off the dinner table. "They still got away with keeping one of us. Saving our human GPS didn't have to mean leaving Manny behind."

Her tone is as dry as my split ends, but ten billion times more annoying.

"So you'd rather Takeshi be their hostage instead?"

"I'd rather we could've stayed *together*, Lana. I shouldn't have to state the obvious."

I'm about to shush her when Joaquín puts his wheelchair between us. He's surprisingly calm for a man whose dad is in danger. "The important thing is we're unharmed, and we can get my father back soon. Besides, have you met Manuel Delgado? What about him is easy to kill?"

Victoria nods. "Yeah, but—"

"They won't kill him yet. If Brunhilde and the others are really traitors, Manny will be used as bait," says Takeshi. He waves us all closer to the lake, where the dragons are keeping an eye out for potential attackers. "We can't do much if we return, but we *will* save him."

I know I can trust him, but something about leaving one of our own behind feels wrong. This is so much worse than fleeing from Nantes before Cecilia fired a spell at Director Sandhar. I'd rather snack on burning stones than drown in doubt over whether they're dead or alive.

I have no choice but to believe Takeshi.

"Welcome to Sanjay Van," he says. "One of New Delhi's forests."

Smiling, Gabriela slaps a hand to her chest. "This is India?"

"Yes."

Gabriela pirouettes twice. "Oh, my God! Bucket list goal achieved!"

"Keep it down," Victoria scolds. "Where's the hideout, Takeshi?"

Still handcuffed, he kneels, wiping the dirt clockwise, revealing a small square of glass. Takeshi puts an eye close to the glass. It emits a flashing silver light that lasts only a second. As Takeshi rises, the glass vanishes under the dirt again. The circle is no more.

He says, "Right here."

I fall through the ground as if it were fog.

I'm immediately standing somewhere else. Mom, my friends, and their steeds have landed next to me. The forest is gone. We're in a bright, marble-tiled hangar. It's almost as big as the wait zone at the Blazewrath stadium; there's enough space for seventy-foot-tall dragons to roam free without bumping into anything. Aside from a set of doors to my left, the hangar is empty. The air conditioning is turned up to the max—a respite from the punishing heat outside.

"Is this… still New Delhi?" Mom furrows her brow. She's been to one magical location before—President Turner's Other Place—and the journey there hadn't been half as confusing.

"Yes. Our hideout is an underground Other Place." Takeshi walks briskly to the doors.

"That's a magical location that can't be found on a map." Mom speaks as if she's reciting something she read in a magical history textbook.

I bump my shoulder against hers. "Good memory, Mom."

"Thank you." She winks.

Takeshi smiles at us like we're the cutest. "It's also where our new hosts will greet us."

Victoria draws nearer to him, an eyebrow raised. "And who exactly are these hosts?"

The doors slide open. A middle-aged man and a teenage girl walk into the hangar.

The man has the same honey hair I'd seen during his execution, but it's not ruffled and knotted. He's dressed in a green sweater and jeans, a stark contrast to his bureau attire. There are no signs of the Sire's fangs on his neck, which had been ripped open for the whole world to see.

Agent Michael Robinson is very much alive.

"Oh, thank God you've made it…" His British accent is different from President Turner's. While the latter is from Leeds, Agent Robinson sounds like he grew up in the East End of London. He runs to Takeshi with the swiftness of a father who hasn't seen his child in years. Takeshi surrenders to his crushing hug, but his handcuffs won't let him return it. Agent Robinson backs away with a sigh. "Bollocks. Let's get you out of those."

He takes out his Silver wand from a leather sheath in his pants. After aiming it at Takeshi's handcuffs, they magically unlock. Then he aims it at Takeshi's black eye and cuts. Within seconds, Takeshi is fully healed and free.

"Everyone, this is my colleague and friend, Agent Michael Robinson." Takeshi turns to the teenage girl. "And I believe you all know the Ghost of Shibuya."

Haya Tanaka, the former Runner from Team Japan, is smiling at us.

"Hello." She speaks in a low, intimidating voice, but she's a ray of sunshine as she waves.

Her outfit is black from head to toe, but her straight hair has been dyed metallic silver. When she last competed in the Cup, it had been orange. This is the girl who won the 2015 Cup for her country, and is the first out lesbian to represent Japan. She runs way faster than me, and she owns every Kawasaki Ninja motorcycle on the market. Speed is her absolute favorite thing.

"It's an honor to meet you…" I don't know why I'm whispering. This isn't the time to be starstruck. At least my mouth isn't hanging open.

Thankfully, my friends are also gawking at Haya.

Especially Victoria.

"You're incredible," she says. "Just… amazing. I literally have no more words."

"Same here," says Gabriela. She's blushing and ruffling the purple side of her hair. I suspect that's Gabriela Code for flirting, but it's too early to tell.

"Okay, okay. Let's keep the fangirling to a minimum." Héctor laughs like he's the most hilarious person ever. He shakes Haya's hand. "Héctor Sánchez, at your service."

"Oh, I know all of you." She peeks over at Edwin. "¡Hola!"

He bows. "Hola, Haya. Un placer."

Someone else enters the hangar.

Her golden scales shimmer under the ceiling lights. So do her spindly wings, which she tucks in as she steadily approaches. Her scarlet horns are as thick and pointy as I remember. The only difference is she no longer has her crystal heart. Before she surrendered it to Takeshi, it had glowed like a small diamond on her chest, marking her as one of the few Fire Drakes capable of granting her rider a wish. Now there's a heart-shaped hole that can never be filled again.

But I'm so happy the Fire Drake from Waxbyrne is still safe.

She halts next to Agent Robinson. Her beady eyes are glued to me, as if she remembers trying to scorch my bones at the wand shop's habitat. Luckily, she's in a better mood today.

"This is Willa," says Agent Robinson. "My steed."

"Willa..." Her name is simpler than I expected, but it suits her.

The Sol de Noches let out soft roars in unison, as if they're saying hello.

Willa returns the favor.

"Why does Cecilia want her so badly?" Victoria blurts out.

"We can discuss that inside. I have a chocolate cheesecake waiting for me. This way, please!" Haya sets off to the doors like a tour guide on a tight schedule. "Careful with the plants. Michael has enchanted some of them to attack. Same with the pool table."

Luis claps. "There's a pool table?"

"And an arcade."

"Oh, my *God*."

Luis and Daga rush after Haya. Daga wags her tail super fast, giving us all a good laugh. Agent Robinson and Willa escort the group inside.

Takeshi hangs back with me. "Are you hungry? Or would you like to rest first?"

He's been snatched from prison, been given cuts and a black eye, was nearly executed in a Dragonblood ring, has fled from traitors, and he's asking *me* if I need rest.

Then there's the way he's watching me. He'd done the same at Andrew's funeral—he stayed focused on me, as if I'm the only reason he still believes in good things. Takeshi had told me I'd helped him find hope again. The sweet, naive boy I once called my forever favorite is gone, but the hardened young man he's become is starting to show me glimpses of his old self.

"Don't worry about me. You're the one who must be exhausted," I say.

He steps closer. The air conditioning system is working, so I don't know why my cheeks are hot enough to fry an egg. "You were also under duress, Lana. It's okay to feel tired or sad."

His voice is so freaking gentle.

It's also a reminder of how fragile Victoria—and the bureau—thinks I am.

Remember, Lana. Don't be a mess.

"I'm fine. Just need to call Samira real quick. You can go ahead."

As I raise my Whisperer, Takeshi says, "Tell her to Transport here as soon as possible."

I give him a thumbs-up, but he's not moving.

"Takeshi. I'm fine. Go show everyone our new headquarters, okay?"

Silence.

Then he says, "Okay…"

He trudges along as if he's wading through quicksand. If I didn't know better, I'd say he'd rather keep treating me like a wounded baby bird than join the others.

I speak into the Whisperer. "Samira, do you copy?"

"Affirmative!" she replies at once. "Are you alone? 'Cause I found some stuff on Sandhar's secret mission you're gonna flip out over."

"Does it involve Dragonblood?"

Samira's gasp could be heard on Jupiter. "How do you know about the tournament?"

"I was there, Samira."

I don't have the strength to tell her everything, but I sum it up as best as I can. Mostly, I focus on Cecilia. Samira confirms she's seen that name in bureau files, but she just knows she's a Gold Wand who's in charge of the vilest sport on the planet.

"She can cast spells without her wand. And the Akarui was *terrified* of her."

"So she's way more dangerous than we anticipated," says Samira.

"Yeah…"

I flash back to how Cecilia delighted in threatening me. The Sire had punished my rebellion with Andrew's murder. He'd needed Edward Barnes's blood in order to break his dragon's curse, but killing him in front of me had been out of spite. Cecilia's even worse—at least the Sire had the guts to show himself to the world. I don't know much about this girl, but every fiber of my being wants to make her sick game disappear. I want *her* to disappear.

And if I can spearhead her downfall, so be it.

"Lana? You still there?"

"Can you search for more files on Cecilia before coming to India? But it has to be quick, okay? If Blood Masks or Dragon Knights catch you, I will set the whole universe on fire."

Samira laughs, but it's not a joke. The last thing I need is my best friend captured.

"I'm dead serious, Samira."

"Heard you the first time! And relax. I'll see what I can do."

"Get here soon."

"Yes, Mother." Samira laughs again. "I'll call you when I get to New Delhi. Love you!"

"Love you, too."

I hang up with more questions than answers. Then I check my texts. Papi still hasn't replied to my message. Searching for Violet #43 can't possibly be *this* distracting. Unless he's already found her? He could be bringing her back to the São Paulo sanctuary right now.

Or he could be in danger. Either the Brazilian Pesadelo is threatening his life or something else is. Normally, I'd have Director Sandhar to help me, but remembering how he could've been killed by now… I'm welling up as my hands start to shake.

No. Don't think the worst yet.

I call Papi. It's a little difficult with my fidgety fingers, but I manage to press SEND.

He doesn't pick up.

It takes me several minutes to type the whole message: *Hi, Papi! Hope everything is well! Please write back whenever you can, okay? There's a lot I have to tell you.*

Keeping my cool during such a chaotic time is a challenge I'm not ready for. My dad is unreachable. The bureau isn't safe anymore. Manny is either dead or being kept prisoner. So are Director Sandhar and Agent Horowitz. The only way I can stop this nightmare from reaching new heights is to end Cecilia's reign. If I could defeat the Sire, I can burn her kingdom, too.

I just need to light the right match.

Most magic schools lost their shroud of secrecy once they welcomed Regular students after the Reveal of 1743. The same can't be said for institutions dedicated to the art of wand-making. Iron Pointe—the most prestigious wand-maker academy in the world—exemplifies how guarded this small section of the magical community is. Everything from the admissions process to graduation requirements is kept close to the vest. Does Iron Pointe fear bureau intervention if their methods are discovered? Or are they hiding something far more nefarious?

—Excerpt from Edward Barnes's journal

CHAPTER TEN

Victoria

THIS PLACE IS MUCH BIGGER THAN THE DUBAI HOUSE.

Agent Robinson has designed an Other Place with *seven floors*. The lowest floor is dedicated to Willa's habitat, which she's offered to share with our steeds. She's giving them a tour on the third floor. I wonder if Daga will force her to play hide-and-seek.

The rest of the house is more suitable for humans. There are two gyms, an indoor garden, a sauna, an arcade, a library, and an infinity pool with crystal-clear water.

Then there's Haya's control room.

"Watch out! That asparagus fern bites!"

She's yanking Génesis away from one of the potted plants by her desk. Aside from the occasional splash of greenery, the control room is bathed in red light, which is coming from the spinning LED bulbs above us. I finally know what it's like to stand inside an ambulance siren.

There's a silver flat-screen TV in almost every corner. Most of them are linked to security cameras outside of this building. I recognize the bureau's New York headquarters in the top left side of the room; it's showing footage from the bustling main lobby. Employees are dashing in and out of the elevators. The large mural with the witch, the dragon, and the Regular man is right where I'd seen it during my post-Brazil interrogation. Nothing unusual is happening yet.

"This is the Cherry Suite. I keep a close watch on everything here. And"—Haya motions to the separate garage on the right—"I build things over there."

Metal scraps litter the area. There are a few finished pieces laying about—a helmet shaped like a hawk's head, a suit of armor with a cobra on its chest, and a sword big enough to take Godzilla down—but it's mostly junk.

A slack-jawed Gabriela reaches for the sword's hilt, then stops. "Does this bite, too?"

"Not yet." Haya grins. "That's a prototype for Willa."

I freeze. "You made a sword for a *dragon*?"

"Why not? They deserve to be protected, too."

"But dragons don't fight with weapons unless they're born with them. Like the Venezuelan Furia Roja and the spears they shoot out of their tails. Or the Scottish Golden Horn."

"That's what we've been told."

Joaquín offers Haya an approving smile. "This is a fantastic space, Miss Tanaka."

She waves him away. "Call me Haya. Now everyone gather around. Gentlemen?"

Takeshi and Robinson take out metal chairs for all of us. Lana sits next to me without a word, her eyes flicking over to Takeshi every five seconds. She's not as excited as someone who's trying to catch a glimpse of her hero, but she's very much invested in what he's doing.

"He's not going to die if you don't stare at him," I say.

Lana almost breaks her neck from turning to me so fast. "What's that supposed to mean?"

"It means you're staring at him, genius. Something you want to confess?"

"Yeah. You're ridiculous."

"And you're frothing at the mouth. Tissues?"

Her cheeks turn slightly red. She's even checking her shirt, as if she's paranoid that saliva has fallen onto it. "Hilarious…" she whispers, way too late.

I've never seen Lana this flustered. Torturing her is a decent form of entertainment, especially since she hasn't been the most… understanding.

She has yet to inquire how I'm feeling after Mami's potential kidnapping. Lana had almost *waged war* against me when I implored her to play in our match against Scotland. She got to act like a complete wreck because her father was going to die. Does she think she's the only one who loves her parents? The only one who's been through shit? Where's the empathy for *me*?

"Before we get to the nitty-gritty of our operation, any questions for us?"

Robinson takes me out of my rage-induced thoughts. He's the only one who hasn't claimed a seat. The former agent stands next to Takeshi, towering over him.

Haya sits to my right, eating her chocolate cheesecake in slow bites.

"How are you alive?" Lana jumps in first.

"Why does Cecilia want your dragon?" I speak louder. Her question isn't as important in defeating our enemy as mine.

"I can answer Victoria's question. You wanna take Lana's?" Robinson asks Takeshi.

"Yes. I'll go first," he says.

Damn it.

I fold my arms as Takeshi continues. "The Sire wanted to broadcast an agent's murder, so I suggested Michael. Then I contacted both him and Madame Waxbyrne. She conjured one of the most difficult spells, even for skilled magic users. You've heard of Other Places."

"Obviously." I'm not even trying to hide my resting bitch face.

"Well, Victoria, there are also Other Bodies."

Now *this* is interesting. "Other... Bodies?"

"Yes, but not many have been successful in casting them. They mostly achieve something similar to astral projection—a person's consciousness is separated from their physical form, but if you touch their projected image"—Takeshi moves his hand through the air—"you feel nothing. The projection starts to fade, too. We needed an Other Body that felt *real*. This is something only one Gold Wand in history has accomplished, and she was very cooperative."

"You told us Madame Waxbyrne and Agent Robinson were lovers," Lana butts in. "After we defeated the Sire, remember? That she was protecting Willa from a former wand-making student. Was that Cecilia?"

Takeshi says, "Yes. And now it's Michael's turn."

Robinson speaks directly to me. "Three years ago, Cecilia Valcárcel was studying at Iron Pointe, a private academy for wand-makers in the Swiss Alps. She was admitted at six years old and left just shy of her sixteenth birthday. Glenda—or as you know her, Madame Waxbyrne—had been Cecilia's mentor ever since she arrived, but she grew more insufferable with age."

Edwin shrugs. "¿Por qué?"

"Glenda only discussed Cecilia's hatred for dragons. When it came to anything else Cecilia had done, Glenda simply said she'd never encountered someone that problematic."

"Was she expelled?" I ask.

"She fled before graduation," Robinson replies. "Glenda had discovered Cecilia pitting two Un-Bonded dragons against each other a few miles outside of school. When Glenda set the dragons free, Cecilia promised to find Willa and me so she could kill us as payback. Then she vanished."

I rise. "This girl has been making dragons tear each other apart for *three years?*"

"We suspect longer," says Takeshi, "but Dragonblood was created after she disappeared. According to witness testimonies, the very first tournament took place six months later, but it was much smaller than what you saw today. Cecilia's illegal sport has only grown in popularity through the years, especially now that the Cup is canceled."

I stand behind my chair. I'm gripping it harder than I would hold onto Esperanza in flight. How can so-called Blazewrath fans support this asshole? There's no way the same people who cheered us on in Dubai are the ones I brushed shoulders with today. They're allowed to hate the IBF for canceling the Cup. They can hate *us* for going to Brazil. But I'd never consider dragons murdering each other a worthy replacement for the best sport in history.

"Why is she doing this?" Lana asks.

"She's an abuser, Lana. What more do you need to understand?" I can't stop my voice from rising with each word—I'm a freight train with no brakes. "People like her are poison, and they don't want to leave this world without making sure everyone else rots."

Haya licks the gooey chocolate off her fork. "She also grew up very poor. Before attending Iron Pointe, Cecilia lived at an orphanage in her hometown of Sevilla. People placed bets on Blazewrath matches all the time. The same thing happens at a Dragonblood ring, but since the stakes are higher, so are the dollar signs. Plus, you can win magical heirlooms and trinkets, too."

So what? I've been poor, too. You don't see me killing dragons to make bank.

"That also explains her love life," says Robinson. "Cecilia likes them rich, but she's only been linked to one boy for more than a few weeks—Antonio Deluca."

Eww. "The sore loser who punched Takeshi at a press conference? What a catch."

"He's a Gold Wand, too, so she could've valued him more," Lana says heavily, as if each word weighed a ton. "How long were they together?"

Robinson shrugs. "Timeline's unclear. They dated after she fled Switzerland. She popped up in a few paparazzi photos with him before the 2015 Cup."

"Then it's possible she confided in him. Any leads on where Randall Wiggins kept Antonio prisoner? Maybe he knows more about Cecilia's magic than us."

Takeshi says, "We believe Randall put him in a skullpit, which is the name he gave the magical traps he conjured for the bureau, but we haven't located it yet. The bureau has spent the past two years trying to find him so he can serve as our informant."

Joaquín draws nearer to him. "Lana told us about the Blood Masks earlier. Why has Cecilia sent them to capture the Sol de Noches? Does she really want them in the ring?"

"Yes. Earnings would triple if a Sol de Noche steps into that ring. They used to be Blazewrath superstars, but now they're legends for bringing the Sire down."

The way he says "used to be" stings—we're *still* Blazewrath superstars. That's a title nobody can ever strip from our legacy. Giving the Sire his comeuppance is one of many things we've accomplished. Will we really be remembered just for defeating him?

Luis says, "Let me get this straight. Either the Dragon Knights free the Sire, or the Blood Masks force our steeds to fight to the death. It's just a matter of who gets them first?"

"I'm sorry, mate. This is a lot to handle," says Robinson.

"It's not." I'm back in my seat, bolt upright. "Nobody's touching our dragons. *Ever*. And I'll die before I let that Gold Wand loser make herself a millionaire on more blood."

Lana's eyes crinkle as she smiles. "Same."

"Really?"

Her silence lasts a beat too long.

"Why wouldn't I mean it, Victoria?" She scowls like an elderly lady scolding a child.

"Past experience."

"What the hell are you talking about?" she hisses.

"I think 'past experience' is pretty self-explanatory."

"Oh, please don't fight…" Héctor is already rubbing his temples.

"A fight involves more than one person," I say. Then I turn to Takeshi. "What about our families? We haven't been able to contact them, and we think they might be in danger."

"Retrieving them is our next step. I need to make some calls right now."

"Who are you calling?"

"Friends."

"Magical friends? Or the Regular police?"

Robinson says, "Our intelligence contacts in the Regular community have been MIA for some time. Dragon Knights first infiltrated Regular security. They've Charmed many high-ranking officials to follow their orders, so their aid is quite limited."

"I see." I turn to Takeshi. "How can you be sure these other contacts are still your friends?"

Takeshi gives me a simple nod. "We can contact them together, if you'd like. Help me see which ones are still worth trusting."

I'm not the hugging type. But Takeshi is tempting me to squeeze the shit out of him. Is he truly offering me the chance to save Mami? To have *agency*? The boy I once considered a terrorist is a better person than the girl who vowed to support me post-Blazewrath.

I say, "Thank you. That would be great."

"Perfect. Everyone, please excuse us."

Takeshi and I walk out together.

I don't spare anyone a glance, least of all Lana. I can deal with her after Mami is safe.

Now to see if Takeshi's so-called friends will help me achieve that goal.

There's a blue door at the end of the western wing. It's always locked.
When I walked past it last night, I heard muffled cries. It sounded like
a girl was in pain.
Tell me what's behind the door, Professor.
Tell me why nobody is stopping it.

—Anonymous note left in Madame Waxbyrne's office at Iron Pointe
Academy

CHAPTER ELEVEN

Lana

MAKING PEOPLE WAIT SHOULD BE A CRIME.

Takeshi and Victoria have been in the library for two hours. Agent Robinson has told us not to worry, and most importantly, not to interrupt. He's clicking away on his laptop while sitting next to the library door, as if he's a nerdy bouncer. Knowing he's on standby to pitch in stresses me out even more—why would they need help with *phone calls*?

Besides telling us not to barge into the library, we have also been instructed to rest. Only Luis and the dragons have taken it to heart. While the steeds are relegated to lounging in their new habitat, Luis is the official guardian of the hot tub. He's passed out, though. And snoring. I've lost count of how many photos Héctor has taken. I'm sure they'll be used for some sort of bribery in the near future. Gabriela, Génesis, Edwin, and Joaquín are all scattered throughout the house. It's like they're too nervous about their families to stay in one place.

Mom's been setting up shop in our bedroom, which I've yet to visit.

Haya is still in the Cherry Suite. I don't know what she could be doing that also takes two hours, but there's a slight chance she won't freak out if I join her. Victoria and Takeshi are doing their part to find the families. Maybe even Manny, Director Sandhar, and Agent Horowitz. Why can't *I* help find Cecilia? Or the next Dragonblood ring? Is that what Haya is researching? I still think they haven't told us everything about Cecilia. Bureau clearance doesn't matter anymore. The whole organization has been upended, so why keep us in the dark? Are there still sensitive things we shouldn't be aware of? Maybe getting Haya to spill the beans won't be too difficult.

She's poring over a stack of pages under the newly changed lights, which glow pumpkin-orange. I'm assuming they help her read better than the emergency-red aesthetic.

"Hey. Would I be bothering you if I hang out here?" I ask.

Haya's gasp is more of delight than shock. "Not at all!" She removes the pile of binders on the nearest office chair. I sit down and roll it closer to her desk, right next to a tiny cactus. The pot has been painted as silver as Haya's hair. "This is Vic. And no, he doesn't bite."

"Perfect."

"But he does explode."

I roll my chair two feet away from the cactus. "Good to know."

The fact that Haya's giggling because of my fear of exploding cacti doesn't bode well for the rest of this conversation, but I still have to try.

"What are you reading?" I stare intently at the pages, wishing my eyes had zoom capabilities. I do catch glimpses of slanted handwriting, so this must not be official bureau documentation.

"I wouldn't want to bore you with this." Haya swiftly puts the stack at the end of her desk, too far from my prying eyes. "Are you hungry? I can get you some chocolate cheesecake." She points at the weapons room. "I have a fridge fully stocked with dessert for any occasion."

That sounds like a dream come true, but it's also a blatant swerve.

She does *not* want me knowing what's in those pages. Which, of course, makes me want to know even more.

It's going to take patience and finesse, though—two things I sorely lack.

"Lana?"

"No treats for me, thanks. So what exactly is your job with the bureau? I mean, when did you even join? The world thinks you're a retired Blazewrath player still living in Shibuya."

"I was." Haya speaks without betraying any emotion. I might as well have asked her what day of the week it is. "My team struggled to recover from Hikaru's murder. We didn't lose a teammate—Hikaru was family. Instead of helping one another cope, we drifted apart. Most of us returned home and didn't keep in touch. We were all mourning in our own ways."

I swallow hard. If anything were to happen to a Sol de Noche, it would crush me beyond repair. Neither Haya nor I are dragon riders, but that doesn't diminish the love we have for our countries' most majestic creatures. Besides, seeing how devastated Takeshi was after losing his steed... I can't even begin to imagine how unbearable that would be.

"Did you join the bureau to find Hikaru's killer, too?" I whisper.

"I'm not actually *with* the bureau. I'm with Takeshi and Michael."

Haya clicks her keyboard super fast. She pulls up a grainy photo of Takeshi that looks like it was taken on a webcam. Those dark bags under his eyes are still noticeable. He's in jeans and a blue FILA jacket—much nicer than his Dragon Knight uniform. Takeshi sits in an abandoned warehouse with one wall missing, as if either a tornado or a dragon has blown it away.

"After Takeshi disappeared," Haya says, "I couldn't focus. My parents were there for me, and so was my girlfriend at the time, but I needed to know where he was. Then he contacts me a year later." She shakes her head. "He interrupted a phenomenal gaming session, too."

I smile. "What were you playing?"

"*Monster Hunter.*"

"Awesome."

Haya sits bolt upright. This is the most awake she's looked. "You play, too?"

"Oh, no. I've just heard of it."

"I can teach you."

"That's very sweet, but—"

"We can use cheat codes."

"No, I—"

"And complete as many side quests as we want!"

I've completely lost her. A part of me wonders if this is Haya's eternal mood whenever she talks about her favorite video game, or if it's fueled by not having other people to play with in real life. Takeshi isn't a gamer. I'm guessing Agent Robinson isn't, either.

She's changing the subject. I shouldn't enable her.

"What did Takeshi tell you?" I wave to the grainy photo.

Haya powers down faster than rival Runners speeding up the mountain. She rolls her chair closer to the desk, turning slightly away from me, and hunches over the keyboard.

"Everything." She's whispering again, but it's not the breathless enthusiasm from earlier. Now it's a disheartened trip down memory lane. "We used to keep one another's secrets. Takeshi helped me so much during our Blazewrath days, too. He was my emotional support. So when he asked me to protect Michael and Willa, I did. Especially when he wanted me to build weapons and armor. Metal forging has been my hobby for *years*, but my parents never approved. It's inappropriate for a lady," Haya says with air quotes. "So was Blazewrath."

"Relatable content."

Haya starts turning toward me again. "Your parents didn't want you playing, either?"

"Just my mom. She came around in the end."

"That must be wonderful." Haya fiddles with the computer mouse, her head low.

Great. How am I supposed to shift the conversation to Cecilia now? Not only will I be the biggest jerk, it could get me on her bad side forever. Waiting to break into the Cherry Suite after she leaves would probably be a mistake—there must be cameras and alarms all around. Maybe even some hidden exploding cacti. And that's *if* I manage to break in.

Unless I strike a deal…

"Actually, learning how to play *Monster Hunter* would be way better," I say.

Haya spins so fast I'm afraid she'll slide out of the chair. "It would?"

"Yeah. I'll join you for a session"—I raise a finger—"after you tell me more about Cecilia."

"Oh, come on! You don't have *clearance*."

"I thought you didn't work for the bureau."

"I don't, but I still can't tell you."

"Why not?"

For a split second, Haya looks over at Vic, and I wonder if she'll blow me up.

"I swear I'm quieter than a grave, Haya. And I'll play *all* the *Monster Hunter* you want."

She beams at me. "Thank you!"

Her gratitude cracks a piece of my heart. Loneliness is such a jerk.

"Ask me anything," says Haya, "and you'll only get one answer."

I could ask a million questions about Cecilia. How can she perform magic without her wand? When did she start hurting Un-Bondeds? Has she ever hurt a Bonded steed? How did she start building her Blood Mask crew? Yet all I can dwell on is that poor Akarui, scared and firing at random. Cecilia had been more than its captor—it listened to her commands.

"How can she control dragons?" I say. "There was an Akarui in the ring and it was… *obeying* her. Would it have done the same if it hadn't been chained? And—"

My phone rings.

I would've ignored it had it not been Monsta X's "Fighter"—Papi's ringtone.

"OH CRAP." I can't remember the last time I fished out my phone faster. Sure enough, the screen flashes an incoming FaceTime call from him. "Sorry, it's my dad! I'll be right back!"

I'm bolting out of the Cherry Suite as I answer. "Finally!"

Carlos Torres—Bond specialist, author, and father extraordinaire—is waving hello at me. His beard is a bit fuller since the last time we video-chatted. All of the lamps in his São Paulo hotel room have been turned on, as if he's allergic to the dark.

"¡Hola, mi amor! I'm good! So sorry for not picking up earlier! This has been a *wild* day. There's barely any signal in these mountains and—" He blinks. "Where are you?"

"I had a wild day, too, but please go first. How's the search going?"

Papi takes a swig of his water bottle. "Unsuccessful," he says gruffly. "I spoke to three witnesses who spotted her feeding on cows at a nearby farm. She fled before I arrived."

I'm not surprised. Retrieving Violet #43 might be Papi's greatest mission in life, but she's still a Brazilian Pesadelo—the world's most dangerous dragon species. She'd been the only Pesadelo to flee the São Paulo Sanctuary for Un-Bonded Dragons after the Sire's attack. She's also the dragon that tried to kill me when I was five. Granted, I *did* invade her habitat, but she seemed super excited to roast me. Over the past twelve years, Papi has been teaching her how to peacefully coexist with humans. I guess Violet #43 was just waiting to escape.

"You'll find her, Papi. I trust it."

"Let's hope so. Now tell me about *your* day, mija."

I leave out how I was almost killed but go into detail about every-thing else: the Dragonblood ring itself, the horrific death match and the witch behind it, that Takeshi had been kidnapped, and our escape into an Other Place. Disclosing our location could put our lives in more danger, so I don't say much more, but I ask if he's spotted any strangers following him.

"None. I'll stay vigilant, though. You need to do the same."

"Oh, we're super safe here, Papi. No worries."

Papi is as sullen as he was when Takeshi held a claw dagger to his neck. It's the look of a man who's trying his hardest not to give into despair, but he's failing.

"That's what you said about the Cup."

Pangolin dragons have almost flung me off the side of the Runner's mountain, yet the force of their bodies doesn't knock my breath away like Papi's words.

I flash back to when he found out I signed my contract. He didn't light up at his only child representing Puerto Rico on a world stage. To him, it had been reckless—a choice made without thinking of the shady circumstances surrounding my invitation. I was a disappointment in the exact moment I considered myself a source of pride. I made mistake after mistake.

I helped the Sire kill Andrew.

Murderer! Murderer! Murderer!

I turn away from the phone. Tears prick at my eyes, stinging with every labored breath. My goddamn hand is shaking. Papi will think I'm either losing my cool, or stuck in an earthquake. I'd pay an obscene amount of money to make him believe the latter.

"¿Mi amor? ¿Qué te pasa?"

His soft voice speeds up the flow of tears. Papi is nothing like the revolting excuse for a cousin I've been doomed with. Todd *wants* to cut me down. Papi would never be that cruel for personal gratification, but he doesn't understand he's doing it, too.

I don't have the strength to explain myself.

"I'm fine, Papi, but I think I hear Génesis calling me. Can we chat tomorrow?"

"Yes, but—"

"Okay, I love you! Bye!"

He calls me three times after I hang up. I let them all go to voicemail, darting up the steps to my room, where I hope Mom is either showering or passed out. I can't let her see me crying.

I can't disappoint her again, too.

Jeffrey Hines @The_Jeffrey_Hines

This is the end of an era, folks. None of these kids wished for this outcome. For most of them, Blazewrath is all they know. So what in the bloody hell could be next?

5:14 AM · August 16th, 2017 · Twitter for iPhone

Jeffrey Hines @The_Jeffrey_Hines

I vote for keeping them together. Not just by country—all of the sixteen teams should join forces somehow. This is the end of an era, but it could be the start of an even better one.

5:19 AM · August 16th, 2017 · Twitter for iPhone

—Transcript from a thread on Jeffrey Hines's Twitter account (@The_Jeffrey_Hines)

CHAPTER TWELVE

Victoria

"I DON'T SEE PHONES HERE," I SAY.

"We don't need one." Takeshi walks to the historical fiction section. Each shelf is color-coded. My favorite is at the top—different shades of red decorate the paper and leather spines.

I can't remember the last time I stood in a library. Mami is the reader in our family, but her reading pile is quite small. Despite Héctor's efforts to steer her into graphic novels, she only likes prose from the romance section and books on the bestseller lists.

Takeshi kneels before the green shelf, which is second-to-the-bottom. He presses the book in the middle as if it were a button.

It slides into a book-shaped hole in the wall.

I can still see the spine, but it's partially hidden in shadow. Nothing else moves.

"Was something supposed to happen?" I ask.

"It's happening now." Takeshi presses the third book on the blue shelf. It disappears like the green one. "Michael figured out how to communicate without being tracked. He calls it the Spine Charm. Each is linked to a different location. Moving them is like speed dialing."

"How many locations are there?"

"A few."

Takeshi presses pink, purple, orange, black, and white books.

Seven.

He picks out a slim book from the horror section and sits in a high-backed chair near the door. "Take a seat," he says. "This might take a while."

"We simply wait?"

"Yes."

"How long?"

"The Spine Charm's limit is two hours."

"*What?* Two hours will crawl by! Our families could be dead by the time we—"

"No one is killing hostages yet. Dragon Knights only execute people they believe are disposable or in their way, and your loved ones are neither. Judging from the way she used Lana in the ring, Cecilia's strategy is similar. If her Blood Masks found them first, they're still alive." Takeshi flips the page while still reading the last few lines. He dives into the next one as soon as it's down. "They will be found, Victoria. In the meantime, read any book you'd like."

"Reading isn't my thing."

I'm grateful Takeshi doesn't extol the virtues of putting my eyeballs on yellowed pages. He reads in silence while I turn into a heap of folded arms and suppressed screams.

My gaze sprints from one pressed spine to another. If there are seven locations, are we waiting on seven people? Takeshi might have a labyrinthine network of allies—he'd been such a beloved athlete. I can believe he collects information from a revolving door of sources, but he'd made it sound like these friends will *extract* our families. Who's competent enough to be trusted with an operation like that? Will I meet the rest of Team Japan? Are more agents involved?

An hour and a half later, no one has answered.

My sneakers squeak as I pace around the chair. "This isn't working…" I mutter under my breath. Saying it louder will result in Takeshi telling me to be patient, and if I hear him even begin to utter that adjective, I'll projectile vomit. "This is such an unbelievable waste of—"

THUD!

The purple book has fallen to the floor.

"Is the message inside?" I match Takeshi's brisk pace.

He grins. "You could say that."

He takes the book and flips it open to the middle. I don't see handwritten notes scribbled in it, no folded pages with fresh ink.

Purple smoke spills out. It hooks around our torsos. A smoky vortex swirls between the pages. I hover three inches off the floor like a stuffed animal in an arcade game.

"What the—"

Takeshi and I are launched into the vortex.

It's fucking cold.

The smoke clears inside a different—and much bigger—library. I'm shivering among rose gold bookcases. Lilacs decorate hundreds of shelves and the ladders attached to them. There's no color coordination here; spines have been arranged by height and thickness. Crystal chandeliers light up all six levels of this freezing tundra.

"Where are we?" I whisper.

"My Other Place. I'm delighted to see you've made it safely," a woman says behind me.

Wait... I know her...

Noora Haddad stands before a glass window. Her professional camera isn't hanging around her neck tonight. Her Silver wand is held tight in her left hand. There's no evidence she works... *worked*... for the International Blazewrath Federation. She's in black, but her hijab is olive. The last time I saw her, she'd given Lana a picture secretly taken at the welcome party. It featured Lana and Galloway by the dragon chocolate fountain—a memento from the night they met.

I don't know what's become of Noora these past few days. Has her life been irrevocably altered, too? Odds are she's been much better off than me. I would've never suspected her of keeping secrets, though, especially ones that involve working with Takeshi Endo.

"The Spine Charm only connects between Other Places," he says. "It's particularly useful for Regulars when we don't have a magic user to Transport us."

"It also serves as the formal invitation you'd need to get inside." I look from him to Noora again, my brow tightly furrowed. "The daughter of an IBF ambassador is one of your secret contacts, and she's going to help save my mother?"

Noora clutches her chest. "What happened to her?" she asks somberly. "And how did you break out of Ravensworth, Takeshi?"

"Let's sit. This will be quite long." He claims a chaise to the left.

When Noora walks over to him, I'm gifted with a full view of a starry sky. This must be a magical projection. I linger on the stars while Takeshi shares our story with Noora. I should be listening intently and cooperating with Mami's rescue. But there's something familiar about this night. It's a photograph I've carried in my memories like an engraved locket.

Then I see the sand dunes.

Even in the dark, I recognize where the Cup protesters held their NO MORE BLOOD signs. Where I stepped on a red carpet for the first time, and felt like a winner long before I competed. My body still vibrates from the shaky trip inside the black SUV with a WRATH license plate. From the shouts of "Boricua!" shooting out of the stands. Shouts I'll never hear again.

"Noora?" I cut into whatever Takeshi is saying. "Are we... Is this... Dubai?"

She nods. "This is the Pink Rock Desert in Sharjah."

The marble walls, the dragon sculptures, the stands. *Everything* has been torn down. It's as if there had never been a Blazewrath stadium here. As if my wildest fantasies had never come true, and my greatness had been a figment of fever dreams.

This is really the end.

With frost-cold hands on my head, I bend over. I'm not a loud crier. Not even when my stepfather lost his shit. My sorrow strengthened him. He'd love to be a fly on the wall now. Watch me wither into what he's always considered me—nothing.

"Victoria?" Noora is beside me, a soft hand on my back. "Do you need anything?"

My life back.

"This was a mistake. I should get her to headquarters," says Takeshi.

"No..." I'm straightening up. "Have you told Noora everything yet?" I peer at her through watery eyes. "How exactly are you qualified to help us?"

Noora sighs at Takeshi. "She doesn't know?"

"I was getting to that." He points to the chair. "Shall we sit?"

"I've done enough sitting today, Endo. Tell me how the fuck a sports photographer is capable of saving my mother. No offense, Noora."

"None taken. But I'm not *just* a sports photographer. I'm also a spy."

"And a very talented one," says Takeshi.

He's serious enough that asking him to repeat the statement would be nonsensical.

The woman who took our first official pictures as a Blazewrath team is... a spy? I've never gotten a suspicious vibe from her. She excels at sneaking around for pictures, though.

"You're a bureau agent," I say.

"No."

"So you're like Haya Tanaka? Working for agents without a direct affiliation?"

"Oh, I'm affiliated. So is Haya, if I'm not mistaken."

"She is," Takeshi confirms.

Are they suggesting there's another organization dedicated to magical law and order? I can't imagine Takeshi following commands— Sandhar and the Sire were the means to an end. Haya, Robinson, Noora, and the six people who didn't answer Takeshi's call... Is he their *boss*?

I've stopped crying. There's no room for despair when confusion has made me its bitch.

"If this is a cult, you can keep it," I say.

Takeshi shakes his head. "My days in a cult are long gone."

"That's what a cult leader would say."

He and Noora laugh.

"I wanted to discuss this with you first, since your steed is the eldest," Takeshi continues.

I step back. "What does Esperanza have to do with this?"

Takeshi fixes his collar, as if he's a politician addressing his constituents. "I've launched a covert special ops team. My objective is to put together a group comprised of both magic users and dragon riders.

In regards to the riders, I'm specifically interested in operatives that have experience in combat or high-risk situations. Blazewrath athletes are the perfect fit."

He pauses.

If he's giving my brain time to absorb every word, I'm grateful, even though it's doing a shit job.

"Blazewrath athletes as secret agents?" I whisper.

"Yes. Our current mission is to protect the Sol de Noches. We must bring down Cecilia *and* the Dragon Knights." Takeshi's firm tone breathes hope into my lungs. "Tonight I'll have you share everything you know about your mother's potential whereabouts with Noora. I've also brought you here to extend an invitation. If you decline, you can still hide in Michael's Other Place for as long as you need. If you accept, your first briefing is tomorrow morning."

I'm close to toppling over—my heart is ramming the hell out of my chest.

When President Turner canceled the Cup, I figured I'd never use my Blazewrath skills again. But this... It's a chance to reclaim a dream I thought was dead. This is an opportunity to train, strategize, and support my colleagues in order to get the job done. We must use our blood, sweat, and tears to save our steeds from the assholes trying to hurt them. This is a *team*.

And I get to be part of it.

"You're asking me to fight evil." I can't believe such cliché words leave my mouth.

Takeshi's smile is warm enough to thaw an iceberg. "You'll be the first line of defense for your dragon. Once we defeat our current threats, we'll defend whoever needs us next."

He might as well have told me I'd won the Blazewrath World Cup.

"This will be an ongoing thing? Like a full-time job?" I say way too fast.

"The pay could be better," Noora jokes. "But yes, it is essentially a full-time job."

I don't believe in describing people as *glowing*. Comparisons between human beings and rays of light are the highest form of cheesiness. But if I could see myself in a mirror, I think I'd set aside my personal beliefs— right now, I could turn a black hole into a warehouse rave.

The view beyond the glass window represents a life that's abandoned me. I will never love anything as much as I loved the sport that defined who I am. Who knows if I'll even *like* this new team dynamic at all? If I'm replacing one pipe dream with another?

But I'd rather lose Blazewrath than Esperanza. If anyone should defend her, it's *me*.

I hold out my hand to Takeshi. "I'm in."

"Excellent." With a bow, he shakes it. "Welcome to Task Force Blaze."

In 1856, an inebriated Calvin Wiles—the first Gold Wand to appear in the bureau's registry—proclaimed he could perform spells using his mind. He promised to bring his mates a dragon's head without using his wand. Calvin traveled to Germany in search of a Schlange. He ventured deep into Teutoburg Forest and found a male Schlange's habitat. The next morning, Calvin's bones were the only proof he was there. The bureau easily confirmed his identity. It has yet to confirm reports his voice could still be heard among the trees.

—*Excerpt from Corwin Sykes's* Dark & Dastardly: Obscure Magical Folklore & Enchantments for Beginners

CHAPTER THIRTEEN

Lana

DEEP WITHIN THE PESADELO SANCTUARY, ANDREW KNEELS beside me.

His blue-and-white Blazewrath uniform is a stark contrast to my black one. We're both on the glass-covered floor, barely a foot away, but I can't reach for him—Randall's Paralysis Charm has locked me in place. Knives shoot into my ribs whenever I move. At least Randall's not here to gloat. The sanctuary is empty save for the Scottish boy crying in silence.

"It's okay, Andrew. We're getting out of here. Don't lose hope."

He won't look at me.

"Andrew? Please. I need you to stay positi—"

"Where's our photo?" he whispers.

I stiffen. "Our what?"

"The photo Noora took at the welcome party. Show it to me."

Even without a Paralysis Charm gripping me, I would have remained deathly still. That picture had been such a precious gift—a balm to my aching soul.

But I left it in Puerto Rico.

"You don't understand... We were in danger... We *had* to escape..."

Andrew stands. I don't know how he released himself from Randall's spell. He's even stopped crying. Now he towers over me, looking down as if I'm filth. "You're erasing me."

"No! I just couldn't go back to—"

"How many times did you look at it? Did you even remember you had it?"

My chin quivers. "I remembered, yes, but... I couldn't... It hurts..."

"You think I love seeing you pretend my death never happened?" He's circling me. His boots grind the glass into tinier particles. With each heavy step, I flinch, driving the invisible blades deeper. "Trying to forget me, are you? Did our friendship mean *nothing*?"

"Don't say that! You know it's not true!"

"You led me here, lass. Brought me straight to the Sire's clutches." Andrew stops before me. "That was the first time you killed me. Now you're killing me again by forgetting me."

"Stop... Please..." I'm bawling. More words stick to the back of my throat, but my sobs won't let them come out. I can't even wipe the tears without breaking into muffled screams.

Silver flames cover Andrew's body. They draw a fiery outline of my friend. A halo settles a few inches above, lighting him up like a diamond in a coal-dark cave.

"Your cousin's groupies are right," he says. "You're a murderer, Lana."

"No..."

"You killed me, and I won't ever let you forget it."

"*No.*"

He snaps his fingers, and the silver fire shoots out at me. My uniform is supposed to be flame-resistant—yet the fabric disintegrates.

So does my flesh. "STOP! IT HURTS!"

I'm flailing, screaming, burning until I'm nothing more than charred bone.

Andrew watches with a satisfied smile. "It should," he says. "Let yourself feel the pain."

"NO!"

"Lana, what is *going on?*"

I crash into Mom, our foreheads narrowly escaping a collision.

She's hugging me. We're both in my bed, and I'm dripping in sweat. Sheets are sprawled all around me; my three silk pillows are on the floor. Maybe I threw them while I was asleep? The sigh of relief never comes—I'd been stuck in a nightmare, but it all felt real.

You killed me, and I won't ever let you forget it.

"Was it a bad dream?" Mom asks.

I don't reply. I'm too weak to even breathe steadily.

Mom checks me for a fever. Then she seizes my hand. "Why don't you go back to sleep, honey?" This is by far the warmest she's sounded since we made up. As much as I love having her treat me like her daughter, staying in bed means more nightmares. It means being watched over by a mother who thinks I'm weak. Making the others think I'm weak, too.

"I'm fine, Mom. Let me take a quick shower. Did you eat breakfast?"

Mom loosens her grip on me. She sighs. "Resting isn't bad, Lana."

"I don't need rest. I need a shower and food."

"How about I bring your breakfast up here?" Mom is as serious as a kick to the crotch.

"I said I'm *fine.*"

Thankfully, someone chooses that moment to knock twice. Mom rushes to the door while I roll under the covers.

Nobody else should see the bird's nest I must have for hair, or the dark bags from a tumultuous sleep. Nightmare Andrew had blamed me for losing our photo, for not even daring to glance at it. He thinks I'm erasing him. How can he—or *anyone*—expect me to cling to the worst day of my life? How is that supposed to help me get over it?

Let yourself feel the pain.

Every breath is a fight against bawling. Talking to Papi last night had been bad—having him call me out last night sucked—but the nightmare was ten thousand times worse. My own brain is working against me. Not even a fake version of Andrew will let me off the hook.

I'm sorry, Andrew. The way forward isn't behind me.

Mom's gasp is loud enough to shatter satellites in space.

"What is it?" I ask.

She steps aside, beaming at me. "Getting out of bed might not be such a bad idea."

"Why?"

Someone barges inside.

"SURPRISE!" says Samira Jones.

I HAVEN'T STOPPED HUGGING SAMIRA SINCE SHE ARRIVED.

Eating my bowl of cereal is a bit difficult, but I'm managing. Agent Robinson has made the mistake of preparing us whatever we ask. I can't decide whose appetite is bigger, Samira's or Luis's—they're both feasting on four different plates. Bacon is a staple in almost everyone's diet, although Haya, Mom, and a constantly yawning Victoria don't care much for it.

Victoria sits across from me at the ruby dining table. Even though she seems tired, her smile makes an appearance here and there, and she's sharing her red velvet waffles with Edwin. I've *never* seen her share food before—she must be in an excellent mood. I've been meaning to ask what happened with Takeshi last night, but when Mom, Samira, and I came to the dining room, everyone else had already arrived. Hopefully, they'll tell us what they learned soon.

"Thank you again, Samira." Takeshi shows off his dragon claw dagger—his weapon from his time as an undercover agent in the Sire's army. He should use it to comb that stray lock of hair away from his face. It's ruining his serious expression with unnecessary softness. Also, why is it *screaming* at me to run my fingers through it? Super inappropriate. "You didn't have to bring it."

"Are you kidding? That thing pierced Randall Wiggins's chest. It is *iconic* and it does not belong in an evidence vault." Samira slurps her grape juice, then dives right into her third serving of piping-hot sausage. "Although I would've dodged those Dragon Knights if I'd left it behind. They were still looking for me in the Department of Magical Artifact Permits and Regulations."

I shudder. The thought of Dragon Knights kidnapping Samira strips me of what little desire I had for breakfast. They'd chanted their heinous, Sire-obsessed prayer right before chasing her down. Luckily, she Transported to New Delhi unscathed. Agent Robinson relayed our location's coordinates through her Whisperer. He had been waiting by the entrance.

"Other than the dagger, what else were you able to retrieve?" asks Takeshi.

"Can she finish her breakfast first?" I squeeze Samira even tighter. "She must be starving."

"Hence the billion plates," says Luis.

Héctor snorts. "You're one to talk. How many pancakes have you gorged on?"

"My metabolism requires me to eat more than a normal teenage boy, Héctor."

"At least you've finally admitted you're not normal." Victoria laughs. When she turns to me, she's still a bright ray of sunshine. "If you keep holding her like that, Samira's eyeballs are going to pop out. Please spare her any more pain."

"Thank you. We could trade seats if you want. It would be a noble sacrifice," Samira jokes.

"Sorry. I like my eyeballs," says Victoria.

"I can pay you."

"Tempting, but it's still a no." Victoria laughs *again*.

"Okay, okay. Point taken." When I let go of Samira, she and Victoria start clapping. Everyone except for Takeshi joins in. He's smiling down at his omelet. Luis has the audacity to give me a standing ovation. "You are *all* the worst."

Victoria shrugs. "Made you laugh, though."

Oh, wow. Did she forget about our fight yesterday? Or is she already over it? Whatever she and Takeshi found out, it's cranked up her Joy Meter tenfold, and I'm *not* complaining.

"Thank you," I mouth the words.

She mouths back, "No problem."

Samira's scraping her plate clean with her fork. She bites into the last piece of sausage, moaning in total joy. "To answer Takeshi's question, I found files on Cecilia in Director Sandhar's computer. Most contain easily accessible details—the orphanage in Sevilla where she grew up, her admittance to Iron Pointe, and the few Dragonblood rings the bureau has been able to locate. But there was a folder in the evidence vault with her name on it."

Takeshi pauses. "I found nothing when I searched that vault for Dragonshade."

"Do you think Nirek tried hiding it there afterwards?" Agent

Robinson suggests.

"Or it could've been a Blood Mask. Nirek's the only employee with access to that vault, but if Samira and I could sneak in, it's likely another person did, too."

"We're digressing," I say. "What's in the folder?"

I might as well have hit the PAUSE button. Nobody makes a sound while Samira pulls out her Gold wand. It's still as lightweight and shiny as I remember it. She fled the bureau before she could finish her Gold Wand certification, but there's no doubt in my mind she was born to level up into the highest category for magic users.

With a flick of her wrist, Samira conjures the notorious folder onto the table. She slides it over to Takeshi. He snatches it like free hot dogs at the state fair and starts reading.

"Cecilia was born on April 10, 1998. Alondra Valcárcel died three hours after giving birth to her. Her mother was a Regular, shunned by her extremely Catholic family for being pregnant out of wedlock. Cecilia's father never came looking for his baby." Samira is laser-focused on Takeshi as he reads at alarming speed. "He also left no trace of his DNA."

"Oh, my God." Now *I'm* the one who's not moving. Randall's smug face crashes into my thoughts—he's the only person whose dad remains a mystery for this exact reason. Could it be the same person? Or their fathers are different men with similar powers?

"What is it?" says Victoria.

"There's no genetic evidence of whoever fathered Randall Wiggins," Takeshi beats me to it. He gives the folder to Agent Robinson. "He and Cecilia share a birthday, too."

Samira points to the folder. "And their disappearances coincide. The day Randall broke out of the bureau is the same day Cecilia fled Iron Pointe."

Are. You. Joking.

"So they're the closest things to magical twins?" I ask. "This must be the same man."

"Or several men from one bloodline?" says Victoria.

Agent Robinson shakes his head. "Gold Wands aren't common. If this is more than one man, the chances of them being related are slim."

Rather than believe we face a bunch of equally powerful people, it's much easier to accept a lone wolf is this powerful. Edward Barnes had cast the first blood curse on a dragon. Madame Waxbyrne can create Other Bodies. Whoever's fathering babies and abandoning ship has to be the most advanced magic user of all time, though. Understanding their psychic abilities could help me defeat Cecilia.

Who are you, strange wizard?

"Madame Waxbyrne never told you about this?" I ask Agent Robinson.

"Not a word. We were together before Cecilia ran away, but even after the bureau became involved and Glenda retired from teaching, she wouldn't talk to me about her. I suspect she was scared of Cecilia. Whenever I mentioned her, Glenda looked like I'd spoken of the Devil."

"Do you think you could contact her so we can try again?"

He slouches. "We don't know where she is. And she's set up traps across the globe to zap whoever tries poking at them."

"She cast an Other Body so you could trick the Sire," I tell Takeshi. "How'd you find her?"

"Bureau records. The organization kept tabs on her, since they were offering her protection from Cecilia, too. But this was long before Dragon Knights infiltrated the bureau. Madame Waxbyrne cut off all ties with us around the same time you and I met at her wand shop."

For a second, I swear he smiles, but he regains his seriousness too quickly for me to be sure.

I pretend I have an itchy spot behind my ear. "There has to be a way to find her."

"Maybe another Gold Wand can do it unscathed. Even then, it's still a risk," says Haya. She's slathering more blueberry jam onto her toast. She offers the jar to Gabriela.

"Thank you." Gabriela takes the jar, even though she doesn't have toast on her plate. She's turning beet red, too, which marks the second time she's blushed in Haya's presence. I don't know if this means she *likes* her, or if she's just starstruck. Either way, it's super cute.

From the way Victoria's smiling at Gabriela, she seems to agree with me. "I think we should hold off on the Madame Waxbyrne search. We're not putting anyone's safety in danger. Any other suggestions for finding more information on Cecilia?"

I'm tempted to contradict her, but she's right. The only Gold Wand here is Samira, and I'd rather get stabbed through the heart than put my best friend in harm's way.

"Um… there's one more thing," says Samira. "Cecilia's Gold abilities are pretty normal save for those mind spells, but she can also… I don't know how to explain it, actually."·

I whirl around, my frantic gaze landing on Haya. From the way she's avoiding me, I know this is what she couldn't tell me last night. "What is it?" I say with bated breath.

Nobody's speaking.

When I face Samira, she's looking from Agent Robinson to Takeshi, her frown deepening.

Takeshi says, "Show them."

Samira takes out her wand. She flips a few pages of the report, then stops on one that is bright red. There's a single black square at the center.

"That icon activates video footage," Agent Robinson clarifies. "Classified surveillance for a *specific* type of content. It'll surely contain graphic violence, so just warning you lot."

"I've fast-forwarded to the last part." Samira sounds like a horrified mother who's found her kids accessing the Internet for the first time.

"Here we go..."

She taps the icon with the tip of her wand.

Light beams out of the page. Outlines crop up in the middle of the table; they're much whiter than the holograms in *Star Wars*, but similar in size. They grow into lifelike depictions of two figures—a girl and a dragon. The girl wears a cerulean-blue blazer with a burgundy skirt. Her brown hair is a tangled mess, as if she's been brawling for hours.

Cecilia Valcárcel aims her wand at a German Schlange.

To the untrained eye, the creature looks like a brown-and-black snake that has been enlarged to skyscraper heights. Schlanges are the only species that can retract its legs. It helps them slither across any surface at the speed of light. This one is baring its venom-tipped fangs at Cecilia. It darts toward her like a viper chasing its dinner.

A golden stream bursts out of Cecilia's wand.

It misses the Schlange by a couple inches. She dashes and rolls over and narrowly escapes fireballs, but her foe is hot on her trail. Cecilia falls. As she tries to stand, the dragon leaps into the air, spreading its wings and unlocking its four legs. Within seconds, it'll crush the evil witch.

She strikes with another spell.

This time, it hits the dragon's chest.

The Schlange freezes as gold light covers every inch of its scaly body. It wails into the sky, a sorrowful tune that rivals what the Sol de Noches once sung. Then blue-white sparks begin to sputter where Cecilia struck. The sparks morph into a glowing orb. Cecilia's magic drags it out of the Schlange as if she's tugging a fistful of hair. More sparks go off. I'm covering my squinting eyes while the orb keeps leaving its host.

Then the orb is launched back into the dragon's chest.

The Schlange collapses. A pool of blood spills out of its lips.

Cecilia's opponent is dead.

It's only when Samira ends the video that I notice my whole face in my hands. Of course I know Gold Wands can kill dragons. I just didn't think I'd ever *see* it. I hope I never do again.

"What the fuck was that magic?" Victoria says. Her Joy Meter has been officially smashed.

"The reason why Cecilia is so respected among Dragonblood fans," a grim Agent Robinson replies. He can barely look away from his pancakes. "She filmed many videos like this one and posted them in online magical conspiracy theory sites. Her network started growing from those posts, and when she became an underground sensation, Dragonblood was born."

Agent Robinson reaches for his shirt's pocket, as if he's searching for a cigarette, but there's nothing. He lowers his hand with a disappointed sigh.

"Cecilia believes souls are divisible from the body," he continues. "Many are convinced Calvin Wiles, the first registered Gold Wand, invented a spell to remove his soul. People have reported hearing his voice in Teutoburg Forest. They say the trees speak as if he dwells inside them. The bureau has never confirmed the rumors are true, but magic users keep attempting similar spells."

I'm spinning despite sitting perfectly still. "Souls can... be... removed?" I whisper.

"Yes."

"And they can be *put into things*?"

"That remains to be seen. The bureau has maintained Calvin's voice is a separate spell meant to feed visitors' paranoia and conspiracy theories. More of a prank than a revelation."

"How can we be sure no one else has mastered this soul trapping charm?"

"We can't," says Takeshi. "But Cecilia seems close to achieving it. That video shows her ripping the dragon's soul out. She failed to fully extract it, though. Sometimes dragons die once their soul returns. On most occasions, they live, but it's like jamming the incorrect piece in a puzzle. It wreaks havoc on their capacities to rationalize and identify their surroundings. Cecilia takes advantage of their confusion, their pain, and they can't stop it."

His expression darkens just like when Cecilia threatened to kill me—he's a fading sunset in the middle of a blizzard. A chilling, hopeless sight. I can't tell if he's really flashing back to Nantes, if he's remembering the dragon we had to abandon.

Hearing about the Anchor Curse had been terrible enough. I still don't know how the Sire was capable of such dark magic, but what Cecilia's doing isn't that far from his wretchedness—they're both using others for personal gain. The only difference is they target one another's kind.

The Akarui in Nantes had been a flailing mess, and it was probably because of this botched soul spell. God knows how much it suffered during and after Cecilia's torturous magic. If it's still alive, the Japanese Un-Bonded remains in excruciating pain.

One day, I hope I can make Cecilia feel it, too.

"She won't get away with this," says Victoria. "Task Force Blaze will make sure of it."

Mom, Samira, and I are the only ones who don't nod.

Héctor is even taking out a black folder from under the table. He flattens it as he takes a sip of his latte. The rest of my friends do the same.

"Should we go over the first mission with our steeds now?" Gabriela holds up her folder.

"Excuse me?" I raise my hand. "Um… What's Task Force Blaze?"

Takeshi pulls out two folders. He slowly sets them next to each other.

"Something I've been working on for a while."

He goes into detail about what he calls a special ops team—how he's inviting magic users and riders into this secret group. Their main job is to keep the Sol de Noches safe, but they're also going after Dragon Knights and Blood Masks. It sounds like a separate entity from the bureau, even though they're in charge of similar activities.

"Before you came downstairs, I'd offered positions to the riders." Takeshi waves at my friends, who are nodding along. "Everyone is on board, but I'm still missing members."

So those two folders are for me and Samira. Of course we'd have a Gold Wand on our side—Samira will smoke any foe in her path. And she's so, so bright. She's the perfect addition to Task Force Blaze. As for me, I'm fast. Tough. Committed. This isn't the Blazewrath World Cup, but I'm still going to work extra hard for my teammates.

Wow. I can't believe I can call them teammates again.

With more resources, I can stop Cecilia now. Takeshi has an actual plan, and I'll be ensuring that evil witch's capture faster if I'm at his side. This is more than a distraction—it's a responsibility. A brand new *purpose*. So many people and dragons need Cecilia gone. They need the Dragon Knights out of the picture, too. Most of all, my country's steeds are relying on our success.

So am I. There's no way I'm failing them like I failed Andrew.

I refuse to let anyone down ever again.

Takeshi slides one folder to Samira. "This is yours if you want it."

"Duh!" She snatches it at once.

He grins as he moves the remaining folder across the table. "And this is yours."

It lands in front of Joaquín.

"Victoria mentioned you helped save President Turner. Keeping him in the Dark Island was a clever way to protect him from the Anchor Curse. We can always use great strategists."

Takeshi's voice sounds a galaxy away, fading in and out. He's completely bypassed me. Is there a super special folder with my name on it somewhere else? And why is he talking about Victoria as if her suggestions have any weight on his decisions? Did *she* tell him not to pick me?

He shakes hands with Joaquín and Samira.

"Training starts in an hour and a half. Meet me in the hangar. The rest of you," he looks over at Mom, then at me, but only for a second. "Enjoy your day."

Takeshi Endo hastily exits the dining room.

You know how some people think dragons choose to Bond? Then there are others who think it's fated? I like the destiny theory, mate. You can't pick out a random stranger and force them to connect with you. A Bond is bigger than dragon and rider—it's the universe giving them permission to share a soul. Humans rarely experience something similar with one another.

—*Excerpt from Andrew Galloway's 2015 interview with*
Sworn Magazine

CHAPTER FOURTEEN

Lana

I've never chased a boy this fast.

"Wait!" I'm gaining on Takeshi as he enters the hangar. My shrill voice bounces off the walls and echoes like I'm miles deep inside a cave.

He ignores me anyway.

"Takeshi, *wait!*" I cut in front of him. "Did I do something wrong?"

"Blocking people's paths is impolite, so perhaps that?" Takeshi flashes me a quick smile, then sidesteps me. "I'm not sure what you're referring to. Could you be more specific?"

"Why don't I get a folder?"

He halts, an eyebrow raised. "I can get you one. Manila. Plastic. Hanging file. Whichever you prefer. Depends on what you'd like to store inside."

I cannot believe this...

"You know what I meant," I mutter as I retreat. I have no idea what I've done to deserve his... whatever this is. The least he can do is give it to me straight. "Why didn't I get invited to join Task Force Blaze? You said it's mostly for magic users and riders, but Joaquín's a Regular."

"He is, yes."

"So am I."

"Correct."

"Then what's the problem?"

"Interesting that you called it a problem." Takeshi hides his hands behind his back.

I do the same, but I'm as relaxed as a heart attack. "What would *you* call it?"

Takeshi takes a careful step toward me. I should back up, but catching a whiff of his mild, flowery cologne tempts me to come closer. The other boy here who wears fragrances is Luis, and he bathes in something that reeks of piping-hot leather. This is a nice change of pace.

"When we were in the arena," Takeshi says, "why did you try to save me?"

My jaw falls. "Excuse me?"

"Your life was in danger. Why worry about mine?"

"Oh, I'm sorry. Was I supposed to let you get killed? Also, *you* begged Cecilia to take you out instead. You can be selfless, but I can't?"

Takeshi's gaze is locked on mine, narrowing even more. "You're defensive over simple questions. You favor feelings—specifically, rage—over basic survival instincts. You could endanger us all if you ignore commands." He takes yet another step. Soon we'll be close enough to dance. For a split second, I wonder if he's a good dancer, and I hate myself. "There's nothing wrong with feelings, Lana. I just don't think you're prepared to master them."

Oh, great. A brand new member has joined the Lana Is A Mess Club. He's the one who went on a revenge mission for two years! How exactly is trying to murder your steed's killer mastering your feelings? If *I* hadn't begged him to spare President Turner, he would've gone through with it! I suppose he takes pride in how detailed and thorough his plan was, though. And I'm sure the Sire gave him plenty of reasons to punch him—I could never be that patient.

Still, I won't be left out of Task Force Blaze.

"Let me prove I *am* prepared, Takeshi. I'll do whatever you say."

"It's not only about doing what I—"

"Give me a million tests. Put me through the ringer. I don't care. Just let me try."

"Lana."

"Please." I stop before tears cascade out of me. If I keep talking, I might get too choked up. Validating Takeshi is the last thing I need right now.

He sizes me up. "You won't enjoy my chances."

"I'll be the judge of that."

"No, you'll really hate them." He takes out a silver remote control from his jeans' pocket. It's thinner than the page with Cecilia's disgusting video. "But if you insist."

He clicks the top button.

The walls flip sideways, revealing platinum screens. They're as big as the Sol de Noches. I think of all the Monsta X videos I could stream here—this is better than a movie theater.

"Runners face many challenges on the mountain. However, each is presented separately. Blocker dragons take turns attacking you. Their riders are only allowed to strike in specific locations." Takeshi lifts the remote. "Everything changes on a real battlefield."

He presses another button.

Flames catapult from the screens.

I drop like a sack of bricks. The fire roars all around me, never relenting.

Then the room shakes with *actual* roars—dragons are zipping into the hangar. I can't possibly count them. And they're moving way too fast to tell them apart; it's a tangled web of spindly wings and bared fangs. I only spot gleaming pink horns. There must be an Irish Spike.

Silver light zooms past me. Gold light follows suit.

Magic users are flinging themselves into the whirlwind of dragons and fire. They scream and punch and wave their wands high.

"Where is the threat?"

I can't believe I still hear Takeshi. He's so, so calm. Not even Yoda could be this chill.

What the hell is he talking about? Everything is a threat!

I stay on the floor, cringing and squinting through the flames. Sweat drenches me like I've been swimming for hours. This must be a sick joke—how can Takeshi expect me to focus during such a disastrous scenario? Yes, battlefields are chaotic, but this is on another level!

"Where is the threat?" he repeats.

"All over the place!"

"Wrong."

"How am I wrong? Are you seeing *any* of this?"

"If you find what's causing the battle, you can end it."

"But nothing's causing it! Everyone's just super furious!"

I'm pretty sure my vocal cords are damaged from yelling so hard, and I feel especially ridiculous considering how Takeshi hasn't spoken any louder.

A child screams.

Right across from me, Dragon Knights are closing in on a little girl.

"Help!" a man says behind me.

A Blood Mask is strangling him. Two more aim their wands at his sides.

More screams, then the sound of a dagger slicing through flesh.

The little girl is still cowering before the Dragon Knights. The man remains at the Blood Masks' mercy. I can't find whoever's been cut. I wipe off sweat from my stinging eyes. Heavy smoke fills the hangar;

I'm coughing hard enough to almost puke out my lungs.

"Where is the threat?" There he goes again.

The roars, the crackling fire, the screams... I can't think... I can't even stand...

CLICK!

Nothing is ablaze anymore. Spells aren't being shot all around me. The little girl, the man, the Dragon Knights, and Blood Masks... all gone.

Takeshi flips the walls back into their original position. They lock with a soft thud.

He says, "What are your thoughts on ice cream?"

NOT EVEN DESSERT MAKES ME FEEL BETTER.

That was so freaking embarrassing. I haven't felt this useless since Edwin first defeated me. The only thing missing is Victoria asking why I suck so much to make this truly iconic.

"I can get you strawberry instead." Takeshi stares at my bowl of hazelnut ice cream. I've barely eaten two spoonfuls. We're sitting right where I knelt like a pathetic excuse for a human being. "Or any other flavor."

"Don't worry."

I take a cautious bite.

Yep, still not helping.

At least Takeshi is savoring his kakigōri. I've never seen shaved ice or syrup this foamy—it's like he's eating a crimson cloud. He's chosen sweet berry for his generous portion, which is turning his tongue red. His lips are stained, too. I picture him cosplaying as a Victorian vampire and stifle a sigh. Frilly collars would suit his bone structure.

"Would you like a taste?" he asks.

I cough. "What?"

Takeshi offers me his frozen treat. "It's delicious."

"*Oh.* No, no, thank you."

I shove more hazelnut into my mouth. Did I really just brain-fart in front of him? And why would I even *think* about his bone structure? That has absolutely nothing to do with anything!

"So when do I train again?" I keep my voice as smooth as possible.

"Before returning to simulations, we should practice a different technique."

"Which is?"

"I haven't named it yet." Takeshi sets the kakigōri next to him. His breathing slows; he's gazing off into the distance. "Hikaru helped me develop it."

Warmth creeps down the back of my neck. Is he about to get personal with me? I'm torn between feeling honored and terrified. It's a privilege to know he trusts me with such private information, especially since it involves the most important connection in his life. But does this mean *I* have to do the same? Will his technique force me to talk about private stuff, too?

What if he asks me about Andrew?

"You don't have to talk about Hikaru," I say. "I understand if it's too painful."

"Not the beginning. That's always my favorite part. When we met, I had just buried my father." Takeshi pauses, as if he's remembering himself as that five-year-old at the cemetery, holding up an umbrella during a downpour in Sapporo. As if he can picture a white-and-red Akarui waiting for him past the tombstones. "Yours has studied Bonds for years, hasn't he?"

"Yeah. They fascinate him."

Takeshi smiles. "No two Bonds are the same. But there's one

similarity—the invitation." He rises, keeping a considerable distance from his dessert breakfast. "Stand up, please."

What is he about to do? Will I have to complete yet another task?

I leave my ice cream behind. My gaze falls, but I quickly stare up at Takeshi again. I can't let him know I'm worried or nervous. "Okay. I'm standing."

He says, "Close your eyes."

"I, um… I have to *close* my eyes?"

"Yes."

I gulp down, fidgeting. "Why?"

"You'll see."

"Not really. With my eyes closed and all."

"Excellent point." Takeshi shrugs. "I still need you to do it."

The longer you stall, the longer it'll be until you join Task Force Blaze.

I hate not knowing what's about to happen. But if Takeshi's convinced this will work, then I have to keep my cool. I follow his orders. The world is dark, cold, and deathly quiet. I'm shivering a little more. Did Takeshi crank up the air conditioning? I'm hugging myself.

"Hands at your sides." There's such gentleness in his tone.

It takes me a minute to let myself go. Not once does he scold me or sigh in exasperation. I actually can't hear anything; Takeshi has become a shadow. As I wait for my next instructions, the hangar grows *even colder*. I'm half expecting to get pelted with snowballs.

Make it stop… It's… so chilly…

Fingertips graze mine.

The sudden warmth shocks me so much I can't even gasp. Heat concentrates in tiny circles as Takeshi pulls my hands into his. Instead of interlacing fingers, he clutches them like a gentleman helping me upstairs, or like he's about to kiss them after polite introduction. I don't know how he hasn't turned into an ice sculpture—his grasp is so toasty, so welcoming.

"Right before the invitation, you freeze," he whispers. It sounds like he's *inches* away from my face. That flowery cologne is attacking me with its sweetness, and so is Takeshi's soft voice. "You can no longer see, either. Then the light finds you." He taps my knuckles. "A dragon's call is holding hands in the dark. The Bond begins if you hold them back."

The last time I held hands with a boy was in middle school, and it had ended in tears. *His* tears. After watching a Blazewrath match together during recess, Charlie Driver tried ramming his tongue down my throat. I punched his Adam's apple. He never bothered me again. I've pictured myself suffering through more boy-related train wrecks. Luckily, I've avoided them.

Never in my wildest dreams would I have pictured *this*.

"You have to let them center you first," Takeshi carries on like I'm totally not on the verge of heart failure. "Sometimes riders struggle because they can't get out of their heads. The Bond doesn't feel strong enough because they're not allowing it." He falls silent, and I can hear us breathing in at the same time. "The world could be ending all around you, Lana, but if you don't focus on what truly matters—the solution—you will help that ending happen faster."

Takeshi Freaking Endo standing so close is enough to make anyone flail. But his barely-there grip isn't only rooting me to the spot—it cancels out the chaos around us. I'm still shivering, I still can't see, and I'm... *fine*. His warmth is a roadmap leading me home.

So I curl my fingers around his. I start off slow, familiarizing myself with how Takeshi feels. The edges are rough, a little cracked. I remember how he wielded a poisoned claw dagger for two years. How he plotted against the Sire with leather gloves that marked him as his servant. This skin tells a complicated story, and I'm not sure I'd like to hear it. I want to center myself.

I want to hold hands with Takeshi Endo for a very long time.

In a totally professional way, of course.

"Open your eyes," he says.

Oh, my God. He's literally inches away.

"Um… okay…"

I comply.

He lets me go.

As he backs away, Takeshi clicks more buttons, cranking the temperature up. He's not even glancing at me—our frozen treats have all of his attention.

"That's all for now." He offers me my hazelnut ice cream. Once I take it, he dives right into his kakigōri again, licking his red-stained lips. "Are you committed to training harder?"

"Absolutely." I reply too fast, but I don't care. This is the only way I can find balance without unlocking painful memories. This is how I get to heal. And I will.

"Excellent. We meet here in the morning for our next Bonding session." He waves me toward the doors. "There's something else I'd like you to do."

While there's no evidence of soul extraction or containment, dragon studies scholars have theorized on the soul's eternal death. Humans and dragons are mortal. Only the former believes in the afterlife. One of the most prominent wand-makers in history, Julia Serrano, dedicated her career to studying a dragon's eternal death. "Bonded steeds have confirmed they possess souls," Serrano has said. "They simply don't know what happens after death. Concepts like Heaven and Hell baffle them—it's as if a dragon vanishes forever once they take their final breath."

—Excerpt from Corwin Sykes's Dark & Dastardly: Obscure Magical Folklore & Enchantments for Beginners

CHAPTER FIFTEEN

Victoria

OUR STEEDS HAVE ALREADY FADED INTO THE HANGAR. Willa arrived last—Robinson had to Transport her. He and Haya are wrapping up our first briefing. On the first pages of our folders, two groups are listed with their respective members:

GROUP #1: DRAGON KNIGHTS

NOORA HADDAD

KIRILL VOLKOV

ANENI KARONGA

GUSTAVO PABÓN

HÉCTOR SÁNCHEZ

LUIS GARCÍA

GABRIELA RAMOS

HAYA TANAKA

EDWIN SANTIAGO

MICHAEL ROBINSON

GROUP #2: BLOOD MASKS

TAKESHI ENDO

ONESA RUWENDE

GÉNESIS CASTRO

ARTEM VOLKOV

WATAIDA MIDZI

SAMIRA JONES

VICTORIA PERALTA

JOAQUÍN DELGADO

Only Takeshi Endo would have the audacity to pull athletes from right under the Sire's nose. Most of these names had been a surprise, especially Noora and the Volkov twins. Edwin had gasped when he saw his boyfriend in his group—even loudmouth Kirill takes his secrets seriously. When I last spoke with Noora, she reassured me she'd have an update on Mami and the other families later today. Their rescue mission better not take much longer.

I rifle through my folder. It has a thick stack of Blood Mask profiles, Cecilia's last known locations, and a list of Un-Bondeds suspected to be Dragonblood competitors. There's a schedule for meetings in the Cherry Suite. It's reserved in the afternoons for my group. Our mission is to find the next Dragonblood arena, catch Cecilia, and set the Un-Bonded competitors free.

Esperanza's drool falls on top of my group's page.

She's peeking over my shoulder, as if deciphering each letter is a matter of life and death.

"¿Quieres que te las lea en voz alta?" I point to the first group so I can read aloud.

She nods, but still speaks in my mind: *Dim... Dim... Diiiimmm...*

"No hagas mucho esfuerzo. Te puedes lastimar."

Essssss... Bieeeeee......

"Tranquila, chica." This is the most she's pushed herself to speak since our time in Cayey. None of the other Sol de Noches can mumble yet, so perhaps Esperanza feels compelled to develop her psychic verbal skills further in order to motivate them.

"All right, people. Let's get to work." Robinson hits a button on a silver remote control.

The walls flip upside down.

Now there are fire blasters and hoops everywhere. Spiked columns have sprouted from the ceiling. They're arranged in a zigzag pattern, as if they've been designed as an aerial obstacle course. Punching bags, boxing gloves, and protective pads appear in the back, right next to red wrestling mats. A track is slowly materializing around the hangar. It has lanes for five runners.

I clutch my chest. This is a *real* training room. It's the closest I've been to anywhere that reminds me of Blazewrath. I look from one spot to the next, wondering if I'm really here.

"Who wants to do the aerial course first?"

I step forward. "*Me.*"

How I missed dodging fireballs.

For the past hour, Esperanza has evaded the blasters like a winged torpedo. She's also contorting her body to glide through the aerial course without grazing the spikes. When she curves her back in between columns, I press myself against her. My biceps and thighs light up with that familiar burn from practicing in Training Room E. I miss my Blazewrath uniform, but these protective pads get the job done.

WHOOM!

I shiver as Esperanza's heartbeats pound through my body. She's sweeping me under a jolt of energy that could power a galaxy. This is our domain.

"¡Dale, mi vida! ¡Más rápido!" I spur her onward.

Esperanza zips past her siblings with a roar. Gabriela and Luis pretend to complain with loud boos and thumbs-down. Héctor, Edwin, and Génesis encourage us to go faster.

"¡Ya bajen!" Joaquín ends our session with high-fives and a chilled bottle of water. When he gives me mine, he says, "You killed it as usual."

It's been weeks since he's complimented my performance. His praise is icing on the cake.

"Gracias, Joaquín." I cuddle up to Esperanza. Her soft purring is the closest she'll ever get to being like a kitten. "What can I do next?"

"You could shower and not smell like a carcass." Luis sniffs me and pretends to retch. "Whew!" He runs away in mock disgust.

I roll my eyes. "We can do another lap around the blasters. How about you time us now?"

Joaquín looks from me to Esperanza. When she nods, he smiles. "You've missed it, too, huh?" he says while patting her nose.

Esperanza shuts her eyes, as if she's relishing his touch.

"That's a yes," I say. "So can we go again?"

Joaquín calls over Robinson. He approaches while writing on a clipboard. I can't tell if I've impressed him. Takeshi isn't here to corroborate my excellence—he's in the library with Lana. I doubt he's introducing her to the Spine Charm, seeing as she's in an infinite time-out. She must be heckling him to give her a chance, and he must be pretending not to care about how sad she is.

He made the right call benching her. Lana isn't fit for the field yet. *But I am.*

"One last lap, Peralta. Then we train the steeds by themselves," says Robinson.

"Yes, sir."

I mount Esperanza at once. She shakes her entire body, as if she's stretching right before lift-off. With a swift push off the floor, we're back in the air where we belong. Robinson lowers the blasters at the same time, aiming at Esperanza and me.

"Time starts now!" he yells.

Two blasters on the left shoot first.

"¡Bájate!" I command Esperanza.

She ducks. The fireballs miss us just as the next two come forward. I steer Esperanza up and down, helping her anticipate each attack before it happens. Whether she's swatting the flames to the side with her wings or tail, diving in and out of their path, or meeting them halfway with fire of her own, my steed makes it to the opposite end of the hangar unscathed.

My team cheers for us below. Even Willa is roaring her approval.

When I'm on the ground again, I ask Joaquín for our time.

"One minute and thirty-six seconds," he says with a thumbs-up.

"Impressive!" Robinson walks up to me. Willa is right behind him, flapping her wings like she's clapping. "Mind if you timed us, too, Joaquín? Seeing Esperanza just made me nostalgic."

"Not at all, Agent. Go ahead."

Robinson climbs on top of Willa. Perhaps it's the adrenaline rush distorting my senses, but did he get on his steed faster than me? And the Fire Drake is ceiling bound a millisecond later.

I sit on the floor next to Esperanza's claw. Sweat keeps getting into my eyes. I split my time between wiping it off and monitoring Willa's progress. Her offensive style is similar to the Sol de Noches's—diving, swatting, and burning the fireballs—but she's also wrapping her wings around flames. Once they're tucked into her sides, black smoke hisses out of them. It's as if her scales are even hotter than the fire attacking her, and she's vaporizing it.

"Forty-two seconds! Wow!" Joaquín shouts.

Everyone claps as Willa descends.

I'm the only one who's not celebrating. *Forty-two fucking seconds?* That makes me look like a slacker! There are obvious things I should take into account. Robinson is older than me, for example, and Willa is older than Esperanza. They're trained bureau agents. And Robinson is a wizard. That might give him an advantage somehow? He's just bested me.

I can't let him do it again.

"Can I have another go?" I ask Robinson.

"Tomorrow. We still have to see what the steeds are capable of."

Damn it.

He rounds up the dragons to the very end of the hangar. I'm relegated to sitting on the humans' side. Robinson and Haya explain the tools Blood Masks use to capture dragons—magical nets, harpoon guns, metal chains—and ask Samira to attack each steed with them.

"Wait. I get to *train with the dragons*?" Samira fans herself. "OH MY GOD."

After her meltdown ends, she casts nets first. Esperanza blows hers apart with a fireball. Titán, Willa, Puya, and Rayo do the same. Fantasma jumps to the side instead, and he's so fast he turns into a dark blur. Daga is the only one who lets the net snatch her. She rolls on her back, bites it repeatedly, and pulls it away like a cat having the time of her life with a ball of yarn.

"¡No estamos jugando!" Luis berates her. "¡Defiéndete!"

Daga does not defend herself.

I've never seen so many dragons cover their faces in embarrassment.

"¿Qué más se puede pedir si su jinete es Luis?" Héctor makes a fair point. Having Luis as her rider *is* indicative of how seriously she'd take this. While Héctor sits next to me, Luis fails at coaxing Daga to break the net. "Let's hope she can break free from a Blood Mask's clutches."

"They'd have to catch her first."

He points at Daga, who's now whining at Samira for taking the net off. "That's looking very likely," he says with a laugh.

"Daga knows the difference between people she likes and a threat. Besides"—I lower my voice—"Blood Masks would have to go through us. They'll never win."

Héctor doesn't put much effort into his nod. His frown reminds me of the morning after I knocked my stepfather out. The day he learned how much shit I'd been dealing with. As happy as Héctor was to meet Esperanza, he offered to sleep over in case we needed anything. Must be that team captain instinct—he can't stop feeling responsible for others even if he tried.

I shrug. "What is it?"

"How are you feeling about all of this? How's Esperanza?"

"We're both great. You? Titán?"

"Oh, he's doing well." Héctor folds his arms. "*I'm* worried."

"Why?"

"This is a lot, Victoria. We still don't know where our families are."

"Noora said—"

"I know. It's nerve-wracking anyway. All we had to stress about was winning the Cup, then about the Sire toying with our fates. Now there's a homicidal witch trying to profit off our dragons. The bureau is a bust, too." He rests his head against the wall. "I wanna fight for our Soles. I wanna free the Un-Bondeds in Dragonblood rings. But I also just wanna be a teenager."

Daga's squeals overtake the hangar.

I can only stare at my childhood best friend. When we were kids, he'd be the first I'd tell anything. Our ten minute walks to school would be ripe with anecdotes—how we stubbed our toes and scraped our knees, and how loudly our mothers shrieked while being chased by flying roaches we had set loose. I don't remember him telling me he was afraid of anything. But not going to college, getting to see his cherished superhero movies on the big screen, or hanging out at the mall… *that* scares him?

"What do you miss about it?" I ask.

"The fact that nobody depended on me. I could go about my day and not care that I hadn't accomplished much. There's freedom in knowing you're not letting people down."

Which is precisely why I need to excel here.

"Don't get me wrong," Héctor adds hastily. "I loved being captain. I'd do it again without all the bad Sire stuff. But yeah, I wanna enjoy my last days before adulthood kicks my ass."

"Our asses have been kicked much more than most adults."

"True."

I lean closer to him. "When our mission is over, you won't stay with Task Force Blaze?"

Héctor pushes his eyebrows together. "Why does it sound like you will?"

I almost tell him I have to. That I refuse to be nothing ever again.

Now's not the time for sentimentality, though. I can't make Héctor worry more.

"Dragon Knights and Blood Masks represent our worst nightmares. But while those specific groups are powerful now, what if someone worse rises next?"

He's starting to smile. "So this is it? Your purpose?"

Whether he approves or not, my future is in this hangar. I need to strategize and train with two former heroes from Team Japan, and a British guy who's better, stronger, and faster than me.

For now.

"Yes," I reply.

"Okay. Just be careful, hermanita. I trust you'll be amazing as usual."

"Gracias."

A siren goes off.

Takeshi speaks through the intercom. "Breaking news. Your families have been rescued."

"ARE THERE ONLY WHITE CARNATIONS?"

Mami is as incredulous as I'd been when I entered the garden.

There are carnations on the grass, inside porcelain vases, and even arranged as wall art. Gabriela would *love* to take selfies here. I can picture her posing on one of the benches carved from gleaming marble, and kicking off as high as she can in the swings with heart-shaped seats.

"Yes. It's quite peaceful."

I'm resting against Esperanza's leg, holding my phone high so Mami can see us both. Esperanza licks my hair so it sticks up—one of the fastest ways to make Mami laugh. I show off the bouquet of carnations Esperanza and I picked out for her. She swoons and blows us kisses.

"This is comforting me so much, Victoria. I almost didn't think…"

Mami sniffles. She turns so I can't see her wiping tears away.

"You're safe now. You always will be."

I owe her life to Noora and the Volkov twins. They Transported to Puerto Rico, searched for each relative at their homes, their workplaces, and left empty-handed. Our manor in Cayey had also been deserted. The Zmey Gorynych steeds followed the scent to where Dragon Knights snuck our families into an Other Place near a mangrove. Now Mami and the others are hiding with Noora in an undisclosed location. The Volkov twins are still searching for Manny.

"Ay, olvídate de mi. ¿Cómo están? How do you feel about your new home? How is everyone treating you?" Mami comes back into view. She's as euphoric as the *Mona Lisa*.

"Everything is great." I point at the bouquet. "Can we talk about how pretty these are?"

"Ay, Victoria... I don't need you to impress me with anything, mi vida, but thank you. I've always loved your gifts."

I haven't bought her anything since I left for Dubai. But even before I played Blazewrath, I'd pick flowers from the bushes in my school's playground. Mami would receive a new flower every day after a screaming match with my stepfather. On the days where he struck her, I'd run back to fetch a handful of them instead, giving them to her while I begged for us to leave him. They're more than a gift—they helped my mother find solace in her darkest times.

I can't let her have dark times again.

"Tell me a happy story, Mami. Your absolute favorite thing that's ever happened."

"Bueno, giving birth to you, of course."

"No. Something happier than that."

"That *is* my happiest story!"

I look up at Esperanza. "¿Quieres que nos cuente algo más?"

Her eyes grow wide with the promise of a story.

Then she tries speaking: *Qu.... Qui... Quiiiiii... Quiiiiieee....*

"Casi, casi." She's truly about to finish her first word! "¿Qué vas a decir?"

"Is she talking to you already?!" Mami's pitch rises as she jumps.

"First word is literally on the tip of her tongue. Or... her mind."

Quiiiiieee.... Quuuuiiiiiiiiiiieeeeeeeeeeee...

"Vamos, Esperanza. Tú puedes."

She twitches. It's brief, but her leg smacks me in the back, hard.

Then she flails as if she's being electrocuted.

She's crying out in anguish. Flames slip out of her snout with every roar. Esperanza's wings are flapping at breakneck speed, shooting carnations into the air. Soon I'm showering in white petals and coiling tendrils of smoke.

"¿Qué le pasa?" Mami yells.

"I don't know what's wrong with her!"

Esperanza faints, but not before she flashes me one last image.

The Sire is smiling.

The boy's parents believe it was an accident. A four-year-old doesn't understand grabbing a dragon's tail could end in disaster. I played along as I healed his burns. They'll never know he pictured the boy's bones at his feet. How his pulse quickened with joy. My steed grows restless with every command. What if I'm not there to save the next child? I fear I must take drastic measures. If the spell doesn't exist, I'll create it, but I won't let my dragon's soul rot further.

—*Excerpt from Edward Barnes's journal*

CHAPTER SIXTEEN

Lana

"HELLO, FRIENDS. CECILIA VALCÁRCEL REPORTING FOR DUTY."

She starts all of her videos like that. Sometimes she speaks in Spanish instead. The gist is the same—Cecilia welcomes viewers, talks about the dragon she'll fight, then the battle begins. There are over two hundred clips of her trying to steal dragon souls. None run longer than five minutes, but that's more than enough time for disgust to overpower me.

Takeshi asked me to study them, though. At least he thinks I'm good enough to find Cecilia's weakness. Since this might be another one of his tests, I'm powering through these videos alone at the library, resisting the urge to set wherever this witch is hiding on fire. It baffles me how she snuck out of Iron Pointe and found random Un-Bondeds to torture. Shouldn't the most awesome school of magic have better security measures?

I suspect she was scared of Cecilia, Agent Robinson had told us about

Madame Waxbyrne. *Whenever I mentioned her, Glenda looked like I'd spoken of the Devil.*

If Randall Wiggins and Cecilia have the same abilities, Madame Waxbyrne must've seen some traumatizing stuff. My efforts to dig up dirt on their magical dad have been useless. Not even researching Randall's mom is helping. There's nothing in common between her and Alondra Valcárcel. Grace Wiggins, the Headhunter of Alabama, was a Dragon Knight with a history of targeted harassment against magic users; Cecilia's mom was a devout Catholic and lauded elementary schoolteacher. They were either chosen at random or impregnated by different men. Randall's mom is still alive, but after being hit with a Truth Charm, she confessed to not knowing how she conceived him. I suspect the wizard responsible erased her memory.

This guy's even worse than his kids.

I toss my phone across the couch. Watching Cecilia's videos isn't showing me much. I can't find a single red flag that screams THIS IS HOW YOU DEFEAT ME. She's graceful and fast and unbeatable. None of these dragons stand a chance. Maybe we don't, either.

Or maybe I don't have all the pieces yet.

Madame Waxbyrne could help. Agent Robinson did mention she's off the grid even for him, but what if he knows something and hasn't realized it's actually a clue?

I head for the Cherry Suite first. After the families were confirmed safe, everyone dispersed to have their private phone calls. Agent Robinson should be done with training.

"You have to *kill him now!*" Haya's yelling greets me as I enter.

She's playing *Monster Hunter.*

Gabriela clicks her controller furiously. "I'm trying!" Her character is driving two blades into a stone beast. It's like a hammerhead shark and a Pangolin had a ninety-foot-tall baby. "It's too strong! Can't those flying thingies help me?"

"Scoutflies aren't around for fights!"

"Then what is the point of having them on my side?"

"They're *trackers!*"

I don't know if I should interrupt. Gabriela is seconds away from video game death, but it's awesome to see Haya share this moment with her. She's on the edge of her seat, directing Gabriela every step of the way and face-palming whenever her advice is ignored.

Gabriela pauses the game. "I just don't see the point. Why can't they coexist peacefully? And his outfit leaves a lot to be desired. I think it's so—" She notices me, letting out a gasp. "Oh, hey! Was I screaming too loud? No one warned me how intense this game was."

"I did!" Haya wipes her forehead. "You were pretty good. I'll take it from here."

"Could we try *Animal Crossing* instead? That one's totally my vibe."

"Ohhh, I *love Animal Crossing.*" Haya claps excitedly. "I didn't know you were a fan. You should've suggested it from the start!"

Gabriela hands over her controller. "Well... I wanted to try something *you* loved first." Her words are a balm to my soul. That wide smile is the softest it's ever been in my presence, too.

Haya is as frozen as my awkward limbs. "That's very kind of you."

I should let them flirt without an audience.

"Just looking for Agent Robinson. I'll check elsewhere. Bye!"

"Wait!" Haya presses the intercom button. "Michael, please report to the Cherry Suite!"

I frantically wave my hands. "To the kitchen!"

"To the kitchen!"

Gabriela and I share a grin.

"You got this," I mouth to her.

She winks.

I exit the Cherry Suite to the sound of Haya scrambling to find her Nintendo Switch.

"THE LAST TIME I SPOKE TO HER, SHE TOLD ME NEVER TO CONTACT her again."

Agent Robinson is pouring himself a spiced pistachio shake. It's as creamy as an ordinary pistachio shake but with lots more cardamom, ginger, and maple syrup. It's also a bit paler.

"Did you have a fight?" My Pepsi can remains unopened. If I put caffeine into my body, I'll blast right through the ceiling. I could be one step closer to stopping the witch who tried to kill me. That's enough to jolt me awake for an eternity.

"No. She said it was for my safety. Cecilia could track her down any day. The less she knew, the better. But it still hurt like hell."

"Did you ever try searching for her anyway?"

He twirls his glass. "She has private residences in the Maldives, Sicily, and Romania, but she's not in any of them. She's definitely not at Iron Pointe. We haven't caught her popping up in security footage from her wand shops or surrounding areas, either."

So she might as well be a ghost.

But I won't accept failure yet. "Do you have messages or letters we could decode? Maybe she did leave you clues, but they're super hard to decipher?"

"Hmm. I wrote five letters before she ever wrote back. Stubborn woman, that Glenda."

I risk a laugh. This is probably not the best time to bother Agent Robinson with details on his relationship, but any information could prove useful. "How did you meet?"

He exhales like he's been holding his breath for ages. I can't tell if he's exhausted, nostalgic, or both. "I investigated a student's disappearance at Iron Pointe. Enid Mendoza. She wouldn't answer her parents' calls.

When we visited the academy, nobody knew where she was. Glenda was her wand lore teacher, but she was also mentoring Enid." Agent Robinson shakes his head. "I met the love of my life because a girl went missing. How twisted is that?"

Okay, that *is* pretty twisted, but beautiful things can come from dreadful things.

"Did you ever find Enid?" I ask.

"No. It remains one of my greatest professional failures."

"Did you interview Cecilia, too?"

He stares blankly at his glass. "She was rather uncooperative."

"You think she did something to Enid?"

"Part of me suspects Enid did run away. But Cecilia wouldn't answer personal questions. We didn't know about her videos then. She was a stranger, and she wanted to remain one."

There's no guarantee Cecilia didn't hurt people long before she touched a dragon. What if this Enid girl is dead because of her? Or worse—she's being tortured. All wand-makers are Gold Wands, and if Enid's still alive, she must be considered useful.

Madame Waxbyrne is hiding something. I need to find out what.

I take a deep breath. This is so intrusive, but I don't have another choice. "Would it be okay if I read her letters? I think Samira and I could—"

"We need to get to the Dark Island *now!*"

A sweaty Victoria sprints into the kitchen. "We have... to hurry... please..."

I shoot out of my seat. Victoria's a trained Blazewrath athlete. There's no way she's exhausted from running down a flight of stairs. "What's going on?"

The other riders arrive seconds later, followed by Samira, Mom, and a puzzled Takeshi.

"V! You okay?" Luis rushes to hold her.

A grim shadow is cast on Victoria's expression. "Esperanza fainted in the carnation garden. She showed... his face and... he was smiling..."

I don't have to hear another word to understand. "The Sire *hurt* her? How would that even be possible? He literally cannot move and—"

Dragon roars shake the whole house—the Sol de Noches are crying. It's not their sad spell song. Fury coils around each note, a call to action in burning red.

"We have to go!" Victoria says. "I don't want him hurting them further!"

"Wait! What if it's a trap?" I hold my Pepsi can like a stop sign. "This is what he does, Victoria. He provokes and destabilizes. Whatever he's up to, it can't be for Esperanza alone."

Takeshi is nodding like I've just aced all of his tests.

"You're right, Lana. We stick together at all times. No sudden movements. No heroics."

Everyone agrees.

"Ms. Wells, you and Lana should stay behind."

I'd appreciate Takeshi's concern if it didn't come with that forlorn expression. Like I'm a hopeless weakling who needs to be removed from Big Girl Stuff. I don't *want* to be near the Sire, but if Takeshi sees how well I behave around him, I'll snag extra points for Task Force Blaze.

Besides, Esperanza is *unconscious*, for God's sake. Is this how I repay her for saving me in Brazil? She'd been the one to insist on helping Papi while Victoria refused. I owe her more than mustering up the courage to face the Sire again, but it's a start.

"I can handle it." I speak a little louder. Hopefully, it'll help me believe it. "Will someone please watch over Esperanza? I don't want her waking up alone and confused."

Victoria is about to say something, but after a deep breath, she bites her tongue. Leaving her injured steed behind has to suck, especially since she's never done it before. I try to console her with a pat on the back. Her silence is as desolate as a winter's night.

"I'll stay with her," says Mom.

My mother is volunteering to *look after a dragon?*

"Are, um… Are you sure?" I almost check her temperature, too.

She looks at Victoria. "If that's okay with you."

"Go ahead. We won't take long." Victoria glowers. "Let's stop that silver cabrón."

Fire rises to the Dark Island's sky.

Clouds of crackling flames swish left and right, lighting up the pitch-blackness. It's a burning tornado in the middle of a beach. And it's coming from the pit where the Sire lies.

The fire is bursting out of his propeller.

The ice cage is gone. Now there's thickening smoke where the frost once was. And his wings… they're not fully developed again, but the stumps at his sides are longer. The silver netting that connects each membrane shines brighter, too.

"How…" The word scrapes my throat like a scissors' edge. This is impossible. The Freeze Charm I'd used on his propeller had been cast with Randall's magic, and his Gold Wand abilities were no joke. It doesn't matter that Takeshi poisoned him to death. His spell should still work.

Crap. The Dark Island removes magic! Could this place have canceled out the Freeze Charm? Is the Sire really healing?

I can't make out what Héctor and Takeshi are saying. My thoughts are tangled in crackling flames and a vengeful dragon. If the Freeze Charm has been undone, and his wings are growing back, does that mean… will he… There's *no way* he's ever breaking free.

Right?

My friends charge ahead with the Sol de Noches. Samira, Takeshi, and I remain by the shore, the waves crashing in harmonious unison, but they're not louder than the Sire's roars.

When the dragons reach him, they blast him with all their might.

The Sire ends his burning tantrum. He whines and sways in a frenetic attempt to escape. The claw towers pinning him are too strong, though. He aims his propeller at Titán.

The fire returns.

He's lighting up the dark with flames I swore I'd taken forever.

The tremors are starting again. Thankfully, Takeshi's focused on the battle ahead, where the Sol de Noches alternate between firing at the Sire and hitting him with their spiked tails.

Make it stop, make it stop, make it stop...

Nothing works, though. The battle rages on with no end in sight. And there's absolutely no use for me here. Not only am I still shaking, I would've been incapable of hurting the Sire in a significant way even if I weren't this nervous. How are we supposed to end his attacks? If the Sol de Noches can't stop him, who can?

WHOOSH!

Esperanza Fades into the Dark Island.

Victoria's yelling at her in Spanish, demanding to know what she's doing here, but Esperanza flies past her without a backward glance. She lands next to the Sire. As the silver dragon scorches her brothers and sisters, Esperanza raises her snout to the black sky.

She lets out a soft, almost whispered note. It starts out like an undulating cry for help, rising and falling in a low-pitched tone. Then it morphs into a full-blown screech. Esperanza's voice is carried up into the stars with the weight of an aching soul.

The other Sol de Noches lift their horned heads high. They join Esperanza with high notes of their own, each one more melodic as they progress, displaying total control of their voices. I stop shaking. The dragons' song—the same mournful spell that began in Dubai—has returned.

It's killing the Sire's fire.

He keeps aiming at a different dragon, but his propeller only casts out hazy rings of smoke. No matter how hard he pushes, the flames never come back. He's been defeated again.

Esperanza lands flat on her face—she's fainted.

"Oh, no! She must've been too weak to Fade," says Samira.

While the other dragons gently poke Esperanza, Daga is biting and tugging on her ear.

The eldest Sol remains unconscious.

"We need to move the Sire." I'm no longer shaking, but I have no idea when I started sweating. I wipe my brow. Sweat sticks to the back of my hands; I quickly rub them on my pants as Takeshi faces me. "This place takes magic away, which could explain why the Freeze Charm stopped working. Esperanza should rest before the next singing session."

"She didn't use magic to rip his wings out. That's a normal injury. And the ice had been intact when we Faded out of Puerto Rico."

I wait for him to keep going, but Takeshi falls silent. "So?" I spur him on.

"Something else is happening here." Samira stares at the Sire with the same heaviness in the Sol de Noches's song. "I wish I knew what."

Takeshi's shoulder brushes against mine.

I don't know if I'm shuddering from the warmth, or from realizing we're in deep trouble if the Sire's fire really has returned. Not only should I worry about Dragon Knights setting him free, now I also have to freak out over him scorching the Dark Island to ashes and killing us all.

Takeshi doesn't look at me. Brushing shoulders isn't a big deal to him.

Then it shouldn't be a big deal to me, either.

When the riders approach me, I say, "We should put him somewhere else. I think the Island is tampering with the Freeze Charm. He could do something worse next."

Luis shakes his head. "It's not the island, Lana. Our steeds can still feel its power. This place had nothing to do with removing that spell or his wings growing back."

Then what the hell is it?

Takeshi says, "Can they still hold him? Or are they getting weaker?"

"Esperanza's tired, but she's angry. I don't see her lowering her defenses anytime soon."

Héctor nods. "Same with Titán. He's confident the Sire won't get away with more."

"Igual con Fantasma," says Edwin.

I speak over the Sire's incessant complaining. "How can you guarantee he won't put the dragons at greater risk of injury? Agent Robinson can build him a sealed chamber."

Victoria lowers her hands, her expression fierce. "Maybe that's his plan—scare us badly enough so we break him out. We'd be doing the Dragon Knights a favor." She peeks at him with the disdain of someone who's fed up with his dramatic antics. "He stays."

"It's much harder to steal a dragon from the Dark Island," says Héctor. "Our guard is up tenfold now. We can take turns monitoring him. The dragons can cast their song spell every day. If he tries anything, he'll wish he'd never been born."

This is ridiculous. Do I want to live with the Sire sleeping close to my room? Hell no. But I won't get much sleep if I'm freaked out over his next move.

As if on cue, the Sire weeps into the night sky.

WHOOM!

The bone throne is on fire.

"What the heck…" Samira aims her wand in its direction.

The flames vanish before she intervenes.

Cracks appear all around the bone, as if the Sire's rage emitted destructive sound waves. I wait for it to collapse or crumble.

It remains.

How did the throne get incinerated? The Sire wasn't even firing anymore!

"Anyone wanna tell me what just happened?" says Luis.

Nobody speaks.

Samira scratches her head. "We are officially out of our depth."

The Sire cries again, which snaps everyone's attention back to him.

I slowly approach the throne. More beads of sweat accumulate on my forehead, but I can't bring myself to do anything other than walk.

"Whoa, whoa, whoa. Where do you think you're going?" Samira hooks an arm around mine. "You don't know what that thing will do."

I stop three feet away from the throne. It hasn't cracked further, but it could mysteriously light up again, and I'm not in the mood to become barbeque. There's nothing remarkable about the broken bone. No smoke or even heat coming off it, though.

"Can you feel how hot it is?" I ask Samira.

She checks its temperature with a spell. "It's… normal."

"So I can touch it?"

"Why would you *want* to?"

"We could study the bone," Takeshi appears to my left. Jesus Christ, he's as quiet as a ghost. "Find out if those sudden flames were tied to the Sire regaining his strength."

I've never been more grateful for how intuitive he is. It's like sharing a language no one else speaks, and it sure saves me some time. "Yeah. I mean, this isn't ordinary magic, so we'd need help from someone who's an expert in more mysterious stuff."

"Headmaster Sykes," Takeshi and I say together.

I haven't seen President Turner's husband since Dubai. They must both be struggling with fallout from the Cup's cancellation, but I'm thinking they'll clear their schedules for whatever this is. I run my fingers down the seat's flat surface. The grooves feel smooth and jagged at the same time. Samira's right—the bone isn't hot at all. I tug on it, but nothing's coming off.

Then a piece falls from the armrest.

I pocket it with a frown. My days are supposed to be devoted to undoing Cecilia's cruelty. Now I have to stress over the Sire *and* whatever's happening to this throne? Forget about acing Takeshi's tests—the Dark Island has provided enough challenges to last me a decade.

I stare at the silver dragon writhing in pain. His anguish delights me, but the fact that he could be regaining the power we stole sends me into a tailspin. I'd rather die than see him as strong as he once was. I'm not letting him get his fire or wings again.

I won't fail Andrew again.

"Take me back to headquarters," I say. "I need to call President Turner."

Teamwork isn't effective without trust, but building it can prove challenging. Antonio Deluca's 2011 Blazewrath debut remains a memorable moment precisely for this reason. A thirteen-year-old Antonio spat on his team captain's face minutes before stepping onto the field. In an earlier interview, he had bemoaned how little progress his captain, renowned Striker Emiliano Cusma, had made during practice. When Italy won their first match against Norway, Antonio was forced to acknowledge that Emiliano scoring first helped him reach the top of his mountain faster. "But if I hadn't spat on him," Antonio said, "he wouldn't have fought that hard."

—Excerpt from Olga Peñaloza's Blazewrath All-Stars, Third Edition

CHAPTER SEVENTEEN

Victoria

IT'S BEEN THREE DAYS SINCE THE SIRE TRIED FUCKING US OVER.

Three days since I've had proper sleep. My after-hour practices are solo—*I'm* slowing Esperanza down. She's recovered nicely, but Robinson and Willa still hold the aerial course record. I suspect it's my steering; weight distribution is tougher during turns. Perhaps I'm too distracted. I keep going from surveillance shifts to Dragonblood briefings.

I don't care. I'm not settling for second place.

"Estás haciendo excelente trabajo. No sé por qué te preocupas tanto."

Edwin wipes the sweat off my cheeks with a dry towel. He's gentle enough to deserve touching me, but he's still keeping a respectful distance. We've been completing a series of simulated attacks—

he shoots fireballs at me, and I evade in sprinting intervals.

I thank him for complimenting my excellent performance, but my concerns are justified. Staying second isn't how I get to stay in Task Force Blaze. That's not how I protect Esperanza.

"¿Tienes sed?" Edwin asks.

I'm not thirsty. I need to train harder.

Before I can refuse, he's forcing a bottle of Gatorade on me.

I narrow my gaze. "Edwin."

"No fastidies más y tomátelo." Héctor is carrying a tray of steaming empanadillas. It is three in the morning, and he craves fried grossness with pizza-flavored filling. He tells Edwin he's made his favorite snack as a treat for suffering through practice with me.

Héctor and I dance between English and Spanish, reserving the latter for the particularly coarse language. Edwin laps it up as a string of orange goo hangs from his lips. The boys are cracking jokes and completely ignoring the point of why we're here.

"I *need* to go again," I say.

"Nope. We're eating. You should, too." Héctor chews with his mouth open. He smiles as I cringe. "Also, some sleep would be nice."

"Not until I go again."

"The hangar will still be here when you wake up, Victoria."

Héctor points out Edwin's shirt, which has Raúl Juliá as Gomez Addams, saying we all should watch that movie, that it's hilarious and laughing is a great way to forget about stress. When Edwin starts explaining why Gomez is his role model, I snatch the hangar remote from him. Robinson let him borrow it for our after-hours practices. I'd wondered how Edwin convinced him, then I remembered it's hard to say no to the sweetest boy alive.

"Gracias por nada," I hiss.

Edwin snatches the remote back.

"Pero—"

"Burnout isn't a myth. How will you save Esperanza if you're exhausted?" Héctor asks. Before my lips can even part, he adds, "And you're great, Victoria. You have *always* been great. I know life hasn't helped you believe that sometimes, but you. Are. *Great.*"

Anyone else could've said that and I wouldn't have cried.

But it *had* to be Héctor Sánchez, and of course I'm tearing up.

"Obviously..." I whisper.

He and Edwin smile.

"Then what's this about?" says Héctor.

Explaining would exhaust me further. It would also motivate him to change my mind. We have enough pretend journalists with Lana alone: She's consumed with contacting Headmaster Sykes, and Samira mentioned helping her reach Madame Waxbyrne, too. And she clearly has no time for me.

After Esperanza fainted for the second time, my friends flooded us with support. Génesis reads picture books to Esperanza so she can fall asleep faster. When she's not engrossed with Haya and *Animal Crossing*, Gabriela cleans my room and reorganizes my shelves. Luis cooks me breakfast. He's even sharing his grapes. Edwin and Héctor take turns attacking me during after-hours practice.

Lana hasn't spoken to me.

There's a difference between dealing with your own shit, and being too selfish to realize someone you call a friend is also dealing with shit.

"Victoria?" Edwin calls.

"Nada. Vámonos a dormir." I empty the bottle of Gatorade in one go. As tired as I am, I don't want to sleep right now, but I favor it over dwelling on Lana's terribleness.

WHOOM!

A boy and a dragon fall from the ceiling.

A *three-headed* dragon.

"That never stops being weird." The boy's blue hair is windswept, but still looks like he's styled it professionally. His lip ring glints as he smiles. "Hello, beautiful people!"

Kirill Volkov has arrived.

"Mi amor…" Edwin drops the towel and Gatorade. He glides over to Kirill, who dismounts his purring steed. Edwin pulls Kirill into a hug, rocking side to side. Their kiss is sweet enough to almost make me believe in love again.

Almost.

"Sorry for barging in. I come bearing the gift of great news." Kirill pulls Edwin back to us, his steed following closely behind. He shakes Héctor's hand. "Captain."

"Good to see you again, Kirill."

"I would agree that it's good to see me, too." The boys laugh at his joke as he turns to me. "Victoria Peralta in the flesh! How are you, Legend?"

This is the first time he's called me that. Paired with Héctor and Edwin's compliments, it's difficult to stop tearing up. The former Russian Blocker has spoken to me a handful of times, and he's treating me better than the girl who promised to help me find a life beyond the gold.

"Happy you're here," I say, and I mean it. This small kindness aside, Kirill is an *excellent* fighter—he blocked with the power and agility of ten Blazewrath champions.

"Likewise." Kirill rests his head on Edwin's shoulder. "Where's Bullet?"

I scoff. That's his nickname for Lana. "Around." It takes so much effort not to say she's probably thirsting over Takeshi in her room.

"Oh. Is everyone else asleep?"

"Most likely," says Héctor. "I have a feeling Luis is watching piano lessons on YouTube."

"Why does that sound like a horrible mistake?"

"Because it is."

Edwin and I laugh.

"A shame to interrupt, but this can't wait," says Kirill. "I found the next Dragonblood ring."

THE SCREENS INSIDE THE CHERRY SUITE ARE FOCUSED ON THE same image.

There's a huge, craggy formation in the middle of the sea. Jagged rock cradles a flattened center. A puffy cloud of smoke is drifting toward the sky.

"Whakaari, also known as White Island, is our target. It's off the northern coast of New Zealand." Kirill taps the smoke with a Sharpie. "And it's an active volcano."

I groan. Cecilia must be protecting the stadium with a spell, but I wouldn't be surprised if she burns someone alive with dragon fire *and* lava.

"How did you find it?" Takeshi asks.

"Artem and I were chasing a Dragon Knight in the area. He escaped when we rescued the families in Puerto Rico. We thought he'd take us to Manny." Kirill frowns at Joaquín. "Your father wasn't with him, but Noora's picking up other leads across the globe. She thinks Vogel isn't actually a Dragon Knight. Wherever she's taken your father could be the same place Cecilia is keeping Director Sandhar and Agent Horowitz... if they're still alive."

Joaquín waves it off like it's not a big deal, but he's not saying anything. This man is rarely speechless. He has to be *dying* inside.

I put his hand in mine. His father risked himself for *me*—the second most annoying person he's ever met after Lana. He would've raged if Joaquín had been in danger. There's nothing I can say to make him feel better, but as long as he knows I'm here, that's all I care about.

"Gracias, Victoria," he says.

I turn to Kirill. "When's the match?"

"Tomorrow at five. New Zealand time."

"What's the plan, boss?" I ask Takeshi.

A brick wall is more expressive than him. He's focused on the biggest screen, his brow furrowed. "Samira, can you falsify tickets for us? I'm assuming Cecilia has increased security after the bureau broke into the last match. We might not be able to Transport inside the stadium."

He might as well have offered Samira a private tour of the *Law & Order: Magical Crimes Unit* set. "Absolutely!" she squeaks.

"What about our masks?" I say. "We could get generic ones on the way there."

"I can make those, too! How about I Charm them to alter our voices?" says Samira.

"Excellent."

Takeshi launches into his plan. He'll ask Onesa Ruwende and Wataida Midzi for backup. He, Samira, Génesis, and I will enter the stadium in disguise. Onesa, Wataida, and Artem will meet us at the entrance. Their steeds will be hanging with Joaquín and Esperanza on the coast. They'll wait for our signal once we corner Cecilia. Joaquín and the dragons will descend upon the stadium, help us fight the Blood Masks, and spring the Un-Bondeds from the ring.

I *have* to do better than my training times.

"Any questions?" Takeshi asks.

"No," I say. "Meet you here in a few hours."

I stifle a yawn as I march outside.

AT FOUR THIRTY IN THE AFTERNOON—NEW ZEALAND TIME—Group #2 is set for Transport to Whakaari/White Island. That's ten in the morning for us.

Which wouldn't have been a problem if I'd slept.

The dark circles under my eyes are hidden beneath a mask. It covers my face in delicate black lace, but when I speak I sound like a chain-smoking senior citizen. Samira's spell is doing one hell of a job concealing my real voice. At least I like the design—Samira made us animal masks. She's a bunny; I'm a lion. Génesis is the most gorgeous swan. Joaquín picked the owl mask, and Takeshi specifically requested a snake.

"Ready?" Joaquín adjusts his mask ever so slightly.

"Ready!" we respond in unison.

Samira raises her wand. "Cecilia, here we come!"

SWISH!

I'm standing on an active volcano.

The soil is rough against my boots, with stray pebbles at every turn, but Whakaari/White Island seems more like a ruddy haven for those seeking solitude than a death trap.

I spot the stadium ten feet away. Every inch of its walls is the color of a Sol de Noche's dark scales. I flinch from the constant *SWISH!* of Transporting guests. People swarm the entrance, where Blood Masks are verifying admission tickets. There's a slight glimmer from the Invisibility Charm cloaking the volcano.

Samira is Transporting Joaquín, Esperanza, and Rayo to a hideout far from the stadium. Onesa, Wataida, and Artem confirmed they're waiting with their steeds. Once Samira drops Joaquín and the Sol de Noches off, she'll hand the other members their masks, then join us.

"How are you feeling?" Génesis asks me.

"Good. I think we should split up, though. One team searches for Cecilia. The other finds where they're keeping the dragons. What do you think, Endo?"

He hesitates. "Cecilia is our first priority."

I must've misheard. So I enunciate each word clearly. "You're letting the match *start*?"

"We have to."

"No, we don't. How is it acceptable to let dragons die?"

"The Blood Masks guarding the cages will do anything for Cecilia. If their master gets caught, they'll surrender. Or they'll try to save her, which will get most of them away from the cages. Even if they don't stand down, we'll have a clearer path toward the Un-Bondeds."

A vein pulses on my forehead. "But we're not leaving without those dragons, right?"

Takeshi says, "You have my word, Victoria."

"I'd better."

I storm off.

SWISH!

"There you are!" a girl says to my right.

Even with her scorpion mask and the vocal fry disguising her real voice, I would recognize Onesa Ruwende anywhere. She's the girl who made Lana's life hell on the Runner's mountain during quarterfinals. The DJ who urged us to dance at the Cup's welcome party.

Now she's the girl rushing over to hug us.

"It's so good to see you again!" Génesis is the first to reach her.

"Likewise!"

When she skips over to me, she settles for a polite handshake. "Hi, Victoria!"

"Hi, Onesa. You're still very tall."

She giggles. "And you're still very short!"

"Proudly."

Wataida Midzi and Artem Volkov approach me. They move like nightclub bouncers on the lookout for foolish behavior. Wataida is warm as he hugs me hello. His mask is my favorite—a phoenix with intertwined black and gold lace. I can't see Artem's piercings behind his tiger mask, and when he shakes my hand, he sounds like a surfer dude instead of a Russian superstar.

"Hello. I am pleased to see you again." He pauses. "Even though your team beat mine."

I can't resist a sly grin. "I'm not sorry."

"Didn't expect you to be." He moves on to Takeshi. "Since my brother is with your other friends, I will pray very hard for their mental well-being."

"So will I. Tickets out, everyone. Showtime."

The tickets Samira gave us are real. She tricked a reseller in a top secret Dragonblood fan forum into a bogus transaction. When Samira Charmed their bank account to reflect the astronomical payment they had demanded, the reseller sent over the tickets, which feature a roaring dragon sigil. I hand mine over to the hulking goon by the door.

One by one, we step into the stadium without being discovered. This place is the same as the one in Nantes, save for the mechanical dragons—other than the iron gates on either side, the ring is barren. I don't know if that means the competitors will be bigger today, or if there's another terrible surprise in store.

"This one's me." I claim the very first seat in the row. Our seats are on the first level.

Everyone else scoots down the line until we're all occupying the seats we've stolen. Happy chatter flies around me as more people fill the stadium. They're munching on popcorn, sipping on sodas and cocktails, as if this is a cause for celebration. At least everyone's too distracted to pay us any mind. I quickly check the seats across the ring. During the previous match, Cecilia hadn't worn a mask, but she might be more careful this time.

"No sign of her yet," I say gruffly.

"She'll surely be here seconds before the match starts," Takeshi reassures.

The iron gates rise on both sides of the stadium.

I cringe as the applause reaches headache-inducing heights. "Wait. Is it *starting*?"

"Apparently," Takeshi says.

"Can't we intervene now? I could distract everyone and—"

"I hate this just as much as you do, but we have to wait for Cecilia, okay?"

This is not okay. A dragon is about to die!

A Norwegian Lindworm exits from the left corridor. This dragon is female—she has seven horns instead of four. Her thin, tawny scales make it easier for her to slither into the arena; Lindworms are the only species with two frontal legs. Lemon-yellow wings sprout from her back, but she has no use for them—chains wrap around her neck and legs.

The Irish Spike coming from the right is also chained. This dragon is male. He has five horns, all as green as his scales, but his whole body is covered in sharp blades. He's the dragon version of the villain in *Hellraiser*. He's already firing at the sky as he storms into the arena.

"Dragonblood! Dragonblood! Dragonblood!"

No one shoots a gun, blasts a horn, or tells the dragons to fight.

The match begins anyway.

And Cecilia isn't here.

Where are you?!

The Spike lodges its fangs into the Lindworm's neck.

"Jesus Christ..." I squirm as the Lindworm shrieks. She coils her body around the Spike's legs, which are the only part without blades. She constricts until the Spike roars to the sun. They retreat. When the Lindworm crawls forward like a winged cheetah on the hunt, the Spike raises his wings, exposing its knives. The Lindworm is about to crash into him.

The female dragon takes flight. She's the one diving into his neck now. It's a quick swipe. As the Spike shoots flames at her, the Lindworm dodges and bites, dodges and bites. The Spike is too furious to notice the pool of blood he's stepping on.

Raise your voice at me again, and I'll make your girl bleed.

That was the first night my stepfather smacked me. I was nine.

When Mami tried to stop him, he broke two of her ribs.

My legs carry me out of my seat.

The Blood Mask at the top of the stairs ignores me. I hurry to the bathroom. The moment I spot a sink, I empty my stomach of bile, since there's nothing else in it to vomit. I'm no stranger to blood—my life has been molded by it.

My stepfather apologized the next morning. He took us to Chili's—the most expensive place he could afford—and painted the house Mami's favorite color. I hadn't thought of that night in years, but pain is like a ghost. It haunts you whether you feel it or not.

"Do you have what I asked?" a boy says in the corridor.

He's talking to a male Blood Mask four feet away from the women's bathroom. The boy hides behind a red devil mask. He has a burgundy crown on. Rubies glint on each spike like the Sire's bloodshot eyes. He's either full of himself, or a high-ranking Blood Mask.

What if he can lead me to the cages?

I linger outside, pretending to wait for someone. Eavesdropping is useless—these assholes are whispering. The boy sounds familiar. His accent isn't registering, though. With a nod, the Blood Mask remains near the bathroom, but the crowned devil leaves at a brisk pace.

"Bathroom is there," the Blood Mask says brusquely.

"I can read, thanks."

This guy will attack me if I follow the crowned devil. Starting a fight will attract unwanted attention, but I can't go back to the arena. I need to know where that guy is headed.

"You have a problem, girl?" He's walking toward me.

Fuck it.

"Is there an open bar nearby? I'm parched," I say.

"The woman in your area can take your order." He's close enough to strike. "Tell her to—"

I punch him in the throat.

He's knocked backwards, and I run behind him to break his fall. Then I choke him until he's unconscious. Luckily, the women's bathroom is empty. I dump him underneath the hand dryer.

Nobody else is outside.

I run after the crowned devil. The corridor winds itself into a circle. Other than a few more bathrooms, there aren't any rooms, staircases, or even more corridors. I'm running across an endless loop of concrete. I curse under my breath—the boy could've been a wizard and Transported out. My hope dwindles faster and faster until I hear him again.

"You're sure she can fight today? That wing looked infected."

"Yes, boss. She'll be going out next. As for the Akarui…"

The other man's voice trails off as I peer down—they're *below* me.

I search for openings, latches, anything that can let me in, but there's nothing.

I check the walls instead. At first, they look as barren as the floor. Then I find a thin slash that curves upward on the left side. It's not shaped like anything; whoever looks at it would think it's just a random imperfection from Cecilia's spell. With what little I know of her, that witch isn't random. Bracing myself for another fight, I put one fist up and touch the slash with the other.

I'm in a different corridor.

This is almost like arriving at Robinson's Other Place—a jarring suddenness that makes you question reality—except this chamber smells like ash and shit that's been festering for days. I gag and pinch my nose. Every part of me is sweating profusely, too. Smoke comes off the walls, as if the volcano's heat is sizzling them. This *has* to be where the dragons are being kept. Unless Blood Masks go to the bathroom here…

I catch snippets of muffled conversation farther ahead.

I clench my fists even more as I tiptoe forward. The chatter dies down, but I push on, eyes wide and ready for anything. Perhaps I should've stuck to the team's plan. They've probably noticed I'm missing by now, but once they see what I've found, I doubt they'll be too upset.

The corridor opens up to an archway. I'm as lithe as a mountain lion, making sure there aren't any hidden doors or crevices for these cowards to jump out of. When I step through the archway, the floor breaks off into a cliff. The stench of dragon droppings has intensified; it's wafting toward me from below. I hold my breath as I look down.

Five cages have been carved out of the volcano's rock.

Three contain sleeping dragons—a Venezuelan Furia Roja, an Armenian Gyurza, and the Akarui that almost burned Lana alive. They're held hostage in spaces much too small for their bodies. The empty cages must belong to the Lindworm and the Spike.

Nobody's standing watch. I'm sure Cecilia must've Charmed the cages, but where did the crowned devil and the other Blood Mask go?

A stone staircase leads down to the cages. If they're locked with a spell, I'll have to bring Samira here so she can open them. First, I have to double-check those locks—but I'll have to be stealthy. Waking those dragons will alert the Blood Masks. As I take a deep breath, another wave of pungent dragon droppings washes over me. I retch.

Give me a break, Peralta. You've lived through worse.

I take precarious steps downstairs. None of the dragons stir. Their slumbering state fills me with hope—stealth is definitely one of my strengths. I pick up the pace, even though I still feel like I'm slogging through mud. I reach the brown-scaled Gyurza's cage first. The rocky bars are three inches apart; I can only squeeze in a few fingers. There's no visible lock anywhere. I search for another slash like the one upstairs, and spot one at the very bottom.

I crouch low.

"Step away from the cage." The crowned devil's voice comes from behind me. For someone whose trapped dragons are about to be sprung free, he's rather calm.

The dragons are still sleeping. Either they didn't hear him, or they're under a spell. I want to kick the walls for not considering they've been Charmed into unconsciousness. Regardless of how quickly I opened the cages, the Un-Bondeds wouldn't have moved.

"Qué mierda…"

"I won't say it again, girl."

"You don't have to." I slowly turn toward him.

He's alone. There's a defiant edge to the way he grips his tux's jacket, like he owns the stadium. His hands are gloved in burgundy leather now; they match the jewels on his crown. An unmoving creep that stands as tall as a king has just caught me off guard. I'm torn between being mildly impressed and extremely irritated. Of course I can take him. I merely didn't want to have to take anybody down until these dragons were out.

"Kneel," he says.

"Okay." I start kneeling.

Then I bolt toward him.

He's pathetically slow—I slam him to the ground. My elbow's pushing down on his neck. That ridiculous crown rolls away. He tries hitting me, but I dodge his fist. I rip his mask off.

Now the voice I vaguely recognized has a face I'll never forget. It's the same face that's graced newspapers for the past two years. Black eyes that look like pools in the darkest pockets of the universe, that button nose that made fans fall in love, and a chin that could cut diamonds.

Antonio Deluca, the missing Runner from Team Italy, is pinned underneath me.

The spell isn't working, Director. I've yet to locate Randall's skullpit. Antonio Deluca may be lost to us forever. But I found an unusual thread of Gold magic circling the area where the Blazewrath stadium had been in Edinburgh. When I unspooled it, a message revealed itself: You will never find him. *I returned weeks later. The thread had been retied, but the sequence and style were different. A new message had been left behind:* I already did.

—*Voicemail left in Director Nirek Sandhar's office, courtesy of*
Madame Waxbyrne

CHAPTER EIGHTEEN

Victoria

"**H**OLY SHIT. YOU'RE ALIVE."

I should be honored he's glaring at me. Only people he deems worthy of his vitriol have the pleasure of being looked at like vermin.

He says, "And *you* won't be for long."

He tries to head-butt me, but I roll off him. The second he's free, Antonio pulls out his Gold wand from the back of his pants. We jump to our feet at the same time.

"Take off your mask, girl."

"Sure. As long as you promise to set these dragons free. I'm not leaving without them."

"You won't be leaving at all."

"Didn't you and Cecilia break up before you were kidnapped? Why are you working with her?" I cock an eyebrow. "You owe her a favor or something?"

Antonio is blinking way too fast. He steps back, squirming. "Take off your mask."

"The world knows you didn't kill Hikaru. You could've walked out of wherever you were a free man, but after this, your life is *over*, Antonio. My team will be very happy to see you."

"So there are more of you here."

Nicely done, Peralta...

"No," I say hurriedly. "But if you don't want to live behind bars, I advise you to help me get these Un-Bondeds out. You still have most of your Cup earnings, right? You're filthy rich, so this isn't about Cecilia paying you. There must be another reason why you're working with her. Whatever it is, my team and I can offer you a much better deal."

I approach him as I would an Un-Bonded in the wild—slow yet alert. There's a high probability he won't take the bait, so I need to get that wand out of his grasp. He's not like Cecilia and Randall. If I disarm Antonio, he can't use magic. And if he tries to fight me, I'll win.

"Stay back!" he yells.

"I'm not bullshitting you, okay? Help me get these dragons to safety and I'll give you whatever you want. Name your price and it's yours."

He sighs in defeat. "You can't help me..."

BANG!

A ray of golden light hits my mask. It flies away before I can catch it.

"Victoria Peralta." Antonio's tone is half-impressed, half-appalled. "My enemy has a face." He hits the volcano's walls with a second ray of light.

A series of blaring alarms echo throughout the underground chamber.

Antonio aims his wand at his neck. "The ring has been compromised!" His voice is magnified as if he's shouting into a loudspeaker.

"There are traitors in the audience! Find them!"

He aims the wand at the Gyurza's cage.

"No!"

I charge him again, but a Blood Mask Transports in front of me. I crash into his bulky chest. He snatches me as more Blood Masks spill into the chamber. While they surround me, Antonio Transports each dragon out of their cages. Only the Akarui is waking up. It starts to open its mouth as Antonio wraps it in the spell's harsh white light.

The Akarui vanishes with an earsplitting roar.

"NO!" I've wasted my chance to free them. Now my friends are in grave danger, and there's a grand total of eleven Blood Masks ready to fight. When I punch one, two more seize me, jabbing me hard in the stomach, and sending me down with a grunt. I push myself up, but they're kicking me to the ground again. I spit out a gob of blood as invisible ropes wrap around me. They tighten until I'm as trapped as the dragons had been in those cages. Even the slightest effort to move sinks daggers into my sides—Antonio's cast a Paralysis Charm.

"Call your dragon," Antonio says. "Or they kill your friends."

"My friends aren't here."

"You have an excellent poker face, but you're lying. Call your dragon."

I spit more blood at his leather shoes. "You're not making her play this fucked up game."

"Your dragon will do anything for you, especially save your life." Antonio motions to a Blood Mask. "Stab her."

The Blood Mask pulls out a knife.

WHOOM!

Esperanza bursts into my thoughts like a comet hurtling for Earth. I'm flinching from the forcefulness of her interruption. It takes me a second to realize she can see what I'm seeing.

¡No vengas para acá! ¡Te van a hacer daño!

My pleas for her to stay put are met with a piercing shriek. Her shadow sails across the ocean waves as the armed Blood Mask draws nearer. Then the shadow disappears.

¡Esperanza, no!

SWOOSH!

She Fades behind Antonio.

He narrowly escapes her stream of flames.

When he lands on the ground, he accidentally drops his wand. My sides are no longer being stabbed; the invisible ropes fall off. I'm free from the Paralysis Charm.

Esperanza burns the Blood Mask holding a knife. When he's a pile of bones in a suit, she scorches two others. One of them is a Silver Wand; the rest are Regulars. Their screams will chase me until my last breath—I've never seen my steed kill humans. They were murderers, but the faster Esperanza melts their flesh off, the more I hate them for turning her into one, too.

While other Regulars scurry up the staircase, Esperanza smacks another Silver Wand with her tail. She flings him over to the staircase. His Blood Mask friends are dropping like bowling pins.

Antonio seizes his wand again.

I run up to him. He might've taken the Un-Bondeds, but if I can bring him to New Delhi, this won't have been such a massive failure. Besides, *he's* the key to locating Cecilia.

My fingers are inches away from his tux.

He knocks me aside with a spell.

"Ugh!" My back slams into a wall.

Esperanza has laid everyone to waste except Antonio. The smell of burned flesh mixes with the dragon droppings. I'm dizzy from the combination of odors, struggling to find my footing again.

Antonio tries to cast a spell on Esperanza, but she turns to roast him. Antonio protects himself with a golden Shield Charm. It's crumbling at the edges like glass under a dragon's claw. Esperanza is showering him with all of her firepower. He'll be dead within seconds.

Cuando te avise, deja de quemarlo. Lo voy a atrapar.

Esperanza keeps firing. As soon as I give her the signal, she'll stop so I can catch Antonio.

Glimmering shards keep dropping from Antonio's shield. He's shaking as he barely hangs on to his wand. Why is he draining himself of all his strength for a girl he broke up with?

¡Ahora!

The shower of flames ends.

Before I can even move, the coward Transports.

"DAMN IT!" I kick the wall as Esperanza runs to me. She's nuzzling my face and licking the blood off my chin with the utmost care.

Do... Doooo... Dolllll...

I think she's trying to ask if I'm in pain. "Estoy bien. Vámonos."

I climb on top of her, throwing one last look at the empty cages. My steed is safe, but I've failed these dragons. I've failed my team. As Esperanza Fades, I brace myself for what I'll find in that wretched arena. Then I realize I can never prepare for such a thing.

SWOOSH!

Everything is on fire.

We fly over the burning Dragonblood ring, but I don't see the competing dragons. Only their chains remain. The Lindworm and the Spike must've also been Transported out. Artem Volkov's steed—a three-headed Zmey Gorynych with glinting emerald scales—is dousing the stands with flames. Onesa Ruwende's sand-colored Pangolin dragon does the same. Wataida's Pangolin slams its curled body into fleeing Blood Masks. They're knocked to the floor at once. People are either scrambling for the exits or Transporting in a rush. Both Génesis and Joaquín are mounting Rayo, who's scanning the stadium.

When Génesis sees me, she steers Rayo closer. "Are you *okay*?"

"Yes. Where are the others?"

"¡Allí!" She and Joaquín are pointing at the ring.

I can't see them at first. Then I notice a fireball to the left.

Samira and Takeshi are inside.

Samira's magic has morphed the flames into the shell that's encasing them. Takeshi has his foot on a female Blood Mask's chest. The woman is unconscious, and her mask's been taken off. Takeshi is also holding onto another Blood Mask, this one a male. He nods to Samira.

With a wave of her wand, the fire disappears.

Takeshi looks up.

He's scowling at me.

Another day for someone with zero talent to get special treatment just because she's not white. I'm tired of people calling you a superstar. I can't even log onto that stupid bird app and not see the Cup's cancelation trending. YOU did that with your crybaby antics. Wherever you are, I hope you're suffering. I hope there's somebody reminding you of your place in this world, which is at the very bottom. I hope they destroy your chances at feeling successful ever again.

—Anonymous comment left on Lana Torres's BlazeReel profile page

CHAPTER NINETEEN

Lana

PRESIDENT TURNER STILL HASN'T ANSWERED THE PHONE.

I've left him twelve voicemails and twenty-two texts. Maybe it's a bit much, but Haya and Agent Robinson can't freaking find him. He and his husband must be hiding inside an Other Place. Thankfully, an online library search led me to the headmaster's textbook. My copy of *Dark & Dastardly: Obscure Magical Folklore & Enchantments for Beginners* might not clear up my doubts, but it could give me a better framework for what I'm dealing with.

I spin the small bone on my desk. Samira's checked it a billion times, but there's nothing unusual about it. Pretending it's a relic from the Jurassic Period makes the disappointment more bearable. Spinning it also helps me endure the long wait until group training is done—Samira's updates on Madame Waxbyrne are a few hours away. She's been scouring Agent Robinson's love letters for clues. Hopefully, she can find something useful soon.

We need great news after yesterday's mess. Takeshi's group only caught two Blood Masks. Interrogation updates trickle in from Onesa, Wataida, and Artem—they're keeping prisoners in a secret location—but still no Cecilia. And Victoria almost got everyone killed. How could she think sneaking away was a good idea? Granted, watching those Un-Bondeds fighting for their lives is the very definition of horrific. She almost died, though, and for what?

Then there's Antonio Deluca. If Cecilia freed her ex from Randall's skullpit, how on Earth did she find him? Maybe only someone as powerful as Randall could've achieved this. Cecilia doesn't strike me as sentimental, so she must've rescued her ex because she wanted a Gold Wand in her army. Much like my theory on that missing Enid Mendoza girl.

Victoria thinks Cecilia is holding something over Antonio's head.

If she had caught him, we could've found out what it is.

"Hey, sweetheart. I found some additional articles and printed them for you. The important parts are already highlighted in red. Where should I leave them?"

Mom carries the stack of pages like a newborn baby.

"Here's fine." I tap the desk.

"Anything worth digging deeper into yet? Most of these talk about blood curses from a historical and cultural perspective, but I can't find much that relates to the Sire's abilities. And there's barely anything on psychic magic." Mom puts the articles on the desk.

"Headmaster Sykes focuses on history a lot, too. I'm only a chapter away from finishing."

Mom slides a chair next to me and sits down. "Let's read it together. Maybe I'll catch something you don't. My brain isn't nearly as weary when it comes to magic." She gives me the kind of warm smile I would've killed to have growing up as a Blazewrath fan.

Some things take time, though.

"Lana?"

I clear my throat. "Yeah, that sounds great."

"Also, your father called again." Mom speaks with such nonchalance. She's looking at my computer screen as if she hasn't upended my entire world. "You should contact him."

My blood pressure skyrockets. We haven't spoken since he threw my failures at my face. Talking to him means exposing myself to further ridicule, and I'm not about to undo the progress I've made during practice. Takeshi is still training me with his Bond technique. I barely shivered this morning, and I can shut out the noise faster. I could be acing his battlefield test by tomorrow.

"Later." I scroll down to chapter twenty-seven, which is titled "Copper, Silver, & Gold: Are Wands All That Matter?" In it, Headmaster Sykes gives a rundown of what each wand level is capable of, but he doesn't explain much about how wands are made. Wand-makers are pros at keeping secrets. Headmaster Sykes jokingly calls Iron Pointe the CIA of wand-maker academies.

But there's a passage near the end that stands out:

> *Many favor wand level above all else. A Copper Wand will never defeat a Gold Wand in a duel. A Silver Wand can never slay a dragon. However, a lesser-known (and unproven) theory revolves around a magic user's intention. Some radical scholars believe a magic user's intention may hold an advantage over their abilities. A Silver Wand could create a deadlier curse than a Gold Wand if their desire to harm others is stronger. The same would apply to save others with a counter-curse. This theory has yet to be universally accepted, but those who support it have requested wand-makers' confirmation.*
>
> *None have come forward to do so.*

Headmaster Sykes doesn't explicitly lean toward this intention theory. How can willpower be a separate form of magic? Even if it's only applicable during curse-casting, it's outlandish.

Then I remember what happened to Samira in Brazil. She shouldn't have been capable of beating Randall, *especially* since she wasn't dueling a normal wizard. What if Samira Ascended to Gold because she countered a curse from the most powerful wizard of our time? He didn't *give* her those powers, but maybe her evolution is unlike anything in history because so was he?

I spin the bone fragment as fast as my racing thoughts. Randall's spell orbs, Cecilia's near-perfect soul extraction, the psychic magic… could their gifts also be explained with the intention theory? And the Sire… his Anchor Curse has never been documented—he *created* it. What if it was born out of his cruel desires? No spell book, no instructions or materials. Just… hate.

It still doesn't make sense. These are still just two magic users and one dragon.

Unless they're so much more…

"Sweetheart, you're spaced out again. What's wrong?" says Mom.

I word-vomit all my thoughts. After ten minutes of ranting, she's furrowing her brow.

"So Samira is a Gold Wand because she went up against Randall, and her wish to save you overpowered his wish to end you?"

"Yeah. Also, let's say intention does outweigh skill when it comes to casting dark magic, and in Samira's case, when it comes to fighting it. What if the hate these Evil Wonder Twins and the Sire feel is actually *connected* to curses?" I read the page's last section aloud. "'Those who support it have requested wand-makers' confirmation. None have come forward to do so.'" I shrug. "Their secrecy could mean the theory is true, and the evidence might be something they're terrified of."

"Or it could implicate them," Mom suggests.

"Exactly. I figured Madame Waxbyrne was our best hope for stopping Cecilia. What if she can help us destroy whatever's healing the

Sire, too? And what if—"

My phone rings.

It's Papi.

"Do you want some privacy?" Mom says.

"No."

I jam the phone into my Wonder Woman backpack, where it rings seven more times.

Mom tries to console me with the promise of mofongo—she's been learning how to cook it—but I need more than one of my country's best dishes. I need to speak with the woman who watched Cecilia Valcárcel turn into whatever she is today.

And did nothing.

"Where is the threat?"

Takeshi is practicing with me for the second time today. He's told me Samira isn't done checking Agent Robinson's letters, and that she wants to be as thorough as possible.

I also think he's trying to wrap up our sessions. He must be swamped with Task Force Blaze stuff. At least he agreed the intention theory is worth considering. He's even asked me to tell Samira—she deserves to hear about what could've helped her Ascend from her best friend.

Fireballs tear through the hangar. The web of spindly wings and bared fangs grows. Takeshi has activated *more* dragon simulations. Spells are being shot from all sides, too.

Takeshi's hands melt the ice caps that are my limbs. They let me steady my breaths, my racing pulse. Noise becomes a faint whisper. A shaking room is a distant buzz.

I search for the battle's culprit. Horns, tails, wands… I'm deep in a burning, blinding sea. Smoke and sweat blur the edges of my vision. The little girl screams as Dragon Knights approach. Blood Masks are about to slit the man's throat. Each plea for mercy threatens to drag me into despair, but I scan the room without pause. Scales and flesh blend into a single thread farther ahead. There's a small opening, though.

A red skirt blows among the flames.

Cecilia wears the same dress she had in Nantes.

She's standing on top of Daga's body.

There's a hole in the dragon's chest. The witch who killed her holds up a glowing white orb—Daga's soul. Its light beats fast. Cecilia turns it ever so slightly. The screams, the roars… everything is louder. Humans and dragons are moving at twice their original speed.

She's the threat.

My fingers still tingle with Takeshi's warmth as I move toward her. I'm hiding behind backs and scales. She cackles at a wizard whose leg has been bitten off.

I sprint up Daga's tail. My hands are outstretched, ready to grab Cecilia's neck.

"You're so right, dude. 'Lana is a pro at crybaby antics.' Good one!"

A livestream is projected on the walls. It's broadcasting from a restaurant, but the angle restricts my vision to a corner tucked near the back.

He sits alone in a black leather booth. A napkin dangles from his VLTN sweater's neck. His knife cuts deep into a rib eye steak while he reads comments on his phone.

"'How long until we make you president, king?' Oh, that's very kind! Fighting winged vermin from the Oval Office does sound awesome. And before I forget, thank you for all the beautiful fan art, guys. The ones where I'm a dragon slayer are the best. *Love* the shirts you've been designing, too. Maybe we'll use them for my presidential campaign."

Todd chews his steak with a smirk.

I can't tell if this is real footage, or if Takeshi's edited a simulation.

I just know I can't move.

"Let's see here." Todd squints to keep reading. "'I hope you ruin what's left of Lana's future like she ruined Blazewrath.'" He sighs. "This is a Blazewrath-free zone, loser. If you supported that stupid game, you're stupid, too. Don't bother me again."

A waiter puts a Perrier bottle next to his plate. Without acknowledging him, Todd slices the rib eye into tiny, juicy pieces. Then he reads on, nodding and smirking.

"Oh, dear. This one's spicy," he purrs. "'Lana should've taken Andrew's place.'"

The boy who's treated me like a lesser being all my life has acknowledged my greatest failure. I'm finally the colossal joke he thinks I am. He can't hurt dragons, but when I remember that Dragonblood exists, how he's getting so much support and *even fan art*... This is Todd Anderson's world. I've given my cousin a new reason to feel validated.

"Lana shouldn't die, guys. She deserves to see her precious dragons go extinct." Todd winks. "Until then, let's get another hashtag trending! How about an Andrew one this time?"

I run away.

He hurt another child today.

Her mother wept as I searched for a pulse.

The more I research, the less I find. And his thoughts… I can't bear them any longer.

Professor Julia Serrano has agreed to meet with me. I'm visiting Iron Pointe in the morning.

I won't give up on his soul.

—*Excerpt from Edward Barnes's journal*

CHAPTER TWENTY

Lana

I DON'T KNOW HOW I MADE IT TO THE POOL.

Technically, I'm closer to the hot tub. Luis has left a note that reads THIS IS MINE next to it.

Nobody else is here. The crystalline water is cool enough for a swim, but I'm on a floating chaise lounge with my sneakers still on. I think it's been, what? Two hours? Three? The point is I've been alternating between bawling and napping. Neither makes me feel any better.

Todd's livestream is real. I checked.

He's done fourteen total, usually while fine dining, and the Internet has unkindly provided them all. I've no need to watch. But the obscene amount of viewers and comments… *Thousands* of people follow him on every social media platform. Some leave him heart emojis. They call him their baby, their king. He's truly thriving with his vitriol-filled bandwagon.

I hate that he has an audience. A *following*.

I hate how little he makes me feel, and how I don't know when it'll stop.

The intercom beeps.

"Lana, I'd like to see you in the garden," says Takeshi. "Thank you."

His message is short, but definitely not sweet. I understand he was testing me. Couldn't he have used another distraction? He straight up sabotaged me, and now he's asking to meet again?

I drag myself off the lounge. If this is for more training, I'll politely refuse. Or scream.

Maybe both.

THIS IS THE WHITEST ROOM I'VE EVER BEEN IN.

Takeshi and I weave through the curving pathway across the garden. I can't even begin to count how many flowers there are. The world's supply of carnations has been stored inside this Other Place. I'm drawn to the swing set at the end.

The seats are hearts, though.

I take a detour to the marble benches. "These look comfortable," I say.

"You were heading for the swings. We can sit there instead."

"Oh... I mean... you don't mind?"

"Why would I mind? I love swings."

Takeshi claims the first swing and kicks off the ground. He doesn't smile when he's lifted into the air, but his eyes are pressed shut, as if he's reveling in the back and forth motion of the ivory chains holding him up.

This is the loveliest he's ever been.

Oh, my God, Lana. Keep it professional!

I sit on the swing next to Takeshi. He glides forward while I run back to gain momentum. We continue in opposite directions, but his eyes are open again. I'm giggling like I'm still that eleven-year-old girl Mom took to the playground once in a blue moon. My weekends were mostly spent catching up on homework and watching Blazewrath matches behind her back.

That little girl wouldn't have believed she'd sit on a swing next to a Blazewrath superstar.

Seventeen-year-old Lana is also struggling. Is this why he invited me? Just to have... *fun*? He hasn't mentioned the Todd incident or further practice sessions.

I swing slower and slower. "So what did you want to talk about?"

"I never said I wanted to talk."

His words should come with that record scratch sound effect. Or a car crash.

"Um... okay?" I don't know how else to address him.

Takeshi brakes abruptly. His half-smile should be illegal in every nation. Thank God he doesn't have dimples. They would've been the death of me.

Wait, what? No, they wouldn't!

"Remember what I said about a dragon's call? How you freeze in the dark?"

So this *is* about training. "Of course."

Takeshi pulls out his silver remote from his pocket. "It's quite unpleasant, which is why the warmth that follows is even more meaningful. A steed wants their rider to trust them, and they achieve it by providing comfort. The same applies to training. We need to feel at peace in order to endure chaos."

"This garden is your peace?"

"Yes. I'd like to share it with you, if that's all right."

As much as I admire Mother Nature, I'm not a huge fan of hanging out with plants. But the way he's asking me to stay with him... This doesn't feel like a test. More like he's trying to help me relax. Maybe this is his apology for showing me Todd?

"I'd love to," I say.

Takeshi nods. "Perfect."

When he clicks the remote, every petal breaks away from their flower.

Soon the levitating petals surround us. They're sucked into a magical whirlwind that moves at a glacial pace, as if they're making sure I know how beautiful they are. How could I not? I'm stuck inside a constellation of delicate, milk-white fluff. I crush a handful of petals to my cheek—a baby's touch isn't nearly as soft. Once I let them go, they slowly float up again.

"Agent Robinson Charmed the garden, too?" I can't bring myself to speak higher than a whisper. It feels wrong to disturb this much peace.

"Yes. Haya and I designed the layout. The swings and benches were her idea. The flowers were mine." Takeshi falls silent as he stares down. "These petals resemble Hikaru's feathers."

"This is your way of honoring his memory?" I ask.

"That's what infiltrating the Sire's army was for." Takeshi rests his head against a chain. "This is where remembering him doesn't rip my heart into pieces. It's where I feel safest. Spending time with my mother also helps, but she's in hiding until we win this war."

I can't imagine what that poor woman has been through. First, her only son loses his dragon steed, then she loses *him*. And long before that, she'd lost her husband to cancer. If anyone deserves a break, it's Sayuri Endo. I hope she's much better off wherever she is.

She should know she's raised a hero. His methods might be extreme, but there's no denying Takeshi is capable of things I never would be.

"You looked the Sire in the eye every day knowing he killed Hikaru. How did you do it?"

Takeshi stares off into the distance, his gaze unfocused. "I reminded myself he would be mortal again, and I was going to end his life."

I swallow hard. "Do you, um… regret not killing him?"

"Sometimes."

I can't blame him, even though *I'm* the one who begged him to spare the Sire. I'd done it to save President Turner—as the Sire's Anchor, he would've died along with the dragon that cursed him. But it had also been moments after Andrew's murder. I couldn't bear to watch Takeshi become the same thing he was trying to eradicate. He deserved a better future than a conscience stained with blood.

"However," Takeshi continues, "I'll never regret putting my faith in you."

My heartbeat outpaces the swirling petals. I could chalk up the compliment to him being nice, especially after bailing on practice. Then his gaze lingers on mine. His breathing matches the steadiness I'm fighting so hard to keep despite the erratic pounding in my chest. We sit there looking at one another, and I'm both infinitely powerful and a speck of nothing.

I'm about to say something—anything to bury my awkwardness—when he speaks.

"We both lost the same friend."

The erratic pounding in my chest grinds to a halt. "Takeshi, I… can we not—"

"But I know you're not ready to discuss it. Maybe you never will be. That doesn't make you weak, Lana. It means we have different ways of coping, and I fully respect yours. All I ask is for you to remember you're not alone. That's why I've brought you to my safe place." Takeshi smiles. "Perhaps it can soothe you, too."

Forget the record scratch and car crash effects. This is exploding planet territory.

The Sol de Noches had surprised me with a welcome message in Dubai. It's the sweetest gift I've ever gotten. This is a close second. Takeshi and I share a deep love for a boy who didn't deserve his fate.

Dancing flower petals won't erase the pain of losing Hikaru or Andrew, but they remind me how lovely this world can be, and how the right people will refuse to let you forget it.

Unlike everyone else, Takeshi isn't pushing me to spill my guts out to him. To act like I'm an injured baby bird who needs saving. But even his offer to spend time in this garden is a sign that I'm doing a bad job of hiding my pain. What if someone asks him why he brought me up here? He'll feed into the narrative that I'm incapable of being in Task Force Blaze.

I'm welling up, but with a few wipes, the tears vanish. "Thank you, Takeshi, but I'm fine."

"I never said you weren't."

"Yeah, but still."

"Congratulations. Would you like a medal?"

I raise an eyebrow. "Since when do you make jokes?"

"Is there a copyright I'm unaware of?" He laughs, but it's that shy, tight-lipped sound older people make when they're pleased with their cleverness.

I don't know why I'm laughing, too. He really needs to work on his so-called humor.

I also don't understand why I can't quit staring at his lips. Why, for the first time in the four years I've admired him, I'm struck with the sudden urge to press mine against them.

Oh, my God. I can't keep denying it. Takeshi Endo isn't my hero anymore. He's my freaking *crush*.

Not that it matters. There's no way this is mutual. He brought me here because he thinks I need healing. He can't have a crush on someone he considers this messy. So I shove all signs of hope and longing for this wonderful boy to the deepest corners of my mind, where they'll remain until my dying day. I have no business seeing him as more than a colleague.

"Um… Yeah, so… this is a lovely flower place," I blurt out.

Did I just say lovely flower place?!

"You're welcome," says Takeshi.

Then we quietly watch the constellation of milk-white fluff together.

CHAPTER TWENTY-ONE

Victoria

"THIS IS BY FAR MY FAVORITE TORTURE DEVICE," SAYS SAMIRA, AS she helps Haya secure a flamethrower to the front of her motorcycle.

The flamethrower is as red as the bike, and as red as the small sidecar attached to the right side. I'm uncertain why Haya is planning on riding such a flashy bike. Our covert ops don't feel so covert with that Kawasaki Ninja looking like a unicorn. Still, these modifications will be useful for Group #1's ambush tonight—Noora located Dragon Knights in the south of México.

I can't let Robinson leave before I beat him at the aerial course.

It's been four days since New Zealand. No one has brought up what happened. I can't tell if they're mad at me or if they're trying not to upset me further. Takeshi's too busy to scowl at me again. His visits to the garden with Lana are becoming more frequent—they must really enjoy making out among flowers. He keeps telling us there are no leads to the next Dragonblood ring, but I wonder if he's paying enough attention.

"May I ride with Haya once it's ready?" Kirill rubs the sidecar's door. I cannot get over his shirt—it's a black-and-white design from Beyoncé's The Formation World Tour. His lip and septum piercings are better suited for a rock show, but I don't think he cares. He turns to Edwin. "My love, I apologize if this is the only thing I talk about for the next five years."

Edwin laughs as he presses the earpiece that interprets what he hears. "No te preocupes."

"That's Spanish for get a new boyfriend," Luis jokes. He's poking Kirill's rock-hard abs. "Move. I want to ride first."

"Not a chance," says Kirill.

"When can we start practice?" I cut in.

Everyone turns to me, but only Héctor sighs. "Victoria…"

"It's okay," says Robinson. "Soon. Willa and I could use a stretch. But first, can we marvel at this contraption? Haya, what do you think of your bike?"

"Oh, it's *perfect*!" She bounces on the balls of her feet.

"Because you made it," Gabriela says. But from the way her eyes are popping out of their sockets, I don't think she meant to say that out loud.

Everyone is staring at her.

Especially Haya.

"You're very sweet, Gabriela." She says it with a smile that could charm even a cold-hearted killer. Haya runs a hand through her silver hair. "Would you like to ride first?"

And there goes Gabriela turning red again.

"Oh… No, no. The others have been waiting for a while. Maybe later."

Haya nods. "Maybe later."

Nobody speaks. Haya and Gabriela build a white picket fence and a three-story house in their minds as they lose themselves in their gazes.

I'd smile if they weren't cutting into my practice time. "Samira? Are you done?"

She flicks her wrist. A clicking sound comes from the bike. When she tugs on the flamethrower, it stays put. "All set! Who wants to ride with—"

"ME!" Kirill and Luis rush her.

Samira jumps back. "Whoa! How about we settle this like adults? Rock, paper, scissors?"

Someone please wake me from this nightmare.

After restarting eight times in ten boring minutes, Kirill is crowned champion. He squeezes himself into the sidecar while Haya mounts her bike. Then he commands his steed to shoot fire at them from across the hangar. Haya darts around the racetrack at full speed, with a howling Kirill raising his arms like he's on a rollercoaster. When the Zmey Gorynych starts firing at them, Haya presses a button on the control panel. Fire blasts off from the flamethrower's tip. Haya alternates between fireballs and a single stream. The Zmey Gorynych bats away each attack with either her tail or more fire, but Haya manages to catch her off guard several times, hitting her square in all three faces.

"Brilliant. We're definitely taking this with us," says a pleased Robinson. He smiles down at me. "Still up for that flight session?"

I almost froth at the mouth. "Yes, sir."

I ask Esperanza to Fade into the hangar, and she arrives a second later. My beautiful girl is already standing at the starting line. She wags her tail as I mount.

"Tenemos que ganarle," I tell her.

With a shy nod, she agrees—we have to win.

I kiss one of her horns. She's been doing so well during our Sire-watching shifts. He hasn't dared to look at her; Esperanza growls whenever he moves. Practices have been good, but those zigzagging towers are still our Achilles's heels. I keep telling her how to twist and duck. I've tried different ways of shifting my weight—leaning forward, to the side—and we're still losing.

"Willa could simply be faster," Héctor had said last night. "It happens." *No.*

Robinson sets off with Willa first. Their performance is stellar as usual. Willa is now crushing *more* fireballs with her wings and vaporizing them. How can she maintain her speed while using her body for additional tasks? If this were the Cup, she'd be the perfect Charger.

"Forty seconds!" Haya says as they land. "Victoria, you're up!"

Héctor offers Esperanza a high-five, and she boops his hand with her nose.

We soar.

Robinson fires up the first blasters. Esperanza dives, rises, and dives again. She's twisting around a spiked tower when flames nip at our heels. Her descent is swift. I'm almost thrown forward, but I grip the reins with all my might. Each time Esperanza avoids getting scorched, she loses her place in the obstacle course, and returning shaves off seconds. Fading ahead would be cheating. I'll win fair and square, but I also want to be clever.

The first time she Faded, she came back to the Blazewrath field wrapped in flames. Her magic protected me. What if the blasters can't hurt her or knock her off course if she's on fire?

"¡Esperanza, préndete en fuego ahora!"

She lights herself up.

I'm cocooned in white-hot brightness. The world is heat and sweat and clothes that stick to me like mistakes I can't live down. Fireballs crash into Esperanza. They're swallowed up into the cocoon, making her burn even more. She stops ducking and diving—her path is steady.

When we finish, Esperanza casts the fire away. I'm unharmed yet sweaty.

"What's the time?" I ask Haya.

Everyone crowds her, but she breaks free.

She says, "Thirty-seven seconds."

Esperanza roars in celebration. So does Willa—she flaps her wings like she's applauding.

"Thirty-seven seconds?" I repeat so I can believe it.

"Yes! Congratulations!"

I fucking did it. I'm finally the best!

I flash my pearly whites as Robinson shakes my hand. The Cup was ripped away before our final opponents could congratulate us. I'm not receiving a trophy today, either. Knowing I accomplished what I set out to do, that I *cannot* be stopped, makes it sting less.

"Bloody good job, Victoria. Using her fire as a shield was brilliant."

"Thank you."

"An amazing session, Legend! You and Esperanza own the skies," says Kirill.

"We do." Perhaps I shouldn't brag, but it wouldn't be me if I didn't.

Héctor pats me on the back. He's about to speak when someone clears their throat.

"Victoria?" Takeshi stands by the hangar doors. "May I have a quick word?"

He doesn't speak all the way to the living room.

I'm surprised his girlfriend isn't here. She must be pining for him in her room.

"Please sit." Takeshi settles on the couch across from me.

I'm tempted to ask if he saw what I did. I can't erase New Zealand from his memory, but I can always do better, and he should acknowledge it.

I take a seat. "What's this about, boss?"

"You were spectacular today."

His monotone doesn't erase the fact that he said it—I've impressed him.

But he doesn't seem too excited.

"Was I the right kind of spectacular?" I grin.

Takeshi's posture is stiffer than a taxidermist's deer collection. He surveys the coffee table. Génesis's *Attack On Titan* coloring book is open on the title page. She doesn't watch that show, but it's the only coloring book Haya had.

"How are you feeling?" He's not looking at me.

"Amazing."

"About New Zealand?"

Guessing Takeshi's intentions is impossible. He hadn't inquired much after Antonio's escape. It's like he was too mad to even speak with me. But I hope he'll be changing his tune soon. I've kept my head down. Trained harder. Today's performance is proof I can do better.

"I'd like to formally apologize. That was unacceptable, and it won't happen again. To answer your question, I feel grateful to still have this opportunity and excited to work harder."

Why is this turning into a job interview?

"You want to work harder," Takeshi repeats.

"Yes."

"That includes following orders."

"Yes."

"Which you didn't do."

"Yes, but—"

"Today you demanded Michael focus on you while he oversaw his group's bike assembly. You've been obsessed with winning an exercise that's meant to foster teamwork." Takeshi tilts his head. "Is that how a team player behaves?"

I haven't glared this hard since meeting Cecilia. "Why are you attacking me?"

"This isn't an attack."

"Yes, it is! You saw how everyone congratulated me. If *I'm* not being a team player, why did they all celebrate my performance? Why have

Héctor and Edwin helped me train?"

"Because they're good people. They want you to succeed. But you"—Takeshi drops his voice—"only want to be better than them."

Is he implying I don't care about my friends? When *he's* been cooped up in a fucking garden with Lana? He needs to do his job already—we won't find Cecilia in the back of Lana's throat.

"Leaders are supposed to work the hardest, not seduce their colleagues."

I shouldn't speak to him like this.

But he shouldn't treat me like *I'm* the problem.

Takeshi hasn't blinked in ten agonizingly long seconds. His gaze bounces from one of my eyes to the other. "You don't take criticism well. I can relate, but it's not an excuse to disrespect me, let alone to disrespect Lana. Her training requires a different approach."

Is it your dick?

"And now so will yours."

I'm on my feet. I bump into the coffee table, but it's as rigid as the guy insinuating I'm about to be punished. "What does that mean?"

"We found the ring," he says calmly. "You won't be joining us."

Shock and fury grab hold of my tongue. I'm stunned into hazy silence as I piece together the meaning behind what he's just said. He *has* been working hard, and he's thrown it at my face so callously, as if he's been saving it for this precise moment—he wanted to humiliate me.

"Are you kicking me off the team?"

"This is a temporary pause in your activities, Victoria."

"But you can't do this. I'm not getting benched."

"Until you learn to take things slow, to truly listen, taking you anywhere is a risk." Takeshi rises, too, but he's back to looking elsewhere. "The match is tomorrow. Our conversation will continue after I return. So will your new training regimen. I recommend you get some rest."

"I said you can't do this to me!"

I'm shouting at my boss. My brain knows it's wrong, but I don't care. This is the same person who kidnapped Lana's dad and forced my team to abandon the Cup. He's pulling the rug from under me yet again—as long as Takeshi's involved, I'll never make any dream come true.

Takeshi starts walking around the coffee table. "Victoria—"

"Fuck off."

I leave before I knock him out.

Enid had been the quietest student in every class. She was always jotting down everything professors said, especially during wand lore lessons. She loved attending Julia Serrano's lectures—her favorite wand-maker. But what I'll miss most is how Enid truly saw me.

One day, you're going to miss what you love, too.

—Anonymous note left in Madame Waxbyrne's office at
Iron Pointe Academy

CHAPTER TWENTY-TWO

Lana

Samira's Tracking Charm is working just fine.

So far, she hasn't landed on any traps. But her spell keeps showing us a blank image. It's a canvas as white as the snowcapped Swiss Alps where Iron Pointe is located. A part of me is impressed with Madame Waxbyrne. I just wish her talents were exclusive to making wands.

I guess Cecilia learned from the best...

"This lady is way more romantic than I ever expected," says Samira.

She's lying on my bed, her legs propped up against the wall. Her group leaves for the ring in a couple hours, and instead of sleeping, she's searching for a secretive Gold Wand with me.

Agent Robinson also has his hands full, especially since his group's operation in México had been a colossal waste of time. There was no trace of Dragon Knights by the time they arrived. Agent Robinson and the rest of his team are poring over every piece of intelligence they've collected, but there's still no sign of the Sire's followers anywhere.

"Are you really focusing on how *romantic* Madame Waxbyrne is?"

"Yup. Gotta see the bright side." She hands me the letter. "Love isn't dead."

"Samira. You're seventeen. You'll have plenty of chances to fall in love."

"That's not the plan, girl. My future's headed more in the ass-kicking direction. Slaying grades and bad guys? Now we're talking." Samira studies her fingernails, which she's recently painted pale blue. "And I've been thinking a lot about your wand theory, too."

Shortly after I asked her to help me find Madame Waxbyrne, I jumped right into explaining what I'd read in Headmaster Sykes's book. We even read it together. Samira's been quiet about it so far, but I'm guessing she's spent the past few days mulling things over.

I'm happy she's finally talking about it, though. "How so?"

"My Gold Wand certification is up in the air, right? Maybe it was the strenuous testing or everything else I've accomplished here, but I'm not as excited about getting certified anymore. The bureau's seal of approval won't tell me *how* I got my powers to evolve so quickly. There's a wealth of information I'm missing out on, and the bureau can't help me access it." She looks me dead in the eyes. "Dark magic lore is only available in one place."

I nod. "Wand-maker academies."

"Yup. I'm thinking about transferring to one. I already talked to my parents, and they were very supportive. They still want to know how they can help us whoop Cecilia's butt, though." She shakes her head. "Anyway, even if we *do* find Madame Waxbyrne and she gives us all the details we need, I still wanna soak up everything I can." Samira taps the wall with alternating pointed toes. "I'm getting a bonus education on how to make wands, which might come in handy for our next showdown! I'm researching scholarships once we're done with Cecilia."

A part of me envies her—her future seems more certain than mine. Here I am wondering if we can defeat the most powerful threat we've ever faced, and my best friend has decided to switch high schools to better understand her magic *while also* helping me end Cecilia's reign. The fact that her decision is because of poor leadership on the bureau's part, that her very existence as a Gold Wand is a question mark in a world with *dragons*, is appalling. As long as she knows I'm always going to support her, that makes their incompetence sting less.

"Wherever you go, they're lucky to have you, Samira. I'm sure you'll find what you're looking for two seconds after walking into the school." I laugh because it's true, and also because I picture her sidestepping everybody to sneak into the library's faculty only section.

"I wish you could join me," she says. "Regulars should be allowed to design wands, too. Can you imagine being allowed to study somewhere as elite as Iron Pointe? You could've been the second Puerto Rican in history to attend! Julia Serrano would've been so proud."

"Agreed. But I can just keep the Cherry Suite's seats warm until you get back."

Samira raises an eyebrow. "You're staying *here*?"

Excellent question. I don't even know why I said that—once this battle is over, I'm sure Task Force Blaze will move into a more secure location in the outside world. I should probably be thinking about school. Also, Mom can't keep neglecting her OB/GYN practice back in Florida. We agreed to visit Puerto Rico for a little while. Now look at us.

Why do we have to assemble puzzles when not all the pieces are available?

"You still here?" Samira pokes my belly.

I recoil with a half-hearted grin. "Yeah. Sorry for spacing out."

"No worries. Just don't do it when I'm calling you with magic school updates, *especially* if I'm mad about liking a rich kid. Although I might not be so mad if they're smoking hot."

I pretend to hurl all over her lap. "Please stop."

"Uh-uh. Don't act like love is icky, Little Miss Endo."

Oh, my God. This is my fault. I shouldn't be going to the carnation garden with Takeshi so often. But it really is the best way to relax! Something about those floating petals makes me think beautiful things can still happen despite the crapfest that is the world right now. And Takeshi's always so… patient. He just sits next to me in silence and enjoys my company.

I enjoy his company, too, but that doesn't mean we're freaking *married*.

"Samira. I hate you. Now can I read in peace?"

"Have you kissed him yet?"

"What? No!"

"Do you *want* to kiss him?"

"SamirapleasejustfocusohmyGod."

She's cackling harder than Cruella de Vil. "Knock yourself out."

While she scoots over to grab her third Sprite, I reread my favorite passage:

Nine days.

That's how long it's taken me to write this. How could I squeeze the contents of my heart into ink and immortalize them on the page? I hope to one day be as talented in this endeavor as you. Above all else, I wish for the gentle ways in which you show me affection to never cease.

I used to think paradise meant an island surrounded by smaller ones, with limestone cliffs and shores as rocky as my past. It used to be daydreams of Mediterranean harbors and colorful boats. But a nighttime stroll across my favorite capital city wouldn't be the same without the hands that hold me like I'm a feather. I thank my lucky stars I'm far wiser now.

Paradise is how much you love me.

When I first read this part, I figured the island she's referencing is Sicily, especially since she already has a house there. But there *are* other islands in the Mediterranean. She's just never mentioned them to Agent Robinson—he'd been clueless as to which one she's referring to here.

And he doesn't remember her mentioning Palermo, which is Sicily's capital city.

"What if you look for her in the Mediterranean instead?" I ask Samira. "Madame Waxbyrne enchanted her letters to stop her Gold magic from being found through them, but she's not as powerful as Cecilia or Randall. There's no way she can cloak her whole existence."

Samira frowns. "Way ahead of you, girl. I already did that last night. There's nothing."

"Where exactly did you search?"

"Sicily and most of the Greek Isles. I have a few left." I'm about to say something when she gasps. Her Sprite almost falls on my bed sheets, but she catches it. "I forgot Malta!"

There's no guarantee Madame Waxbyrne is in any of these places.

Still, a suspicion is better than nothing.

"Let's start with Malta."

I've never seen Samira whip out her wand this fast. She conjures a black-and-white blueprint of Malta into the middle of my room. It's complete with grooves and squiggles to represent the country's roads and steep cliffs. Samira jabs her wand into the blueprint. A bright spot of gold bursts across the map like an exploding star. It splits into hundreds of smaller lights. They hover over different areas. Samira taps the first spot on the right.

Gold lightning flies toward her chest. She's thrown off the bed, convulsing from the shock.

"Samira!" I help her up, thinking she'll rest, but she's already tapping a second spot.

Another lightning bolt hits her.

"OH, YOU WANNA PLAY GAMES, HUH?" she screams.

"Wait! You are *not* getting zapped again!"

"You're damn right I'm not!" Samira lets me sit her next to me. The intensity in her scowl could scare the toughest bodybuilder on the planet. She's studying the map in silence. I'm trying to do the same, but I keep thinking about how freaked out Madame Waxbyrne must be to pull such heinous trickery.

"What exactly are we looking for, Samira?"

"A pattern. Or anything that seems off."

The spots are all the same shape, size, and color.

I'm two seconds away from throwing in the towel. Still, I reread the letter. "A pattern or anything that seems off…" We guessed the location references correctly, but other than that, she only mentions an amount of days and how much she loves Agent Robinson.

"Nine days." I look at the map. "How many spots are there?"

"Thirty-four."

I do a quick Google search on Madame Waxbyrne. There are no nines in her birth date. I can't remember any nines displayed in her wand shop, either.

My heart speeds up. "The hexagon…"

"The what?"

I grab Samira's shoulders. "Waxbyrne's floor plan in the cash register area. It's a hexagon. So is the store's entrance. And the Dragonblood ring in Nantes… it was *also* a hexagon."

Samira tips her head back. "Madame Waxbyrne was Cecilia's mentor. Maybe that specific shape has something to do with wand-makers?"

"And it could be what we need to break this spell." I point to the map. "Should we try it?"

"Let's go." Samira connects the gold spots until she's drawn a hexagon.

Nothing happens.

Then the particles become a single dot.

It's right on top of Valetta, Malta's capital city. Samira and I flash our teeth at one another.

"You freaking did it!" I say.

"Does that mean you'll repay me by letting me call you Little Miss Endo?"

"Absolutely not. Now get dressed. We have to—"

Papi is calling me again. He keeps leaving me text messages and voicemails. Usually, it's to wish me a good day.

"Why are you ignoring him?" Samira asks. "Did something happen?"

I haven't told her about our last chat—I can't have her worrying. Ever since Takeshi has been helping me, I feel like I'm stalling on talking to Papi. What if he makes me spiral back into those feelings of failure? I shouldn't risk it.

But I miss my dad. I wish I could share *everything* with him. I couldn't make him proud with a golden Cup. I couldn't even properly save him—Takeshi did. The least I can do is show him how great I'm doing, that I'm not a disappointment, after all. And if it makes me cry again, I'll promptly hang up and hide in the carnation garden.

"No. I've been too tired to talk." Papi's already hung up, so I start a video call. He picks up after the third ring.

He's crouching under a tree. Dirt is smudged on his forehead along with beads of sweat.

"¡Mi amor! How have you been? It's wonderful to see you!"

My father is panting.

"Um… Where are you?"

"Just a few feet away from where Violet #43 was rumored to be seen last. I think I can hear her snoring, but it could be another Un-Bonded. Fingers crossed!"

"Wait, you're calling from the field?"

"Yes! I've been trying out different hours to see which ones fit best with your research schedule, and this one happened to coincide with mine." Papi's smile breaks my heart and glues it back together again. "I've missed you so much, Lana. You look beautiful as always."

I can't believe I was afraid of feeling like a failure because of him. He must've felt terrible after how I reacted. Or maybe Mom spoke to him? Either way, I'm so relieved.

"Gracias, Papi."

"De nada. So what's in store for today? Are you eating well? Did you sleep okay?"

A dragon cries out.

Papi's eyes grow three times their original size. He's sprinting for dear life, putting the phone as close to his panicked face. "Te tengo que enganchar, ¿okay? I'll call you later!"

He hangs up.

"Whoa! Do you think that was really the Pesadelo?" Samira asks.

"I don't know. I just hope he doesn't get hurt. And I hope we don't, either." I grab the bone fragment from my desk. "Let's go pay Madame Waxbyrne a visit."

Samira nods. "Better hope your boyfriend gives you clearance."

"He is *not* my boyfriend."

"Sorry. I meant future husband."

"Stop!"

I playfully elbow Samira as I open the bedroom door. I walk outside. And I slam right into Victoria.

Professor Serrano is wrong. He can still be saved.

I'm going back to see what's behind that blue door. She and Glenda are hiding the missing piece.

They can't stop me from casting the spell.

If they try, they'll regret it.

—*Excerpt from Edward Barnes's journal*

CHAPTER TWENTY-THREE

Victoria

LANA AND SAMIRA BELONG IN THE LOUVRE. THEY'VE TRANSFORMED into marble sculptures with matching deer-in-headlights expressions. The only difference is Samira reaching for her wand.

"Relax. Getting blasted is the last thing I need," I say.

"My bad. Gotta be ready at all times."

"I can respect that."

"Victoria…" My name is a question mark on Lana's lips. "What are you doing here?"

Perhaps I shouldn't be surprised *she's* surprised. We've avoided each other for days. Does she have to sound like seeing me is a tremendous shock, though?

Don't get confrontational. You've been through enough today.

Besides, she's the only person who can empathize with me—we've both been sidelined.

She's been a selfish mess. But Lana knows how much it hurts to lose. The Cup, her friend, her future… I don't need Esperanza's images or sweet, half-formed attempts at speech. Everyone else will scold me for telling Takeshi to fuck off. Lana will, too, but she'll understand my rage.

"Can we talk? I know it's late. This is important, though."

"Oh." Lana furrows her brow. "Did something bad happen?"

"Yes."

Samira's wand is out. "Who are we fighting?"

"Take it easy, Gandalf. It's not life or death." I shake my head. "Actually, it is. More Un-Bondeds will die tomorrow morning, and Takeshi won't let me save them."

Lana and Samira gasp. "He found the ring?" Lana says.

How is *that* the part she's focusing on? I've just told her I can't go on the mission!

"We have to talk to him now. He might leave super early," Lana tells Samira.

"Agreed."

"Talk to him about *what*?" I fold my arms.

Lana smiles like she's been awarded the Blazewrath World Cup. "Samira found Madame Waxbyrne! We need to corner her as soon as possible." She points from me to herself to Samira. "Would you like to come with us? The more muscle we have, the better."

So now I'm muscle.

I'm not someone she trusts or even cares about.

And she wants me to help her interview a witch. In what world is that a suitable replacement for smashing dragon cages apart?

"She won't do shit to help us," I say. "Just like you."

I march down the corridor.

"Excuse me?" Her irritated squeal is less than an inch away. This girl really broke into a run to sass at me. She stares me down like we're rival cowboys in a spaghetti Western.

"I spoke perfectly clear, Lana. That witch must have more traps around her hideout. Not only are you risking your and Samira's lives, you're wasting time focusing on the wrong things. Those dragons need us *now*. I'm not interested in babysitting some old lady."

"She's in her fifties," Samira says.

"Whatever!"

Lana steps even closer, her boiling-hot glare incinerating me. "I'm always focusing on the wrong things to you. Figuring out President Turner's secret, saving my dad... but you still rescued me in Brazil, Victoria. You did what your steed, your whole team, knew was right."

"That's all I'm good for, huh? Cleaning up your messes? I can't have my own plans? I have to support you or I'm a bad person?"

"Okay, this is taking a turn." Samira puts an arm between us. "Let's back up."

"When have you *ever* supported me?" Lana has the cojones to say. "I hated myself so much in Dubai because of you. The first day we met, you freaking threatened me! You put a trophy over our free will and acted like being under the Sire's control wasn't a big deal."

"Yeah, that's not what backing up means..."

"And you have the nerve to call me out for trying to stop a killer again?" Lana's crying. It would be more dramatic if I didn't expect it. "I might be a mess, but you're poison."

"Lana!" Samira yanks her away.

Too late—the damage is done.

When you grow up with someone calling you nothing, you get used to it. You even believe it. Then one day the weakest girl you've ever met calls you destructive.

You believe her, too.

Because all you want is to rip the wallpaper from her room's walls, and set her bed on fire.

"When the Cup was canceled, you told me there was life beyond the gold. Is this it, Lana? A so-called friend, who holds my hand while I'm sad at a press conference, yet demands I feel excited about returning to where my stepfather beat me and who never asked how my steed was doing after fainting and who just ignored how upset I am about what her stupid boyfriend did?"

I never knew I could speak so fast. Losing my Cup dreams had been the first lesson—I'll never amount to anything if I hope for validation from others. Task Force Blaze is merely an excuse for Takeshi to feel relevant. To reclaim the power he's had stolen.

It's time I did the same.

Lana and Samira are statues once again.

But Lana is frowning.

"Victoria, I—"

"You can fuck off with Takeshi. I'm done with all of you."

"Wait."

"Don't ever speak to me again. Wouldn't want you getting poisoned."

I walk past her and Samira. Even if they insist on wasting time, I won't.

I have a ring to sneak into.

The online forum Samira browses is a dead end.

Users post random locations based on speculation. I click on links, hoping none turn out to be a virus-infected site or weird shit. More forums appear instead. These are dedicated to Dragonblood fans sharing their likes and dislikes. I scroll faster whenever I catch glimpses of video thumbnails from past matches. Soon I'm swirling down a wormhole of complaints about the disaster in New Zealand—a lot of people want to kill me.

I smile. This is by far my favorite compliment.

It particularly helps after watching Lana and Samira Transport to

Malta. Of course Takeshi gave them clearance—he couldn't stop ogling his girlfriend while she brainwashed him. I suspect he has no clue I spied on them chatting in the living room. Lana and Samira left fifteen minutes ago. Takeshi's group leaves for the ring in a few hours.

I must find it before then. Picturing their faces when I free the dragons and catch Cecilia... Takeshi thanking me for doing his job better... That'll be such a glorious occasion.

Leave Victoria alone. She's iconic, one kind user writes, *and we all screw up sometimes.*

Their screen name is SolNocheblood5ever. I check their previous activity. Nothing related to ring locations or ticket selling; they're simply raving about me. I follow their every cyber move until I land on a password-protected page. The hashtag #destroythering appears under an X. Users need an eighteen-character keyword to enter.

Samira is in Malta. Without her magic, this will be much harder.

Don't give up. Those dragons need you.

I type different word combinations, all related to Dragonblood. When those are rejected, I type code words associated with me, my Blazewrath records, even my birthday.

ACCESS DENIED.

This page is better protected than the Pentagon. I *have* to message SolNocheblood5ever. What if I'm reaching out to a stalker? Creating a fake profile and using a pseudonym would be good for keeping my identity a secret... unless I'm dealing with a hacker. If this user is smart enough to build a page this heavily protected, figuring out who I am might not be a stretch. And if they find Robinson's Other Place, I've truly put us all in grave danger.

But whatever this user knows, I need to know, too.

Heaving a sigh, I return to the fan forum and send SolNocheblood-5ever a private message: *Hello. I also want to #destroythering. Do you have any information on the next match? I can repay you with a personalized autograph from Victoria Peralta. No charge.*

The page says they're online. My hopes of getting answers have skyrocketed.

Twenty-five minutes later, I get a response: *WHAT??? HOW DID YOU GET IT???*

I have connections. Would this be an acceptable form of payment?

YES.

Very well. Send me an address and it'll be in the mail soon.

Wait! What kind of connections? How can I trust you? For all I know, you're lying just to get your hands on the ring's location.

So you do have it.

SolNocheblood5ever stops typing. The ONLINE next to their name is gone.

My webcam light turns on.

"ÁNDATE PA'L CARAJO IT'S REALLY YOU." A voice comes out of the speakers.

I slam the laptop shut. God fucking damn it. "You hacked my computer!"

"I'm sorry! I had to know! I'm shutting the camera off now!"

When I reopen the laptop, my webcam's light is off again.

"Victoria Peralta is talking to me," the voice says. "Am I dreaming? Is this the afterlife?"

"You're thinking out loud, friend."

"EN SERIO YOU JUST CALLED ME YOUR FRIEND."

I'm powerless against the giggles. They keep speaking in Spanish, and their username makes a reference to my country's dragons. "Are you from Puerto Rico, too?"

"Yes! Comerío!"

"Nice. So can I get that ring location?" I hesitate. "Sorry, I don't know your name."

"Kenny!"

"And your pronouns, Kenny?"

"They and them. Thanks so much for asking! Not many people here at Iron Pointe are—" Kenny gasps. "Uh… could you pretend I didn't tell you where I am? I might not be a student, but we're all prohibited from engaging in extracurricular activities while the term is in session."

"That won't be a concern."

Kenny sighs. "Gracias, Victoria. Oh, and here you go!"

The page reloads. My screen is filled with spreadsheets that contain match dates, times, and names of the competing dragon species. All of the matches have already happened, but the last column has a fight that's taking place six hours from now.

It also lists a location: Perito Moreno Glacier. Argentina.

I bite down on my fist. Even though the guttural scream I'm holding in is of absolute joy, everyone will think I'm dying if I release it.

I *can* save the Un-Bondeds.

"Kenny, you've done an honorable thing. Tell me where to send my autograph and I'll—"

"Psssh, forget about it! I just spoke to an *icon*. That's all the payment I need."

I wish I felt like the icon Kenny—all of Puerto Rico—deserves. But the more I think about my Blazewrath legacy, the less it shines when compared to what I hope to do with Dragonblood. Getting those Un-Bondeds out of their cages might make me an icon, albeit a different kind. What matters is that I don't fail again. Not those dragons. Not *myself*.

"Gracias, Kenny. Have an excellent day."

"You, too! Go kick some ass!"

There's a *click* once they're done speaking, as if they've hung up.

I reach out to Esperanza and tell her to meet me in the carnation garden. She whines and flashes me wholesome images of the team, as if she's imploring me to follow Takeshi's orders.

Takeshi no confía en mi, Esperanza. Pero tú y yo podemos hacer esto juntas.

Reassuring her we can do this together doesn't keep her from whining more. Neither does explaining how little faith Takeshi has in me. But after insisting this is our best shot at ending Dragonblood, my stubborn steed falls silent, and the images disappear.

With a winning smile, I hurry into new clothes so we can Fade to Argentina.

I found the spell.

At long last, his soul will be saved. The world will never witness his cruelty again.

Now I must finish what I started.

—Excerpt from Edward Barnes's journal

CHAPTER TWENTY-FOUR

Lana

MADAME WAXBYRNE'S VILLA IS SECLUDED AT THE END OF AN empty street.

It sits right across from the sea, tucked in a pocket of sand-colored stone. Locals and tourists enjoy cocktails by the docks several feet away. It's nighttime in New Delhi, but it's almost four hours earlier in Valetta—a pink-orange sky serves as a canvas for the setting sun.

Thanks to a Cloaking Charm, Samira and I hurry down the street undetected. I narrowly avoid brushing three different guys' shoulders. Once we reach the villa's arched entrance, Samira drops the spell, but keeps me close to her.

"Are you gonna be good cop or bad cop?" she asks.

I can't stop hearing Victoria's last words to me. I'm the bad cop in her story. Part of me agrees. Calling her poison was horrible—she's had enough insults thrown at her. And the fact that I hadn't considered how painful it was to return to Puerto Rico… I deserve her fury.

Then I think of all the times she's put me down. How she treated me like filth while demanding I perform better in the Cup. Tough love isn't the same as being cruel.

Victoria can't understand what she's never been taught.

"Are you listening to me?" Samira pokes my belly.

I try a smile, but it feels too heavy to keep. "This isn't *Law & Order*, Samira…"

"I know, but choosing our roles is a crucial part of the interrogation."

"Oh, my God. Fine. You're good cop. Now can we break into this house?"

Samira's eyebrows shoot up. "We're not knocking first?"

"Why would she answer the door if she's hiding?"

"Bad cop indeed." Samira points the tip of her wand to the door. "I don't know what kind of tricks this lady has up her sleeve, so stay close to me *at all times*."

"Got it."

"Also, I really wanted to be bad cop, but you'll—"

The door opens.

A spacious living room lies ahead. It has a ceiling high enough to feel like I'm stepping into a Mediterranean palace.

"Get in quick." An American woman's voice echoes throughout the house. It's the same voice that greets customers in her recorded welcome message at Waxbyrne.

"She must've enchanted the walls to make them see-through," Samira whispers. "Clever."

And creepy…

Samira and I make our way into the house. The door slams shut as soon as we pass the archway. Madame Waxbyrne isn't on one of the mahogany leather couches, at the L-shaped dining table placed farther back, or on the small staircase leading to the second-floor balcony. Nothing here betrays a witch's presence. Not that I'm expecting smoke-filled cauldrons and Charmed grandfather clocks, but this is a surprisingly boring home for a Gold Wand.

"Sit," says Madame Waxbyrne. I still don't know where she is, but she sounds close.

"Yes, Ma'am." Samira rushes to the couch. I'm not sure if it's part of being the good cop, or if she's a little scared. She taps the spot next to her. "You heard the woman."

I join her on the couch.

Madame Waxbyrne says, "Why have you come?"

Wow. I figured the first thing she'd ask is how we found her, but I guess Samira's been in the news long enough for the world to know how awesome she is. Of course she must know who I am—how many teenage girls have rescued Fire Drakes in her wand shop? Maybe she suspected this would happen. Madame Waxbyrne doesn't sound upset. Her tone is... weary.

"We have a few questions regarding Cecilia Valcárcel," Samira says.

"And her relation to Randall Wiggins," I add tersely.

Crickets.

I check the staircase, but there's nobody. "Um... you still there?"

A door creaks behind me.

Its oval frame materializes under the stairs in a bright, golden thread. A middle-aged white woman flings it open. Her pale blue heels scrape the floor in soft, melodic *clicks*. Most of her hair is gray now, but there's some dark brown sprinkled here and there. Even without the heels she would be tall. I should've suspected her body had been edited to look slimmer in the dozens of magazine covers she's graced. Today she flaunts her curves in a pink sundress that matches Malta's afternoon sky.

"Samira Jones and Lana Torres." She says our names gently as she takes a seat across from me. "There are questions you're better off not asking. Knowing the answers could be far worse."

Not exactly encouraging. "Okay?" is all I can say.

"With all due respect, Ma'am, we still need to know them. The Sol de Noches are in grave danger." Samira is taking her good cop job *very* seriously. She's even keeping her voice down.

Guess I should fully embrace my bad cop persona.

"So is Willa," I say. "I doubt you'd want to repay the people helping Agent Robinson and his steed with silence, so spare us the theatrics. We're not leaving until we get answers."

Madame Waxbyrne places both hands on her lap. She sizes me up, then Samira.

"I am indeed in your debt, girls. But I also admire you. Samira's the only person who's ever found me. The amount of magical strength required... I can't even describe it. And you"—she peers at me—"what you did in Florida was heroic. Cooperation is the least I can offer."

Good.

I say, "We know about Cecilia's psychic magic and how she can remove dragon souls. We also know she freed Antonio Deluca. I think she and Randall Wiggins share the same dad, but there must be something else binding them. Are their powers tied to a curse?"

Madame Waxbyrne's hazel eyes grow three times their size.

"Am I right?" I prod.

"Partially." She crosses one leg over the other, holding onto her knee. "But none outside of the wand-maker community has even come close to guessing."

"Or maybe they've been too scared to consult you?" Samira says. "No offense, but when it comes to being approachable, wand-makers get an F. What's with the secrecy?"

"Precisely because of what your best friend just said. Dark magic permeates many aspects of a wand-maker's world. This isn't something we enjoy boasting about."

Any other day, I'd spend hours asking her for more details, but I only have time for one.

"What do you mean I'm *partially* right?"

"Cecilia and Randall possess similar abilities, but they're not bound by blood."

So the dad theory is out the window.

Madame Waxbyrne conjures a steaming mug of hot chocolate. She sips carefully, her gaze shifting from one heeled shoe to the other.

"How did they get their powers?" I ask. "Were they tampering with dark magic? Did their mothers do something weird? I mean, neither has a biological father."

"Both moms are Regulars, too," says Samira.

"You've done your research." There's something eerie about how Madame Waxbyrne whispers, how she keeps glancing down. "Cecilia and Randall were born on the same day from the same circumstances. Their stories don't begin with their mothers' pregnancies. But in order to understand them, I must tell another." She places the mug on her knee. "How's the Sire?"

Samira and I share petrified looks.

"His wings are growing back. And his fire's returning." Mentioning the bone throne isn't safe yet. I won't confess until Madame Waxbyrne gives us something to work with. "I struck him with one of Randall's Freeze Charms. But he's being kept somewhere that removes magic, and I wondered if that's why the Sire's getting stronger."

"This isn't his prison's doing." She nods. "It's starting."

"*What's* starting?" Samira sounds just as freaked out as I am.

"The Sire's case is unique because so is he. Everyone's tired of hearing how he's the first dragon to break his Bond, but they don't know how he did it."

"Holy crap. Do *you* know?" I'm almost dangling off the couch.

Madame Waxbyrne sighs as she conjures a another object.

It's a black Moleskine journal. Save for a few scratches, it's been preserved well.

The initials E.B. are engraved on the front.

"Is that… Did you just… How is it…" Samira can't finish a sentence. I have a feeling I wouldn't either if I tried.

"Edward left this with me before his death. It details many things I suspected, and one thing I did not. The Sire grew more disdainful with time. He took lives long before his Bond broke." Madame Waxbyrne presses her mug to her lips, but she doesn't drink. It's like she just wants to feel something as she speaks. "Edward was convinced he could save his soul. That he could find or create a spell to make him good. This desire led him to… experiments."

Samira grabs my wrist like she's watching a scary movie. I envy her—I can't move at all.

"He came to Iron Pointe asking for help. My colleague and I warned him not to pursue this further. Wand-makers understand souls better than anyone. But we didn't know the whole truth. The consequences we feared relate to a living soul—something the Sire doesn't posses."

Okay, now I'm flailing. "Why the hell not?"

"The Sire didn't fly out of the North Sea. Edward created him."

The first time a dragon and its rider meet is known as the Discovery. Whether it's a few minutes or several days, they share their innermost thoughts and get to know one another at a soul level. This doesn't mean they know everything by the time the Bond is sealed. They may spend their whole lives redefining their identities. Only one constant remains—both would die for the other.

—*Excerpt from Carlos Torres's* Studying the Bond Between Dragons & Humans

CHAPTER TWENTY-FIVE

Victoria

I'M EMBARRASSINGLY UNDERDRESSED FOR THIS COLD-ASS WEATHER. The Perito Moreno Glacier floats in the freezing southern waters of Patagonia. It reaches for the Argentine sky with its jagged teeth in gleaming turquoise. The snow-capped mountain where Esperanza and I are hiding is much bigger, but the glacier still seems like an imposing sea creature, covering close to ninety-eight square miles of the frigid Pacific Ocean.

Cecilia's ring has been placed at the glacier's center.

It has two additional floors today. There are longer lines outside. I didn't see which dragons were on the roster, but the crowd size makes me think it's a coveted matchup.

What a lovely day to rain on their parade.

Esperanza is scoping out the perimeter for Antonio Deluca. Cecilia could still be avoiding the ring, but he should be here. Instead of blindly searching for cages, Esperanza and I will corner him and demand he takes us to them.

I wish the search had ended twenty minutes ago, though. My black FILA jacket isn't thick enough for these harsh winds.

More people file into the stadium as the minutes tick by. I keep peeking behind me, but we're alone. Most of the Blood Masks are down by the stadium's entrance and surrounding areas. They scan tickets and closely monitor every attendee.

WHOOM!

Esperanza pauses the scene in my head, then replaces it with her view. She's looking at a narrow road behind the stadium. A lone Blood Mask is walking in circles as he speaks on his phone. He's waving his free hand around, seemingly upset. His suit is dark blue today. He's wearing a black parka and matching boots. But his devil mask is the same.

I rub her neck as a thank-you. "Muy bien, chica. Vamos a decirle hola a Antonio."

She disconnects me from her eyesight with a purr. After a quick Fade out of the mountain, we land right behind an unsuspecting Antonio.

He turns.

Esperanza slaps the phone away with her tail. Then she pins Antonio down. His abrupt fall carves brand new cracks in the ice. Esperanza Fades us back to the exact spot we'd been hiding on the mountain, miles away from his homicidal friends.

I dismount. "Where are the cages?"

"What… How did…" A flustered Antonio breaks into a sweat as Esperanza growls.

"Answer the question, Antonio."

"I don't know!"

"*Liar.*" I crouch next to him and seize his collar. My shivers are gone—the fury coursing through me is hotter than a Puerto Rican summer. "Don't make this worse for yourself. Tell me where they are and I promise you'll have less jail time than your girlfriend."

Antonio spits on the snow.

I pray he tries that shit with me. He'll be eating out of a straw for years.

"She's not my girlfriend!" the fool says. "And I swear I don't know where the cages are. I've been *trying* to get the dragons here, but she's not cooperating."

"What do you mean? Isn't the fight starting soon?"

"Yes! Master still won't answer me."

I open and close my mouth. Then I say, "Master?"

Antonio looks like he's about to spit again, but he lays his head back, as if our exchange is draining him. He's breathing steadily despite Esperanza's claw on his chest.

"She only responds when I call her that," he says.

"You narcissists deserve each other."

"It's not just her narcissism..."

I nod. "Go on."

Antonio curses in Italian. It's similar to Spanish, so I understand what he'd like me to eat.

"Don't make me repeat myself, Antonio."

Esperanza adds dramatic flair with a soft roar.

"Fine!" Snot hangs from Antonio's nose. It's such a rush to see the most obnoxious Blazewrath player cower at my mercy. "Six months ago, Cecilia freed me from a magical maze, after I was left to rot among hungry shadows and shrieking specters for two years. When she tore Randall's skullpit apart, I thought my mind was deceiving me. It was so... *easy* for her."

"She did you a favor. You should be thrilled."

Antonio looks like he's about to vomit.

You can't help me, he'd said back in New Zealand. That hadn't sounded like someone who's here voluntarily. Antonio doesn't care about a lenient sentence. If I find out why he's really helping Cecilia, I can offer him what he's desperate for. Searching for the Un-Bondeds will still take less time with him on my team—he understands Cecilia better than me.

I loosen my grip on his collar, but only slightly. "You're not working with her to pay a debt. There isn't an honorable bone in your body. You never do as you're told, either, which is why serving her has to be an involuntary act. How is she forcing you to obey her?"

Antonio turns his face away. Esperanza's growl is louder, but he doesn't look at us.

"Answer me!" I punch the snow. Not even the powder sticking to me can cool me down.

Esperanza digs her claw deeper into Antonio's chest.

He winces, then glances at me. Antonio bites down hard, drool slipping down the sides of his mouth. He's trembling. "You can't... help me..." he repeats in a weaker voice.

The blackness swirls out of Antonio's eyes.

Now they're the same hazel as Cecilia's.

He says, "Hola, Victoria."

But it's her voice.

I push away from him, gasping for air like I'm underwater. Lana had told me she'd seen this happen before. The Sire had hijacked President Turner's body in his own home. He'd been the Sire's Anchor—a magically tethered vessel that could feel excruciating pain whenever the Sire did, as well as his puppet. The Sire had *murdered* President Turner before cursing him. He'd been revived hours later, doomed to spend the rest of his half-life working for a monster.

Antonio isn't another Blood Mask.

He's Cecilia's Anchor.

"You're dead... I mean... you're undead..." I don't even know how to speak anymore.

"Antonio's not here right now. Would you like to leave a message?"

Cecilia's self-satisfied chuckle makes me want to sink her in the icy waters below. "Or better yet, say it to my face."

SWISH!

Cecilia Transports beside me.

I try decking her, but the conniving witch casts a Paralysis Charm. The invisible daggers begging for a taste of my ribs have returned. I whimper as Esperanza roars at Cecilia. The Gold Wand hits my steed with the same spell. Esperanza's body jerks, then stiffens. She's using all of her energy to crack Cecilia's magic apart, but it's a fruitless endeavor.

"Il mio amore?" Cecilia calls Antonio. "Stand up."

"Yes, Master." He hadn't moved this fast in any of his Blazewrath matches. With a gentle touch, Antonio dusts the snow off her daisy-white coat. He stands at attention once he's done.

Cecilia runs her fingers through his hair, but her expression is as cold as the glacier below. "I'm so happy you could make it, Victoria. For a moment, I feared you wouldn't take the bait, but you've done precisely what I expected. Having Antonio out in the open so you could catch him has been one of my cleverest ideas. Wouldn't you agree?" She pinches Antonio's cheek.

"Yes, Master."

My knuckles long for Cecilia's bones. This was a goddamn trap. I fell for it just like Lana had fallen for her dad's kidnapping. I'd given her so much grief, and I'm outshining her as the fool of the century—at least she had backup.

A thunderous roar rips out of Esperanza.

The sky suddenly feels like it's cascading down on me. I've brought my steed right to Cecilia, who's smiling at her like she's received the greatest birthday present of all time.

"No te preocupes. Nada le pasará a Victoria… si compites en el torneo."

She's just told Esperanza to compete in the tournament. If she refuses, I'll get hurt.

"¡No le hagas caso!" I tell Esperanza not to listen. She's huffing like this is the most indignant thing she's ever heard.

"Esperanza will fight today," says Cecilia. "Otherwise, she'll have to watch her starved opponent feast on you in front of our beautiful crowd."

"Go ahead, then! Just leave Esperanza alone!"

Of course I don't want to die, especially not in such a horrible fashion. But if I must choose between death and watching Esperanza in a Dragonblood match, I choose death.

Cecilia says, "Esperanza, ¿vas a competir?"

As soon as she's done asking her if she'll compete, my steed starts crying.

Her tears reflect my look of despair back at me. I wish I could use my sleeves to pat her eyes dry, and hug her as tight as possible. I keep yelling at her in Spanish, trying to convince her not to fight, but she's only focused on Cecilia.

Then Esperanza bows her head.

"No…" Her consent is a bullet to my soul. I'm nothing more than a pile of fast falling tears. "Esperanza, por favor… no lo hagas…"

"Very good!" A smirking Cecilia claps. "Time for the main event!"

CHAPTER TWENTY-SIX

Lana

"**E**DWARD BARNES CREATED A DRAGON?" EVEN AS I SAY IT, THE
words don't quite click. The most respected bureau agent Charmed a
creature to life. He registered a sentient spell as his real steed. Legalities
aside, how is that magic even *possible*?

Madame Waxbyrne puts the journal beside her. She runs a finger
down the spine. "He didn't understand why dragons seldom Bonded
with magic users. The more he studied the Bond, the more he desired a
steed. His expertise as a dragon anatomist helped him design the perfect
Fire Drake. He didn't want a crystal heart—the dragon itself would be
his wish-come-true."

"Was this like your Other Body Charm?" I say.

"No. What I did to fool the Sire wasn't meant to last. We also used
different ingredients." Madame Waxbyrne's upper lip twitches. "But
when he started losing control of his steed, he stuck his nose into my
school and made everything worse."

Samira shrugs. "Did he steal? Learn something he shouldn't?"

"Both."

I can't fault Edward Barnes entirely. If *my* dragon were hurting people, I'd try to save him.

Barnes duped the whole world, though. Is this why he sacrificed himself? Had the guilt eaten him alive? He was never meant to be a rider. And what's worse, he brought a killer to life. *A dragon's call is holding hands in the dark*, Takeshi had said. Barnes ripped the dark open and forced his way into it. Now we're all paying for his mistake.

His own son paid the highest cost.

Don't dwell on that now.

I say, "You said wand-makers understand souls better than anyone. How did Barnes use this knowledge? And what does he have to do with Randall and Cecilia?"

There goes that lip twitching again.

Madame Waxbyrne empties her mug, then shakily places it on top of the journal.

"A wand-maker's job is to channel magical energy into inanimate objects. We must ensure these vessels never break. Some materials are stronger than others. At Iron Pointe, we worked with an extensive variety, but one has been more commonly used in recent times."

God, she loves talking herself in circles.

"And that material is?" I coax.

Madame Waxbyrne looks me dead in the eye. "Dragon souls."

I shoot up. "*What?* You're killing dragons?!" Samira is restraining me, but I'd never lay a hand on this pathetic excuse for a woman. She's seriously admitting to such a revolting act? No wonder Iron Pointe is wrapped around secrecy. This isn't about having their methods stolen.

They're covering up crimes.

"No," Madame Waxbyrne speaks. "When a dragon loses its soul, it may still live."

"*May?*"

"I know it sounds horrible, Lana."

"Oh, you can't even imagine."

"Soul extraction *and* containment," Samira interrupts. "They're both possible."

Madame Waxbyrne nods. "Not every wand-maker can achieve this. My colleague, Julia Serrano, perfected the craft. Edward Barnes walked in on her shaping a Gold wand with a Schlange's soul. He wanted to learn how to put another dragon's soul into the Sire's body. Julia and I explained the dangers of such complex magic. And Julia always extracted souls from dragon eggs. When they hatched, they grew up without the capacity to Bond."

I can't pinpoint when the bile started rising in my throat.

I'm thrust back to the couch. The first Puerto Rican wand-maker to have studied at Iron Pointe created Un-Bondeds. Others before her have also cast this atrocious spell. Papi's hard work, his tireless studies… Greedy magic users are to blame. They'd rather make a quick buck than preserve Earth's greatest marvels.

Samira covers her mouth, sitting beside me at a snail's pace. Her plans to study at Iron Pointe have just crashed and burned. So has everything we ever believed.

"This is too much to take in. I apologize," says Madame Waxbyrne.

"Did Barnes steal the soul?" I *have* to move on before I punch a hole in the wall.

She glances at the journal, sighing. "Yes. When he tried containing it, the link between him and his false steed snapped. The Sire's true nature was unleashed. This also led to Doomfall." She tries to meet my gaze but can only focus on her hands. "Dark magic begets greater darkness. A curse created two more, and these were born in *human* form. They were wicked enchantments in the shape of wicked children."

Holy crap. The Evil Wonder Twins aren't actually *people*.

They're curses.

"They were always meant for terrible things…" I whisper.

"Theoretically, but they have free will, too. However, their circumstances didn't steer them away from embracing their cruel nature. For Randall, it was being raised as a weapon. And Cecilia… She had a best friend. Enid."

"The girl who went missing?" I ask. "Agent Robinson said Cecilia hadn't given him any information regarding her disappearance. Did she hurt her?"

"Never," Madame Waxbyrne says curtly. "I did."

Samira's hands fall. "You hurt a student?"

"Enid had been… chaotic. She and Cecilia were convinced they could run Iron Pointe in my and Julia's absence. It started as pranks— dead animals hanging from our doorways, stolen possessions that were Charmed to attack us. Then secret visits to the extraction chamber grew frequent. They also snuck out to practice with Bonded dragons. When Julia and I discovered Enid fighting a steed, she struck to kill us. But we were faster. By the time Cecilia realized what we did, Julia had joined the search for the Sire, and I was left to face her alone."

I don't know what's crueler—the truth behind Randall and Cecilia's powers, or knowing this whole mess could've been avoided. Randall's deterioration took longer. Still, finding out your teachers murdered your best friend, and that they covered it up… I would've gone feral, too. Dragonblood remains Cecilia's *choice*, though. My pity for her can only extend so far.

"How do we defeat her?" I say. "I mean, Randall's dead, but I'm not killing Cecilia." We can take her powers with Dragonshade, too, but I can't let her drive me into the most bitter, vengeful version of myself. It's like our former stylist, Marisol Cabán, had said: "You're not on the menu, mamita." Regardless of how helpless I want Cecilia to feel, I'd rather lock her up without her magic.

Madame Waxbyrne's expression is grim. "My time has been consumed with finding Doomfall's counter-curse. I have been unsuccessful thus far. Some curses never truly die."

I'm knitting my eyebrows together. "What are you talking about?"

"Doomfall might not be reversible, Lana. Cecilia, the Un-Bondeds, they could outlive us."

"Okay, but—"

The right side of the house explodes.

I'm launched to the opposite wall. My left shoulder takes most of the hit, but my head and hip slam into concrete, too. Samira lands beside me with a yelp. The living room has been turned into Ground Zero, dust and smoke flying everywhere. There's a loud ringing that drowns out whatever Samira's saying. She's frantically pulling me behind her, but I can't hear a word.

Dragon Knights spill through the hole on the wall. There are five, ten, twenty, then way too many to count. Two steal Samira's wand while another locks his arms around her.

Dragons stand watch just outside the smashed wall. Four Irish Spikes, three Scottish Golden Horns, three British Fire Drakes, five Norwegian Lindworms, and two Brazilian Pesadelos.

When another explosion goes off elsewhere, I know two things for sure.

My hearing is back.

And we're under siege.

"What a charming place you have here, Glenda."

He's the only one not wearing his hood up, exposing the pale skin covered in coal-dark veins. His blond hair is swept back, but it's stringier and greasy, as if he hasn't washed it in weeks. The spring in his step remains. So does the stone-cold grin I thought I'd never see again.

"Now take me to those beautiful Sol de Noches," says Randall Wiggins.

Enid and Cecilia were inseparable. Whenever one displayed bad behavior, the other defended her. I still remember the day I caught Cecilia hanging a classmate's decapitated rabbit outside his window. Enid said the rabbit's owner had Charmed the animal into attacking them. Although her claim was verified, we wondered how Cecilia could be capable of such violence.

She simply replied: "Hurt my best friend, and I'll hurt you worse."

—Audio sample of Madame Waxbyrne's interrogation after Enid Mendoza's disappearance; property of Iron Pointe Academy

CHAPTER TWENTY-SEVEN

Victoria

CECILIA SITS ME ON A HIGH-BACKED CHAIR NEXT TO HERS.

They're cushioned in plush velvet, as red as the banners hanging around the stadium.

Cecilia and I sit on a separate platform that floats between the pit entrances. The platform is solid gold, and so are these seats. She's showing us off like queens at a royal ball.

I'd enjoy the glitz and glamour if I weren't magically tethered to this chair. The Paralysis Charm is even crueler when I'm sitting down—the bone-numbing pressure on my ribs ripples down to my hips and thighs. Moving feels like tearing through concrete with a jackhammer.

But it can never hurt more than Esperanza's psychic block.

I bang on her psychic walls while waiting for her match to begin. I don't know where Esperanza or her opponents are being kept. The worst part is she's *choosing* to be alone. I understand she wants to spare me from whatever she's experiencing, but we've been caught because of me. *I* should be the one in that ring.

"Are you excited?" Cecilia's voice is like that jarring motion after a rollercoaster car sets off. Even if you brace yourself, it still gives you whiplash. The sadist takes a steaming pink teacup from Antonio, who I'm positive must be sulking behind his devil mask.

"What exactly would I be excited about?" I grumble.

"Esperanza's grand debut! She'll be spectacular, I'm sure."

"Is that what you tell yourself before bed every night? How you justify killing innocent dragons? That they'll be *spectacular*?"

"Ay, Victoria. No seas una gilipollas." After calling me stupid, Cecilia sips on her tea, pinky up and all. She couldn't be more of a wannabe rich girl.

I almost gasp—money isn't everything she's after.

She also wants Willa.

Killing her is *personal*. With a Sol de Noche in her grasp, Willa remains Cecilia's biggest failure. I doubt someone as conceited as her appreciates being labeled a loser. I would never betray Willa's true hiding place, but what if I convince Cecilia to free Esperanza in exchange for the dragon she really wants? I'll give her a fake location, tell Esperanza to alert the other Sol de Noches, and have Task Force Blaze trap Cecilia like the rat she is.

We're in a sold-out stadium. She's not canceling this fight. Either a riot will ensue, or they'll ask for their money back. Unless I suggest *adding* Willa to the match... It would be the first three-creature Dragonblood event in history—well worth the price of admission.

"I asked you a question," says Cecilia. "Where's your head at, linda?"

I've never hated being called pretty more. "Do you want a legendary match?"

"I already have it." She drinks more tea.

"Who's Esperanza's opponent?"

"A dragon," she says with a giggle.

"I have a better suggestion."

"Ooh, look at you. Il mio amore"—she pulls on Antonio's coat—"Victoria has a *suggestion*." When she faces me again, she rests her chin on one hand, holding the teacup high. "Which is?"

I say, "Willa."

Cecilia loses her grip on the teacup, but she clutches it quickly. Antonio almost breaks his neck turning to me so fast. When he stares at Cecilia, she licks her lips, then bites down on the lower one. She's looking down at the icy pit with longing.

"Did you hear me? I can give you Willa. You can have the first Dragonblood match with *three* dragons. One of them will be the steed you've been dying to find."

Her silence is worse than her giggles—she could suspect I'm lying.

Try harder.

"Think about it," I say. "After two years, she'll finally be yours. No more searching."

Cecilia's perking up again, smiling at her teacup. "She'll finally be mine…"

"Yes."

"And you'd betray her so easily?"

"The more distracted Esperanza's opponent is with Willa, the better Esperanza's chances are of winning. My steed will be the queen of the ring. Your audience gets a show they'll never forget, and you'll have your long-awaited revenge."

I desperately need to wash my tongue with bleach.

Cecilia relaxes her shoulders as she leans back. "You'll take me to Willa. That's not up for discussion." She sips her tea. "But it'll be *after* Esperanza's fight."

Oh, I think not.

"Don't you want to make Dragonblood history?" I ask as calmly as possible, even though I'm screaming on the inside. *This fight cannot happen!*

"Willa doesn't belong in the ring. Her execution is for me alone. I have very special plans for her." Cecilia hands over the empty teacup to Antonio. While he passes it on to another male Blood Mask, she says, "Thank you for making my dreams come true."

This twisted witch isn't taking the bait. I can't save Esperanza.

But I can still delay the fight.

"Why do you hate Madame Waxbyrne so much?" This is my last resort. If Cecilia goes on a rant against her former mentor, it'll give me time to finally contact Esperanza.

She says, "She killed my best friend."

I was *not* expecting it to get this dark. "What?"

Cecilia laughs at my expression—it must be hilarious to watch me almost have a heart attack. "You look a little bit like her. Her name was Enid, and she was perfect."

If she's expecting me to be honored, joke's on her. I'm as frozen as the glacier below us.

Then I realize this is yet another prime opportunity to distract her.

"Why did Madame Waxbyrne kill her?"

A dry laugh escapes Cecilia. "You don't need my past."

"But I want it. The last thing I expected was for you to *care* about someone." I almost turn to Antonio. Then I remember how horribly painful that would be. "What happened to Enid?"

Cecilia's sad smile would break my heart if I gave a shit about her.

"I'd been a runaway orphan for three months when the staff found me. They lured me in by promising free meals and a bed. How could I say no? But when I arrived, my classmates made fun of my dirty clothes and shoes. They called me La Callejera."

The street urchin. "Did the staff intervene?"

"Enid did. She defended me constantly. Sometimes she protected others from my wrath." Cecilia flips her hair like she's in a shampoo commercial. "I wasn't very nice."

I can relate. Growing up, I wasn't the most fun person to be around, especially the day after my stepfather would hurt Mami or me. I was too small—too scared—to fight him. My classmates usually found themselves in screaming matches with me, and I'd start them all. Even the littlest thing sent me over the edge. It was the only way I could feel in charge again.

"Why did Madame Waxbyrne kill her?" I insist. I can't wrap my head around the most famous wand-maker being a murderer, and I don't even *know* her.

Cecilia takes a deep breath, glowering at the floor. "She's evil, Victoria. And she was always so jealous of my powers. She went after Enid first. As if a broken heart would lessen the strength of my spells. I found my best friend's body at the foot of a mountain. She looked like she was making a snow angel—arms and legs splayed, a bloody smile carved on her face."

This still isn't adding up. "Why didn't the bureau arrest her?"

"The school covered up Enid's death. Her parents only called the bureau because they hadn't heard from her in weeks. She's still considered missing."

"Why would Iron Pointe cover up murders? And why didn't *you* come forward?"

Cecilia runs a finger across her seat's armrest. "Iron Pointe will never fall. If I wanted Madame Waxbyrne to pay, I'd have to take everything she loved."

A teacher murders her student, keeps it secret, and runs a global empire in hiding. Her cowardice led a teenage girl to unleash her inner John Wick. Enid must've been as dangerous as Cecilia, though. Otherwise this personal vendetta goes beyond anything I've ever seen.

Cecilia lost her best friend. Now she's about to take mine.

She's using Esperanza just like the Sire used me—we're part of agendas we never asked to be included in. I know what it's like to be someone's toy, and another person's punching bag.

But I'll never allow Esperanza to suffer.

"You don't have to go through with this," I say. "You already have enough money to live comfortably for the rest of your life. Take it and disappear, Cecilia. These dragons have *nothing* to do with what happened to Enid. Why do you want to hurt them?"

"Madame Waxbyrne said I'd never be stronger than a dragon. She called me their inferior. A month before she killed my best friend, I told her she was wrong. I promised to prove it, but I didn't know how. Then Enid died. My rage showed me the way."

"Enid wouldn't have wanted this for you. She would've tried to—"

"Ay, you're boring me, linda." Cecilia nods to Antonio. "Let's start the show."

Antonio signals to another Blood Mask near the arena. When the Blood Mask walks off into the corridor, I poke at Esperanza's psyche, but her wall is still up.

"Wait! Let me take you to Willa! She can—"

Horns blare across the stadium.

The crowd cheers as Cecilia rises, her brown hair flowing down her back. She waves at her admirers with a queen's poise. "Welcome to Dragonblood, everyone! What a lovely day for a match!" Her silky voice echoes throughout the glacier. "Bring out the dragons!"

It's been three days since his poisoning.
There are no signs of further deterioration. He just keeps repeating their
names.
Takeshi Endo.
Samira Jones.
Lana Torres.

—Director Sandhar's notes on Randall's progress, three days after his
fatal poisoning; property of the International Bureau of Magical Matters

CHAPTER TWENTY-EIGHT

Lana

ANDREW'S KILLER IS STILL ALIVE.

Some curses never truly die.

Randall casually strolls toward me.

"Leave them alone!" Madame Waxbyrne implores. A Dragon Knight holds a knife to her throat, but she's still courageous enough to address Randall.

He cups my face in his gloved hands. Even if I could knock him out, his goons will retaliate. I'm not about to let my best friend die.

"Lana Torres." He says my name like it's a song he's rehearsed for years. It spills out of him in such an easy, familiar way. "I've been dreaming about you for weeks. Along with you"—he looks at Samira—"and Takeshi Endo, of course. I'm saving all three for last."

His threat takes me back to Brazil. I scream as he drain's Andrew's blood. When his heart stops, Randall celebrates. Now he's come to stop mine, too.

I unravel into tremors.

Randall cackles. My weakness has probably added ten years to his life.

"Glenda, it's been a pleasure destroying your ugly home. After weeks of surveillance, I'm happy I don't have to see it again." Randall looks over her shoulder. "Or you."

Madame Waxbyrne is a bone-white painting. Her dread overpowers any instinct to survive.

Then she says, "I can help you free him."

"Wish I could believe you. Besides, your successor has already made a better offer."

Oh, my God. Does he mean Cecilia? These wicked enchantments are working together?

"Randall, I—"

He aims Samira's wand at her, then flicks his wrist.

Madame Waxbyrne disappears. The Dragon Knight holding the knife is also gone.

"Where did you send her?" Samira yells.

"Somewhere she can watch her lover die. But first"—Randall touches his cold forehead to mine, and my shivers grow stronger—"I have a meeting with Puerto Rico's dragons."

An ivory veil wraps around the room. It vacuums us all into a white blur. Randall is still holding me, still cackling, as I sob into the void.

I'm back at the hangar.

I kneel in front of a killer, watching my mother and friends realize we've returned.

"Lana!" Mom runs to me, but Agent Robinson grabs her.

Dragon Knights and Un-Bondeds guard Samira and me from the steeds roaring at them. Esperanza isn't here. She and Victoria must be in another room.

"This can end quickly if you cooperate." Randall releases me; my cheeks still tingle where leather met flesh. He walks closer to an open-mouthed Takeshi. "But *your* death will be slow."

Takeshi only looks my way. It's the same expression he had in Nantes—I have just ruined his plans, and he's scrambling to figure out how to save me.

My limbs are boulders, weighed down and useless. The shivers won't go away, either.

"Where's Esperanza?" Randall asks.

"Missing," is all Takeshi says.

"Interesting. And her rider?"

"Also missing. We were about to search for them."

"How sweet." Randall presses Samira's wand against Takeshi's chest. He runs the tip up his shirt, stopping at his Adam's apple. "I hope the Sol de Noches can free the Sire without her."

"Let Lana and Samira go first." Takeshi's tone is much calmer than my racing pulse.

"You're in no position to propose a trade, Takeshi. Free my master now."

"Once the girls are safe, the steeds can—"

Randall presses the tip deeper. "I won't repeat myself."

Daga wails to the hangar's ceiling. She's stomping her back legs, too. Fantasma and Rayo are cuddling up to her, purring in unison, as if they're trying to comfort her, but she keeps crying.

When Randall laughs, his protruding veins wriggle. They're black cobras searching for an escape. "I know, baby. This is all so upsetting. But your friend here is being a little bitch. Hand over the Sire, or I crack open his skull."

If I don't do something, Takeshi will die *and* the Sire will be released. But I don't have the counter-curse to defeat Randall. How am I supposed to fight him?

He thinks he's in charge. But if he's working with Cecilia, he's just her pawn.

Turn the curses against each other.

"What did Cecilia promise you?" I dare to ask. "Was she the one who healed you? Did she send you to watch over Madame Waxbyrne? You're too strong to be someone's servant, Randall. First the Sire, now Cecilia… Why would you let them treat you like their inferior?"

All eyes are on me. I want to scream at the dragons to Fade, but there's no way I can communicate without actually screaming, so I settle for staring at Héctor.

His nod is almost imperceptible. He closes his eyes, as if he's trying to reach out to Titán.

Randall turns ever so slightly. "She speaks."

"Lana, please don't," Takeshi begs. His Adam's apple bobs up and down.

"Oh, no, let her go on! I've missed her nonsense." Randall is fully facing me now, but the wand is still on Takeshi. "I serve the Sire. Cecilia is merely my accomplice."

"Did she spring you from the bureau?" Samira chimes in. God bless her soul.

"Her Blood Masks saved me, yes. The Dragonshade almost ate me alive. She told me my magic would slowly defeat it, and she was right. Then she showed me Antonio Deluca." Randall sighs happily. "Only a legendary witch could destroy my skullpit. So we struck a deal. I'd find the Sol de Noches and free my master. Then I'd hand the dragons over."

Like I said—total pawn.

"How did you even track this Other Place, Randall? How did you get through Madame Waxbyrne's traps? Your *magic* helped you, not Cecilia. She knows you can get her what she wants, and she'll betray you once these dragons are hers."

He narrows his gaze. I've never seen him confused, but it's a glorious sight.

"Betray me how?" As he's shaking his head, Génesis and Gabriela close their eyes, then Luis and Edwin jump in. They must be reaching out to their steeds.

Keep going.

I say, "She'll use your curse against you."

Randall is on the verge of launching a thousand ships to war. His black veins swirl faster. "What are you talking about? I'm not cursed!"

"That's what she wants you to believe. Let me help you, Randall. I can stop it."

"WHAT ARE YOU TALKING ABOUT?" Randall is seconds away from ripping his matted hair out. He holds up his hands, realization dawning on his face. "What did Madame Waxbyrne tell you, huh? Did she put you up to this?"

"Let me help you," I repeat. "Together we can find a—"

"SHUT UP!"

Randall shoots a black lightning bolt at Takeshi's arm.

"Argh!" Takeshi convulses on the floor.

"Get the Sol de Noches!" Randall yells.

Flames and dragon roars erupt all around me.

The lightning around Takeshi's arm is gone, but smoke still coils around it. A jagged scar swirls from wrist to elbow. It's as dark as Randall's veins. And it's writhing in the same pattern.

"Always happy to return the favor." Randall points at his veins.

There's no darker magic than a cruel heart. Ill intent is a necessary component of curse casting, but there are worse things than condemning your enemies to a lifetime of misfortune. We don't require metal wands to ensure suffering—they're mere conductors of our terrible wishes. The wish itself is the root of evil. So is the joy that comes from knowing the wish has come true.

—Excerpt from Corwin Sykes's Dark & Dastardly: Obscure Magical Folklore & Enchantments for Beginners

CHAPTER TWENTY-NINE

Victoria

MY BEAUTIFUL ESPERANZA ENTERS THE RING FIRST.

Her neck and legs are chained. She sluggishly plods onward; the ice is sturdy despite her weight. Esperanza keeps her head down as Cecilia's audience cheers her on.

"She's the first dragon born in Puerto Rico! The first Sol de Noche to ever compete in Dragonblood! Everyone, put your hands together for the one… the only… Esperanza!"

Cecilia claps along with the other creeps here. Perhaps I should be thrilled to see how much support my steed has—she's the clear favorite. But it doesn't make this impending battle more bearable. Dragons don't get voted off the glacier for being unpopular.

Esperanza patiently waits at the center of the ring. She's a black dot in a frozen sea.

My psychic nudges are a waste of time. That dark wall remains.

Why isn't Task Force Blaze intervening? Are they even here yet? I hate the sudden pang of guilt that washes over me. If I had obeyed Takeshi, Esperanza and I wouldn't be in this mess. I'd give anything to have him run into the ring like I did in Nantes. Lana would be much faster, though. She could've gotten Esperanza to safety while Takeshi fought off her captors. Samira could've given Cecilia the duel she deserves.

And I ruined everything.

Lana was fucking right—I *am* poison.

I scrunch my nose as tears fall. I stomp the floor in protest. Daggers drive themselves into my ribcage. They hurt like hell, but I'd rather be in extreme pain than witness Esperanza's murder. I have to bring that psychic wall down. Two minds are so much better than one.

Today the wall is as tall as the dunes Lana ran up in Dubai. Scaling it would take too long. I have to go *through* it, but how do I shatter this stony contraption?

"This next fighter is also entering our ring for the first time!" Cecilia says. "Our youngest competitor at eleven months old, please give it up for Argentina's Garra de Hierro!"

My jaw drops. "Shit."

As the applause grows louder, a new dragon enters the ring.

The Argentine Garra de Hierro is the closest thing to the sun in dragon form. Its scales are dandelion-yellow, and its beady eyes shimmer in mesmerizing gold. It's one of the smallest species—about forty feet tall—but those silver claws make up for its petite body. They can grow three times their original size, and the Garra de Hierro is capable of extending them from ten to twenty feet, depending on its age. And it can morph its extremities into blades.

I need to get Esperanza's wall down *now*.

"Dragons, wait for my signal!" says Cecilia.

The Garra de Hierro lowers itself until its chest touches the ice. Then it lifts its wagging tail, which moves as slow as a pendulum. Esperanza doesn't even blink. She's not showing any signs of fear, but that doesn't mean I'm the only one who's terrified.

I return to the psychic wall, which suddenly seems even more daunting. I visualize it crumbling into a pile of rocks. I picture a fireball piercing through the stone, then more fireballs, until my mind becomes a low-budget production of the Apocalypse.

The wall is still up.

Esperanza, ¡déjame entrar!

She can't hear me begging her to let me in.

"These are the rules! Esperanza isn't allowed to Fade. She's not allowed to communicate with her rider, Victoria Peralta." When Cecilia mentions me, people clap like I'm part of the main event, too. I glare at the stands. "If she disobeys, her rider will be executed!"

The cheering reaches astronomical levels. I never thought so many people would be this excited about my death. Now I want to spite them even more and make sure Esperanza wins. I just don't know how to get that Argentine dragon to stand down without injuring it.

Forget about the Garra. Focus on the wall!

Cecilia says, "Let the Dragonblood spill!"

A horn goes off.

The Garra de Hierro springs into the air.

Esperanza wraps herself in flames. I don't see how that helps—fire is no match for those steel claws! The Garra takes three swipes at her face, but Esperanza jumps back unharmed. She's roaring at her opponent, too. The Garra responds with a full display of its pearly fangs.

Then its claws start growing.

The dragon is still too young for them to reach twenty feet, but they're at least ten.

Esperanza isn't moving.

"¡Vuela!" I yell at her to fly.

My plea falls on deaf ears. She's not even looking my way.

The Garra propels itself forward. Its broadswords are extended toward Esperanza's chest.

"ESPERANZA, ¡VUELA AHORA MISMO!"

I scream as steel finds fire.

BOOM!

The Garra is shot backward. Its twisting body nearly collides with the side of the ring.

People are either gasping, swearing, or staying silent. As the dragon regains control of its limbs, more gasps ensue.

Esperanza's fire is still covering her.

But it's hardened into rock. It has a bumblebee-colored sheen, and it's thin enough to see her safely encased within—she's turned her flames into a *shield*.

"How did she do that?" Developing a brand new ability during a fight isn't ideal, but this is so much better than getting stabbed through the heart.

Now back on its feet, the Garra leaps over Esperanza, striking its swords against the shield. They keep sliding like socks on a wet surface. When the Garra lands on the ice again, it charges Esperanza with double the speed. The blades make no headway on shattering Esperanza's fire shield. With every failed stab, the Garra shrieks in desperation. It flies around to find new angles to attack.

"This is wonderful." Cecilia turns to me, hands clutched to her chest. "Does she have more tricks up her sleeve?"

"Not that I know of," I say.

"Did you know about this ability?"

"No."

Cecilia nods. "I do love it, but avoiding a fight will only make things worse for you."

Her frosty gaze isn't exactly comforting. Will the match get canceled so the Garra can kill me instead? I suspect Esperanza will be forced to watch my execution. It doesn't matter how honorably my steed is acting. Cecilia wants blood, and she'll have it.

The longer the Garra tries to smash the shield, the heavier it pants. Giving up isn't in its vocabulary. Its sole purpose is to get Esperanza out of her fire, even if it's exhausting.

Of course... Esperanza isn't avoiding a fight. She's tiring her opponent out! Once the Garra is close to either fainting or throwing in the towel, she'll strike.

"She's only trying to drain the Garra of energy," I tell Cecilia. "Esperanza will fight once it's easier to win. You'll see."

"I'd better." Cecilia points her wand to her neck, activating that annoying loudspeaker spell. "Esperanza, baja el escudo y pelea. Si vos rehúsa, Victoria muere."

She's threatened to kill me if Esperanza doesn't drop the shield.

Esperanza closes her eyes. Even though I can't feel what she's feeling, that heavy look on her face tells me she's devastated. I wish I could tell her to Fade. She'd never abandon me. If this must end with death, she won't let it be mine, but if that shield goes down, it'll definitely be hers.

WHOOM!

The black wall goes down.

I'm hit with a kaleidoscope of rainbows. They swirl in waves of eye-popping brightness. Then a single cloud of neon red explodes into view—my favorite color burns bright and hot. Its warmth drapes itself over me, heating me up better than any winter coat.

Esperanza's roars sound far away. When they draw nearer, each note changes into a series of soft, constant mumbles. If the Paralysis Charm wasn't gripping me, I'd fall off from the shock—she's forming her very first words. The mumbles continue for only a second.

She finally wrangles them into a coherent message: *T... te... amo.*

I don't need Cecilia's magic to hold me in place. My body is frozen stiff. After two years, Esperanza can speak. Yet her message isn't a cause for celebration.

It's a goodbye.

Esperanza, ¿qué estás haciendo? Por favor, no–

Her shield morphs back into crackling flames. She's shooting them out to the Garra de Hierro, who narrowly escapes the blast with a wicked smile.

"Perfect! Now *this* is what I signed up for!" says Cecilia.

Esperanza whips around as she lights her tail on fire. The Garra swings a blade at her neck, but she rolls to the left. Her tail slaps the Garra hard across the face. Even though it yelps, the Garra shakes the fire off, then lunges at Esperanza. She sinks her fangs into the claw. With a jerk, Esperanza flings the Garra behind her. The Argentine dragon fans its wings to stop its momentum. Then it flies down, both claws extended toward Esperanza's eyes.

A surge of adrenaline crashes over me—I'm locked into her emotional state again. The kaleidoscope is now a grayscale painting that's as chilly as this glacier. Either Esperanza's too distracted to block me, or she's choosing to let me help her.

There's not a second to waste. *¡Vuela!*

Esperanza leaps seconds before the swords find her eyes. She's bounding over the Garra like a Runner in a Block Zone, fast and frantic. She's about to land behind her rival.

The Garra whirls around.

It drives a sword into Esperanza's side.

"NO!" I foolishly try jumping to my feet. Cecilia's spell is ripping me apart, but the pain is nothing compared to seeing Esperanza topple down with a gut-wrenching wail. She hits the ice on her injured side and slides away in a spiral. There's a bloody trail in her wake.

"Garra! Garra! Garra!" the crowd chants.

¡Párate, por favor!

Even though Esperanza starts to stand, the Garra sinks its fangs into her neck. It pins her upper body against the ice. Then it alternates its claws, stabbing her repeatedly.

"STOP IT! PLEASE DON'T KILL HER!"

Tears and snot mix together. My best friend is dying. Two years of the strongest love I've ever known are being ripped out of my life. I keep psychically imploring her to leave. My addled mind races with thoughts of shrouding Esperanza with her fire shield. *Protégete*, I tell her, but the world she's showing me remains a grayscale painting. Her energy wanes with every breath.

She lights herself up again, burning the shit out of the Garra de Hierro. As it retreats in agony, Esperanza's legs are shaking. She keeps falling like a hatchling learning to walk.

I can't see the ring anymore.

There are only silver scales that shine like diamonds.

The Sire's scarlet eyes flash before mine.

Lightning seizes me in a fist of punishing bolts. I'm writhing, screaming.

Dying.

The Weekly Scorcher: Why would Lana be scared of facing herself?

Todd Anderson: She's deeply insecure. And she's not as nice as people believe. Growing up, I couldn't do anything without her undermining my success, but the worst thing is her pathetic faith in dragons. One day, she'll realize she's been duped. They're going to let her down when she least expects it, and she'll regret ever choosing them over family.

—Excerpt from Todd Anderson's exclusive with The Weekly Scorcher

CHAPTER THIRTY

Lana

I DUCK AS THE SOL DE NOCHES' FIREBALLS FLY PAST ME.

They scorch a handful of Dragon Knights. Soon our enemies are piles of bones and soot. This is the second time I have seen a Sol de Noche burn our enemies—Titán had defended us from other Knights at the São Paulo sanctuary. It still doesn't make me feel any better. What a horrifying way to die.

My head and ears pound something fierce. The hangar becomes a festival of screams, roars, and the constant blast of killing spells. The riders are mounting their steeds; Mom and Joaquín are huddled behind a fire-breathing Willa.

Samira connects an uppercut to Randall's chin as she wrests her wand away with the other hand.

I drag myself toward Takeshi. He's too weak to move, groaning with every tired breath. Hugging him probably isn't helping, but I don't know what else to do. I'm shaking and ruining his clothes with never-ending tears. Randall has scrubbed the world clean of hope again. Takeshi only has three days to live… if he even makes it out of here.

His best friend is dead because of me. Now I'll lose him, too.

"Lana…" His whisper brings me back.

"No, don't speak. You need to save your strength."

"Don't… feel sad… Just go…"

"Stop talking."

"Please go…"

Takeshi slurs the rest of his words. I've never seen him this pale, this helpless. He's not the boy who wins Blazewrath World Cups and infiltrates the Sire's army.

He's the boy I like, and he's dying.

I cry into his shirt. The sweet smell of flowers still clings to him. Takeshi tries running a hand down my back, but he can barely lift it. His sigh is as cracked as my heart.

Samira casts a golden Shield Charm around us. She's pushing the shield farther out to cover the rest of Task Force Blaze. The Un-Bondeds try to burn us, too, but the shield is too powerful.

"Let me look at him!" Samira bounds toward Takeshi. "Maybe we can treat it!"

"Dragonshade has no treatment or cure. He's going to…" I can't say it in his presence. Of course he already knows, but spelling it out makes it so… *final*.

"YOU'RE NOT GOING ANYWHERE."

Randall unleashes a wave of golden light from his hands. He directs his spell at Samira's shield, which is crumbling at the edges.

She's not falling back, though. My best friend keeps her defensive stance.

I spot Mom on the floor—she's right outside the shield's edge. Randall is either too angry to notice, or he'd rather kill Samira first.

"Help her!" I yell. I can't unglue myself from the poisoned boy in my arms.

The fight rages on.

I look back to Mom. She's right in front of Randall.

She thrusts a merciless hook into his stomach. The Gold Wand doubles over in surprise and pain, and his golden light disappears.

A Dragon Knight lunges for Mom's ankles. She drags herself past the shield a split second before they reach her. The Dragon Knight's hand is singed right off.

Titán grabs Mom with his tail. Fire and magic keep striking the shield. It's a light show brighter than a Magic Kingdom parade and an EDM festival combined. It's also messier—dragons are slamming into one another, and even stepping on their Dragon Knight allies.

BOOM!

Samira's shield blows up into a huge cloud of gold dust.

I'm launched to the floor. "Ow!"

Takeshi's chilled hand finds mine. "Lana… *Go!*"

"Will you shut up? I'm not leaving you!"

My clothes stick to me as I stand. Héctor and Titán leap in front of me, alternating fireballs between a Spike and a Pesadelo. While the Spike hogs most of Titán's attention, the Pesadelo flies high, then dives for his black wings—it's trying to bite them.

The Sol de Noches whine together.

Their cries are unbearably loud, but Daga's are the loudest. She's screeching as if her very soul has been shredded into ribbons. My country's dragons are swaying erratically. Their riders wince with every jerk. Wisps of smoke blow out of the dragons' horns. Whatever's happening has Randall's full attention, too. When the riders scream in matching agony, the smoke thickens, billowing faster to the ceiling. The tips of the dragons' horns glow with white-hot light.

"What's going on?!" I say. "Why are you—"

A massive lightning bolt zaps the Sol de Noches. They collapse one by one, taking their riders down with them. A black hole appears above their backs, expanding like a window as the curtains are drawn. Crashing waves echo from beyond the darkness, as does a familiar dragon's roar.

I see his wide-open mouth first. The red eyes soon follow, and those silver, spindly wings flap into view a second later. As he flies out of the hole, the darkness comes out *with him*. Sand, sky, and stars are sucked into our world.

An earthquake ensues.

I throw myself at Takeshi, covering him from the crumbling walls. The Dark Island's ocean washes concrete and metal away, then Sanjay Van's trees and foot trails. Foamy water soaks my jeans before it retreats. I'm sinking into wet, black sand, the tiled floor long gone.

Behind me, a strange, bold, crimson glow emanates from the bone throne. The dragon claw towers that once trapped our enemy are in splinters. He flies low over the destruction, weaving in and looping, basking in his victory.

The Sire is free.

"YES!" Randall breaks into applause. "All hail the Sire!"

Dragon Knights and Un-Bondeds bow to their master. A crying Randall falls to his knees.

Despite Haya and Kirill's efforts to wake them, the riders aren't moving. Neither are their steeds. Could Esperanza and Victoria be gravely injured, too? Is that how he got out?

My tears mix with saltwater and sweat—the Dark Island had been no match for Doomfall.

The Sire is even more dangerous now, and we can't stop him if we're this heavily outnumbered.

I pull out my phone. It's barely at fifteen percent of battery power, but it's enough. I don't have numbers for the other members of Task Force Blaze, but the BlazeReel Live app is the next best thing. I open it and hit the LIVE button. My broadcast starts a second later. Viewers trickle in faster than I hoped, so I aim the phone's camera at the silver dragon above me.

"This is Lana Torres! I'm at Sanjay Van National Forest in New Delhi, India! The Sire has returned! I repeat, the Sire has returned! If you're a dragon rider or a magic user, my friends and I really need your help! He's hurt the Sol de Noches and their riders! His Dragon Knight army has brought Un-Bonded dragons to attack us! Please send help! He's going to—"

The sky rumbles with the Sire's furious roaring.

Comments flash by too fast to read, but I continue, "He's going to kill us!" I aim the camera at myself. "We need you *now*."

The silver dragon descends.

The worst thing about pain? I couldn't possibly answer that. My suffering will never be the same as another's, and theirs will differ from the next person. But I can tell you the worst thing about the Anchor Curse. It's not the intrusions into your thoughts, or the inability to say no. It's the fact that you'll wake up in the morning and feel it all over again as if for the first time. Our aggressors shape our lives into a continuously drawn circle, then blame us when the ink runs dry.

—Excerpt from interview with Russell Turner, former president of the International Blazewrath Federation, in The Weekly Scorcher

CHAPTER THIRTY-ONE

Victoria

I'M STILL TRAPPED IN THIS INFERNAL LIGHTNING.

My body vibrates as I spit out blood. My guttural screams are the only thing I can hear.

Then the bone-breaking pain stops.

I tumble out of the chair. No dagger stabs me—Cecilia must've removed her magic. Antonio pulls me up. Sits me down again. He's asking if I can hear him while Cecilia claims her throne. Even though she's looking at me, too, her true interest lies in the ring.

"Es... Esperan... za..." I can barely utter her name.

She's unconscious. The Garra de Hierro has even retreated while Blood Masks rush to her aid. They're checking her pulse, her dilated pupils, but she's not moving.

WHOOM!

Sssse… essss… ca… pó…

As much as I hate her telling me the Sire has escaped, I'm relieved to hear her again.

Lo sé, chica. ¿Estás bien?

"Are you speaking with her?" Cecilia asks.

"Yes. She's too weak."

"She has a fight to finish."

Cecilia is lucky I feel like three dragons are sitting on me. Her pretty face wouldn't have stayed pretty otherwise. "But… she… lost…"

"You only lose Dragonblood when you die." She gives my hand a gentle squeeze. This asshole is convinced I'm the closest thing to her dead best friend. "The match isn't over yet."

"No…"

"Tell Esperanza to stand, or the Garra de Hierro kills you both."

"Do what she says," Antonio implores. Another fool who needs to keep his mouth shut.

Esperanza shows me the bone throne, which pulses with red light. Blood seeps from the cracks. It swaddles each armrest tight. Two golden threads hovers over them—two wands. I ask my steed what it means, but she doesn't know.

My heart sinks. This mystery is better suited for Lana and Samira's brains.

Where are you?

"Why isn't she getting up?" Cecilia's nagging is worse than being struck by lightning.

She wants a fight? She'll get it, but it won't be the one she wants. If I can muster all my remaining strength and sneak up to attack her, Blood Masks will come for me. Esperanza will have the chance to Fade out of her chains and burn them all to the bone. Even with just a drop of her normal energy, she's still a *dragon*. They can't stop her.

I share my plan with Esperanza. She tries to dissuade me from lunging at Cecilia, but I'm too fired up to listen. I can even feel my arms and legs again. Who said rage isn't healthy? I tell her to forget about the bone throne. Right now, our mission is freedom.

Esperanza slowly pushes herself up. Applause soars beyond the stadium's walls, even though it's taking her longer than usual. Blood Masks retreat toward the Garra. I almost expect the Argentine dragon to seize its chance. Thank God it's not attacking yet. It gapes at Esperanza, as if it can't believe she's attempting to stand.

Cecilia makes it onto the balcony's railing within seconds. Her giggles are my personal definition of Hell. "Yes, Esperanza! Let the match continue!"

Antonio's eyes linger on mine. When his back is fully in front of me, I try moving my fingers and toes. Everything works again.

I ask Esperanza if she's ready.

Her response comes quickly: *Sssssí.*

I leap out of the chair. The punch I drive into Antonio's head is strong enough to knock him back to fifth grade. As he drops, a gasping Cecilia starts to lift her hand at me. I've never charged at anyone this fast. My jabs connect with her shocked face. I kick her legs from under her, too. When she lands on her back, I give her a final uppercut.

She twitches before passing out. Blood drips down her nostrils and bottom lip.

I might not be a witch, but I'm still damn powerful.

"Grab her!" a Blood Mask yells. Five more are running to me.

WHOOSH!

Esperanza is flying next to the balcony's railing. Her chains have been left behind in the ring, where the Garra de Hierro stares at them in awe. Esperanza roars at the cretins who think they can stop us.

I jump onto Esperanza's back. The whooshing sound of a spell chases me.

Esperanza casts her fire shield around us, and the spell ricochets.

More spells bounce in every direction as the shield burns brighter.

"¡Llévame a las jaulas ahora!" I'm not in my best fighting shape, but I can't leave those caged Un-Bondeds. I'm half-expecting Esperanza to Fade to New Delhi against my wishes.

She flies back into the ring.

I'm holding onto Esperanza tighter than ever—she's heading toward the Garra de Hierro.

Please don't attack us…

The dragon is too confused to move. Esperanza pushes her fire shield farther out, enveloping her slack-jawed rival. It crouches into fighting position when Esperanza tries to approach, but it's not baring its fangs or growling. This is simply what it knows best—survival. Esperanza aims her snout at the dragon's shackles. She flashes her teeth. The Garra de Hierro looks from her to the chains around its legs. As more Blood Masks descend upon us, it moves closer to Esperanza. With a forceful tug, Esperanza chomps on each shackle like a starved hatchling. She spits out the steel with more disdain than I have for anything.

The Garra de Hierro is huffing and whimpering, as if it can't believe it's free. Argentina's most lethal weapon meets Esperanza's gaze. Its eyes are glassy with tears.

Both dragons nod.

With their sides pressed against one another, they light the ring on fire, scorching every Blood Mask within reach. Those touched by Esperanza's fire are burned to raw bone. Those who suffer the Garra's fury take longer to die, their skin peeling off in soot-covered clumps.

Magic users are Transporting outside; either Antonio or Cecilia lifted the shield to let them flee. Regulars are fleeing and screaming.

Cecilia is still on the floor. A few Blood Masks are trying to wake her up, but I must've hit her harder than I thought. I could pat myself on the back—what a legend.

She can still rise at any second.

"¡Esperanza, las jaulas!" We're winning, but we can't waste more time.

She ceases fire and taps the Garra with her tail. When the dragon turns, she points to the sky. Both beauties push off into the air. As the stadium becomes a blip in the distance, the Garra slips out of the shield. Then it takes flight to the east as a free dragon.

I smile. One down, God knows how many to go.

WHOOSH!

Esperanza has Faded inside a rock-laden chamber. It's much bigger than the one in New Zealand, and the stench of dragon droppings is fouler. The grimy walls are the same color as the mountain we'd used as a stakeout point—the cages had been below us!

Boots crunch the soil, hurriedly. They're coming from the dark tunnel ahead.

"Ahí vienen," I warn Esperanza, but of course, she's already in firing position. A dozen Blood Masks race out of the tunnel. "Túmbalos con el escudo."

Esperanza pummels them with the shield like I command. The hardened flames burn them faster than her normal fire. We forge a path littered with bones and blood. I feel nothing when their cries ring throughout the chamber. I no longer have pity for these killers.

The tunnel isn't as dark with Esperanza's shield lighting the way. It reminds me of a popular saying Mami would use as I was growing up, "como boca de lobo." Even though it means "like a wolf's mouth," it refers to how little visibility we have at our disposal. The darkness continues for a few feet before opening into another chamber.

Eight Un-Bondeds are trapped in cages too small for their bodies.

The Japanese Akarui is here. The other seven are months-old Garra de Hierros. They must be from the same mother; it's one of the few species that can lay more than one egg at a time. My heart tumbles into my stomach. The Un-Bondeds in New Zealand are either dead or being kept in a different prison. Even after I release these dragons,

Dragonblood won't end today.

But at least Cecilia will be short of eight fighters.

I dismount. That magical key slash is located at the bottom of the bars again. I show it to a panting Esperanza. She's already losing steam; I hate myself for tiring her out. I offer to unlock the cages alone. She carefully nudges me to the right and heads for the first cages.

I hurry to the Akarui. The magical bars roll up like a curtain as I press the slash. I move on to the next dragon, then the next one, until every cell has been opened. The cave rumbles with each key's unlocking.

All eight dragons are startled awake.

I run to Esperanza's side. She covers me under her wing, assuming a defensive stance.

The Garras are smaller than the Akarui, so it takes them less time to squeeze out of their cells. None pay attention to Esperanza. They're scrambling to leave those tiny hellholes behind, squealing in what I can only assume is euphoria.

The Akarui uses its wings to pull itself out. As it is freed, the grubby wings spread out before me. Esperanza keeps her position, but the Akarui looks from her to the Garras. Finally, it finds me.

The dragon bows its head.

The baby Garras bow, too. They're wobbling, though—they're not very coordinated yet.

Fighting back tears is worthless. They creep up on me faster than Antonio on this very mountain earlier. These creatures don't know me, but they understand what I'm doing for them, and they're showing me *respect*. Having fans is amazing, but setting dragons free…

It tastes sweeter than winning a golden Cup.

I say, "Let's help you get home."

A chilled hand clamps around my neck.

"Nobody is going *anywhere*," Cecilia says.

She tosses me down.

When I'm on my back, she pins me with a spell. I scream—she's dropped a wall on me. Esperanza attacks with flames, as do the other dragons, but Cecilia creates a shield from orange-yellow light, reminding me of Esperanza's fire magic. Yet another thing she's stolen from a dragon.

Antonio is hiding behind her. He doesn't have his devil mask on. Now I can see that same pained expression he showed me moments before Cecilia took over his body. Except for him, there are no other Blood Masks here, and he's not doing anything to help his master.

He's my only chance at getting out of here alive.

"She doesn't own you, Antonio! Fight back!"

"¡Cállate!" Cecilia's nose is bleeding faster. She cares way too much about me to wipe it clean. "You're going to die today, Victoria Peralta, and it'll be your own fault."

"You can resist her! You just have to—"

"Don't speak to my Anchor!"

Cecilia lifts the hand she's using to pin me. It's glowing as if the sun itself is nestled in her fist. She'll most likely squash me when she brings it down. No matter how hard Esperanza and the Un-Bondeds fire at her, they can't even put a dent on the shield.

Antonio is pathetically rooted to the spot. He's a kicked puppy waiting for a treat.

"Antonio, please! You're nobody's Anchor! *Fight back!*"

With a laugh as cold as the glacier, Cecilia stands on her tiptoes, lowering her fist.

A bolt of golden lightning strikes her.

She's blown across the entire length of the tunnel. Her high-pitched scream will forever be my favorite sound. As she's flung out of sight, her shield disappears.

"Hurry!" Antonio helps me stand. His wand is still aimed at the darkness ahead, but I can't hear Cecilia. "Go back to your friends and hide! She won't stop until she finds you!"

"I know, but she'll kill you if you stay. You're coming with us, Antonio. The Sol de Noches helped President Turner block his Anchor Curse. I'm sure they'll help you, too."

He's smiling and crying. "It's too big of a risk."

"Shut up. You saved me. Now I return the favor." I nod to Esperanza. "Vamos a New Dehli, por favor." I point to the Un-Bondeds watching me with expectant eyes. "Y ellos vienen."

We're *all* going back to headquarters together. We can figure out how to get these dragons into safer territories later. Right now, Task Force Blaze's hideout is the best choice.

Esperanza beckons the dragons toward her. They quickly oblige. Antonio and I mount her back. Once we're secure, Esperanza unleashes a final roar toward the cave's ceiling.

The Fade sucks us back into familiar darkness.

He's on a greater path of destruction now.
And he's been hurting Russell in secret. My best friend's will belongs to
the dragon I once called the other half of my soul. If I kill him, Russell
dies. I must take his fire and wings instead. My next curse will bind him
to an immortal vessel.
If he ever rises again, I pray others will do what I could not.

—Excerpt from Edward Barnes's journal

CHAPTER THIRTY-TWO

Lana

THE SIRE STANDS BEFORE HIS MOST LOYAL DOG, RANDALL. He curls his wings inward and snarls.

"This is for those who thought this day would never come," says Randall as he stands. "The true king of the skies is back! Bow to him!"

I'll never bow to Andrew's killer. That's worse than spitting on his grave.

None of my friends obey, either. Agent Robinson is riding Willa, who bravely snarls back. Kirill hugs an unconscious Edwin. Haya holds Gabriela. Both steeds and riders remain out of commission. Mom, Joaquín, and Samira place themselves between my teammates and the silver dragon.

"How *dare* you defy him?" Randall looks like he's been fed a spoonful of guano.

"You have your master back. What more do you want?" says Samira.

"You, of course. Along with you"—he points at Takeshi, then at me—"and you."

"Then take us, but let everyone else go!" Takeshi is trying to stand, but I keep him locked in my arms. He speaks into my ear. "Run to Samira. She can Transport you."

"*No.*"

"You're not dying today, Lana Torres."

"Neither are you!"

"Technically, I still have three days left." He insists on standing, but he lets me hold him up. That wretched black stain keeps wriggling like a serpent. Takeshi huffs as he leans into me.

He grabs my hand.

He's frigid and frail—the very things I was when he first held me in the dark. But I have no warmth or comfort to provide him. Our fingers intertwine anyway, as if we can force hope into our souls with a simple touch. I need to keep him away from danger.

And I need to wake my friends up.

"Look at you two cuties!" Randall claps. "I didn't know love was in the air! How about I kill you together? Wouldn't that be romantic?"

The Sire's roar rattles my bones.

"But first!"

Samira is flung across the beach. She lands at the black-veined killer's boots.

He rips her wand out of her grasp.

"No!" Samira and I are one desperate voice.

Randall snaps Samira's Gold wand in half.

It turns to dust, blending with the dark sand.

I'm not shaking nearly as much as Samira. Her tears flow fast. She can't perform magic without her wand. She's still powerful, but Randall's made sure she doesn't *feel* powerful again.

He and the Sire are grinning.

"Get away from her!"

Agent Robinson leads Willa toward them with a battle cry. She tries burning the Knights, but two of them block her fire with Silver wands.

One of the Scottish dragons drives its horn through Willa's side.

"NO!" I punch the sand.

The worst part isn't hearing Willa's cries.

It's the Golden Horn swinging her around like a carousel made of icy-blue scales. Agent Robinson is slipping off his steed, but he manages a spell at the Golden Horn's face. The injured dragon tosses Willa into the air. She and Agent Robinson crash-land where the Cherry Suite once was. I wait for Willa to move, to cry out again, but Agent Robinson is the only one stirring.

I don't notice Mom helping me carry Takeshi until we're about three feet away from the fallen dragons and riders. She sets him next to Fantasma and Edwin. I'm rocking them with all the strength I can muster. Either it's not enough, or they're beyond my help. None of the other riders or dragons respond—my friends are deep in magical slumber.

"Cecilia! I have your dragons. Follow these coordinates and get them yourself."

Randall speaks into a golden mirror in the air. When he finishes, the mirror disappears.

I can't let her take them!

"What the hell is this magic?" I keep rocking everyone, patting their heads, checking their pulses. "Come on!" I yell their names over and over.

BOOM!

I'm lifted into the air.

Screams and growls reverberate across the beach. When I fall, sand buries itself into my eyes and nostrils. A small sandstorm blocks my view.

"Lana!" Mom. She sounds miles away.

So do Samira and Takeshi... They're yelling my name, too...

I wipe the sand off, but it's sticky from my tears.

There's a black coat in front of me.

"Your loved ones belong to my master. He hasn't fed in weeks," says

Randall. "But killing you in front of Takeshi Endo... Now that's a show."

Wings flap in the distance. The Sire's roar shakes the earth, followed by familiar screams.

No!

Randall blows me a loud, wet kiss. "Tell Andrew it was a pleasure to kill him."

A fireball blows him away.

He's rolling even faster than Zimbabwe's Pangolins. His burning body nearly slams into the throne's pulsating red shield. The second he touches sand, Randall starts flailing like a fish that's jumped onto a dock. He's still alive, but at least he's not close enough to kill me.

Tar-black claws are right where Randall stood. They're attached to a violet dragon.

I flinch. There's a Pesadelo in front of me. It's much bigger than the ones Randall brought, though, and it has a wider neck and wings. This is a female. I'm about to bolt, but the dragon lowers its head, revealing the last thing I'd ever expect to see.

A rider.

"Are you okay, mija?" he asks.

It takes me a second to fully believe what I'm seeing.

Because if this is not, in fact, a hallucination, my father is on top of Violet #43.

"Papi? Is that... *you?*"

"Mr. Torres!" Samira is rushing toward me. If she can see him, too, this is definitely real.

"Are any of you hurt?" Papi dismounts the Un-Bonded, whose eyes are glued to mine. I wait for her to remember me. Maybe she'll barbecue me as payment for our unfinished business. But all I get is sneaker sniffing and a bored huff. Whether she remembers me or not, she's over it.

As Papi helps me up, he checks me for bruises. "Lana, *are you okay?*"

"How did you convince her to ride with you? And how did you even get here so fast?" I shake my head. "Wait, what the hell am I doing? Forget about me! Go help *them*!" I point to the battle raging on near the Sol de Noches. Mom still shields Joaquín, but Haya and Kirill are moving slower. So is Kirill's dragon—the Sire beats all three heads with his tail.

"On it!" Papi gets back on his saddle. He motions to my right. "It's a long explanation, mi amor, but I *can* tell you they brought me here. Please stay by their side!"

Violet #43 flies off.

I search for Papi's allies.

Noora Haddad holds up her wand. She's Transporting new arrivals to the beach. Some are bureau agents, who run up to Willa and Agent Robinson.

The rest of Task Force Blaze appears.

Onesa Ruwende, Aneni Karonga, and Wataida Midzi's steeds have curled into balls. The Pangolin dragons cut through the Knights' formation like sand-scaled bowling balls. When the Irish Spikes barrel into action, the Pangolins make way for Willa again. Hell itself shoots out of her snout—she's using more firepower than I knew she had! The Spikes wail in unison as they're scorched mercilessly. They retreat with their singed wings.

Gustavo Pabón and his Furia Roja flank the Golden Horn. The Venezuelan dragon's tail opens up like a red rose in bloom. Crimson spears soar out of it. They connect with the Golden Horn's side, back, and face. While the Scottish dragon unleashes wails of agony, the two Pesadelos charge Gustavo and his steed. Artem Volkov intercepts them atop his roaring dragon, commanding all three of the Zmey Gorynych's heads to bring the heat against the Brazilian dragons. Soon the sky becomes a cloud of flames. I see tails whipping tails, heads butting into backs and chests, and the Furia Roja's spears cutting through the flames at breakneck speed.

"Thank you for the location, Miss Torres," a man says. "We certainly would've taken much longer to find you without it."

A black-eyed Director Sandhar stands next to me. Agent Horowitz is beside him, with only a few scratches on her cheeks.

"Oh, my God. You're *alive!*" I hug them tight enough to cut off their circulation.

"We owe it to Brunhilde," says Agent Horowitz. "And Manny."

"That's right. Don't you forget it, nena."

I jump back with a gasp. "MANNY!"

Miraculously, he lets me hug him. I don't care how he got hold of the metal bat he's wielding, or why he puts an arm around a displeased Agent Vogel once we separate.

She glares at me. "I will never forgive you for abandoning me with this man."

"Oh, come on. You love me." Manny leans forward. "She loves me."

Director Sandhar shushes him. "Sienna and I will need you to fight the Sire with us," he tells Samira. "Until those Sol de Noches wake up, you're the only one who can trap him again. Brunhilde and Noora can Transport everyone. Lana and Manny can help the Sol de Noches."

Samira shows him her empty hands. "Randall broke my wand."

"Fuck." Manny speaks for us all.

"Let's not panic. We can still stop him." Agent Horowitz rises with a fierce expression unlike anything I've seen from her. It's like she's ready to tear this whole beach apart.

The Sire's roars grow louder. He smacks Violet #43 out of his way, causing Papi and the Pesadelo to spiral farther and farther off course. The Sire flies low, his mouth open wide, preparing to shoot a fireball at Mom.

"We have to hurry!" I snatch Manny's arm and run.

The poor guy's slower than me, and he complains the whole time we're tearing through the sand, but he's still trying to catch up.

Director Sandhar and Agent Horowitz are already launching spell after spell at the Sire.

He dodges every single one.

"KEEP HITTING HIM!" I say.

More spells follow, but they miss. The Sire flies lower until he's almost nose-to-nose with Mom. Joaquín tries pulling her back, but she insists on shielding him instead.

I ramp up my speed, leaving Manny in the dust. "YOU HAVE TO STOP HIM NOW!"

A dragon swoops down next to me.

"Need a ride?"

Victoria is patting Esperanza's back.

Dark magic always requires blood, but not every spell that requires blood is nefarious. Charms experts have spent centuries studying its healing properties. Some discoveries have proven useful in the treatment of magical maladies. Dragon blood, for instance, contains nutrients and proteins that can reduce the effects of these ailments, if not obliterate them entirely. Blood curses can also be broken the same way they were cast. The end of a dark spell is its beginning.

—*Excerpt from Corwin Sykes's* Dark & Dastardly: Obscure Magical Folklore & Enchantments for Beginners

CHAPTER THIRTY-THREE

Victoria

I DON'T KNOW WHAT THE FUCK IS HAPPENING.

Well, I can clearly see the Sire is back. Randall Wiggins is somehow alive.

And Lana's father is riding a Pesadelo. The world's most dangerous dragon is hitting the Sire with everything it has—fire to the face, tail to the legs, claws to the horns.

The Akarui and the Garras de Hierro are flying behind us. Antonio rides with one of the Argentine dragons. He's struggling to hold on while the dragon does cartwheels. Its siblings are also joining in on the fun. These poor babies are ecstatic they can fly again.

I can also see headquarters has been replaced with the Dark Island.

Was this what happened when the Sire broke free? How did he do all this?

Esperanza's fireball strikes him in the neck. He's thrown fifty feet away.

That adds a few more minutes in our favor.

I'm reaching out to Lana, but she seems as if she's seen a ghost. There's a heavily panting, hairy man swinging a bat farther back. He's doing his damnedest to keep up with us.

Wait... is that...

"MANNY!"

"Yes, it's me! Now go rip that guy a new one!"

Lana climbs on top of Esperanza without taking my hand. Seconds later, she's squeezing the life out of me. "You don't know how happy I am to see you're both okay! I'm so sorry for—"

"We can apologize after we make it out alive!"

"Okay!" She squeezes even harder.

The Sire is circling back to the Sol de Noches.

Esperanza Fades in front of them. She douses this silver prick with more fire. When he tries firing back, the Akarui pummels into his shoulder, followed by the Garras. Each launches an assault on a different part of the Sire's body. This is a Dragonblood match on steroids.

Those babies are going to die without my friends' help.

"VICTORIA!" Lana is screeching in my ear.

"What?"

"Get us down now!"

I tell Esperanza to descend. Once we're down, Lana runs to her mother and Takeshi, who is covered in black swirls.

Swirls I've only seen on Randall.

"That's not..." I can't even mention Dragonshade. Seeing Takeshi on his back, his eyes darkening, his skin growing pale... He doesn't deserve this.

"It is," says a frowning Lana. I can't imagine how much she's hurting.

I hate that I hurt them both even more now.

"I'm sorry," I manage to speak.

"You didn't do this." Takeshi tries to smile, but he groans in excruciating pain.

"Besides, we can apologize after we make it out alive." Lana motions to our friends. "Help me wake them?"

"Of course."

I shake Héctor first, shouting his name. I move on to the others. Esperanza whines as she presses her nose against Rayo's. She even pokes Rayo's wings with her claws.

No response.

When the Sire attacked Esperanza, she recovered on her own. She's bigger than her siblings, and as the eldest, her magical strength could be greater. They always depend on her to initiate their song, too. What if they don't do that out of respect?

What if she's *the only one* who can start the spell?

"Esperanza, necesito que cantes."

My steed furrows her brow. Suggesting she sings to them might sound ludicrous, but if she's capable of building an entire island through music, it's safe to assume it'll help here.

Dozens more Transport Charm lights are going off around the beach. The new arrivals are cloaked in black and silver—Dragon Knights. I stop counting at fifty and curse under my breath.

I grab Esperanza's nose. "Canta."

With her eyes closed, Esperanza carries a high note straight to the stars. She sounds like a broken heart with scales and wings. There's a rough, winding pattern in the way she's singing. It rises and falls in quick jerks. My steed has turned her voice into a violin, and she's playing each string with the same fire nestled within her.

The new song shrouds my mind in black. I can't see anything, let alone think.

Then a small flame appears at its center. It grows into two flames, which become three, four. When the fifth one burns into existence, Esperanza stops singing.

Fire shoots out of her chest.

It connects the Sol de Noches in a single flaming thread. This is much thinner than the ring of fire they cast during our quarterfinals match, but it's just as bright.

The dragons rise.

While they roar and bite and flap their wings, their riders jump to their feet.

I can't stop clapping. "IT WORKED!"

Daga's sloppy kiss prevents me from saying anything else. She's licking my face and wagging her tail like the happiest puppy alive. Even Puya and Rayo sneak kisses in, too. They almost drop Esperanza on her back with their aggressive cuddling. Titán and Fantasma are whining at them to back off, especially at a clingy Daga, whose head is on Esperanza's shoulder.

But even after she's left alone, my steed can't get up.

The song and her battle wounds are too much to handle.

"Descansa, mi amor. Te voy a proteger, ¿okay?"

I seal my promise to protect her with a kiss on her cheek.

Esperanza closes her eyes, sighing with exhaustion.

"V!" Luis pulls me into a hug. "Where the heck were you? I was so worried!"

Héctor waves Titán over. "She can explain later! There's a whole-ass *war* going down right now, Luis! Everybody, to your steeds!" He gives me a side-hug. "Gracias."

"De nada," I say.

The sand rumbles. Willa and Robinson are speeding toward us. She has a silver bandage covering her side, which I suspect her rider conjured. He's also magically dragging metal objects from underneath the sand—a red Ninja motorcycle with flamethrower and sidecar attached, a spiked bat, an extra flamethrower, and the Godzilla sword.

Haya's inventions!

Robinson flings the sword over to Willa, who catches it with her tail. She spits fire onto the blade. The Fire Drake advances with her burning weapon held high. Robinson Transports the rest of the inventions to where Haya and Kirill are breathlessly sparring with three Dragon Knights.

Haya gasps when she notices her gadgets. "My babies!" She hurriedly snatches the extra flamethrower and jumps onto her motorcycle. "Joaquín, do you want a free flamethrower?"

"We haven't formally met, but you're my favorite person!" says Manny. He and Lana's mom make sure Joaquín is safely seated into the sidecar. "¡Quémales el culo, mijo!"

"What does that mean?" Haya says.

"You don't want to know!" Joaquín takes his flamethrower while she grabs the one on the front of her bike. They speed off into battle. A screaming Haya shoots at the Un-Bondeds that are attacking Task Force Blaze dragons. Joaquín is targeting Dragon Knights.

Lana's mom takes the spiked bat. She and Manny are now a tag team, ready to crack as many Dragon Knight skulls as possible, and I fully support them.

"We have to hurry!" Kirill is climbing on top of his dragon. One of its three heads is barely conscious. The other two have black eyes, but they're still alert. "The Sire *cannot* escape!"

My friends lift off.

Antonio slips off the Garra's back. He plummets toward us.

Esperanza breaks his fall with her tail. When she sets him down, he's writhing the same way he did on the mountain.

Cecilia is trying to take over again.

"Is that Antonio?" Lana asks. "What's happening to him?"

"He's Cecilia's Anchor!"

Lana freezes. Which is the exact opposite of what I need her to do. "Her Anchor?"

"Yes! If she seizes control of him, he'll strike!"

"Okay, but look at him! He's surprisingly strong, Victoria. Maybe he can hold her back for longer. Touching him might worsen his pain, or even make him lose focus."

Why is she choosing this moment to be the logical one? But the more Antonio presses his head against the sand, the less his body convulses. He alternates between yelling in rapid Italian and English. This silly little rich boy is tougher than I thought.

With Esperanza down, I can't join my friends in the skies.

Then her warning washes over me.

"The throne is trying to ask for something!" It's only glowing bright red, though—the gold wands and the blood are missing. Still, I tell Lana about what my steed showed me.

She's as confused as I am. "You're sure you saw two golden wands?"

"Yes. Do you think they represent Gold Wands?"

Lana's eyes are saucers. She pulls out a small white object from her pocket.

Bone.

"We need to smear Randall and Cecilia's blood on this," she says.

"What the hell are you talking about? The blood was coming *from* the throne."

"But it's not there right now, see? What if the throne needs blood from the twin curses?"

Now I'm the one with huge eyes. "The twin *what*?"

SWISH!

Dozens of Blood Masks have landed on the Dark Island.

Cecilia is at the helm of their brigade, casting more Transport Charms for her soldiers.

"Blood Masks, charge!"

They scatter like ants fleeing a toppling hill, joining ranks with the Dragon Knights. It doesn't matter who fights for whom. Our two greatest enemies have become one.

I turn to Lana. "You're sure it's her blood?"

"I'm ninety-nine percent sure," she says, raising her fists. "It's worth a shot."

Manny gets to Cecilia first. Each attempted blow is a waste of time—the witch is Transporting all over. She appears close enough to hit, then vanishes. I try to figure out a pattern, but she's too erratic. The only predictable thing is her cruel laughter. This is yet another game to her.

"Can you access her thoughts?" Lana asks Antonio. "Or at least make an educated guess?"

"No! She's too strong!" he laments.

I look at Lana's hand. "Give me that bone."

"Why?"

"Just *give* it to me."

When she obeys, I study Cecilia's movements again. Her pattern draws into a solid shape in my head—each Transport Charm is a different part of a hexagon.

Being a great Striker takes practice. Training won't help much without talent.

I'm Victoria Fucking Peralta, and I have both.

When Cecilia vanishes from the topmost right corner, I fling the bone to the left. It sails past hooded figures and masked killers.

SWISH!

Cecilia reappears.

The bone crashes into her cheek. Blood drips from a deep gash.

"Ahhh!" Her scream is the soundtrack of my happiest memories.

"Bring that over here!" I tell Antonio.

He's recoiling from the strike, too. The more we hurt her, the more we hurt him, but he summons the bone back into my grasp. There's a thin coating of blood on it.

"Get Randall's blood." I toss it to Lana. "*Run!*"

When I arrived at his house, Edward was already dead. The amplifier was still there. I believe he used it to harness the Doomfall. I've taken it before the bureau comes. Powerless or not, the Sire remains free, and he'll surely kill again. I must find the counter-curse. Those dark enchantments can never be born, Glenda. If they join forces, our world will meet its end.

—*Voicemail left in Madame Waxbyrne's cell phone*

CHAPTER THIRTY-FOUR

Lana

Tℍɪs ɪs ᴛʜᴇ ᴍᴏsᴛ ɪɴᴛᴇɴsᴇ ᴠᴇʀsɪᴏɴ ᴏꜰ ʜᴏᴛ ᴘᴏᴛᴀᴛᴏ I'ᴠᴇ ᴇᴠᴇʀ ᴘʟᴀʏᴇᴅ. If only I could move. What if my theory is wrong? Could the bone throne really be demanding the Evil Wonder Twins' blood? Does that mean the throne is sentient?

Someone's shaking me hard.

"What are you waiting for?!"

Victoria.

Then Samira.

They're speaking over each other as the battlefield sinks into deeper chaos.

"What do you need?" Samira yells.

Blood Masks are closing in. Cecilia isn't far behind.

Takeshi's coughing up black blood. His eyes… they're fully dark… Esperanza rests beside him, whipping her tail at approaching enemies. But she's moving slower and slower.

"Lana! What do you need?" Samira again. "Maybe I can will some psychic magic into being, you know? There's gotta be a way to heal Takeshi and stop this battle and—"

"EAT SHIT!" Victoria is fending off two Blood Masks. Samira pulls me behind her, as if she knows the first thing about throwing a punch. Bless her. She's lost her wand, and if I don't do something, she'll lose her life, too. We *all* will.

Where is the threat?

There's a silver dragon, a magical girl, and a magical boy.

I only need the boy.

He's locked in a duel with Noora and Agent Vogel. The throne is about twelve feet away.

Takeshi is still coughing. Esperanza cries out. Victoria screams her head off.

"Tell me how to help you!" Samira is about to pull a muscle from yelling.

"I'm fine," I say. Then I'm off.

Randall is distracted. I aim full steam ahead for his left side. Nerves sink their claws into me, but I'm not shivering even though I still fear this magical boy.

He should fear me more.

Noora sees me approaching. She forces Randall's attention on her, turning him a little.

I smack Randall. The bone collides with the bridge of his nose.

"Ahhh!"

Randall crashes to the sand. His poisoned blood drips on the bone next to Cecilia's.

"Excellent technique," says a smiling Noora.

"Now get out of the way!" says Agent Vogel.

I flee. Randall's outraged cries trail behind me, which makes me pump my arms faster. I can also hear the continuous zapping from spells, the endless cries for help.

I forge ahead.

Silver wings creep up in my peripheral vision.

The Sire is flying toward me. His flames nip at my aching heels. Why is he coming after me? It's like he knows what'll happen once I get this blood to the throne.

Keep going!

This is the closest thing to a Blazewrath match I've experienced in weeks. The Cup was actually a warm-up in comparison. There are no winding paths upward, and I'm even happier about the absence of Block Zones, but I'm too tired. Knowing the Sire is trying to kill me isn't adding much momentum. I'm zigzagging and ducking and exhausting myself further.

I trip.

My left knee hits the sand first. As the rest of me falls, the bone somersaults out of my grasp. The Sire hovers on top of me. His roars unleash a flurry of tremors. With shaking arms, I cover myself and look away. Running is useless. Even if I can get the bone, he'll burn me alive.

I've failed Andrew.

I've failed my country, the future I thought I could have…

"NO!" a girl says.

Heat lingers close, but never touches me. I can hear the fire crackling inches away.

I risk a tearful peek at the Sire. His flames are almost on me. With a hunched spine, he looks in my direction, aiming straight for my head. But he and his fire are trapped inside a net. Black, coiling tendrils slither in the same pattern as Randall and Takeshi's veins. The Sire tries to blast it apart, but the dark net grows thicker.

Behind him, tendrils burst from Samira's right hand. Her left hand is aimed at a wailing Takeshi.

She's ripping the Dragonshade out of his wound. When the black gobs of poison travel toward her, she leads them to the Sire, strengthening his new prison.

"I got him!" Samira is all smiles, even though she's trembling harder than I am. "Go!"

I'm laughing through my sobs. Samira Jones is *using psychic magic.* What I'd give to see if she fully heals Takeshi. I force myself up, but I might as well be wearing a backpack full of bricks. I grab the bone and keep a steady pace toward the throne. Its red light glows fainter.

It pulls itself aside like a curtain.

My whole body slumps on the throne. When I'm properly seated, the light covers the entire area again. I slide the bone fragment from where I took it. A loud clicking noise ensues.

Then nothing.

Maybe I shouldn't sit?

I get up. Still nothing.

I take the bone out again and sit back down. Crickets.

I kneel before the throne, offering the bone as a gift. "I have what you asked for. The blood of the twin curses is now yours."

Not. One thing. Happens.

I sigh. "Fine. I'll just have to—"

"Welcome to the dragon maker's throne," a woman's voice sends chills down my spine.

The Weekly Scorcher: When Lana can't trust dragons anymore, what do you predict she'll do?

Todd Anderson: Cry a lot. After she's done with her pity party, I hope she realizes there's only one right thing when it comes to dragons.

The Weekly Scorcher: Standing against them?

Todd Anderson: Yes. We should be putting our faith in magic users, especially Gold Wands. Their powers can change this world for the better. And unlike dragons, they'll never hurt us.

—*Excerpt from Todd Anderson's exclusive with* The Weekly Scorcher

CHAPTER THIRTY-FIVE
Lana

"FORGIVE ME FOR DELAYING. I HAD TO VERIFY THE BLOOD YOU brought. One of the samples has been poisoned, which made it harder to corroborate. You may take a seat now."

I'm not terribly excited about talking to a disembodied voice, especially one that's inviting me to sit on what could easily turn into a death trap. But if this voice will really stop the Sire and the twin curses, I should trust it.

I carefully settle into the throne as if it had always been mine.

"What's your name?" says the woman.

"Um… I'm Lana… Who are you?"

"Nice to meet you, Lana. I'm a soul."

"Wait. Souls can stay alive even *inside* objects?"

"Depends on the spell. This one preserves the soul, but it can also do the opposite…" Regret hooks onto every word. "Before my death, I was a Gold Wand from your island."

I choke on my own spit. After a few coughs, I whisper, "Julia Serrano?"

She laughs warmly. "You know your history."

Oh, my freaking God. I'm talking to the most powerful Puerto Rican witch ever! I'm suddenly swept away to Malta again, where Madame Waxbyrne is telling me about how Julia helped her kill Enid Mendoza. How she vanished to stop the Doomfall.

"What is… How did you… Why…" I have no idea where to start.

"The Sire kidnapped me when he was still human. My death was quick. I wouldn't help him become a dragon, but I vowed to end him. My soul clings to his rider's most treasured artifact—a throne he built from the bones of dragon hatchlings. Edward used it to amplify his Extraction Charm. Now I'm using it to destroy his curses."

Wow. I aspire to be this petty someday.

But there are a few things I'm not quite getting.

"Does that mean you found a counter-curse? And if this throne belonged to Edward Barnes, how come the Sol de Noches had it?"

"I stole the throne prior to my death. When my soul left my body, I had already enchanted it to latch onto the bones. I hid us deep within my country's soil. For the past two years, I've been putting out something like a distress call, searching for a magical being strong enough to help me strike Edward's curses down. Our island's dragons answered that call."

So their song spell helped created the Dark Island *and* set Julia's soul free. They didn't build the bone throne, but it still belongs to them. So will our victory today.

"And the counter-curse?" I ask.

"There wasn't a preexisting spell, so I created it. You've brought two of its ingredients, but we're still missing the last one."

Every muscle in my body ties itself into knots. "How do we find it?"

"With a simple request," Julia says. "The Doomfall tarnishes souls, Lana. Its counter-curse requires a soul in return, but it needs one that still inhabits its human vessel."

Silence falls between us. Despite the chaos outside of the red light, I can only hear her words on a loop in my frazzled brain. Julia needs a living person's soul.

I'm the only one who can give it to her right now.

"I… have to die?" I whisper.

"No, brave girl. You must sacrifice a *piece* of your soul. You will still live afterwards."

That's definitely better than dying. It's still a tricky thing for me to grasp, though. "Okay, but if I'm missing part of my soul, what will happen to me?"

"I have many theories. Unfortunately, we'll only be certain once the spell is cast. This is an irreversible act. It's not a decision you must take lightly. Do you accept?"

Why is she trying to scare me? Doesn't she *want* me to complete her counter-curse? The last thing I need is to lose even a slice of myself, especially when I'm still trying to figure out who I am in a world without Blazewrath. Stopping Cecilia was supposed to be the answer. So was Task Force Blaze. I never realized embracing my new future would cost me.

"Do you accept?" Julia's insistence is a cold dagger's edge. I understand she's desperate, but why is she being so ominous? That doesn't exactly inspire confidence.

Not that it matters. I might not know what I'll become after my sacrifice, but it'll be the most important thing I'll ever do. I wasn't born to win a Blazewrath World Cup, let alone to save the world. I'm neither curse nor blessing. There was no predestined roadmap for me to break the Doomfall. I *choose* to. Not to spite Cecilia, Randall, or the Sire. That had been the mission of a vengeful girl. One doesn't get rid of their pain by hurting others.

But if losing a piece of my soul *also* means losing the guilt from Andrew's murder… I wouldn't feel so much remorse, so much rage. My heart would free itself from this grief.

"Lana, do you accept?" Julia asks again.

She needs me to agree, but so do I. This is how I finally save myself.

"Yes," I say.

Julia sighs. "Thank you."

A beam of red light stabs me through the chest.

A throne unfit for kings,
Carved from dragon bone,
A red light glows and sings,
And turns your heart to stone.

—Excerpt from Edward Barnes's journal

CHAPTER THIRTY-SIX

Lana

EVERYTHING IS ON FIRE.

I've been dunked into lava, and it sears my veins at a billion miles per hour. With my back arched, I launch a thousand screams to the stars. I can't hear the dragon roars, the jarring detonations of Transport Charms, or the ocean waves. I only have the raw, unfiltered sound of my agony.

Something spreads from within. It starts at my chest, opening up like a giant Venus flytrap. Whatever's inside me expels a spine-tingling chill. A blast of cold air sweeps over my heart, which beats at supersonic speed. The ice carves a path to the rest of me. Instead of lava, now I'm stuck in a snowball. This pain is no better—every inch of me winds itself into crystallized knots. I try to keep my breathing steady, but the more I inhale, the sharper it stings.

"What the hell is happening?" I ask Julia.

She doesn't reply. Maybe she'll ruin the counter-curse if she intervenes? I should keep quiet, too, but this is messed up. How can doing the right thing hurt so much?

A chainsaw is going to town on my insides. I flail harder with each slice.

But my body has it easy. The grief remains, tethered tight and unyielding. Andrew's dying screams are almost as loud as mine. Sacrificing a piece of my soul means watching the scalding summers on the island I love fading to a joyless, dull gray. It's biting into my favorite fried dishes and tasting tar. It's reaching for the friends I made when my wildest dream came true, the best friend who's always been by my side, the tortured boy I long to kiss—and hugging smoke instead. Six black dragons are flying into the night and shattering like false promises. My parents are walking away forever, abandoning the child who's always coming up short.

It's living in a world I never asked for, and knowing I can't change it back.

Or can I?

"Stop! I don't want this anymore! Julia, please make it stop!"

The chainsaw slows, slows, then halts. I still ache, but the pain has lessened.

"Do you really want to stop?" Julia's voice offers no comfort. "If you quit now, the counter-curse will be useless! I'll need another sacrifice quickly!"

Another sacrifice. Someone else will have to go through with this if I chicken out. Their happiest moments will be stripped of joy, of purpose, and all because I'm too scared.

I can't let anyone else suffer. This is my choice. Besides, my agony is temporary—it'll end once I save everyone.

"Just... take it already... hurry..."

"Lana, are you *sure*?"

"Yes!"

The chainsaw returns even faster. Big and little moments blur into a film reel. I'm signing my contract at President Turner's Other Place and jogging around my neighborhood in Naples for the first time. I'm fleeing from the Volkov twins on the mountain and learning about the Dark Island in the locker room. I'm talking to Andrew next to the dragon chocolate fountain and watching him die in Brazil. The world is light and bleak, great and terrible.

The chainsaw is gone. So is the insufferable cold, the film reel of blended moments. I wait to feel discomfort, pain, or overall weirdness, but I'm... fine? I still remember my whole life. I'm still devastated about Andrew. For all intents and purposes, I'm back to normal.

"Did it work?" I say.

"It's done!" Julia rejoices. "Thank you, Lana! Now let's get this curse underway!"

The red light howls like a tropical storm. A beam reaches out for the bone fragment. When I give it away, the light gobbles it up in one huge bite. I'm thrust backward. My head slams against the throne, but the snowball freezing me from within hurts so much worse. Everything tightens, hardens, again. I can't even speak—my mouth is frozen shut.

"One soul to unleash, one to seal forever," Julia recites her spell. "Keep one soul in half, take the other whole. Let our love drive out the Doomfall, and return our world from hate."

White light pours out of the Sire's scales. He shrieks and slams into the cage's walls.

Stardust explodes within the dark cage.

The Sire is dead.

The cold is knocked out of me. Even though I shudder, I can't move at will.

As the carnage ensues, the black sand sinks underneath Sanjay Van's soil. The foot trails and trees are springing back out. The black ocean vaporizes until all that's left is steam coming off the forest river. I drop onto a patch of grass—the bone throne is gone.

I hear Julia one last time. "Muchas gracias, Lana. Lo logramos."

I try to move, but I can only scan the battlefield. Randall's poisoned body lies on a black, viscous puddle. His blue eyes are shut, hopefully for good.

"WHERE IS MY MAGIC?!" Cecilia is throwing a temper tantrum farther behind him. She still tries to cast killing spells at Victoria, but nothing shoots from her hands anymore.

Victoria looks at a kneeling Antonio. Even though he's wincing, he nods.

She clocks Cecilia on the chin. The Gold Wand drops like a pin two seconds later.

The girl behind Dragonblood has no magic. Her twin brother appears to be dead.

The Doomfall is broken.

"Lana? Can you hear me?"

Takeshi.

He holds me in his arms, warming me up with both his body and his kindness. There's a black, squiggly scar where Randall struck him with the Dragonshade. A rough sketch of the sky in a Van Gogh painting. It is hideous and lovely at the same time.

My shudders slow to a stop. The boy I like isn't dying anymore. He's holding me as if he's afraid *I* will. He keeps calling my name, asking me if I can hear him, and indulging me with sweet caresses on my cheek. Thinking up words is frying my brain.

So I curl my fingers around his neck and bring him down closer.

"What are you doing?" he says.

I kiss him.

His hesitation only lasts a second. He's pushing me so close; our bodies merge into a single entity. He's gentle despite his eagerness. His lips aren't as soft as the carnation petals we watch every night. They're a little chapped, hot from the inferno all around us.

But they're *his* lips, and they're perfect.

Then I crumble in his arms as the darkness claims me.

It's impossible to describe how freedom feels. After so many years under the Sire's control, I couldn't pick a toothbrush without waiting to hear his voice. I'm embarrassed to admit I'm still struggling to accept his absence. I have much to consider in regards to my professional future, but nothing will ever be more difficult than learning how to think— and live—for myself.

—Excerpt from interview with Russell Turner, former president of the International Blazewrath Federation, in The Weekly Scorcher

CHAPTER THIRTY-SEVEN

Lana

I HAVE NO IDEA WHERE I AM.

I'm cracking one eye open, squinting from the lamps overhead. Who thought it was neat to shine such a painfully bright light at me? At least the bed is comfy. So are these fluffy pillows. The pale blue sheets are quite warm. I grip them too tightly as I prop myself up.

"Careful. You don't want to hurt yourself further."

Even though he's sitting next to me, his friendly smile as wide as I remember it, I'm still processing the fact that he's... wherever here is.

"How are you feeling, Miss Torres?" says President Turner. He's in a plain black shirt, an emerald cardigan, and jeans. I didn't think he was capable of dressing casually. But when you lose your job in the world's greatest tournament, I guess suits become unnecessary.

But that doesn't explain why he's at my side.

"I'm..."

How *am* I feeling? My insides aren't freezing to death, but something stirs in my chest.

Seeing President Turner again... I should be happy, right? This man made my Blazewrath dreams come true, even though it hadn't been his choice. He treated me with kindness despite the excruciating pain he was constantly subjected to. I even convinced Takeshi not to kill the Sire so President Turner would still live. He'll always be one of the most important people to me.

Yet I feel nothing.

"Are you hurting?" President Turner points to the door. "I can call a doctor right now."

"No, no... I'm just... surprised to see you. Where are we, by the way? And how come you're here? What about my family and friends? Takeshi?" Even as I utter each word, none tug at my heartstrings. I'm spewing them out of curiosity, not nostalgia or concern. I might not be freezing, but I'm as cold as the frost that sliced my soul apart.

Don't freak out. Maybe you're still struggling with the spell's aftermath.

"We're currently in London. And this is an Other Place. Corwin's, to be exact. He built it a while ago, but he's expanded a few rooms to fit Task Force Blaze comfortably. This hospital wing is new. There's a separate one for dragons. Your friends, family, and Takeshi are also here. Some are still nursing injuries. Luckily, there were no casualties on our side."

"Why aren't we at the Bureau? Is it still under attack?"

President Turner hangs his head low. "The bureau's headquarters in New York is in ashes. The organization is in peril at an international level, as well. Dragon Knights and Blood Masks have infiltrated every department in every country. The ones you defeated in New Delhi have all been apprehended, and some in hiding have also been captured, but there are still traitors among us." President Turner offers me a hopeful smile. "Nirek and his agents will catch them soon."

I wish I shared his optimism. We might've won the battle at New

Delhi, but the war is far from over. Stopping the Sire and the twin curses is only the beginning. There will always be another threat. I wait for the inevitable shot of adrenaline that comes with realizing I have evil to bring down... that overwhelming desire to stomp on everything that makes this world unsafe... to fill my days with the purpose I've fought so hard to find...

I yawn. "What happened to Randall and Cecilia?"

"Dragonshade finally killed Randall. Cecilia has been sent to Ravensworth Penitentiary. She's currently locked up in what used to be Takeshi's cell. I'm told it was his idea."

He pauses, as if he's expecting me to laugh. Or maybe he's waiting for a funny comment?

"Cecilia is in prison," I say.

"Yes."

The one thing I've spent so long coveting is now a reality.

And. I. Feel. *Nothing*.

Is it wrong that I'm not motivated to search for answers? To seek out possible reasons why Julia's spell has left me so... whatever this is? She warned me there would be consequences, that they would hurt, but this doesn't compare to almost dying on the bone throne. I'll take being drained of emotion over the torturous minutes I endured under the counter-curse's hold. This is still so confusing, though. If I can't feel anything, what the hell have I become?

I try another question. "So no more Dragonblood?"

"That's our hope, but we believe a few Blood Masks could still be trying to kidnap Un-Bondeds. Just because their leader is gone doesn't mean they can't profit. I'm certain a new one will rise in Cecilia's place. And speaking of dragons"—he leans closer to the bed—"Samira told us about the Doomfall. She and Corwin share a theory that you sacrificed something for the counter-curse. We've been waiting for you to wake up for the past four days."

I knit my eyebrows together. "I've been unconscious for four days?"

"Yes." President Turner reaches out for my hand. When I take it, he puts the other one on top. The gesture leaves me as unmoved as everything he's told me. "The moment you cast the counter-curse, you also destroyed the Anchor Curses. Antonio Deluca and I are truly free now. From the bottom of my heart, Miss Torres, thank you."

He's tearing up. He swallows, checks the door, then looks back at me.

He says, "Forgive me if I sound selfish. Whatever it is you risked, I'm happy you did it. But I'm also concerned. A counter-curse that strong can't have demanded something trivial. I suspect you're in unimaginable pain right now. Is this correct?"

That stirring in my chest persists. It's still pretty tolerable, though.

"I'm actually fine, Mister President. Oh, wait. I shouldn't call you that, huh?"

"It's okay. I rather miss the title."

We stare at each other in silence.

I break the ice. "So we won?"

He laughs. "Yes, Miss Torres. We won."

I should be throwing a party. Scratch that—a whole damn parade. Everyone must be thrilled about what I've done, even if they also understand I've lost something valuable. But knowing a piece of my soul is gone will freak them out.

Which is why I need to keep it to myself, especially since this is the most confusing thing I've experienced. I don't want answers or sympathy. I just want space more than ever.

"Would you like me to leave you to rest? Or are you willing to speak with the others?"

Ugh. I don't *want* to. But if I must keep up appearances, so be it.

"I'm good to go, yeah. Help me up?"

"Gladly."

After President Turner gets me off the bed, he whispers, "Thank you again."

I can only nod as he escorts me outside.

THE LIVING ROOM IN THIS OTHER PLACE IS COMPLETELY DIFFER-ent from President Turner's.

Headmaster Sykes enjoys a darker palette than his mahogany-obsessed husband. The walls and furniture are spider-black, but the chandeliers are much lighter graphite. Lamps hang like crystal chestnuts, some higher than others. They seem better suited for a French palace. I'm making my way down the staircase, which is shaped like waves in a parted sea.

Everyone smiles and waves as I descend. I don't see Victoria, Agent Robinson, or Antonio Deluca. None of the dragons are here. They must be in their habitat.

Papi and Mom are the first to grab me.

"How are you, mija?" Papi says. He rubs my back in a circular motion. "I'm good."

My arms remain limp at my sides. Even when Mom hugs me, I'm not compelled to hold her, either. She also asks how I'm doing. I repeat what I told Papi.

Samira and her family are next, followed by my former teammates, Joaquín, Manny, the Volkov twins, Wataida, Aneni, Onesa, and Gustavo. Their excited words blur into one long ramble. I can barely keep up with what they're saying, let alone with the amount of hugs I get. Luis and Gabriela linger the longest. Haya has to physically remove Gabriela from me. When Gabriela complains, Haya plants a sweet kiss on her mouth. I guess they're official now.

Headmaster Sykes, Director Sandhar, Agent Horowitz, and Agent Vogel don't touch me, but they're reassuring me all is well, and that I've done the world a great service.

Takeshi is the only one who doesn't approach me. He's hiding his hands in his pockets, and watching me with unparalleled caution, as if I'll blow up into ash if he looks away. For a second, I swear he takes a step forward, but he stops.

"Hi, Lana." His voice has never sounded so husky and fragile at the same time.

I wonder if he's nervous, or maybe even scared? I remember how I kissed him four days ago. How he held me like I was long-lost treasure, and he was about to lose me for good.

I wonder if I should be nervous or scared, too. If he wants me to ignore everyone watching us right now and kiss him even harder. If he'd rather initiate instead. Above all, I wonder if kissing him would cast that slow stirring in my chest into the farthest abyss on Earth, restoring the sacrificed piece of my soul. But the thought of pressing my lips against his…

The stirring speeds up, growing into an ache that stabs me in small bursts.

I rub my chest. Then I remember I'm being watched. The weirder I behave, the more worried everyone will become, so I stop rubbing and smile at Takeshi.

He doesn't smile back.

"Hi," I say as convincingly as possible, but he's still not cheering up.

"Would it be all right if we chatted later? We have so much to discuss," Headmaster Sykes says. There's a bit more stubble on his chin than when I last saw him at Andrew's funeral. It suits him. "Please know we're at your beck and call, Miss Torres. You're not alone."

Mom nods as she kisses my forehead. "You're *never* alone."

"Thank you," I say in a tone drier than Pink Rock Desert.

Samira asks, "You sure you're good?"

This is my best friend in the whole world. She's capable of using psychic magic now. I should be asking her how *she* feels, right? Maybe take her to the side so we can talk about what's happened with her powers ever since I blacked out? Even when I try forming the words, my lips don't move. I'm drowning in a sea of indifference, and there's no harbor or rescue ship in sight.

"Perfectly fine," I whisper.

There had been way more eyes on me inside the Blazewrath stadium. The ones in this living room are much worse, though—these are the people who know what I used to be. They have expectations and demands far greater than those of complete strangers. With every breath, my chest tightens into knots with steel-tipped edges. I'm being cut from within again, but it will never be as insufferable as the pressure to be who they all want me to be. I need to be Lana Aurelia Torres, and I don't know how to be her anymore. I'm not sure I ever want to again.

Get out of here. They're only making things suck more.

"I'm going to lie down for a few more hours," I finally blurt out. "Sorry, guys. I promise to be more talkative soon."

"No need to apologize, nena. You've been through hell. Welcome to the club." Manny is raising a glass of whiskey at me. He downs it all in one gulp.

Any other day, I would've giggled. Now I can't even force out a smile.

"Rest it is," says Papi. He's holding me like fine china, leading me back upstairs.

I take one last look at the boy I once liked. It's so wild to think I kissed him only four days ago, and now I can't even bear to imagine us kissing without shuddering.

Takeshi glances at the floor as he retreats.

"Gracias, Papi," I say, "but I can get upstairs myself."

I leave everyone behind.

For Un-Bonded dragons, the line between aggression and survival instincts is blurred. How can we help those who think they don't need it? Those who refuse to allow us into their space? Perhaps the answers will be found after I'm gone. But I've taken the first step into a world without hate, and I urge others to keep going.

—*Excerpt from Carlos Torres's* Studying the Bond Between Dragons & Humans

CHAPTER THIRTY-EIGHT

Victoria

"AND *THIS* LITTLE PIGGY BROKE THE BLOOD MASK'S FINGERS."

I tap Esperanza's claw. Lifting it is impossible for me, so I've tweaked my rendition of "This Little Piggy" accordingly.

Esperanza simply huffs. She's already been subjected to my edited version in Spanish. Sharing it in English isn't making her any more of a fan. She's lying on the bed Headmaster Sykes built for her. It has feather-soft sheets and pillows shaped like dragon scales. I don't know why the headmaster included a stone fountain. It spills water into a base that's as big as my steed's head. Everything else in this hospital wing is exactly what one would find in a Sol de Noche's habitat—towering palm trees, an abundance of coconuts, and dim lighting.

Esperanza is the only Puerto Rican dragon here. Willa is recovering next door. The others are in a separate habitat right below us. They play games loud enough for our floor to vibrate.

It's been four days since Esperanza survived her Dragonblood match. Lana's dad brought over a few trusted doctors to check on her. Even though she can walk, fly, and Fade, she gets tired easily. Her siblings have tried to help with a song spell. All it's done is cheer her up. Doctors have recommended an extended resting period. She's not even allowed to psychically communicate. I've been feeding her and making sure she doesn't try to exert herself.

I've also been worried about Mami and Lana. My mother's still hidden somewhere safe, and Director Sandhar has given me clearance to reach out, but I haven't called her yet—I want Esperanza to be fully healed. I'd hate to stress her out even further, especially when I won't be able to tell her where we are, or when we'll meet again.

As for Lana… whatever she did on that bone throne almost *killed* her. Now she's been unconscious for four days and counting. Luis and Gabriela think she'll wake up soon. Edwin, Génesis, and Héctor suspect it'll take much longer. I've been dividing my time between visiting her and caring for Esperanza. I'd rather be there than mope in bed all day.

At least Lana has Samira to watch over her, too. Even *Antonio* stopped by yesterday. I did catch him checking Samira out on four different occasions, so his intentions aren't entirely centered on Lana's well-being. To no one's surprise, Takeshi's also been up to her room multiple times. I think he'd sleep in the hallway if they let him. That must've been one hell of a kiss.

Esperanza whines as she flips over to rest on the opposite side. She's been mostly silent and detached. I hope that means she's on her way to a clean bill of health soon.

"¿Quieres más agua?" I ask if she wants more water.

Esperanza shakes her head, then yawns as if she hasn't slept in weeks. "¿Carne?"

She doesn't want meat, either.

"Okay. ¿Quieres dormir?"

Esperanza closes her eyes. Sleep seems to be the winner.

The double doors slide open.

"Bad time, Miss Peralta?" Director Sandhar walks in. Shockingly, he's alone. I assume this means he's taking a break from his many enemy-hunting duties.

"What's wrong?" I say.

"I'd like a quick word. Best not to bother your steed, so can we chat outside?"

"Do I have a choice?" It's meant as a dry joke, but Sandhar isn't laughing. "Fine."

The air conditioning is lower in the corridor, which is a relief. Living on a tropical island for fifteen years has spoiled me into thinking any place under seventy degrees is the North Pole.

I haven't spoken to Sandhar since we won the battle of New Delhi. He explained what happened to the captured agents, and I'm certain he's skipped over the rougher parts. Cecilia locked them in a fortress at a remote countryside village near Madrid. According to Sandhar, it was similar to Randall's nightmarish skullpits. They tried to escape several times, but their efforts only paid off when Noora found them. Agent Vogel and Manny had been at her side. Then Noora saw Lana's distress call, and Transported everyone to New Delhi.

"I'll start with the news," Sandhar says. "Lana is awake."

I can't remember the last time I gasped this loudly. "*What?*"

"She came to just a few moments ago. Russell brought her downstairs so she could say hi, but she's back in bed." He's not looking at me when he says this; the floor has all of his attention. "I think we should abstain from visiting her until further notice."

"Why?" He's telling me the girl who almost died for us is finally conscious, and now that we can comfort her and ask her what she went through, we have to back off?

Sandhar sighs. "She's not well."

"Of course she's not well. That's why we should rally around her.

If she sees how much we missed her, and that we're here for whatever she needs, she could feel better faster. That's what I've been doing with Esperanza." I pause. "I think she's tired of my jokes, but she can always count on me being there for her. Doesn't Lana deserve the same?"

"Indeed, Miss Peralta, but Lana... something is... *off.*"

I back into the wall, cocking an eyebrow. "Off?"

"She doesn't seem like herself. It's like she's analyzing her surroundings in a very... detached manner. Almost as if she doesn't know how to react."

"Has anyone *asked* her how she feels? Or about what happened on the throne?" I say.

"Yes. She says she's fi—"

"Fine." I should've known.

"Corwin will try to gather more information on the state of her physical and mental health. This will take a while, since he thinks the counter-curse affected her irrevocably. No one is allowed to bother Lana. We don't want to delay or hinder her progress. Is that understood?"

Oh, I completely understand. I just don't agree. Something's *been* wrong with Lana for weeks. Ever since Andrew's murder, she's had a tough time dealing with her trauma, mostly because she hasn't confronted it. There's a possibility the counter-curse's side effects could be aggravating her heartbreak. *She doesn't seem like herself.* Is she pushing everybody away harder than before? Or is this new Lana much worse than I suspect?

"Has Samira been helping the headmaster? I think she can figure this out quickly."

"She has, yes. The order still stands, Miss Peralta. No visitors."

"But I—"

"As for the offer"—Sandhar speaks louder—"Takeshi and I have been meaning to discuss Task Force Blaze's next steps with you."

That's a curveball if ever I've seen one. "Really?"

"Yes. I intend on salvaging what remains of the bureau and

transforming it into something greater. Once our organization is back on its feet, I'm reestablishing the Department of Magical Investigations. Takeshi has agreed to cooperate in making Task Force Blaze a *permanent* bureau program. In the meantime, I was hoping we could continue to train current and new Blaze agents. I'm here to ask if you're willing to commit to such an endeavor full-time."

His change in subject gives me whiplash, but I'm as still as a rock. He's giving me a job? Not just *any* job—I'd officially become a bureau agent. The future I'd fought to shape for myself when Takeshi first offered me this path... now it's actually happening. I no longer have to prove I'm worthy—that I've *always* been worthy—of this title, and of respect. My purpose in this great, big world has finally been made clear. I thought an offer like this would set my soul ablaze.

But I'm not on fire.

My thoughts are flashing the same image—Lana.

I'm too worried about her to focus on anything else. Otherwise, my apathy would mean I no longer care about saving lives. Getting paid to bring our enemies down would be a privilege.

I need to see Lana. Talking to her will ease my concerns, and I'll have a clear head. I could be accepting Sandhar's offer before dawn.

"Miss Peralta?" His tone is as tense as the episode of *Law & Order: Magical Crimes Unit* Samira made me sit through last night—I need to see the next one ASAP, so I will know if they caught that Silver Wand grave robber.

"How long do I have to think about it?" I say.

He smiles. "Take all the time you need."

"Thank you." I walk back to the double doors. "See you at dinner."

"Till then, Miss Peralta."

He goes over to Willa's room.

Once he disappears inside, I'm off to find the girl who's supposedly no longer herself.

LANA'S DAD IS FAST ASLEEP OUTSIDE HER DOOR.

I forgo knocking and twist the knob. Mr. Torres doesn't stir. The hardest part is complete.

Lana is indeed awake. She's sitting alone in bed, but she's staring blankly at the wall. I expect to see her mom walk out of the bathroom, but there's nobody else here. I no longer know if that's a good thing.

I shut the door. "Hi," I whisper.

Lana looks over to me. "Oh. Victoria."

That's it. Not even a formal hello.

I wasn't expecting a flash mob and confetti, but this is underwhelming. I'm suddenly standing in a kitchen in Dubai, where the excited stranger who'd rescued a Fire Drake at a wand shop is introducing herself. The girl in that kitchen had been this one's complete opposite. Her warmth was a nuisance at the time. Now it's a memory I hold dear.

How do I talk to someone I don't recognize anymore?

"Can I help you?" she says.

I wish she'd sounded angry—that would mean she still cares. But there's only boredom. Her expression makes it worse. It's like someone vacuumed every emotion out of her. What if that's exactly what happened? Could the counter-curse have sucked her dry of feelings? Samira and Headmaster Sykes have so much work to do.

I can try to provide them with *some* information, especially if I can get her to open up.

"I wanted to see how you're doing." As I approach the bed, Lana returns her attention to the wall. "So. How are you doing?"

"Good."

"Really?"

"Yes."

"You don't look good."

Lana is quiet. Then she shrugs. "Nobody looks good all the time."

"But you never look good." I try making a quick, silly joke, which is what *she's* good at.

She lays her head back on the pillow. Her silence would give anyone chills. Sandhar had been right. This girl isn't ready for visitors, and it might take a *very* long time until she is.

"Do you remember anything about the battle?" I risk a hand toward hers. She doesn't flinch at my touch, but she's not reciprocating, either.

"I remember everything."

"And the throne?"

"That, too." She closes her eyes. "I remember it the most."

"Can you tell me what happened?"

Lana doesn't reply.

"Hello?" I check her pulse. She's very much alive.

She's just dead inside.

Either Lana is feigning sleep, or she's really unconscious. There's a chance the counter-curse has weakened her. But if she's trying to avoid this conversation, this is quite pathetic.

I'll still worry about her when I leave this room. I'll wake up every morning and wonder about her health just as much as I'll wonder about Esperanza's. Coming here hasn't helped me put Lana's well-being to the side—it's jammed it front and center.

I let go of her hand as if it's wrapped in barbed wire. Lana's not reacting.

Fuck that throne and whatever it did to my friend. I can't imagine how that living room looked when Lana greeted everyone. The way Sandhar spoke made it seem as if they'd all attended a funeral they were never invited to. Her parents… Samira… Takeshi…

I'm so happy I missed it.

"Lana? Do you want me to go?"

She's not speaking.

I walk to the door.

"Why are you sad?" she says. "Did something happen to Esperanza?" Her eyes are open, but she's still blank-faced and unapproachable. She's sitting up again.

"Esperanza's fine. And I'm sad because... you're not... yourself?"

She pats the sheets down. "I'm just tired, Victoria. I'll be more peppy soon."

"It's not about being peppy." I march back to the bed. "For instance, how did you treat Takeshi when you went downstairs?"

"I said hello." She says it with knitted eyebrows, though, as if she's not sure if she did.

"Did you want to kiss him again?"

"I need to rest." Lana is rubbing her chest with a fierce grimace. She's sinking into the mattress as fast as my hope flickers out.

I hightail it back to the door. Her reluctance reminds me of every caged Un-Bonded I've met. She's not snapping at me or cursing me out, but her insistence on being left alone is as devastating as those dragons' rage. It wasn't until Esperanza and I freed them that they trusted us. It took a leap of faith and plenty of perseverance, but we did it.

I stop. It's been four days since I've interacted with Un-Bondeds. The Garras de Hierro and the Akarui fled without saying goodbye. None of the Un-Bondeds that fought against us were caught. It's like they served their purpose and left before they could experience human contact.

Lana has Samira and Headmaster Sykes to help with her recovery. Un-Bondeds in the wild have no one. And if Sandhar's guess is correct, they're still in danger of being captured.

"Why aren't you leaving? Don't you have somewhere else to be?" Lana's indifferent tone remains, but she's still rubbing her chest like it's a genie lamp. "Maybe Esperanza needs you."

I grin. Esperanza will *always* need me.

Sandhar wants me to be a more intimidating version of a police officer—one that chases enemies on her dragon steed. I thought I wanted this, too, but I was craving something to live for. The very organization I'm supposed to serve doesn't exist anymore. Perhaps it's best if it doesn't return to how I once knew it. Task Force Blaze might be a thing of the past, as well.

At least for me.

I say, "She's not the only one."

Students often ask me about the most powerful spell a Gold Wand can cast. Most guess it's the dragon-slaying spells. Others inquire about their Love Charms (hiring Gold Wands to perform one remains a highly pursued yet illegal practice). What unsettles me is the emphasis on power as a show of force. The ability to take life or to manipulate others into entering relationships without consent shouldn't be considered the standard. Both are crimes for a reason. My answer is always the same—the most powerful spell a Gold Wand can cast will never be stronger than choosing to build a better world, especially for those who struggle to belong.

—*Excerpt from Corwin Sykes's* Dark & Dastardly: Obscure Magical Folklore & Enchantments for Beginners

CHAPTER THIRTY-NINE

Lana

VICTORIA PRACTICALLY LIVES IN MY ROOM NOW.

It's been a week of insisting I eat three times a day despite not being hungry, fluffing my pillows, changing my sheets, and asking if I need to pee. She'd read bedtime stories if I let her.

Samira has been worse. Between treating me like a murder suspect with her out-of-the-blue interviews and sneaking broccoli into my soup, it's overwhelming. Not that her questions bother me. She hasn't brought up the throne. Neither has Headmaster Sykes. They mostly stick to checking if I'm in pain. I've caught Headmaster Sykes staring. I always tell them I'm fine.

I wish my body would let me lie better—the chest pain flares up whenever they're near.

My parents haven't been a comfort, either, even though I don't hurt as much around them. Mom keeps holding my hand as if it's supposed to offer consolation. She throws in a kiss on the forehead, too, but her lips smell like apricot and coffee, so I recoil.

Papi shows me clips of Violet #43 every night. He updates me on how well she's adapting to sanctuary life. She even poses for photos with staff now. While Papi can't formally Bond with her, rescuing the Brazilian Pesadelo from dragon trappers softened her up. Instead of flying away while he fought, Violet #43 stayed with him. They've been a tag team ever since.

My father shows her off during his FaceTimes with staff. I always tune his chatter out—there's nothing exciting about watching a Pesadelo eat grapefruit. She also cries at the end when they have to say goodbye. He reassures her he'll visit soon while I yawn.

"She used to be *obsessed* with dragons," I overheard Samira tell him two days ago. "It's like she doesn't care about them anymore. Or about anyone, really."

The way Papi's shoulders sank suggests he didn't take it well. It hasn't stopped him from bringing me more Violet clips. It's noon right now, but I'm sure he'll have a new batch tonight.

Lucky me.

"Are we having cobbler again for dessert?" Victoria asks Samira. The three of us are the only people in my room. They're sharing a pint of Ben & Jerry's Half Baked ice cream while I observe in abject boredom. "I really liked the peach one from yesterday."

"It's my momma's recipe! I've been eating it all my life." Samira waits for Victoria to remove her spoon, then hurries to grab more ice cream. She stops, risking a glance at me. "Lana and I ate it during our study sessions."

"Mm-hmm…" Those days, which were once a vibrant mural, have been painted over in the blandest shade of white. Even if I *wanted* to chip away at it, the paint wouldn't come off.

Samira goes back to her pint. "Maybe I can bring Esperanza a slice."

"Thank you. She'd love that," says Victoria. "I'm so relieved she finally left the hospital wing this morning. That cobbler can be her celebratory treat."

"Ugh, that's such great news. She truly deserves the world."

"And so much more."

"Do you know anything about Willa, by the way? I think Agent Robinson said she's getting discharged soon. I hope he's right. I'd like to say goodbye before I leave."

Something pokes my heart. I flinch from the surprise flash of pain, which is what I imagine getting dunked into an ice lake would feel like, but it's only for a second.

Samira's going on and on about Willa's health and making sure she packs everything and fawning over suitcase designs and eating her Ben & Jerry's with an abominably huge smile.

"Where are you going?" I say.

"Oh." Samira seems more shocked than me. She and Victoria share a look, then a nod. "I'm going to Iron Pointe. Director Sandhar has asked us if we wanted to become bureau agents, but we've turned him down. The academy sent in my acceptance letter this morning."

She takes another spoonful of ice cream. Her nonchalance almost rivals mine.

I'm shaking my head. "Wasn't Iron Pointe done after our chat with Madame Waxbyrne?"

"It's because of her I'm attending. She's coming back as headmistress. Her commitment to reform the craft will include safer and ethical practices. All the wands she's sold with dragon souls are being decommissioned, and she's launching a new line. I've been asked to design it. Antonio Deluca will be working with me, too. Can you believe *he* offered to help out?"

Victoria coughs, but she's smiling. "I wonder what his motivation was."

Samira rolls her eyes. "Anyway, Madame Waxbyrne wants to put souls back into their vessels. Julia's magic killed most, but a few are still sentient, such as the Pesadelos at your dad's sanctuary. Madame Waxbyrne will serve less time if she returns what she and Julia stole."

"Why are you leaving so soon, though? I thought you would stay here with me or... I don't know... keep being a member of Task Force Blaze."

Samira swallows her frozen treat before replying. "Never say never, but right now, I really want to finish my studies and do volunteer work, especially with other teens from low-income households and disenfranchised communities. Victoria and I are launching a program with funding and educating as a starting point."

"The educating part was her idea," Victoria adds.

"Yup. I was thinking about offering the resources they need to pursue careers in magical studies and improve their living conditions. And I'm also hoping to do further research on psychic magic. Headmaster Sykes has already offered to mentor me. Maybe I can convince him to rent a chateau in the South of France to try new spells on the weekends!"

She and Victoria laugh.

I say, "But this is what you excel at. Kicking butt. Taking down bad guys."

That insistent poking is back. No matter how hard I try to ignore it, the damn thing keeps digging into me like a dart in search of its bull's-eye.

Samira's eyes are as wide as coasters. "It's not completely off the table. It's just not what I'm most passionate about right now, especially when I haven't even graduated. And I know rebuilding the bureau into something greater is important, too, but I don't want to miss out on being a teenager. This journey into breaking Doomfall has been fulfilling *and* taxing, Lana. One day I'll be ready to take bad guys down again. For now, I'd rather build the heroes up."

I turn to Victoria. "Are you leaving, too?"

"Yes. I'll be home-schooled, though. Esperanza and I will be too busy flying around the world. We're going to find Un-Bonded dragons in the wild and help them develop social skills. Your dad has already put me in contact with a few sanctuary employees in different countries. They'll be training me and coming along for the ride whenever needed. Also"—she motions to Samira—"I'll be donating my Blazewrath money to Samira's causes."

"And the rest of our team?"

Victoria says, "They're going home, but they'll be part of Task Force Blaze in a limited capacity. They're working with Director Sandhar so they can reach out to other dragon riders, especially older ones. Takeshi's also helping, but he'll head back to Sapporo in the morning."

The freezing pain is so much sharper now.

No amount of rubbing will get rid of it, and I don't know why I insist.

Then it fades like the last smoke tendrils of a cigarette. I can breathe better now.

So I say, "Why is Takeshi leaving?"

"He wants to be with his mom. President Turner is throwing a farewell breakfast for him." Samira looks at me like she's not buying Takeshi's excuse.

I don't doubt he misses his mother. I also don't think this is a choice he's made out of nostalgia alone. What if he's trying to get away from me? The way I treated him wasn't exactly welcoming, so I can't blame him, but the thought of never seeing Takeshi again…

The cold returns in a swift, bone-crumbling wave.

I'm kicking off the sheets and gripping them at the same time.

"What's wrong?" Samira and Victoria say.

When Samira touches my forehead, the chills triple. She backs away. Even though the cold is receding, I'm still pulling on the fabric, searching for comfort in its softness, finding none. Why is thinking about Takeshi doing this to me? And even before him, learning of my best friends' new plans… it's like they're… hurting me? How can they hurt someone who can't *feel?*

Unless my soul is trying to stitch itself back together, and the counter-curse won't let it.

There's a war raging inside me, and I don't know whose side I'm on.

"Lana! Tell us what's going on!" Victoria is as loud as a ringing bell.

I whisper the only thing I can, "Nothing."

Thankfully, they don't persist. After they make sure I'm comfortable again, they keep eating their Ben & Jerry's and talking about life outside of this Other Place. Soon I won't have my best friends hovering over me. The boy I once liked will be gone. So will most of the people here. Even if I see them again, their lives will carry on as if I'm a distant memory, a passing thought in a string of experiences I'll be excluded from. They might never think of me at all.

I'm not sure I'm okay with it anymore.

I CAN'T EAT OR SLEEP FOR THE REST OF THE NIGHT.

My brain repeats the news until reciting it becomes second nature. But the more I dwell on it, the quicker the cold comes back. I sink into a pattern of refusing to remember, and failing to forget. Monitoring the clock isn't helping. Nobody's told me the exact time Takeshi's leaving, but I'm assuming it's early. Will anyone come find me so I can say goodbye? Is he planning on coming up here instead? Do I even want him to see me?

I'm a mess of freezing insides and shaky limbs, but I keep my breaths steady, pushing the pain away with the might of a Sol de Noche. If it's true that my soul is fighting to be whole again, letting it do so means succumbing to the same agony I endured on the bone throne, and I don't think I could ever survive another round of that. As much as it hurts, I have to watch the people I cared about (*care* about?) move on without me. Being near them is what's causing me to suffer, after all. They're doing me a huge favor by walking away, and hopefully, never returning.

I must start by watching Takeshi leave.

I sneak downstairs for his farewell breakfast. My parents had offered to fetch me clean clothes and help me to the living room, but I declined. It's better if I keep to myself in the back, where no one can make me the center of attention, or make me hurt worse.

I press against the wall, careful to move as quietly as a spy in enemy territory. The edge of the staircase creaks a little. My steps become even slower.

When I peek down to the living room, only Takeshi is standing. The black scar on his arm has faded just a smidge, a tattoo he can't erase. Everyone's backs are to me. They clap while Takeshi bows.

He says, "I've done many things alone, and I've done them well. When I joined the bureau, I only wanted revenge. My purpose was as bloodstained as the Sire's hands. Even though that purpose changed"— he stops, thoughtful—"I still question the person I became. I never want to lose myself like that again." He pauses again, this time glancing down. "I haven't had the chance to properly heal after Hikaru's murder. Everything has been… difficult. But there's hope for better days, in large part because of you."

Whatever's jabbing at my chest grows tenfold. I try to ignore the pain, but my thoughts rush back to our first night in the carnation garden, where a boy made petals float and cracked open his heart to me. Where he confessed to never regretting putting his faith in me. That night meant something once, and I think it's meaning something again.

If only the counter-curse would let it.

"Stop hurting… please stop…"

"I can see the sunrise again because you've helped me find it," Takeshi says. "And I can never thank you enough. From now on, I vow to—"

I interrupt him with a loud sob.

My whole body is racked with tremors. I spill out more tears than ever in my life.

I'm running despite the detonations in my chest making every breath a challenge. I can barely see where I'm going.

I run right into him.

"Lana…" Takeshi's whisper is as soft as his grip. He keeps his distance, though, as if he's worried about upsetting me further. "You should be resting. Can I help you back to your room?"

More hurried footsteps rush toward us, but Takeshi holds out a hand, his expression stern.

"Would you like me to find your mom? She can help you get back to bed," he says.

"No… I…" I'm sobbing even harder. I don't know how to make this agony stop. I don't even think it's possible. But I can't keep hiding from the ones who want to see me well.

From the ones I'm hurting, too.

Takeshi says, "You don't have to force yourself to—"

"I'm not okay, Takeshi. Everything… it all hurts *so much*… I can't do this anymore."

He's smiling. "I know, and I've got you. I won't let you go."

"What? No…" I'm wiping my tears, but more keep coming. "I'm not your burden."

"You're nobody's burden, Lana. Don't ever call yourself that. If you let me, I'll be by your side. We can go through this together."

"No… That's not… Your mom… You have to *go*."

"And I will. After I spend time with my mother, I'll come visit you."

"But you said you wanted to heal. I won't take that away from you."

Takeshi laces his fingers around mine. He pulls me closer—just enough for our hearts to pound against one another.

"*You* are part of my healing, Lana. This"—he motions to our held hands—"is what I've been hoping for since you scolded me in Brazil. Sometimes I think it might've started when you pummeled me in the wand shop. If you need me by your side, that's precisely where I'll be."

I can't speak. My own words choke me along with the curse's hold.

So I stare into his eyes, and he stares into mine. They don't save me from the agony. They're not a magical gateway into a better world. Everything that's ever sucked about my life still sucks. But there's something soothing about looking into them—a promise of that sunrise he says he's found. My forever favorite isn't my salvation. Nobody is. I have to save myself, but I can't do it alone, and I'm finally willing to admit it.

Takeshi wipes my cheeks. "Am I allowed to be by your side?"

I reply with a kiss. It's much, much softer than the one in New Delhi, and even if I wanted to speed it up, the pain is too unbearable. Takeshi doesn't rush me into it, either. When we separate, he steals a quick peck.

My parents hug me first, followed by Samira. They help me sit, even though I'm no longer a sobbing disaster, but even the smallest movement wipes me clean of strength. Samira and Victoria sit at either side of me on the couch. They hold my hands while I take a deep breath.

President Turner offers me a plate of bacon and scrambled eggs. Luis tries to sneak in a baguette slathered in peanut butter, but I politely refuse. He shares it with Kirill instead.

I finally tell everyone about Julia Serrano's counter-curse. There are no gasps when I admit a piece of my soul is missing. My friends and family are just... listening. Headmaster Sykes is taking notes on his phone. A few weeks ago, facing the people I love in such a weakened, troubled state would've been a nightmare. I'm a pro Runner even when it comes to my problems. But the time for running is long past me, and I'm the last one to catch up with the truth.

"Thank you for sharing your story with us," Joaquín says. "How can we help?"

"Say the word and it's yours." Luis is still chewing on his baguette.

President Turner nods. "We're all here for you, Miss Torres. Through thick and thin."

Even if I wanted to continue with Task Force Blaze, I'm not ready for any kind of labor. I don't know if I'm ready to sit in a classroom, either. Going to school would mean learning from home, at least temporarily, but would I do that back in Florida? Or is the island still calling me?

I look at Samira and Victoria. These amazing girls are choosing to do what's best for their souls. Mine might be incomplete, but that doesn't mean I'm broken. I can choose to be happy, too. Does that include seeing a therapist? Searching for magical treatments that could minimize this abominable pain instead? I don't know yet. I don't know *a lot* of things.

There's only one certainty.

"Thank you. I'd like to stay in Puerto Rico, if that's okay. For good."

Mom is on the verge of crying. "Of course, sweetheart."

As the farewell breakfast resumes, I'm still aching, still short of breath and wrapped in chills. But a huge weight has been stripped off my bones. I'm sharing one final morning with a group of people I cherish more than I could ever say.

"You're the bravest girl I know," Victoria tells me. "And you'll always have me."

If I try to speak, I'll just break down again, so I nod. She nods back. For the first time in a long time, I feel like I'm home.

Do I think Blazewrath will ever return? You're asking the wrong person, my dear. The fate of the sport has always belonged to dragons. Perhaps the world will be rid of Dragon Knights soon, and steeds will flock to training centers again. That doesn't strike me as the most plausible option—would you go back to a stadium when you can have the whole sky?

—*Excerpt from interview with Russell Turner, former president of the International Blazewrath Federation, in* The Weekly Scorcher

CHAPTER FORTY

Victoria

"ARE YOU SURE I CAN'T SAVE YOU SOME SANCOCHO? IT'S THE BEST one I've made so far," Mami says. Our FaceTime call has reached the fifteen-minute mark, and it's mostly consisted of her boasting about tonight's menu. She's cooked more Puerto Rican dishes here in Switzerland than she has in all of our years in the Caribbean.

"Eat it. I think we'll be late anyway."

"Why? Didn't you girls find that dragon already?"

"Sort of." I peer down at Esperanza. Her bandages have been off for a month, and she's shown constant progress ever since. We can communicate psychically and fly together without her tiring. I sit in my saddle as she scours the frosty mountains below. We have an excellent vantage point from inside our cavernous hideout in the Swiss Alps. I still hate the cold, but I'd be foolish not to admit how stunning this view is. I'm grateful for the absence of glaciers, though.

"What do you mean *sort of*, Victoria?"

"We've heard the dragon, but we haven't met her yet. She's quite the loud eater."

According to my contact at the Bern Rescue Sanctuary, my latest case is finishing up a meal near the Matterhorn—the highest peak in Switzerland. Sunlight has turned its tip into a reddish pink arrowhead. Sanctuary staff set up camp at the edge of the dragon's habitat. They confirmed she has scars from her Dragonblood days. She hasn't tried attacking them, but she's cowering at their approach and hiding between boulders. The only upside is she's allowing them to feed her. Once she's full on cow meat, I'll get the signal to descend.

"Ay, pues tengan cuidado. I know you've been doing a wonderful job with these poor creatures, but you can never get too comfortable. I don't want anything to happen to you girls."

Keyboard clicks fill in her silence. She must be checking Facebook again.

If she sends me another text chain, I'm hanging up. "Sí, Mami."

"Y mira, any updates on Lana and mis otros bebés?"

I sigh. Lana and her other babies FaceTimed me right before she did.

That had been our first successful call in weeks. Last month, Hurricanes Irma and María devastated our country. My friends have been flying all over the island donating food, clothing, and medical supplies. While some private and public properties have been rebuilt, and magic users have helped repower our towns, there are still people who don't know where their loved ones are, or how they're doing. Rivers have drowned our roads and homes. Trees have smashed our windshields and windows. We can certainly lift Puerto Rico again.

But these hurricanes are bullshit. Our people don't deserve to go through *any* of this. So much more would be accomplished with Esperanza and me there. Lana's threatened to sue me if I come home. She's looking healthier and happier, even though she trembled during most of the conversation. She still spoke like a high school principal. Héctor and Génesis said they'd start a rumor that I suck my thumb. Gabriela and Luis will make a Reddit thread with videos of me dancing. Edwin just laughed hard as they spoke.

My friends have asked me to follow my dreams. The island is aching, and even though my steed hasn't asked me to go home, I don't have to be Einstein to guess where her heart truly lies.

"Everyone is tired, but determined to make things better," I say. "I wish I could help."

"You *are* helping. Puerto Rico needs people on the ground to provide essential supplies and construction materials, but it also needs hope."

I laugh dryly. "I'm in Switzerland trying to get an Un-Bonded to trust humans. How is that giving Puerto Ricans hope?"

"They'll know what another Puerto Rican is capable of! What *they* could be capable of, too, once the country is back on its feet. Carlos Torres is a pioneer in understanding the dragon-rider Bond, but he's not a rider. He doesn't have any experience freeing Dragonblood fighters, either. You're not only following in his footsteps, mi vida—you're breaking new ground."

Technically, she's right, but this feels like I'm betraying those who chanted my name during the Blazewrath World Cup. The ones who supported me should receive support—my blood, sweat, and what's left of my money. I care about helping Un-Bondeds. I also care about helping Puerto Rico. One shouldn't matter more than the other, but what if it does?

WHOOM!

La isla tiene a nuestros hermanos, Esperanza says. Her enunciation has gotten so much better this past month. *Este dragón solamente nos tiene a nosotras.*

Our home has our siblings. This dragon only has the two of us.

When it was in a cage, it had no one. How she escaped… I might never know. It's possible the Blood Masks grew weary of her.

But freedom is more than stepping out of the walls that confine us. Our memories come along for the ride. Those who've hurt me left lasting handprints on my soul. I still feel them sometimes. I have to live with the worst while fighting for the best.

This dragon's scars don't matter more than the ones every Puerto Rican has.

But I still want to heal them—they could help *me* heal, too.

"¿Victoria? ¿Estás en un viaje?"

"I'm here, Mami. Go eat your sancocho and please know how much I love you."

She smiles like she's about to cry. "I love you more. Both of you."

Esperanza purrs into my phone's camera, then puckers up like she's going to kiss it.

Mami can't stop giggling. After we blow each other goodbye kisses, I promise to bring her flowers, and she promises to stay up until we get back.

Five minutes later, we're called to the Matterhorn.

Esperanza turns to me. She's patiently waiting for a command.

I press my forehead against her snout. "Vamos al Matterhorn."

Vamos, she repeats.

With a leap, we soar across the cold Swiss sky.

There's a reason why we call Puerto Rico la Isla del Encanto—the Island of Enchantment. You can search for magic in its rivers and crops, in the capital's cobblestone streets and the smallest town's narrow roads, or even in the rainforest's winding trails, but what you're looking for lies in the heart of its people. Oh, and in our dragons, too. You don't wanna mess with them.

—*Comment left by SolNocheblood5ever on Lana Torres's BlazeReel profile page*

CHAPTER FORTY-ONE

Lana

THE BEACH LOOKS SAD TODAY AGAIN.

There aren't any people here in La Posita, for starters. A few seagulls glide low over the foamy waves, but even watching them fish is depressing.

Maybe it's the heat playing tricks on me, or the exhaustion from speaking with displaced teens all morning. Then I remember what I've seen since our rebuilding efforts began. Loíza has always been poor. Despite a spot on the world map thanks to Piñones—a coastal haven for Afro-Latinx music, culture, and fried foods—Loíza remains my country's most neglected community.

Which is why this sucks even worse. Hurricane Irma laid waste to about ninety houses in Loíza alone, but María cranked up the devastation to three thousand deaths across the country. The Río Espíritu Santo has spilled over to the streets. The elderly and the sick have lost what little medical resources they relied on. Whenever I think there's no more debris or trash to remove, we find more.

My family home in Cayey is gone, too.

I'll never retrace my first steps, or relive my happiest childhood moments.

Of course, getting help from a brigade of magic users has been invaluable. The combined efforts of Director Sandhar and President Turner have sped up our recovery process, especially since Loíza has power again, but that doesn't take away the fact that people have died. Official numbers are still being counted across the island—the death rate rises every day.

I'm used to horrible things. It's just not the same to experience them in my home, not when the spell that took my soul is still hurting me.

Therapy has helped me control the chest pain and tremors. Although I'm not shaking anymore, and the ache has mostly dulled, I still feel that pinch of cold and a constant tugging. Any progress is a miracle considering my sessions have been via Skype with a psychologist in the States. Mom found me someone here, but we're waiting for her to start seeing clients again. Even psychologists need a break during a crisis.

Samira has also been a lifesaver. Not only is she Transporting canned goods and medicine, she's reading up on soul extraction at Iron Pointe's library. She and Antonio Deluca are the first students to enroll in a new program on curse studies. Madame Waxbyrne splits her time between supervising their wand designs and reconnecting souls with their vessels. Agent Robinson and Willa have joined her on each trip—their little family is back together.

"Your ice cream is melting. Would you like me to eat it instead?"

Takeshi grins like he's so satisfied with himself. I've been lucky enough to enjoy that grin in person for the past three days. He'd wanted to come earlier, but I insisted he remained with his mom. She didn't waste a single opportunity to bow in gratitude during our phone chats.

My own mother almost broke Takeshi's spinal cord with a hug when he arrived. Papi's his biggest fan, though. He's mentioned Takeshi rescuing him in Brazil one billion times.

I'm lying on his chest in the sand. He's right—all two scoops of my chocolate ice cream are dripping down the cone. I've been so caught up in my thoughts that I forgot to eat. At least some of my appetite is back. I lick the chocolate off the cone before I'm left with a puddle.

Once I'm done, I show Takeshi the empty cone. "You can have it now."

He bites into it faster than Daga can wiggle her tail.

That gets a laugh out of me. Despite the sharp twist near my heart, I can bear it. Being with my friends, my parents, and Takeshi has made the post-hurricanes reality a little better.

The bleakness creeps in when I least expect it. There's still so much to build, to nurture. Takeshi and I will go to the afternoon session with the teens I've been helping, once our lunch break is over. Héctor and the other riders are busy with a supply drop-off down south, and since the press got wind of it, they'll be gone for a while. We're meeting for dinner at Victoria's old house. After it was magically rebuilt, her mom let us borrow it as headquarters.

But there are other things that will need more than magic to be built again.

"Thank you for sharing your dessert," Takeshi says. "Ready to leave?"

"One second."

I unzip my Wonder Woman backpack. The memento is right at the top. I hold it up high, and it looks like we've been painted in the sky.

My photo with Andrew is as good as new.

Takeshi had been the one to find it back at the manor. Sometimes I talk about Brazil during therapy, and it helps to have a physical reminder of the friend I lost. Not because I'm forgetting or erasing him—Andrew Galloway will last forever. But the way forward isn't to pretend that what's behind me never happened. I have to lock hands with both realities, and march onward steadily.

"You're so beautiful," Takeshi whispers.

"Thank you. Andrew's outfit is pretty cool, though."

"I'm partial to his hair."

"We were robbed of the best shampoo commercials."

"Indeed."

Our playful back-and-forth lasts several minutes. This dynamic has helped us discuss deeper stuff when it comes to our respective links to Andrew. It's helping us heal *together*.

I don't know what's next. Not with our relationship. Not with Samira's research, Victoria's mission, or my country's recovery. Not even with me. A month and a half ago, I was hiding in the mountains, wishing I could return to my family home. My wish came true—just not how I hoped. That doesn't mean I no longer have any hope left.

The beach looks sad today again, but I love it anyway.

I say, "I'm ready now."

Takeshi helps me up. I hold my favorite hands as we walk away from the shore. Waves crash harder the farther we retreat. It's like a blender has been turned on in the deep. Or maybe Poseidon is throwing a temper tantrum at one of his brothers. I hear the seagulls chirping louder, too. I pretend the ocean and the sky have joined forces to mourn my departure.

Still, I keep moving. The seagulls' call grows fainter and fainter.

In the distance, a dragon's cry echoes behind me.

THE END

ACKNOWLEDGMENTS

I CAN'T BELIEVE I WROTE A SEQUEL.

In two months.

In 2020.

Those three facts would seem ridiculous if it weren't for the immense amount of support I received. Debuting as an author in 2020 was a surreal experience, and I feared this book wouldn't get written. It did take me two extra weeks to complete my first round of revisions. Typing that extension request email made me feel like a total failure.

Luckily, my editors are GOLDEN. Tamara Grasty and Lauren Knowles, you took me under your wing at a very chaotic time in both publishing and the world. It's because of you I knew I could finish this book. Without your guidance, vision, and support, the last half of Lana's story would've never seen shelves. #TeamBlazewrath for life!

Ashley Hearn, another key member of #TeamBlazewrath, and the reason why Victoria has her own POV! I never thought I could write dual narrators, but here we are!

My agent, Linda Camacho, you helped make 2020 the year where some of my wildest dreams came true, and this book is further evidence that you're never wrong, lol! Thank you for everything you do!

Page Street Publishing & Macmillan! Everyone who worked hard to bring *Blazewrath Games* and *Dragonblood Ring* to shelves deserves a medal. Specifically, I'd like to thank Kayla Tostevin and Lauren Cepero for helping me connect with readers, teachers, and librarians. Carolina Rodríguez Fuenmayor, for illustrating *Blazewrath Games*'s STUNNING cover and bringing my dragons to life. Molly Gillespie, for designing my debut novel's cover. Melia Parsloe, for designing *Dragonblood Ring*'s gorgeous cover, and Setor Fiadzigbey, for ABSOLUTELY BLOWING MY MIND with the illustrations! I am obsessed!! Shout-out to Franny

Donington for helping me strengthen this book further after reading circulation pages! Your suggestions were chef's kiss! Editorial interns, marketing, sales, artists, you are all my *heroes*.

The Iron Keys, Natasha M. Heck (Commander) and Karuna Riazi (Once and Future Queen), critique partners extraordinaire, beloved friends, and fellow fantasy fans. This book centers around two girls who struggle with what success and worthiness means after surviving their darkest days. Knowing you both makes me feel like a winner.

Adriana M. Martínez Figueroa, your friendship is like a sandwich de mezcla. It can never be topped. Thank you so much for supporting *Blazewrath Games*, and for providing such an outstanding sensitivity read on this sequel! My soul left my body when you refused to reference Todd by name. Also, thank you for enduring my Husband DMs.

Adriana De Persia, the first person to ever read this book, your comments made me laugh out loud and get super emo at the same time. Please keep writing your BRILLIANT stories and keep showing the world how amazing you are, thanks.

The Latinx book/blogging/vlogging community, I literally owe you all my money, okay??? Your support still leaves me speechless, but I'll gladly accept it whenever it comes. Special thanks to these absolute wonders: Vic (@mmmmsunlight), Jayden, Paola (@Guerrerawr), Gabi (gabi_morataya), Andrea (@andreabarango), Wilmarie (@lesbe_reader), Arthur (caro_guayaba), Kirstie (@BorikenHazel), John (@Johnlikestoread), Cande (@iamrainbou), Ursula (@gemchronicles), Jocelyn (@joceraptor), Josie (@TheJosieMarie), Gaby (@gaby_burgos27), Valerie (Insta: @starrynight.reads), Sofia (@SofiainBookland), Carmen (@tomestextiles), Linda Raquel (@linda.reads), and Astrid (@astridpizarro). Last but not least, to my nemesis, Adri (@perpetualpages), the perfect foil to everything I do. Bring on the memes!

Book bloggers/vloggers/readers who shouted about *Blazewrath Games* and *Dragonblood Ring* online, I see you. I also owe you my money.

To Shealea (@shutupshealea) for hosting my very first blog tour and helping me connect with such amazing content creators! Also, Fadwa (@litfever), Joel (@joelrochesterr), Brad Krautwurst (@snarkbybrad), Alina Sergachov (@AlinaSergachov), Olivia Vaughn (@olivaughn), and Solange (@and_shereads), for making such GORGEOUS content and being so kind to me?? As if I deserve it????

Linda Raquel Nieves, for the BEAUTIFUL pre-order campaign character art featuring Lana, Victoria, and Cecilia! I can't tell you how excited I was every single time I refreshed my inbox and saw one of my girls in your illustrations. Mil, mil gracias.

Lisa Iki, for the jaw-dropping beauty that is my Takeshi and Hikaru pre-order character art. Seeing my vengeful boy and his best friend through your talent has left me speechless. Thank you for being just as enthusiastic about such a heartbreaking image as I am!

Natalia Martínez, for inviting me to my very first festival as an author and for hosting a *Blazewrath Games* blog tour for #ownvoices readers!

Christina Orlando, for being "a hot bitch" and for buddy reading with me, even though you fly by pages faster than a Sol de Noche!

Peter López, you incredible soul. All the hugs for my lovely Twitter and website graphics! Also, YOUR WRITING WILL CHANGE LIVES. Keep going.

Las Musas, for helping me find a space that allows me to feel valid as a creator. Specifically, huge thanks to these gems: Mia García, Adrianna Cuevas, Yamile Saied Méndez (work wife alert!), Nikki Barthelmess, Francesca Flores, NoNieqa Ramos, Jonny Garza Villa, Anna Meriano, Zara González Hoang, Laekan Zea Kemp, Maritza and Maika Moulite, Chantel Acevedo, Zoraida Córdova, Ann Dávila Cardinal, Nina Moreno, Laura Taylor Namey, Tehlor Kay Mejia, Aida Salazar, Crystal Maldonado, and Romina Garber. Gracias infinitas, mis vidas.

Author/publishing friends, especially fellow 2020 debuts, you're all so near and dear to my heart! Special shout-out to these incomparable

humans: Katie Zhao, Adiba Jaigirdar, cara davis-araux, Gabriela Martins, Cam Montgomery, Rebecca Coffindaffer, June Tan, Destiny Soria, Camryn Garrett, Diana Urban, Torrance Sené, Sonora "Soni" Reyes, Shveta Thakrar, Roseanne Brown, Lori M. Lee, Prerna Pickett, Racquel Marie, Kalynn Bayron, Emery Lee, Laura Genn, Tashie Bhuiyan, Dante Medema, Tracy Deonn, Aiden Thomas, Claribel Ortega, Jennifer Iacopelli, Julie Abe, Jamie Pacton, Dahlia Adler, Adam Sass, and Chloe Gong (#FreePain). Thanks to you, my debut year was so much more bearable!

Family and friends, thanks for encouraging me to keep going on this wild publishing journey. Mom, Dad, and Renis, for enduring me while I'm on deadline. Love you! Gabi Morataya, for knitting me a baby dragon and making the best K-pop shirts ever. Melanie Pacheco, for designing the gorgeous Funko POP! versions of Lana and the Sol de Noche. Marianne Robles, for your K Drama recommendations, fangirling over all things Victon with me, and creating the most aesthetically pleasing character profiles of all time. Adrianna Cuevas, for being my virtual BTS concert buddy and posting the best pics of baked goods. Melanie Barbosa, Paola Nigaglioni, and Xavier Torres, the Holy Trinity of *Blazewrath Games* hand-sellers at my local indie bookstore. Josie Marie and Gabriela Burgos, for the excellent movie recs and *John Wick* debates. Se les quiere un mundo.

To the readers, teachers, and librarians who carved a space for my duology on their shelves, I'm forever in your debt. Lana, Victoria, and the rest of Team Puerto Rico have lived in my head for many years. Knowing they can now live in your homes and libraries as two halves of a heart humbles me. With all that I am, thank you.

Until the next ride.

ABOUT THE AUTHOR

AMPARO ORTIZ WAS BORN IN SAN JUAN, PUERTO RICO, AND currently lives on the island's northeastern coast. *Blazewrath Games* is her debut novel (Page Street Kids, 2020). Her short story comic, "What Remains in The Dark," appears in the Eisner Award–winning anthology *Puerto Rico Strong* (Lion Forge, 2018), and *Saving Chupie*, her middle grade graphic novel, comes out with HarperCollins in 2022. She holds an MA in English and a BA in Psychology from the UPR's Río Piedras campus. When she's not teaching ESL to her college students, she's streaming K-pop music videos, vlogging for her eponymous YouTube channel, and writing about Latinx characters in worlds both contemporary and fantastical. Follow her shenanigans online at www.amparoortiz.com.